AWAKENINGS

AWAKENINGS

EDWARD LAZELLARI

TOR®

A TOM DOHERTY ASSOCIATES BOOK
NEW YORK

AWAKENINGS

Copyright © 2011 by Edward Lazellari

Edited by Paul Stevens

A Tor Book
Published by Tom Doherty Associates, LLC
175 Fifth Avenue
New York, NY 10010

www.tor-forge.com

Tor® is a registered trademark of Tom Doherty Associates, LLC.

Library of Congress Cataloging-in-Publication Data

Lazellari, Edward.
    Awakenings / Edward Lazellari. — 1st ed.
        p. cm. — (Heroes of Aandor ; bk. 1)
    "A Tom Doherty Associates book."
    ISBN 978-0-7653-2787-1
    1. Amnesia—Fiction. 2. New York (N.Y.)—Fiction. I. Title.
    PS3612.A983A96 2011
    813'.6—dc22
                                            2011018989

First Edition: September 2011

Printed in the United States of America

0 9 8 7 6 5 4 3 2 1

To my sister Pamela,
the first audience for my narrative musings

ACKNOWLEDGMENTS

It took more folks than I can name to produce this finished work, but I'd like to start by thanking the following people for their contributions to this effort: Seth Kramer, Lisa Ryan-Herndon, Alice K. Turner, Seth Lerner, Tom Doherty, Paul Stevens, Ron Gwiazda, Katherine N. Munn, Erich Schoeneweiss, Merav Hoffman, George (Geof) Smith, John McClure, Evan Gunter, Pamela Small, Mary Ann Yashima, Lisa DuMond, Dale Hrebik, Louis Lachance, John Bligh, Keith Clayton, Phyllis Wender, Sonia Pabley, and Edward Hibbert.

AWAKENINGS

PROLOGUE

THE BAD GUYS

TWO DAYS AGO

Colby Dretch cleaned out the empties from his office wet bar. Only half a bottle of vodka and a bottle of peach schnapps remained. He threw the clinking bag, along with a valise full of his laundry, into the bathroom and hoped the new clients had good bladders. Once he had folded the bed and threw the pillows into the closet, the place looked almost ready for business. It would be a no-frills meeting.

Carla would be bringing the new clients in any minute. Colby put on a fresh shirt and tie. He tied his knot using the reflection in his office window and surveyed the bustling masses on Third Avenue. An image of dressing up a pig popped into his head; he had to chuckle. While it might hide his varicose veins, no shirt and tie could detract from his dark puffy eyes, thinning hair, gaunt cheeks, pasty pallor, and hawkish nose. He looked like Ichabod Crane on that ill-fated night, and he was only fifty-two. But it was all part of the game.

Carla led an odd crew of three men into the room. One man had to crouch to get through the door frame. He looked almost deformed—his jaw was thick as an anvil, his fedora was too small for his head, and cigarette smoke wafting from his lips caused a

11

cloud that partly obscured his face. His stylish suit barely contained him, and dandruff lay on his jacket collar and breast. The other two looked like fashion models. Same height and build, they both wore their hair slicked back in ponytails and could have passed for twins, except for their coloring. One was light-skinned and blond, the other swarthy and dark. Carla rolled her eyes as if to say, *Who let these guys out of the sideshow?* She tossed him a wink and sashayed out of the room. Colby smiled; she would have made a great gangster's moll.

A cold chill went through the detective. He checked the radiator dial to his right and saw it was already in the on position. *Fine time for the heater to go on the fritz,* he thought. He rubbed his hands for warmth before offering one to the blond man Carla had pegged as the ringleader.

"Hi. I'm Colby Dretch. Take a chair, please."

"Dorn," the blond man said, waiting a moment before accepting the detective's hand and taking the seat on the other side of the desk. He failed to introduce his silent colleagues.

Colby noticed a trace of an accent, but couldn't place it. Dorn exuded confidence, like someone raised in an exclusive Northeastern boarding school; the kind with crested jackets and ties, where teachers lived in fear of their students. He took his seat behind the desk. The others in the room chose to remain standing. Colby lit a cigarette and offered one to Dorn. Dorn politely declined.

"What does someone with your kind of money want with a broken-down detective like me?" Colby asked. "Did Pinkerton go under?"

Dorn studied the autographed celebrity photos around the

room; Colby knew they looked impressive, even through the dust. Dorn picked up a framed photo of the detective and his boy. "Your son?" he asked.

In happier days, Colby thought. He was unimpressed with Dorn's forward style. "His name's Tory." He waited for Dorn to put the photo down before continuing. "I should tell you, I'm suspended from practicing for the time being. A small disagreement with the district attorney's office."

"Your abilities are still intact?" Dorn inquired.

"Yeah. As long as we keep things on the down low, keep it strictly cash, it shouldn't be a problem." Carla was right. These guys were oddballs. Anyone with common sense would have walked out already.

Dorn pulled out a piece of paper and handed it to Colby. It was a long list of names with short descriptions of age and race, some of them various versions of the same name spelled different ways: Cal MacDonnell/McDonnell, Callum MacDonnell/McDonnell . . . et cetera.

"Could you locate the people on this list?" Dorn asked.

"Assuming how accurate the names are . . . probably in two days."

Dorn looked to his swarthy colleague, who offered an ambiguous, yet approving, shrug. The giant just kept blowing smoke.

"Are you boasting?" Dorn asked.

"I can cross-reference multiple government databases."

"We tried other agencies with similar resources," Dorn said.

"I've got access to deep systems that are normally off limits to private firms. The fringe benefits of twenty years in the NYPD." Colby also had a network of strategically placed bribed informants.

He wondered why he tried to impress clients that, as far as they knew, needed him more than he needed them. *Old habits die hard,* he thought.

Colby waved the paper with the names in front of Dorn. "Is this it? The job?"

"Large agencies have too many eyes and ears, Mr. Dretch. I value discretion. I also want someone desperate. Are you . . . desperate, Mr. Dretch?"

"Hardly," Colby lied. He started rubbing his hands again to keep them warm, and regretted that it looked like an act of weakness. He turned up the thermostat in the heater behind his chair.

"Don't be offended," Dorn said. "I insist that people who work for me make my interests their only priority. There's a refreshing lack of activity at this firm due to your dubious practices." Dorn's smile was shark white. He pulled out a recent copy of the *New York Post* and scanned an article. "'Colby Dretch . . . under government indictment for nine counts of embezzlement and blackmail of his rich, deeply troubled, and well-connected clientele . . . infidelities, pedophilia, domestic abuse,' et cetera. And, you never reported your 'moonlighting' income to the government. Why, they have you on tax evasion alone." Dorn moved to the second half of the article on a different page. "Eight civil suits, resulting in your property and finances being placed in escrow. Suspended operating license, at least until the verdict, after which it will be fully revoked. A bit redundant," Dorn said turning his attention back to Colby. "Not really much use in prison. The vultures are circling."

"Innocent until proven guilty," Colby said, calmly. He was

losing patience with this lot, but he wouldn't let them see him break.

Dorn's cohorts made a poor attempt to suppress chuckling. "Mr. Dretch, you're not just a thief—you're an accessory after the fact in your clients' illicit affairs. You'd be lucky to get out in thirty years."

"I think you ought to leave," the detective said in a steady voice.

Dorn reclined in his chair and smiled as warmly as his features would allow. "Colby, you misunderstand. I'm interested in doing business with you *because* you're guilty. Putting the screws to anyone naïve enough to trust you with their deepest secrets is an admirable trait. That's a sign of intelligence where I come from."

Colby had never before been complimented for being a complete bastard. His crimes were many—far more than the indictments that had been handed down already. Friendless and penniless, his passport revoked by the courts, the future looked bleak, and now he was taking crap from some rich boy with an agenda.

Colby tossed the list of names on the desk in front of Dorn. "Many agencies can find these people for you," he said. "You don't need me."

"That's not why I'm here, detective. The real job is for a name not on this list—a young man. His name could be anything by now; even one of these," Dorn added, picking up the list.

"Not interested," Colby said.

"You cannot find him?"

"I can find anyone. But as you just pointed out, I have many problems."

"Name your price."

"It's not that easy."

"It really is."

"Fine. A million dollars as a retainer, ten thousand a day plus expenses, twenty-five thousand for each name on the list that I locate, and another million when I find the boy with no name."

The two men stared each other down; Colby waited for Dorn to leave.

"Done," Dorn said.

Colby almost did a double take straight out of the movies. "What?"

"I agree to your terms."

Colby shifted in his chair to find a more comfortable position. It was his worst tell when playing high-stakes poker and had lost him a lot of money through the years. *What cards does Dorn hold?*

"Those fees are unreasonable," Colby said, cautiously.

"Are you that good?"

"Yeah, I'm that good, but . . ."

"Others have failed. I need results."

With two million dollars cash, Colby could buy his way off the continent without a passport. He could start life over in a country without an extradition treaty. He could even set up a trust fund for Tory, try to make up for being a lousy father. He had just been handed a way out of the mess that was his life.

"You can wire these funds internationally?" Colby asked.

"Even to Antarctica," Dorn said, smiling.

"Tell me more about the kid."

"I have never seen the child. His last known location was Dutchess County, New York, thirteen years ago. He bears a red birthmark above his left scapula. Symian will provide a detailed file."

"Symian?"

"Our colleague. He is taking care of business with your woman."

Colby grinned. "Ms. Hernandez is engaged to be married to a Marine. He's back from Afghanistan next week."

"Symian is adept at winning women's hearts," said the swarthy twin in the corner, with an amused expression.

"This boy," Colby started, getting back to the job that would save his life, "are you his biological father?"

"Relative," Dorn said.

"You're a relative, but you've never seen him, you're not sure of his name, and you believe he was somewhere in Dutchess County about thirteen years ago."

"You're on top of the situation already."

A heavily swathed man Colby assumed was Symian walked in from the reception area and gave Dorn a nod. "Just them," he said, in a raspy whisper. He wore gloves, his hat was too big and his raincoat collar and a scarf hid much of his face. Colby noticed that under the brim's shadow, where the whites of the man's eyes should be, they were egg-yolk yellow.

"The file," Dorn ordered.

Symian placed a portable flash drive on the desk.

"Is this kid in witness protection?" Colby asked. "Those FBI guys are hard to crack."

"Why would they be involved?" Dorn asked.

"Well, I assume . . . the mother took off with the kid because she didn't want him raised in a 'connected' family."

Dorn laughed. "A compliment, Mr. Dretch. Alas, I do not bear the honor of belonging to that distinguished group."

Colby was amused. After years on the job, he knew a thug when he saw one. If Dorn hired him for his scruples as he claimed, then he'd also know working for organized crime posed no problem.

"I guess that's not important, as long as your money is good," Colby said.

"Shall we secure his commitment, my lord?" Symian asked.

"And *your* loyalty, Colby, how do we ensure that?" Dorn's tone changed, making the previous conversation until now seem almost jovial. "Are we to trust you with our secrets?" Dorn's voice exuded a deep severity.

For the first time, the detective wondered if he was in over his head. He wished he'd replaced the clip in the Beretta sitting in his bottom drawer.

Colby took a deep breath and convinced himself he had the upper hand. After all, if other detectives had failed before him, and they went out of their way to hire an indicted, unlicensed detective, he must be exactly what they need.

"Look, Mr. Dorn—I'm smart enough to know who not to screw with. I promise, the retainer will assure my loyalty."

Dorn gave a nod to Symian. The bundled-up man pulled a small velvet sack out of his coat pocket.

"I disagree," Dorn said. "Where I come from, fealty is a matter of life and death. Since your oaths mean little, you have to give us something very important to you. Something you could never live without."

That's a new twist. Colby had never been asked to put up collateral for a job. "I thought you read the *Post* article. I put up most of my money for bail. The government took my passport and froze my assets until the investigation is complete. I sleep on that fold-out couch over there. I got nothing to give you." Colby glanced at the photo of Tory, and immediately regretted it. "My boy's a quadriplegic. I won't lift a damn finger if you bring him into this."

"I do not want your son," Dorn said. "Some creatures throw their young to the wolves if it means one more day for themselves. I have something more dear to you in mind. Hesz."

The large man scurried behind the detective in a flash, faster than Colby thought possible for someone so big, and locked him in a full nelson.

"What the hell are you doing?" the detective shouted. "Carla! Call the cops!" The detective struggled, but Hesz's grip was like refrigerated steel. It was only when Hesz was breathing right on top of him that Colby finally realized the mist coming out of his mouth wasn't cigarette smoke . . . it was frost. As was the "dandruff" on the man's suit.

"Call the cops!" Colby shouted again.

Symian walked up to him. He glanced at Dorn and said, "Bet you a purse of Krakens it bursts. He doesn't look too healthy."

Dorn gave Symian a fierce look and said, "If he dies, I'll braid your liver into a rope and hang you with it."

Symian's grin revealed canine teeth. He turned back to Colby and put two small pills into the detective's mouth and said, "Swallow these."

Colby spat them out. "Fuck you! Carla!" A frightening thought occurred to Colby. Carla might be dead.

"It's just nitroglycerine," Symian said. "Trust me."

Symian gripped the detective's face, pried his mouth open,

slipped two fresh pills under the detective's tongue, and Hesz clamped the detective's jaw shut with a massive hand.

When Symian was sure the pills had dissolved, he ripped Colby's shirt open and drew a circle in the center of his chest with a foul-smelling, thick, cloudy liquid that he seemed to be scraping off his own forearm. Using a Sharpie marker he drew five symbols around the circle and then spread more of the goop over the symbols. Then he placed the fingers of his right hand on the circle under each symbol. He uttered an undecipherable word.

Pushing forward, Symian's hand sunk into Colby's chest up to his wrist. Colby's eyes almost came out of their sockets. He anticipated the agony of such a violation, but as the seconds passed, he realized it was a numb sensation, like pins and needles.

At the door, a shocked, hysterical Carla crawled in, sobbing. Her torn blouse revealed symbols drawn around a red welt on her chest. "Give it back!" she cried at Symian. "Oh, Colby, make him give it back!"

Colby never screamed louder in his life. He could feel the gray man's hand clamping his heart, but was too gripped with terror to realize there was little blood coming forth. Symian's hand pulled the organ free of its attachments. Within moments, Symian held Colby's still-beating heart in front of his face. He put it in the velvet bag, thumping like a trapped rat, and pulled the drawstring shut.

CHAPTER 1

HERO SANDWICHED

1

Callum MacDonnell woke up in a cold sweat and managed to stifle a yell at the last minute. He caught his breath, then rolled out of bed as softly as possible so as not to disturb Cat. Not easy at six foot five, and two hundred and fifty pounds. The light from the street tinted him the same shade of blue as his eyes, like snow under moonlight.

"You don't really think I'm still asleep?" his wife said groggily from the other side of the bed. Catherine MacDonnell propped herself up on her elbows. "You were thrashing around like shark prey."

"Sorry," he said, and sat back down on the bed.

Cat hoisted herself up from the mattress and rested her chin on his shoulder straining to keep her eyes open. "Bad dreams again?" she asked, rubbing his back.

The same dream had plagued Cal for almost two weeks now. He tried to retain the peculiar details of his nightmare even as they dissolved into the ether of his memory. The lack of sleep affected him on patrol, and in New York City that could get a cop killed, especially in his precinct.

"Want to talk about it?" Cat asked.

"It's probably just stress," Cal said.

"Maybe you're worried about the ESU exam?" She slid her fingers up to the back of his neck and kneaded the tension out with an aggressive thumb. Cal responded instantly. His shoulders dropped, his head bobbed to the side, and his muscles softened.

"No," Cal said. "I'll ace it."

"Maybe you're stressed because you're having reoccurring nightmares." She kissed his cheek.

Cal smirked. "You missed your calling as an analyst." He let her dig into his neck and shoulders for a little while more. He'd been reluctant to discuss the dreams because of how strange they were—both in content and familiarity. "This dream feels like I'm living a memory," he said to his wife. There, it was out.

That prospect brought Cat further out of her sleepy haze. "Cal, could it be you're remembering something from before the accident? From your childhood?"

"I don't think so. What I'm dreaming . . . it's surreal. I'm in a stone building; there's a fight; someone tells me to go through a door."

"Who told you? Did you recognize a face? A landmark?"

"I was with a group. We were going on a trip. We had a talking horse . . ."

"A what?"

"It's weird. At the end, there's this intense grief, a pressure like a moose standing on my chest. Like somebody died."

The thought of that pain made Cal tense up again. He squeezed the bridge of his nose hard and realized he needed an Advil.

"And then . . . ," Cat prodded.

"That's when I usually wake up. This is the kind of stuff a fifteen-year-old boy dreams of," he said, frustrated. "I just want a full night's sleep. I am feeling stretched thin."

They heard a shuffle in the hallway. The door to the bedroom creaked open.

"Hi Pa," said their five-year-old daughter, Brianna, in a sleepy voice. She stood in the doorway in her flannel *Dora the Explorer* pajamas, clutching her Elmo doll in her hand. A testament to modern-day marketing.

"Bree, you should be in bed," Cat said, a bit annoyed.

"I heard talking," she offered as her excuse.

Catherine MacDonnell was the law in the MacDonnell home, which was the way Cal liked it in lieu of life in the outside world: long patrols, city politics, and administrative headaches. Her temper was legendary in the neighborhood when someone broke that order. Her hypnotic gunmetal-gray eyes and raven hued tresses—a gift from her Sioux grandmother—gave her a formidable presence, despite her small stature. She could turn whatever spot she stood on into the center of the universe when the mood suited her.

But, despite Cat's protestation, Cal was happy to see Brianna. She was his anchor—his only known blood relative in the world, and he never lost his patience with her. "Don't you have school in a few hours?" Cal said halfheartedly.

Bree looked at her father seriously and said, "It's only kindergarten. All we do is color and play games. And then they make us take a nap so the teachers can relax."

Cal laughed. Even Cat had to fight off a chuckle. "When did you get to be so smart?" Cal asked, holding his arms out. Bree jumped into her father's massive arms, the safest place in her universe.

"Oh, don't encourage her, Cal. We *all* need to go back to sleep," she said looking at their daughter.

As if on cue, Maggie trotted in wondering who had called a family meeting at this hour and could she get a cookie out of it. The pit bull–lab mutt barked to announce her arrival, then jumped on the bed and proceeded to lick Bree like an ice cream cone.

"Brianna MacDonnell, get to bed this instant," Cat said. "Maggie down!"

Cal knew better than to push his luck. He gave Bree a peck on the cheek and put her down with a pat on the butt. She left the room with Maggie in tow. Cat shook her hair, a bit flustered at the chaos. She studied her husband.

"You've got to see someone about this. You can't keep going to work strung out on no sleep. It's affecting all of us."

"I know. I'll make an appointment with one of the department shrinks."

"Today?"

"Yes, right away," Cal said, rolling his eyes. He lay back down on the bed facing the window, staring out at the winter sky.

Cat snuggled next to Cal and put her arm around him. She kissed him tenderly on the temple and then rested her head against his. "Don't be mad," she said. "That little girl needs her daddy to come home safe every day."

"What about this little girl," he said stroking her arm.

Cat snuggled closer and wrapped her leg around his. They stayed that way until they both fell asleep.

2

It was the silliest domestic dispute Cal and his partner, Erin Ramos, had ever been called on. The complainant was a seventy-three-year old recent émigré from El Salvador who accused her seventy-eight-year old husband of hiding her teeth because she refused to have sex. Perhaps the ambience of the South Bronx was not as conducive to romance as the Salvadoran countryside. A shouting match ensued, followed by the husband's playfully spanking his wife on the rear end with a spatula. She responded with a rolling pin to his head. One of the neighbors called it in.

"Technically, he battered her first," Erin noted.

Embarrassed by the sudden appearance of the law, the wife was on her third straight minute of explaining her story without coming up for air. Erin tried to keep up for Cal's sake.

"She says she's in America now," Erin translated. "And doesn't have to perform 'wifely' duties when she has a headache. There was an article in the Spanish *Cosmo* at the manicure shop."

Neighbors spilled into the hallway to witness the commotion.

"Everyone back in their apartment, *por favor!*" Cal said. He squeezed the bridge of his nose, trying to drive the fatigue from his mind. "I don't have the energy for this tonight. What's the husband say?"

The husband, holding an ice pack on his little bald head, stood about four-foot-nine in slippers. His green pajamas and large thick eyeglasses gave him a tortoise-like countenance.

"He's been getting—'*it*'—daily since they were married almost fifty years ago," Erin said. "They have fourteen children. All of

a sudden, she started putting him off. And you think *you* have
no energy?"

A trickle of blood slid down the side of the man's age-mottled
head. The wife, alarmed, used her dishrag to stop the bleeding
and led her husband to an armchair in the living room. At first, he
sat stone-faced with wounded pride, but soon patted her arm. She
kissed his cheeks even as tears began rolling down her own.

"We're not arresting him," Cal said.

"But . . ."

"Two hours in Central Booking over *this*? Look at them.
They adore each other. She probably got razzed at the manicure
shop for being old-fashioned. My own wife used to read *Cosmo*—
I'm aware of the consequences. If we arrest him, she's going to
feel awful."

"Well, short of booking them separate vacations, what do
we do?"

"She *is* seventy-three. We should probably cool him down a
bit." Cal pulled out his ticket book and wrote, "conjugal engage-
ments, three times per week, only." He tore out the ticket and
showed it to Erin.

"Translate this and inform them it's an official warrant. They
can have sex three times a week."

"This isn't legal," Erin said.

"*They* don't know that."

"But . . ."

"Erin, who's going to know their business? If she's in the
mood, they'll think they're being naughty. If she's not, he'll be
too worried about what the next cop will write up to push it." Cal
gave his partner a big smile. "For God's sake, Erin, the woman
can't chew."

Erin laughed. "Okay, but Lord help us if she turns frigid and he whips out your 'warrant' to the next unit that answers the call."

The old woman gave some rosary beads to Erin and a tin of butter cookies to Cal before shutting the door. Cal called it in to Central, and they left.

Rain pattered the roof of their cruiser as Cal and Erin resumed patrolling the South Bronx. The drumming water had a pacifying effect. No one knew better than Cal how the four-to-twelve shift could put a kink in a person's biological clock. Add to that his insomnia and it was a recipe for bad judgment on a dangerous job. He'd promised Cat he'd see a department therapist, but had yet to make an appointment. As of 11:00 P.M., Cal was willing to give out slaps on the wrist until midnight so that he wouldn't have to pull overtime booking suspects. He prayed the rain would keep people indoors and out of trouble. He was determined to hit his pillow before 1:00 A.M.

Erin had a passion for Latin music that she foisted on her partners. Cal was grateful for the upbeat tempo that helped counter the lulling effects of the rain.

"You're gonna love this one," she said with one hand on the wheel and the other jiggling a CD into the deck. "I recorded it when Tito Puente came to Orchard Beach. You never heard percussion like this."

"Look, all this Latin stuff sounds great to me," Cal said. "But I can't tell the difference between salsa, calypso, or marinara," he yawned.

"Marinara is a pasta sauce."

"Whatever. The music is keeping me awake. Your lecture does the opposite."

As Erin continued, Cal closed his eyes, convinced it would help him stay awake if he focused on the music. Twice, he jolted as he faded toward slumber, shaking his head and forcing his eyes open to their extreme. Erin hadn't noticed. He concentrated on the music, tried to single out each instrument, an exercise that would keep his mind alert. He was not going to sleep. Erin's chattering grew fainter. He fell toward slumber, like a kid hurtling down a slide . . .

They were all dead. The blood-drenched valley was littered with corpses and broken bodies, many belonging to those who were barely yet men. Smoke billowed from burning towns and the nearby forest, painting the sky charcoal. Winged cavalry fluttered before them like a swarm of locusts. The last remaining defenders clustered on the battlements.

Royal guardsmen were building barricades throughout the castle—every man was ready to go down fighting. "You can't be serious, Father?" It was the first time Cal had ever questioned his commander's authority.

"Listen to me," said the old man. "The boy must be protected on this journey." It smelled like a parent trying to send his son away from a slaughter.

"My duty is to defend this castle until my last breath!"

"Your duty is whatever I . . . !" The old man's nose and cheeks shone like hot iron against his white whiskers. He let out a big breath, and his face softened.

Cal looked into the old warrior's piercing blue eyes and wondered when this tired old man had replaced the robust warrior who was permanently etched in his mind. It was not so long ago he was jumping into the man's arms, pleading for a fencing lesson. He felt like that boy again.

"This building keeps the rain off the regent in a storm. Our responsibility lies with the kingdom, with the family. I've no idea if the hell I'm sending you into is any better than the one we're about to face. I only know that the boy's chances fare better under your watchful eye."

"This is it, then?" Cal said.

"I still have a few tricks up my sleeve," the old man said with a smile.

No child was closer to his sire than a MacDonnell. It was their strength. Cal could see his father's heart breaking for not giving him a better world to inherit. He wanted to tell the old man that he had done better than anyone else could have, but before he could utter a word, his commander said:

"Go! They're waiting on you. Take any servant that swears fealty to his lordship. Wherever you end up, remember your duty to the kingdom. Our family has protected this dynasty for seven generations."

A loud crash sounded a few rooms away. Metal clashing. Screams of butchered men echoed across the palace. Cal raced down the hallway without looking back. A blinding light emanated from the pantry as though a thousand candles burned. From inside the room he heard a voice.

"Idafor . . . susma . . . lewear . . . respond . . ."

Erin was shaking his arm. "Cal, wake up."

The radio blared, *"Four-One Ida, ten-thirty-one reported at nine hundred fifty-seven, Kelly Street. Suspect is a large Caucasian male, in a suit, wearing a black fedora, last seen heading for the roof."*

"Ten-Four Central, Four-One Ida responding," Erin reported into the radio. "Do you have a call back, over?"

"Affirmative on call back. What is your position?"

"We're two blocks from site, Central. We got it."

Cal was shaking his head, trying to wake up in a hurry.

"Can't blame you for being tired, partner . . . I wouldn't get any sleep either if Cat were *my* girl," Erin said with a smile.

"Very funny. What's going on?"

"It's a prowler. He'll probably be gone when we get there."

"Should we wait for backup?"

"Nah. One look at your nine-foot ass and he'll surrender on the spot."

In spite of himself, Cal hoped the perp would be gone by the time they arrived.

They rolled up in front of the building. Cal picked up the radio. "We're eighty-four at nine-five-seven Kelly Street, Central," he said. "What's the response on the call back?"

"Four-One Ida, suspect threatened tenant with an ax, last seen heading toward roof. He's described as a large Caucasian in a raincoat. No confirmation that he has left the area yet, over."

"Why did this skell stick around?" Cal grunted. "We're dealing with a moron."

"Crack addicts, murderers, and rapists, oh my," Erin said. "You want easy, move to Iowa."

"Four-One Ida requesting eighty-five forthwith at present location, over," Cal said.

"Affirmative, Four-One Adam responding to request for backup. ETA is six minutes."

"Thank you, Central," Erin said airily.

"Wait by the entrance," Cal said. "We'll flush him out."

Erin looked at her partner with amazement. "You want to flush him down alone?" she asked.

"Sooner we nab him, the earlier we book him and the faster I get to bed."

"What confidence. Nice having muscles to spare."

"Speed and leverage can beat raw strength in hand-to-hand," he said.

"Easy for you to say."

Cal looked up at the tenement. It was a five-story walk-up, the kind with a great crown at the top of the façade, one that had seen better days. He entered and searched the ground floor. Paint peeled off the heat pipes. It smelled like rice and beans and greasy chicken. Trash bags were piled in the corner by the basement door. Cal checked it. Locked. Erin stood in the vestibule by the mailboxes . . . no room to slip past her. Cal heard a noise from above, and looked up the stairwell. A woman was peering down from the fourth floor. She waved him up. He climbed the stairs slowly, making sure each landing was clear of people before proceeding.

The woman was a young Hispanic, short with brown eyes and cropped curly hair, in a loose tank top that barely contained her. Cal could see and hear a group of children peering through the crack in her apartment door.

"Cállense!" she yelled at them. Then she turned to him. *"Fue grande, mas grande que usted. Se fue a través del techo y hacia el edificio abandonado al lado."*

"I'm sorry, I don't speak Spanish. Here," Cal said, pulling his radio mouthpiece toward the woman. "Say it into this."

"He went next door through the roof," Erin translated.

"Shit. That's great. Poking around a decrepit building in the dark. If the perp doesn't get me the tetanus will."

"I can go," Erin offered.

"No. You stay downstairs. Same plan, different building. I'll follow him through the roof and flush him out."

With a little luck, their backup would arrive by the time he got there.

3

It took Erin Ramos a few minutes to pull the wooden boards off the doorway. She walked into the vestibule holding her nightstick like a club. The smell was suffocating, like an unwashed hospital bedpan. She propped the front doors open with the boards to let the air in. The streetlights illuminated the vestibule and some of the lobby. Rain streamed in behind her—it felt good, natural. There was something about this building besides the odor that gave Erin the heebie-jeebies. The first thing she noticed was the cold, as though someone were running an air conditioner in the middle of winter. She was glad it was still Cal's turn to flush out the perp. Since they alternated the task, Cal could have claimed he'd done his turn at the last building. A pang of guilt came over Erin about letting Cal go through the roof alone. It was a good thing her partner was a man without any known fears.

Finding Cal's phobia turned into a mission at the precinct. Everyone had one thing that spooked them, but MacDonnell's fear eluded the gang. During a nightcap at a local bar, Cal admitted the only thing he dreaded was losing his family. His coworkers razzed him. They wanted to hear he was afraid of snakes, heights, or clowns. Sergeant O'Malley made a crack about wishing someone would make his own wife and kids disappear. Cal was angered by the remark, and it almost came to blows. He refused to speak to O'Malley the rest of the night. The others refused to believe he wasn't afraid of anything. Just the AIDS test alone every time a suspect bled on you was enough to make even the toughest cop balk. Erin knew better. Cat and Bree were as much a part of Cal as his limbs.

Erin walked past a line of battered mailboxes. The floor was inlaid with white and black hexagonal tiles, many of them chipped and cracked.

"Four-One Ida, what's your status? Over," the radio blared.

"Eighty-five is still requested, Central," Erin responded. "What's the ETA? Weren't they supposed to be here by now?"

"Four-One Adam unable to respond due to vehicular accident en route—redirecting Four-One David to your location. ETA is ten minutes. Recommend you wait for backup, over."

"Negative, Central. Officer already in pursuit, over and out."

Erin was not happy with the turn of events. Ten minutes could be an eternity. A shadow at the top of the stairs dissolved into the darkness. If Cal had scared out the perp and he spotted her, then he'd be looking for another exit. Her plan was to sandwich the suspect between herself and Cal. Erin took out her Maglite and crept up the stairs.

At the top of the stairs she shone her light across the landing. Nothing.

She walked across the hall to the second set of stairs and put her foot on the first step. She heard a creak behind her. Before she could turn, there was a swish, like the sound of a switch whipped through the air. Then silence. Not a drop of rain, not a squeak; someone had pulled the plug on the whole world. She realized she was tumbling forward, only because the floor raced toward her. An odd sensation, like gravity had been turned off. She was floating. The moment slowed (a Hollywood special effect) and her view rotated, like clinging to a ball in flight, past the floor and back to the scene behind her. Her temple bore the weight of the fall, hard—she couldn't move. A beautiful man with long dark hair and bronzed skin had one arm across his chest, and in his hands he held a gleaming sword parallel with the ground. He was the second-to-last thing she witnessed before everything went dark. The last thing Erin Ramos saw was her headless body falling toward her.

4

Cal searched the roof thoroughly before hopping over the brick divider between the buildings. He landed in a puddle. The cold rain was still coming down hard, and the door to this roof creaked open and shut at the wind's whim. It was bent, which kept it from closing completely and there was a rusty hole where the lock had once been. He turned on his Maglite and carefully opened the roof door. Something scuttled on the floor below beyond the range of his light. He entered the access way and proceeded down the stairs, his white breath trailing behind him.

The dilapidated tenement, once a shelter for many, now reeked of must, urine, and burnt ashes, the by-product of transients trying to keep warm. Patterns pressed into the tin ceiling reflected a previous era when intricate moldings, rich with details and fancy woodwork, were built into every structure by skilled immigrants. Slumlords turned these edifices into havens for rodents, roaches, and drug addicts.

Cal started to unholster his gun, then changed his mind in favor of the nightstick. He was worried about squatters who might be living there. Nothing hurt worse than accidentally killing someone already down on his or her luck.

The air was colder inside the building. Cal took that as a bad omen. Back at the precinct, the veterans told stories to spook the rookies. The most popular was about taking statements from a person in a building who they later found out had been murdered there years earlier. When they checked photo records it would be a perfect match. Others spoke of homes, which even during winter, were colder inside than outside; it was as though they were no longer connected to the natural world. Nothing good ever came of these places. What they stressed most was, turn around and leave. Just get out of there. Cal chuckled at their intensity, especially Mookie Malone, who would get that glassy stare and even forget his beer. Grown men with guns getting spooked by bumps in the dark. Cal assumed those stories were an elaborate prank to haze the younger officers. He was sure of it—until he entered this building.

The hairs on his arms bristled and he could not shake the feeling that something was wrong. His decision not to wait for backup haunted him.

In his career, Cal had performed a wide range of unpleasant and dangerous tasks. He had recovered decomposed corpses, faced down drug dealers and violent addicts, and broke up angry mobs, while suffering the protestations of a police-wary citizenry. Each day, he left for work confident that he could handle anything "the citizens" threw at him. Now, he felt beyond the safety of that assurance. And, he thought he was being watched.

He landed softly on the top floor and threw his light up and down the hallway.

Clear.

The scuttling resumed in one of the abandoned apartments at the end of the corridor. Cal crept down the hallway to 5E. The door was off its hinges. He peered into the void and listened before shining his light through the doorway.

The radio suddenly blared.

"Four-One Ida, what's your status? Over."

His heart almost burst from his chest. Cal turned the volume down and left the response to his partner. He cursed himself for not turning it down earlier. His position was now compromised, which could be bad if the suspect turned out to be a full-blown wacko. Few assailants would actually attack a police officer, but any cop who depended on that to keep him safe had one foot in the grave.

A few tense seconds passed with no response.

Cal secured his nightstick and drew his pistol. He walked through the doorway and shone the light around the room. It was a studio apartment; the kind coveted by creative types in Manhattan. Beer cans, old newspaper, and dirty dishes were scattered across the wet floor. Plastic buckets caught leaks from the roof, but not enough. A stained mattress lay flopped in the corner. Cracks in the plaster exposed wooden slats in the walls. He could see into the bathroom, the only extension of the single room. There was nowhere to hide, not a corner or a box from which to conceal anything larger than a cat. The room was empty. Yet, something was wrong.

If Cal really had a sixth sense, it was the ability to know when he was being stalked. The image of a gazelle in high grass kept popping into Cal's head. Every nerve in the cop's body fired up, his hackles stood on end.

He started to back out of the room slowly. Someone was in there with him, he just was not seeing them. He shifted his light around as he backed up. Rain dripped on his shoulder . . . and something gooey, too. It smelled acrid, its texture like melted glue. He spun around, ready to fire. No one was there. Then a frightening thought occurred to him. He looked up. Pressed against the black ceiling, two yellow eyes and a fanged grin looked back.

CHAPTER 2

SHE'S CRAZY 'CAUSE SHE'S BEAUTIFUL

1

Seth Raincrest slammed the snooze control for the fifth time. Each nine-minute reprieve was, of course, the last before he would drag his lanky frame from the mattress, but the slow roll down to his pillow appealed more than the walk to the bathroom. The day officially began when Hoshi—fully aware that it was within her master's power to end the incessant buzzing—planted her furry rump on Seth's head until the bad noise stopped.

Seth sat on the edge of the bed and clicked on the news. A student in Queens had been murdered, a baby in Cleveland was kidnapped from day care, India and Pakistan were pointing nuclear missiles at each other again, Meredith Vieira started her five-part series on colon cancer, and Mafia capo Dominic Tagliatore, the Debonair Don, was finally indicted on thirteen counts of racketeering. "Yay for the good guys," Seth grunted.

He lit a Camel and decided he could get by another day without showering or shaving, so long as he changed his underwear. Seth could stretch a bar of soap for two months, a technique he had perfected in foster care. In the bathroom, his reflection studied him—bloodshot hazel eyes shaped like crescents standing on their tips, a Roman nose, and greasy brown hair. He hadn't a clue which side of the family he took after. All record of his past had been destroyed, along with his parents, in a house fire thirteen years earlier. And, Seth could not recall anything from before the day of the fire. Because of a passing resemblance to John Lennon, friends teased he was probably the Beatle's love child. Seth always felt more like Ringo.

He shuffled into the spare bedroom he used as his photo studio. The answering machine beeped. He ignored it. The ashtray on the work counter, piled high with bleached white carcasses of Seth's addiction, overflowed with a halo of ash around the base. The workspace was decorated with small figurines of Bugs Bunny, Minnie Mouse, Porky Pig, and other cartoon characters, positioned in ways that would perturb any censor. Behind the figurines, an eclectic collection of bongs loitered against a wall marked with vertical measurement like that of a police lineup. A sign over the bongs read *The Usual Suspects*.

He pulled out a nude photo layout he had shot earlier in the week. Six days overdue, Seth just couldn't muster the interest to get the job done. He attributed his procrastination to working best under pressure.

Seth studied the layout. The girls, a blonde and an Asian, were going at each other with rubber sex toys. The story began with them in a doctor's waiting room. Since the doctor was taking so long, patient and nurse decided it would be the perfect time to get each other off. *Just like it happens in real life*, Seth thought. He'd hired them through an ad for models in the *Village Voice*. Seth was amazed that he could always find someone willing to do a shoot for a few hundred bucks or less. He had yet to encounter the girl, filled with righteous indignation, who would accuse him of being a pervert and a detriment to humanity. Apparently, those types did not read the *Village Voice*.

The girls who answered Seth's ads always needed more money than their social situation or education would allow them to earn. The blonde in the photo, a coed, needed airfare to Cancún for spring break. The art store she cashiered at paid crap. So there she was, naked, with her head between a stranger's thighs, clueless that this easy-money moment was going to follow her for the rest of her life like herpes. Most girls didn't realize that the sets were resold to multiple publications; that they were uploaded to Web sites and downloaded by tens of millions everywhere throughout the world.

Seth lit a fresh cigarette as his roommate Joe walked in.

"Who's on the machine?" Joe asked.

"Dunno."

Joe played the message.

"It's Carmine. Where's my goddamned photo shoot?! You screw me on this and you're not only fired, but we'll come at you so hard you won't be able to afford a disposable camera! Hell! You won't be able to hold a disposable camera!"

"Crap! Are you gonna make the rent?" Joe asked.

Seth took another drag on his Camel and began to thumb through an issue of *Penthouse*.

"Man, this routine is getting old, Seth."

Seth shuffled to the window. Cracked open, the winter air brought sounds of commuters, shopkeepers, and local transients beginning the day's hustle. From his five-story perch, he followed the line of Avenue A past Tompkins Square, through the heart of the East Village, until it disappeared at Houston Street. Tenements once home to a million immigrants were now filled with artists, musicians, actors, students, and outcasts. Ramshackle shops and bars, clustered around the foundation of every building, were the best way landlords could afford the taxes on their rent-stabilized properties.

"I'm serious, man," Joe continued. "You quit school, you bagged on Kevin's wedding without a word, you dumped Mindy the day you were supposed to take her to the clinic. You never come through for anyone."

Across the street, an old hooker hustled a man sweeping snow off his stoop. Her skin, dry and brown, sagged from her bones like she had just walked out of the desert. She had to work mornings because she couldn't compete with the new girls at night. There were always new girls.

Their voices bounced off the buildings and echoed through the nearly deserted street. The man shouted about children living there and kicked her off the stoop. The hooker stumbled to the corner. Her erratic footprints in the snow traced her muddled perceptions.

Outside the Korean deli, a stray mutt pissed on a crate of oranges. Mr. Cho chased it away with a broomstick, then hosed down the oranges and put the fruit out on display. Kids hurled snowballs at a city bus. A beautiful redhead with map in hand searched for the right street.

Red was tall, with a regal air. She walked with an odd gait Seth couldn't quite place. He imagined she had hooked up with a well-endowed stud after a night of clubbing and was now trying to make her way back to New Jersey. If Red starred in one of his sets, he could sell porn to the Pope.

"Seth!" Joe shouted.

"What?"

"What are we going to do with you? We're tired of your shit."

"We? Who's *we*? You're *all* discussing me now?" He threw his cigarette butt out the window and lit another one.

While crossing the street, the old whore was hit by a garbage truck. Her body landed in the middle of the intersection. Traffic stopped. A crimson army marched outward from her broken body.

"My God!" Joe screamed. He grabbed a blanket off the couch and ran from the apartment.

The whore had solicited Seth on his stoop once. Her teeth were rotted, her eyes bloodshot, and she smelled like piss. Seth wondered if she was better off dead.

A man in a long leather coat and Dalmatian-print Stetson elected himself to be in charge. Joe handed him the blanket. Seth chuckled. Joe, a transplanted Californian, was the only one in the crowd who came out of his home to help. He never got over his small-town habits.

The doorbell rang.

Seth was surprised to find the redhead with the map waiting on his doorstep. She was taller than he was, filling the door frame. A tan suede coat ran down the length of her body. A leather satchel hung over one shoulder. Her hair was long and unnaturally bright against her swarthy complexion. Random blond streaks gave the impression that her head was aflame. Her eyes, set far apart, were the color of moss under a full moon.

She held up an index card, and in what sounded somewhat like an Eastern European accent, stated, "You are Seth Raincrest."

"Yeah . . ." Seth took a drag on his cigarette. "You're answering the ad?" he asked, licking his lips.

"No."

"Too bad." Seth exhaled smoke slowly while he studied this Amazon beauty. "Look—I'm not interested in joining any cults, even if you're a member."

"Excuse me?"

"I'm not buying."

"I'm not selling."

"Do I know you?"

"We have met before. Are you going to invite me in?"

Seth was suspicious. Relatives of the girls he photographed sometimes blamed him for their disgrace and tried to hold him accountable, especially when a model OD'd on drugs. The dope was inevitable when you did that kind of work, but it aged them to where they weren't even useful for sets. Finding new girls was easier than trying to save one. He merely chronicled one stage of their downfall. He wasn't their friend and certainly wasn't their analyst. Seth was concerned he'd someday be the target of a family's vigilante wrath.

"Sorry, but I'd remember *you* if we met."

She peered at him. "My name is Lelani. We met long ago. A place called Aandor."

"And-or? That's in Canada, right?" Seth took another drag.

"It's complicated. Are you going to invite me in?"

"What's complicated?" he asked.

"Really . . . have you no sense of etiquette?"

There was a glimmer of condescension in the way she spoke to him. She had an air about her. An image of Lelani, naked with her head between some girl's thighs, entered Seth's thoughts. *How's that for etiquette,* he thought. Sensitive due to his vocation, any buzz or whisper often gave Seth the impression he was being talked about. He dealt with perceived slights by imagining the offender in a compromising situation. This time it didn't work. Lelani came off so confident, so superior, that the thought of her nude only made him more insecure.

"I flunked finishing school," he said. "And, you're weirding me out. I wouldn't invite you in if you offered to jump my bones."

"That will not happen."

"Then I'm real busy. B'bye . . ."

Lelani braced the closing door with her foot. "You were put into foster care when you were thirteen. You have no recollection of your life prior to that year."

Seth felt a tug of curiosity, but suspected this was a scam. "I already know that, honey. My parents got turned into crispy critters in a fire. There's nothing mysterious about amnesia induced by trauma."

"Yes, but you don't remember anyone from before that time."

Seth's oldest memory was of sitting on the curb outside his burnt home, breathing with help from an oxygen tank. A medic placed a blanket around his shoulders and told him lies about how everything would be all right.

Seth's instincts were telling him she was trouble, but he couldn't figure out her angle and curiosity got the best of him. There was also the chance that he might convince her to pose. He released the door. "You knew me before the fire?"

"Give me a chance," she implored. "I assure you, my intentions are not malevolent."

Thirteen years ago his case had stumped everyone from police to social services. No one, not relatives, friends, neighbors, or teachers, came forward to claim him. Social services concluded that his family had just moved to New York. The fire destroyed all evidence of his origins. They could not trace his next of kin. He was placed into foster care until someone claimed him.

On the eve of his eighteenth birthday, Seth had prayed that someone would come for him before midnight. It was the last time he ever made a plea to a higher power. The next day he was discharged from the foster home. His disappointment festered until he wanted nothing to do with the people who abandoned him. Now, someone was laying claim to a part of his past he had put to rest.

"Are we related?" Seth asked.

"Definitely not."

He was pleased to hear the news.

"A cup of tea would be appreciated," Lelani prompted. "It is freezing outside."

"This is New York. You might be psychotic for all I know."

"You would be dead by now," she said, calm.

Seth wasn't sure if she was joking.

Joe returned from the street, shivering.

"Poor lady—the paramedics said she isn't going to make it," Joe said. "That guy in the Stetson took it really hard. I think he knew her."

"The only thing that guy's upset about is his lost income, you yokel. He's her pimp. Are you even living in the real world?"

"What's the real world, Seth? One where you never lift a finger to help someone else? You barely help yourself. You're the most negative . . . Who's she?" Joe asked, pointing to the girl.

"Joe, meet Lelani. We met in Canada a long time ago."

"It was not Canada . . ."

"Look Seth, we need to finish our talk—" Joe said.

"Sorry, dude. We were just heading out for some tea."

"Tea? You can't just—"

"Lelani came a long way just to see me, and I won't be rude. We'll talk later."

"But . . ."

Seth grabbed his coat and led Lelani down the stairs.

2

Fresh snow rushed from the sky to join its graying counterpart on the streets of Alphabet City. People huddled in their overcoats, trying to keep nature's cold bite from their collars. Seth tried to lose the girl, but she kept pace with him.

"Is it far?" Lelani asked.

"Is what far?"

"The café."

"Café?"

"The tea?"

"We're not going for tea. I just said that to get Joe off my ass. I'm picking up some . . . uh, supplies."

They arrived at a tenement on Avenue C. Two young girls were building a snow wall around the stoop.

"Hey, Mr. Picture Man," one of them said. She raised her hand for a high-five slap.

"Hey, Ms. Sassafras, what's happening?" Seth obliged.

"When you gonna take my picture and make me famous?"

"Caitlin, you don't want to be famous. You want to read

books and work in an office. And don't tell anyone you have money or they'll all come a-borrowing."

"I already got a moms, Mr. Picture Man. What I need you for if you ain't gonna make me a star?"

"Just keeping you honest. Building a fort, huh?"

"Them stupid boys from the projects come 'round and throw snowballs at us. We just minding our own business."

"Why are you even out here in the cold?" Seth asked.

Caitlin gazed at her boot. She ground the snow beneath her toe.

"Your mom?" Seth guessed.

Caitlin looked up. "I hate it when she all shaking and throwing up."

"Is your mother ill?" Lelani asked the girl.

Caitlin remained quiet. Seth felt pressure to say something right, but nothing came into his head. He pulled out five dollars. "Here. Take your friend to the pizza shop. Have a slice, play video games."

Caitlin and her friend were halfway down the block when she turned around and shouted, "When I'm famous, I'ma buy you a limo, Mr. Picture Man!"

"What color, Sassafras?" he returned, but the girls were long gone.

Lelani looked confused. "Should we look in on your friend's mother?"

Seth considered it, but decided against it. "None of our business," he responded.

They entered the building. Five flights up, Seth rapped a coded beat on the door. There was a rustling in the apartment.

Through the door a muffled voice sang, *"The time has come, the Walrus said, to talk of many things: of shoes—and ships—and sealing wax—of cabbages—and kings . . ."*

"Open the fucking door, Earl," Seth said, pounding.

Earl, in his boxers and tank top, looked like he just awoke from a long sleep. He showed them into the kitchen while ringing out his ear with a finger and said, "You know . . . the code's for everyone's protection, man."

"Is the *insignificant* other around?" Seth asked.

"At work. Who's the chick?"

"Nobody. Ignore her."

"This is my place of business, man. How do I know she's clean?"

"You don't."

"You think with your dick, man."

"Hey, can we get on with it? I've got deadlines."

Earl disappeared into the back room. They heard a window open and then the clang of boots ascending a fire-escape ladder. Seth sat next to a peeling radiator pipe on a wiry kitchen table chair.

Seth pointed to the other chair and said, "This may take a while."

"I'll stand, thank you."

"Really, make yourself comfortable. He has to go up to the roof, across two buildings, and down three apartments. Most paranoid fucker I ever met."

"Paranoia is just another form of awareness. These chairs do not look sturdy."

"I've sat in them a dozen times. They've never let me down."

"You're mocking me."

"Suit yourself."

"You think I'm strange."

"Well, you're beautiful—that makes you crazy by default."

Lelani took her overcoat off, revealing an olive turtleneck knit, blue jeans, and black riding boots. The pattern of her shirt ran vertically, hugging the contours of her body. Seth took measure of her in his professional capacity—too meaty for the scrawny centerfolds in his third-rate periodicals, since the camera added pounds, but perfect in reality.

"You find me comely?" she asked, smiling.

Seth blushed, a first for him. His world was full of promiscuous women, desperate for money, for whom no breach in decorum was likely. Lelani, however, had him on the ropes. He got the impression she knew something he didn't—something profound. A face like hers could land the cover of *Playboy*. Red could have any straight man she desired, and convert a few souls from the *other* team as well. What did she want from him?

"You still think you know me from before the accident that killed my folks?" he asked.

"I recognize many things about you."

"People change."

"So far, I haven't been surprised by what I've found. Character stays constant, and you are who you are. Incidentally, what is your trade?"

"'Mr. Picture Man.' I'm a photographer."

"An artist? No one at school expected you to succeed. At anything."

"We went to school together?"

"The best in Aandor."

"So I *am* Canadian?"

Lelani's watch alarm went off. She pulled a pill case from her satchel. "Does your friend have any tea?"

Seth checked the refrigerator and found a can of iced tea.

"Cold tea?" Lelani said, examining the can.

"Beggars and choosers . . ."

She placed a purple pill into her mouth, then washed the pill down with the tea. Seth wondered if it was Prozac or some other mind-stabilizing substance.

"Vitamins?" he asked, innocently enough.

"Allergies."

"Right. So tell me about our school. Did the girls wear those plaid micro skirts?"

"Why you were permitted into our school is a subject of much speculation. There was no evidence that you were intellectually gifted. And no, you are not Canadian."

"Did you *search* for me just so you could insult my intelligence?"

"I found you because you have a duty to complete for some very important people, and I intend to see you fulfill it."

"How could I possibly have had any important obligations at thirteen? Let me guess . . . I'm royalty."

Lelani laughed. "Your mother was a tavern wench."

". . . Okay, you're a time traveler. We have to save the future!"

Her cool manner and the earnestness of her gaze were unsettling. This was either the most amazing prank ever or the woman was deeply disturbed.

"You're mocking me again," she said. "You do have a healthy imagination, though. Good thing, because you'll need it."

"Now *you're* mocking me," he said, throwing her vernacular back at her.

"Things are seldom what they seem. There are thirteen years of your life which you cannot account for. Open your mind. Your origins will challenge everything you hold to be true—about your role, your world, even your universe."

Seth burst out laughing. She was a sideshow drama queen; part carnie hack, part Rod Serling. "You're so full of shit, sister . . ."

They heard shuffling in the bedroom, the clatter of blinds. Earl reappeared a moment later. He threw a ziplock bag full of herb on the table. "You owe me a hundred."

"Put it on my tab."

"Dude, you already owe me for last week. I'm not running a charity."

"*Dude*, I'm tapped out right now. I'm good for it."

Lelani picked up the bag and examined the contents. She arched an eyebrow at Seth. "Supplies?" The wave of contempt he imagined earlier had returned.

"Look, we have nothing to talk about," he said, grabbing the bag from her. "You're a space cadet."

Lelani pulled out a photograph from her satchel and put it before him on the table—a man and a woman embracing cheek-to-cheek and smiling.

"Who are they?" Earl asked, craning his neck.

Seth was silent. He stared at the photo in disbelief, picked it up with both hands as though to disprove its existence, and fondled the glossy image with his thumb as one would a fine piece of velvet. A match had been lit in the dark recesses of his mind.

"Where the hell did you get this?"

"We have something to talk about after all."

3

Alphabet City was a freshly shaken snow globe—four inches already on the ground, with no end in sight. Lelani's hair billowed against the white backdrop of Tompkins Square Park like a flame. Its only competition came from the lights on a fire engine that blared past them on Tenth Street. Lelani refused Seth's suggestion that they take a taxi back to his apartment.

"I'll pay," he insisted.

"I wouldn't fit."

"Do you mean physically?"

"Yes."

"Are you kidding?"

"Quite serious."

The knowledge she held boosted Seth's tolerance for her eccentric nature.

"So dish," he said.

"Dish?"

"How'd you come by a picture of my parents?"

"Parham and Lita Raincrest were not your biological parents."

Seth's heart sank into his gut. "I've been an orphan my entire life?"

"No. It was a cover. You were part of a group that emigrated here years ago to raise an infant. The environment at home was not safe. We lost contact with the group shortly after your arrival."

"Where's the kid now? Where's the rest of the group?"

"I wish I knew," she said. "You are the first one I've tracked. Luckily, you retained your name."

A name that belonged to people who allegedly weren't even his parents, Seth realized. "Who were my parents, then?"

"Your mother is Jessica Granger, a tavern wench at the Grog and Grubb Inn. Your father . . . unknown. A merchant who visited the pub. Once."

"What city? Toronto?"

"You are not Canadian."

From orphan to bastard in less than five minutes, Seth thought. "You said Jessica *is* my mother."

"To the best of my knowledge she still works at the Grog."

The flood of questions came too fast for Seth to absorb: What was his mother like? Was coming to the U.S. his own choice? A fear grew within. To his surprise, Seth realized he was not ready for the whole truth.

"How'd I get into your school?" he asked, changing the subject. "If you're any indication, it was probably a snob society. 'Tavern wench' doesn't sound like a high-paying career."

"Magnus Proust gives scholarships to the less fortunate. He believed in your talents . . ."

"Magnus Proust?" The name rattled around Seth's mind with no slot to settle in. It sounded more like a new brand of Trojan condom than a headmaster at some elite school.

"What's the school like?"

"Thirty students spend their first year as Novitiates. The subsequent cycles are two-year programs: twenty from the first year advance to become Apprentices. Ten are graduated from this lot to be his Acolytes. Of them, only four finally achieve the honor of becoming Magnus's Adepts. I am an acolyte. You are an apprentice."

The titles were odd, but Seth had heard stranger things.

Some of his models came from the well-to-do class—rebels acting out against their banishment to Exeter and Vassar. But more important, Seth had found a big chink in her story. He was five or six years older than she was. No way was she a senior classmate to him. The suspicion that this was an elaborate con or the musings of an unbalanced mind crept back, but this time he experienced trepidation, as though he might lose something important—something he *wanted* to know. "What did we study?" he asked, playing along.

"Alchemy, transmogrification, sorcery, enchantments, curses . . ."

Seth stopped. His teeth ground together painfully. He turned away from Lelani.

". . . You were the group's mage," she went on. "Though little true magic remains on this world, it was considered a necessary precaution."

His lips clenched into a line. Seth hid his trembling fists in his pocket. The brick wall he faced, with its perfect uniformity, beckoned to be punched.

"Is something wrong?" she asked.

Seth took three deep breaths and turned to face her. "You forgot to mention the talking hat that chooses which house we belong to."

"What talking hat?"

"I'm a schmuck for buying your crap! You think this is funny? Leading me on to think I'll finally know something about my past?"

"Seth . . ."

"Shut up! Just shut up. I've spent years in a dozen homes. You'll never know what it's like, walking the streets, wondering if the hotdog vendor or subway clerk or the bum on the corner is a cousin or an uncle. Do you even have a clue what it's like to not know who you really are? Where you come from?"

The stiffness of her lips broke. It was the first time Lelani looked unsure about anything. "No," she responded. "I'm not aware of what you have endured."

Seth had her on the defensive for a change. He closed the gap between them and stared into her eyes. He was hoping for just a hint that Lelani was being sardonic, an invitation to smash her pretty mouth. Instead, for the first time since they'd met, that air of condescension receded from her. She gazed back into his eyes and touched his soul, a warm hand on a cold spirit. She put her arms around him. Her body was strong and comforting—a shelter in the snow. Her cheek touched his. What surprised him most was the sincerity she exuded. His anger drained through their embrace.

"I'm not handling this very well," she said. "I apologize."

"Yeah," he said, and walked off without her. Then Seth stopped. There it was again, that nagging curiosity. *Is she crazy?* Even the most ambitious swindles used pieces of truth to snag victims. "Is there any way we can get to the facts without the crazy talk?" he asked.

Lelani bit her lip as she considered it. "I'll try."

A minute later, they turned the corner onto Avenue A to spot a cluster of red flashing lights down the street. The moment turned surreal when Seth realized his building—his apartment—was the subject of the attention as smoke belched from his living room window.

They passed a group of local youths who raised their arms pushing against the sky and in unison chanted, "The house—the house—the house is on fire!" Then they broke into laughter.

Seth didn't see the humor. He checked his watch. They'd only been gone for three hours. How could he lose his home— again—in such a small span of time? No one should be so un- lucky as to have his home burned twice in one lifetime. He hid his ziplock full of pot behind a neighbor's trash bin and ap- proached a police officer who ordered him to step back behind the line.

"That's my place, man!" Seth shouted.

"When we get the all clear from Fire, we'll let you up, sir," the officer said.

Seth spotted two of his neighbors, Ramone and Chad, huddled beneath a quilt under Mr. Cho's awning. Ramone held Hoshi in his arms.

"Oh Seth! Thank God you're okay," Ramone said.

"What happened?" he asked them.

"Explosion," Chad said. "It tore through our wall."

"An explosion?"

Lelani stepped away from them to face the activity. From her satchel she pulled something that looked like a compact. *Great time to fix your face,* Seth thought.

"Where's Joe?" he asked.

Ramone and Chad looked at each other, expecting someone to answer.

"Where's Joe?" Seth asked again.

"We thought you . . . we heard shouting from your . . . We didn't realize . . ."

"Where is he?"

Chad pointed to an ambulance outside the cordoned off area. Sobbing, Ramone braced himself on Chad's shoulder. Seth ran toward the ambulance. The surreal scent of barbecue permeated the air. He saw a draped body inside. The paramedic held him back.

"Whoa, where do you think you're going?"

"My roommate is in there. How he's doing?"

"He's not— Look, I'm sorry. There was nothing we could do."

Seth felt punch-drunk. His breakfast clamored to come up. "But . . . I just talked to him an hour ago."

"It was a powerful explosion. He died instantaneously."

Seth burped. He could taste his stomach acid. It was short warning—he threw up on the street, just missing the paramedic's shoes. The medic pulled paper towels from his truck and handed them to Seth.

"Sorry," Seth said, then hurled again.

"Don't worry. Here, take these with water. They'll settle your stomach." Seth accepted the tablets. "You should talk to that detective," the paramedic added, pointing to a fiftyish-looking man in a brown trench coat. "And I'm sorry."

Lelani joined him as he approached the detective. She looked concerned. "We should leave," she said. "It's not safe here."

"Shut up."

"This fire was not an accident."

He faced her. With a stiff accusatory finger he said, "What did we say about the crazy talk?"

Lelani bit her lip and remained quiet. She looked up and down the street, examining the crowd surrounding them.

"Hey you!" Seth called to the detective. "The guy in the ambulance is . . . was my roommate."

"Sorry," the detective said. "If it's any consolation, Mr. Raincrest died quickly."

"I'm Raincrest. My roommate was Joe Rodriguez."

"Oh," the detective said. He scribbled the correction into his notepad. "Good thing I hadn't started the paperwork yet."

"What happened?"

"Near as we can tell, the gas line erupted and a fireball engulfed the place. Took out your neighbors' apartments, too. They said they heard some yelling and your name came up a few times. Maybe that's why they thought it was you in the blast."

"Joe and I had a disagreement before I left, but we weren't yelling. Maybe he was on the phone."

"Where were you?"

"At a friend's house. I was with her . . ." Seth realized that Lelani wasn't behind him. She was scouring the crowd again.

"Who?" the detective asked.

"Her."

"The redhead?"

"Yeah, that's the one."

"She a roommate, too?"

"No, I just met her today. I think she escaped from Bellevue."

"Lucky you. Look, I can't let you in yet. Once the Fire guys give the okay . . ."

"Thanks."

Seth walked over to Lelani.

"We should go now," she repeated.

"Hey, nutjob, my goddamn home was fireballed! I'm not going anywhere. I have to see what I can salvage."

"Do it quickly."

"We can't, yet."

Lelani took him by the arm and led him toward the entrance. She mumbled as they walked. Seth expected to be stopped at any moment. They were already up the stairs before he realized they'd snuck through. When they got to his floor, she told the firemen they had permission to be there. The city workers handed them face masks.

"How'd you do that?" Seth asked.

"They teach us these things in Bellevue," she said, with a wry smile.

A gray haze saturated the room. Even through the mask, the acrid air made its way into his mouth and nose. Piles of black ash sat where walls once stood. Charred floorboards remained of varnished woodwork. They had to watch where they walked. Electrical wires dangled from the ceiling. Lelani hung back. Seth made his way to his studio. All the photos were melted into slag. His cameras were destroyed, his computer, his stockpile of film—everything was gone. A puddle of plastic sat where the phone used to be.

"Motherfucking goddamn shit!" he yelled. "It's gone! All of it! Everything I own is shit." He shoved his fingers into his hair and balled his hands into fists. Seth was on the verge of crying, but didn't want Red to see him that way, so he swallowed the pain and pushed it into his gut.

Lelani pulled her compact out again. She held it before her and gingerly circled the room.

"Why are you doing that now?" Seth demanded.

"Pardon me?"

"You just had that compact out ten minutes ago. Your face needs less work than anyone I know."

Lelani followed his line of sight to her hand. "I'm not putting on makeup," she said. "I'm checking for residual . . . well, it's more 'crazy talk.' I'll spare you the details." She handed him the device.

It was a heavy, ornate brass disk. There was a concealed hinge on one side and a clasp opposite it. On the inner lid was a mirror, but not the cheap kind mass-produced by Revlon. This was the cleanest reflection Seth had ever seen, pure liquid silver, as though you could stick your hand through it to the room on the other side. On the inner base were a series of assorted gems, and lines of pearls embedded in the brass. Around the jewels were intricate designs and patterns etched into the metal. Some jewels blinked, others remained lit. They cast a laser-like grid onto the mirror. It looked like a Victorian-era version of a Palm Pilot.

"What the hell is this thing? A tricorder? It must be worth a fortune."

"It's hard to explain. Just think of it as a Geiger counter for now. The gas line did not cause this fire. The explosion was the result of an attack. I'm quite certain you were the target."

"Oh, here we go again."

"Listen, before you lecture me; I've come a long way to find you—not to insult your intelligence, not to make your life miserable, not to start a friendship, but to help you discover yourself and in so doing, help my cause. I don't want money and I don't want pity for my mental state. I understand what you are going through . . . the loss of a home and friends is a terrible thing. I know because I have lost my own home."

Her fierce sincerity almost succeeded in making Seth forget she was a nutjob.

"I don't know what to make of you," he said. "And I don't have time to figure it out. My roommate's dead. My home's a cinder. I might be sleeping on a park bench tonight."

"Then perhaps I can give you some practical help. I have a room on Twenty-third Street. You can stay with me until you decide your next step."

"What's the catch?"

"You accompany me to the Bronx. I have to find someone. This attack means that my timetable has been shortened. I can't leave you alone."

"Screw that." Seth dug out a tin box from the burned out closet. Inside were two twenty-dollar bills and a ten. "Who has time to trek up to the Bronx? All I have to do is get to a pay phone." Then he stormed out of the remains of his apartment.

4

Seth bought a five-dollar phone card at Mr. Cho's. By four thirty, the sun was sliding past the horizon and a cold drizzle replaced the snow, washing away the pristine blanket of white. Seth had only a dollar credit left on the card. He was still struggling to find a place to stay. A few friends offered to put up the cat who slept peacefully on the stoop. Lelani stood at a respectable distance from the deli payphone. Seth knew she wasn't there for moral support.

"Hi Earl. I need a favor . . . can I crash with you tonight? No, Kevin's still away on his honeymoon. Why not? She's still pissed at me? Look, I'm in dire straits, man. My place burned down. I'll sleep on the floor. C'mon, she's not even your wife. You're gonna pick a chick over your bud? Yeah, thanks a lot, man. Happy fucking holidays to you, too." Seth slammed the pay phone. "Asshole."

"He's being unreasonable?" Lelani asked, breaking her silence.

Seth's first instinct was to tell her to buzz off, but he realized her offer of shelter was the only option on the table at the moment. It was looking better with each call.

"No."

"Then why would he not . . . ?"

"I sold photos of his girlfriend to the amateur section of a few nude magazines—without permission. She got drunk at a party and stripped. Got off on my taking photos of her."

"Hmmm?" Lelani murmured.

"I gave her half the money. She's hot. It was a good way for me to get noticed at these publications. *She* needed the cash because she was about to get evicted from her apartment."

"Clearly, she has no sense of gratitude. So you photograph nude women for cheap periodicals?"

Seth regretted bringing it up. He heard condescension creeping back into Lelani's voice.

"I don't photograph anything anymore. I'm out of business. My cameras, my archives, a thousand dollars' worth of film, all gone. Even the graces of my employer . . . gone. I missed an important deadline today."

Seth picked up the phone and dialed another number.

"No one will help you," Lelani said.

"I'm getting that, yeah. Did you cast a spell on me?"

"You do not inspire loyalty within your circles."

Once again Seth made his appeal on the phone, this time to

an ex-girlfriend who always needed money. He offered to pay her rent and then heard the click of the disconnect.

"Why is this happening to me?" he wailed.

"You have disappointed these people once too often. They feel no allegiance to you."

Again, Seth suppressed the urge to punch her out. He considered a homeless shelter, but knew he'd never make it out by morning with the few dollars he had left.

"These friends of yours, did they know your roommate as well?" she asked.

"Yeah, so?"

"You did not mention his death. Not even once."

Seth realized she had a point. Concentrating on his own problems, he had neglected to mention Joe's death to anyone. What was worse, he couldn't undo it. His friends would be furious at him once they learned about it. The chasms he had just discovered expanded faster than his ability to bridge them. He had helped foster this shortage of goodwill toward him through the years. Joe probably put in a lot of effort on his behalf into soothing the rifts among their friends. Now his advocate was dead and he had yet to shed a tear. Add in a crazy woman's accusation that he was partly responsible for Joe's death—a case of mistaken identity—and his shame only deepened. He sat on the stoop in front of the deli stroking Hoshi's neck. No progress had been made since his eighteenth birthday, he was still alone, and he couldn't blame the fire this time.

"Come with me and you'll have a place to sleep tonight," Lelani offered. "Do it for the cat."

"At this point," Seth said, "I don't have anything more to lose, right?"

Lelani remained quiet for a moment. Then she offered her hand and helped him off the stoop. "We'll drop the cat off at my room, first," she said.

"Uh—I don't have *anything more* to lose, *right* . . . ?" Seth repeated.

"Certainly," she answered—but would not look him in the eye.

CHAPTER 3

THREE-RINGED CIRCUS MAXIMUS

1

The man with the yellow eyes dropped from the ceiling and knocked the pistol out of Cal's hand. Cal tried to twist away in time, but found himself pinned under this strange person with oozing pores. Sharp talons slashed at him and tore his bullet-proof vest. Cal couldn't get any leverage. Every way he twisted, the assailant was able to twist just as far. His assailant's proportions were off, as though his limbs were stretched beyond human capability; the lack of sleep must have been screwing with Cal's perceptions. Although he couldn't get free of the perp's viselike grip, Cal was stronger and could move the attacker's limbs wherever he brought his own arm, so he brought the full force of his steel-jacketed Maglite against his attacker's head. The man yowled and fell off.

Cal rolled out from under the man-thing and quickly checked the cuts on his face and chest. His attacker now stood between him and the hallway. That little bit of distance between them gave the officer his first full view of the creature. It looked gaunt and emaciated, its skin dolphin gray, but it was essentially a person, albeit disfigured, and there was an intelligence in its gaze. It had no intention of letting him leave. He scanned the floor for his gun, but it had fallen into the darkness. There was no time to search. He quickly pulled out his nightstick and stood up.

"You're under arrest for assaulting an officer!" Cal shouted. "Please, feel free to do this the hard way."

The yellow-eyed perp smiled. Cal was perplexed when it attempted to throw a punch from ten feet away. He was more confused when the fist actually connected with his jaw. Just as his vision cleared, he could see the creature's arm snapping back to its former proportion. *This isn't sleep deprivation,* Cal thought. Whatever it was, the assailant moved like it was triple-jointed and stretched better than his wife's yogi.

They circled, trying to decide their next move. The gray man never relinquished his position at the doorway. It didn't run, even though the element of surprise was gone, and this worried Cal. He was much larger than his attacker, and despite its unique abilities, this thing was not as strong as he was. Something else occurred to Cal. This assailant did not match the description of the suspect. *It was waiting for backup! It was stalling.*

Cal lunged, swinging the nightstick hard. The man-thing ducked, avoiding the blow. Instead of bringing the nightstick back around, Cal brought the Maglite in his other hand down, smashing it into the top of the man-thing's skull. Then he backhanded his nightstick into the assailant's face to finish the job.

The creature crumpled to the floor, groggy with pain. Cal snapped his handcuffs around the thing's wrists. The attacker had residue on his skin, like the sticky stuff he had touched earlier. It had an acrid organic smell. He searched the floor with his light and recovered his gun.

"You have the right to remain silent," Cal recited. "Anything you say can and will be used against you in a court of law."

The officer continued reciting Miranda while shoving his prisoner into the hallway. Crossing the threshold, he caught a glimpse of someone from the corner of his eye and raised his Maglite in time to deflect a sword from cleaving him in two. Sparks flew as old steel met new steel. Cal could tell from the force of the blow that this new attacker, a bronze-skinned swordsman dressed in a black leather jacket and jeans, was Mack-truck strong.

Cal pushed his prisoner down the stairs, grabbed his steel-jacketed Maglite like a rolling pin and warded off a second thrust head-on only to find himself holding half of the cleaved flashlight in each hand. Cal drove a hard kick into the assailant's solar plexus. The swordsman went down gasping for breath. Then Cal kicked him in the head. He was going for his pistol again when the little gray man grabbed him from behind. Its arms, free of the manacles, wrapped around Cal like a snake. They continued to coil until Cal was bandaged tight, his right arm pinned underneath. Then, the gray man bit him in the neck.

Cal lunged backward, smashing into the corner of the door frame repeatedly until the arms loosened. Reaching over his own head with his left hand, Cal grabbed the gray man by the scruff of his neck, then leaned forward, pulled his attacker over him, and slammed him hard into the floor at his feet. The swordsman came at him again. Cal picked up the gray man like a shield just in time to block a thrust, which came through the gray man's rib cage just under the heart. The man bled blue. Shocked by the act of piercing his associate, the bronze man hesitated.

Cal pushed the gray man toward his friend, giving him the second he needed to pull his service revolver.

"You've got a lot of nerve to ambush a cop!" Cal yelled. "You guys on drugs?"

The swordsman propped his companion against the wall and pulled out his blade. The gray man coughed dark ink. He held his side where blue liquid seeped into his shirt from the wound.

"I can get an ambulance here in minutes," Cal said. "Put down your weapons."

"Symian will be fine," the swordsman man said, with no indication of haste. "His kind's constitution is different than ours. Like stabbing putty." It did not look that way to the gray man, who was in great pain, but declined to object. The swordsman kept his weapon between himself and Cal.

"Put the weapon down!" Cal repeated.

"Time has done you justice, my captain. If you had fought this well in Aandor, the city would have never fallen."

Cal thought the bronze man mentioned something familiar, but he had trouble wrapping his mind around all these events. Guys with swords. Gray men with blue blood that clung to ceilings and contorted like they had bones of rubber—nothing in Cal's training had ever prepared him for this. These attackers have climbed out of a Cirque Du Soleil sideshow. Maybe the butter cookies the old lady had given him were spiked. If this was the new breed of perp, the NYPD was in serious trouble.

"We should have waited for Hesz," the gray man said, through a fit of coughs. "Captain MacDonnell is formidable."

"I haven't even made lieutenant," Cal interjected. "You morons don't even have the right cop."

"That's what you think," the gray man said in a raspy, guttural voice.

Cal was confused. Being called "captain" had a familiar ring. *Aandor?* Things were making less sense by the minute. This mess was just a routine call over a trespasser. But these perps knew things Cal didn't even realize he knew until they spoke them aloud.

Cal's eyes went wide. *Oh my God! My dreams.* He stood there frozen with his gun trained on them, wondering if this was a dream. Was he really still in the cruiser, dozing, as Erin blasted Tito Puente from the stereo?

Cal never heard the person creep up behind him. A hulking figure in a black fedora slapped the gun out of his hand and grabbed him by the throat. The giant's irises were blue as a Siberian husky's. His cold breath numbed Cal's face. Cal punched the man in the jaw and nearly broke his hand. The giant lifted the officer off the ground with one arm and crashed him against the wall. Cal slumped to the ground against the door frame.

"Dorn said to wait for me. You are lucky to be alive," the giant said in a voice that rolled like thunder.

"Not at all," said the gray man. "It never even occurred to him to kill us. Thirteen years have taken the edge off the good captain."

Spots appeared before Cal. He concentrated on the new assailant's deep baritone voice and tried not to black out. The man had to be close to eight feet. He had a jutting jaw and heavy brows. His lips were like two fat bloodworms copulating. His nose was broad, his bottom teeth protruded, and stuck out even when his mouth was closed. They were speaking in a foreign language he never studied, yet he understood every word. The giant called them Symian and Kraten. They called him Hesz. Cal committed the names to memory.

Kraten found Cal's wallet and pulled a photo from it. "Mac-Donnell has a woman," he said, showing the picture to his cohorts. "And a brat. Many will find that very intriguing back home," he said with a grin.

"He does not even know who he really is," Symian continued. "Besides, if we had guns this would have been easier."

"No!" said Kraten. "I'm a warrior. I want to touch death through my sword. Bolts are for children and archers."

"How will they take to you running through maidens and allies with your sword back in Aandor?" Symian said. "Perhaps we can run it through MacDonnell's wench next, *great* warrior."

The swordsman was ready to run his accomplice through again when Hesz interceded.

"ENOUGH!" he bellowed. "Guns are loud. They draw attention."

"This mission was a waste of time," Kraten said. "MacDonnell is a pawn waiting for his pension."

Cal tried to get up and stumbled. Hesz put his foot on the officer. Hesz crouched low to look Cal in the eye and in a mocking tone whispered, "Is this lie you live so complete, MacDonnell, that you will die a stranger to yourself?" Frost clung to Cal's cheeks and they turned numb. "Where is the boy? I promise your death will be quick."

Cal threw a right cross at Hesz's face. The blow glanced off his jaw with little effect. It was like hitting a wall of bone. Hesz grabbed him by the throat, lifting him off the ground. Cal went numb; Hesz's breath was giving him frostbite and he couldn't inhale for the grip. Cal kicked Hesz in the groin with little effect. The other two laughed.

"If only his father could have seen that wench's move," Symian said. "What would his father have thought?"

"You know Hesz's grandsire was a frost giant, boy," Kraten said. "The family jewels are recessed to keep from freezing."

Cal started to black out. He wished he'd had more time to sort things through . . . to say good-bye to Cat and Bree, to learn the mysteries of his past. So many things undone. He wondered if the blinding ball of white light flashing across the hallway was the gateway to the afterlife.

2

Symian screamed as the side of his face burst into flames. He covered his face with his hands, trying to smother the fire as blood poured from his eyes. The shock caused Hesz to loosen his grip, which allowed Cal to gasp a gulp of sweet air.

An insight about frost giants danced beyond the reach of Cal's mind. If only he could remember. Hesz and Kraten looked in the direction of the flare. They failed to notice the figure coming from the other direction. All of a sudden, Kraten's head was introduced to the broad side of a Louisville slugger. He fell like a sack of bricks.

Hesz hit the batter with a backhanded slap, which sent the man tumbling down the stairway. He turned toward the floating flare, which had subsided to mere illumination. A tall young woman with red hair held a ball of crackling blue-white light in her palm. Hesz released Cal and charged her. Cal leaned on the door frame and tried not to slip down farther as he watched the fight, unable to help. A devious smile graced the woman's lips. She turned around, exposing her back to Hesz, then bent over as though picking up a penny. Hesz had nearly reached her when suddenly he went flying across the hall in the other direction, and smashed through the wall at the end of the landing.

Hesz shook his head. He slowly got up and brushed the debris from his suit. He looked to the girl across the hallway with some understanding of what she had done. A murderous smiled spilled across his face. "Your bag of tricks is small, acolyte. Could they not find a grown-up for this mission? Or are all your sorcerers dead?"

"They may well be, giant," she answered, solemnly. "But you are one mage short at the moment, and all the dead sorcerers in Aandor are of no advantage to you right now."

Cautiously, Hesz stepped through the hole. He ripped off a large chunk of the banister to use as a club, and moved toward the girl. The woman stepped back into a defensive stance, her arms and hands raised, elegantly poised in a precise manner.

The giant hesitated a moment . . . then continued toward the girl, raising his club, intent on creating carnage. As he did so, Hesz exposed his underside to Cal, who was still groggy on the floor braced against the door frame and trying to pull himself up. Then it occurred to the policeman, the thing that was just beyond the border of his thoughts a moment before; something about a nerve cluster. Cal braced himself against the door frame, gathered his remaining strength, and kicked upward, hitting Hesz's external oblique muscle. Hesz let out an inhuman howl. He dropped his club and fell to his knees, clutching his side shaking. Pleased, Cal slumped back to the floor.

The woman approached Symian, who still lay on the floor holding his face and whimpering. Blue streams like ink from a busted pen flowed from his tear ducts. She pulled a small piece of the flare out from the larger ball, which crackled in her palm, and dropped it on the gray man. The residue on his skin caught fire, burning blue like a gas jet. Symian screamed again and tumbled down the stairs.

"YOUR RACE WILL DIE, WITCH!"

"Hey," Cal managed, attracting his female rescuer. He pointed to Hesz. The giant had gathered the bronze swordsman and went through the hole he had made. They could hear his clanging as he flew down a rear fire escape.

"We had the element of surprise," she said to Cal. "I was able to incapacitate their magic user before they realized they were under attack. Only a fool stays to battle a sorcerer without protection. It's best not to push our luck." The young woman crouched over him. Her face was broad and her eyes were deep as fjords, repositories for all the deep mysteries of the world.

The man with the bat rejoined them. He had a great welt on the side of his face. He reminded Cal of a young John Lennon.

"Fucking shit! This isn't worth having a place to crash!" he yelled. "I'm better off at a shelter! You never said we would be fighting eight-foot linebackers with fucking swords!"

"Are you with Anti-Crime?" Cal asked. He could hear sirens approaching. He felt hot and groggy.

"The troll bit him," she said. "We have to treat the wound before it festers."

"Take him to the hospital! I'm done with this crap!" John Lennon insisted.

"What's going on? Where's Erin?" Cal insisted.

"Your partner? She's on the second floor!" John Lennon said. "Both pieces!"

"The hospices won't know how to treat him. We'll take him to my place," the woman said.

"No," Cal said. His strength was draining every second. He struggled to talk. "Cat! Bree! They know where . . ."

John Lennon found Cal's wallet and revolver on the floor and handed them to the woman. "They know where he lives. We need to tell his cop friends and let them handle it."

She studied the wallet. "He has a woman and child," she said, pondering. "This will cause problems for his family."

"Please," Cal said, barely conscious.

"Will they really go after his family?" the Beatle asked.

"Anything's possible," the woman answered. "At some point maybe . . . if they're desperate."

The sound of police running into the building echoed up the stairwell. Radios blared, footsteps pounded, threats were issued. Cal's vision turned gray. The girl pulled an ornate compact from her satchel. *Great time to do your makeup,* Cal thought. Then everything went black.

CHAPTER 4

HARD-KNOCK LIFE

1

Daniel Hauer worked at his latest masterpiece: an ink drawing of the Green Lantern blasting away a Khund armada with his magnificent power ring. The hero's primary weapon being in fact a ring and not a lantern never seemed odd to Daniel. What made a hero great was his strength of character; he must be a true paladin of virtue and honor. Although there were many manifestations of this hero, dating back to the 1940s, Daniel preferred the second variation, test pilot Hal Jordan. He suspected that other incarnations since Jordan had been designed by a marketing department that had read too much Spider-Man (a good character in his own right, but not appropriate for the Green Lantern).

The ballpoint scratched a groove into the varnished wood as it traced the pattern of the lantern logo on the hero's chest. As Daniel put the finishing touch on it, a gray shadow sprawled across his desk. The young man looked up into the dour face of Mr. Palumbo.

"That's a beautiful illustration, Mr. Hauer. Can you explain to the room how this drawing relates to societal class structure in precolonial India?"

Daniel glanced at his friend Adrian Lutz and flashed him a look that said, *You should have warned me.* Behind Mr. Palumbo hung a series of world maps showing the evolution of political boundaries over the centuries. Daniel locked on to India, circa 200 B.C., and called up the proper information from his brain.

"Huh . . . sure."

"Really?" said Mr. Palumbo.

"Yeah, see . . . Green Lantern is a Kshatriya warrior who takes his orders from the priestly Brahmans represented by the Guardians of the Universe on Oa. The Khunds are a warrior race trying to expand their influence, in much the same way as Alexander the Great. And this drawing is like . . . when the Indians fought off the Greek general Seleucus Nicator as he tried to invade Punjab."

Adrian rolled his eyes in disbelief. Giggles erupted throughout the classroom. Mr. Palumbo, aware that few students were as well read as Daniel, nevertheless was not going to suffer any excuse for ignoring his lesson.

"I'm giving you a zero for the day. And, one other thing . . . all of your desks throughout the school are covered with these drawings. You're destroying public property."

"Destroying? You can still use them."

More chuckles erupted.

"One of your pictures ruined Katie Millar's white blouse after she rested her arm on it," Palumbo said.

Daniel's heart sank. Katie was one of the few kids to befriend him after he had transferred to George Fox Middle School two years earlier. They sat at the same desks in shared classrooms and left notes for each other (and the occasional test answers when one's exam preceded the other). With the onset of acne and wet dreams, Daniel realized Katie was more than just a school buddy. Her skin had adopted a sweet fragrance, and he was extremely aware of her budding chest, especially when she innocently bent over in a loose top. He often woke up hard at the thought of her, something he wished he did not do because he was embarrassed to face her at school, but he didn't have any control over it. Her eyes wandering toward older boys, especially with letters on their jackets, frustrated him, and now he was responsible for ruining her expensive clothes.

"Sorry," he said.

"I'm not the one you owe an apology. We've discussed your drawings at the faculty meetings. Principal Conklin made it clear that next time you were to be sent to his office. Since you are not prepared to take my lesson seriously, please leave the room."

Daniel packed his books slowly in hope Mr. Palumbo would change his mind. No such luck. All eyes stayed on him as he shuffled out the door. Standing in the empty hallway, Daniel wondered what to do next.

Only 10:00 A.M. and the day was already a bust. If he went to the mall there was a chance he'd be caught playing hooky. Then, his stepfather would get dragged into this, a situation Daniel wanted to avoid at all cost.

2

Principal Conklin sat back in his ergonomically correct executive chair like a man who thought he ran the Seventh Fleet. He was in his fifties, wore a brown suit, and his arms were up and resting on his bald head, while his gut protruded like a Butterball turkey hanging from a sling. The leather squeaked as he rocked back and forth. Daniel associated the noise with a common bodily function.

Plaques and trophies from a distinguished career as a high school athlete and medals from military service decorated the office. On the desk were pictures of the principal's wife and his two daughters, who no doubt got their good looks from the other side of the gene pool.

The man's legendary gaze made you feel as though he knew everything you thought you'd gotten away with. As Conklin blustered on and on about school property and the taxpayer's burden, Daniel considered his role in the scheme of life.

Not to be a jock, cheerleader, metal head, or standard-issue redneck increased the odds that you were a school geek. Soon, everyone would know what had transpired in Mr. Palumbo's class. That was all he needed in a school where he could count his friends on one hand. Then the words, "your father," broke him out of his trance.

"My father?" Daniel repeated, rejoining the discussion.

"Yes, Daniel, your father," Conklin drawled. "Since your arrival, fourteen desks have been mutilated thanks to your hobby. Your pappy will pay for the damaged desks so that the good taxpayers of Glen Burnie County can rest assured their money is going toward books and teachers, and not for repairing the hobby of a juvenile delinquent."

"It's not like I took a hacksaw to those things. I can wash those drawings off with soap."

"Those desks have grooves in them 'cause of your ballpoint. Son, I look good when the school looks good."

"Look, I'll never do it again, and I'll pay for the desks out of my own money. I have a part-time job at Pathmark. There's no need to bring my stepdad into this."

"I respect a boy that fears his father. Means there's hope for you, son. Tell you what . . . can you give me five hundred dollars by Monday?"

"Five hundred dollars? Those desks can't cost five hundred dollars. Who are we buying them from, Dominic Tagliatore?"

"I'll take that as a no," Principal Conklin said.

"Look, my stepdad's been out of work for a while," Daniel said. "I don't want to add to his troubles. Can't we work something out? I'll throw in extra money . . . we can call it interest. You have my word."

Conklin considered the offer for an eternity. Daniel sat there tense, wishing for the words "it's a deal" to come out the fat man's lips.

"I have to submit a budget by Wednesday. I can't take a chance that you won't make due. Everything's got to be by the book."

"But if you'd just—"

Conklin hoisted himself out of his chair and opened the door. "No means the same now as it did five seconds ago. I've got to know for sure where the money's coming from. Now get on, go to your next class."

The boy left the office uncertain of what to do next. If a bolt of lightning had hit him right that second, he would have considered it a stroke of good luck.

3

Daniel liked stocking the aisle ends at Pathmark. In addition to the unobstructed view of the cashiers—of which Katie Millar was one—he usually stacked the sale items into intricate patterns, a more appealing labor than just placing boxes on an aisle shelf. He designed the stacks so that there would never be too many extractions from one area, thus bringing the construction down. Daniel employed pyramids, helixes, double helixes, and a few shapes of his own invention, which he was unaware that engineering students spent entire semesters on. The patrons deconstructed these temples of frugality without realizing they were part of a preordained strategy.

Daniel finished setting up boxes of Honey Nut Cheerios just as Adrian polished off his third low-fat ice cream sandwich.

"Your shift's over," Daniel said. "Don't you have anything better to do than to watch me work?"

"Nope."

Daniel glanced at register three where Katie Millar scanned items and made small talk with the locals.

"Well, go home or something," Daniel said.

Adrian looked like the Antarctic explorer whose mission commander just ordered him to go for a stroll in the middle of July. Daniel glanced out the store's big front windows at the clear night sky, but from his expression it was obvious Adrian saw a blizzard.

"I ain't botherin' no one. So what happened in Conklin's office?" Adrian asked, changing the subject.

"He slung some bullshit. No, that's not right . . . first he bored me to tears, then he slung the shit."

Daniel thought about the actions that led to his predicament.

The real world vanished when he drew pictures. His mind took him to better places, where the lines between good and evil, right and wrong were crystal clear. It was like stepping into a different universe.

"The school's going to tell Clyde he owes them five hundred dollars for the desks," Daniel said.

Adrian perked up. "No! Can't you talk them out of it?"

"Only if I come up with the money by Monday. How much you got in your pocket?"

Adrian checked his pockets. He looked like a lost cause with crumbs on his lips and collar and cream dotting his ample chin. Daniel rolled his eyes.

"Hello . . . sarcasm," Daniel snapped, handing his friend a napkin.

"Oh," Adrian blinked, "no need to get snippy."

"Sorry." Daniel stole another glance at Katie. She saw him, smiled, and waved before resuming her scans.

"Conklin always hires his cousin to do carpentry jobs," Adrian said. "Guy can't keep regular work 'cause of the hooch."

"Alcohol seems to screw me no matter who's drinking it," Daniel said.

"Spend the night at my house," Adrian offered. "You can walk home with me."

Daniel cocked a suspicious eyebrow at his friend. "Not for nothing, Ade, but you wouldn't by any chance be in trouble with them Grundy boys again?"

Adrian's face dropped all pretenses. "They got it in good for me, Danny."

"Take a swing at them for once, Ade. Jeez, you outweigh both of them by twenty pounds."

"I can't. I don't know why I get so scared. My feet don't move. I feel heavy, like in a dream when you can't run."

Daniel felt a momentary disgust toward his friend. If only his own problems came in the stature of the Grundy boys.

"Ade, what are the odds that the Grundy boys are lying in wait for you, tonight?" Daniel asked. "They're probably home tonight watching *WWE SmackDown*. I think their aunt's in a cage match."

"You don't know that."

"Why are you so sure they're looking for you?"

"I didn't let them copy off my math test."

"You suck at math."

"I got a C plus. They didn't do as well. Like it's my fault they're stupid."

"So, let them cheat."

"Mama said it ain't right to cheat or help a cheater."

"Then let Mama come get you. Go home."

"Aw hell, you just wanna walk with Katie alone after shift."

"It's the only chance I get anymore. She's having lunch with the 'in' crowd these days."

Daniel realized how much he had taken Katie for granted over the past two years. He thought they would be buds forever. Things were changing. As his desires for girls grew, he noticed Katie's new interest in facial hair, driver's permits, cars, and a voice in the low-octave range—all things he lacked. She was still friendly, but always asking him for his locker room–privileged facts about one guy or another: What does so-and-so say about me? Is so-and-so still seeing what's-her-face? It was clear she saw Daniel mainly as a search engine.

"I appreciate your offer to sleep over, Ade, but that'll just piss Clyde off more. He's already madder than a hornet on good days."

"Dan, please," Adrian begged. "I'll walk behind . . . or, up front. I won't listen. Just don't make me walk home alone."

The shift was over. Katie began cashing out. Daniel threw the last few boxes on the pile and headed for the employees' room.

"Danny?" Adrian implored.

"Fine. Walk behind us. Don't talk."

Daniel launched into a trot and nearly ran over his crush flying through the employees' lounge.

"Jeez, Dan. Slow down," Katie said. Her hazel eyes had a calming effect, even when she didn't mean to. Her long auburn hair had developed a distinct scent of its own. Daniel was both numb and energized in her presence.

"Sorry. I was hoping to catch you."

"Well, make it quick. I'm getting picked up."

"Cool. Can I hitch?"

"Not my mom. Josh Lundgren."

"Captain Baseball? What makes him so special?"

"He's got a motorbike."

"Oh. I was hoping we could talk."

"About?"

"Uh . . . well, sorry about your blouse. The one you got ink on."

Katie smiled—cancer and AIDS would be cured, Israel and Palestine would settle, and solar energy would be practical—to Daniel, everything would be okay.

"I heard you got sent to Conklin," she said.

"Yeah."

"Well, don't worry. I switched desks in most of my classes so it won't happen again."

It was a bomb. Another perk of being Katie's friend severed. No more secret notes. No more lingering scent from the previous class, her residual warmth on the seat. He couldn't think of anything to say. Should he ask her not to switch? Promise never to draw again?

Instead, he said, "I see."

"Look, Danny . . . I don't know how else to say this, but . . . you got to stop watching me—in the hall at school, at lunch, here at work—I can feel your eyes on me. It makes me uncomfortable. I care about you, but not the way you want me to. I don't see you as a 'guy.' No! . . . I didn't . . ."

"I know what you mean," Daniel whispered. The shrill beep of a scooter horn cut through the thin store windows.

"I hope we can still be friends," she said.

"Sure. Of course."

Katie danced away to Josh's persistent tune. Daniel waited for the world to end. It stubbornly continued, so he grabbed his coat and left. Adrian followed.

4

Daniel and Adrian were halfway home when two large shadows burst out from behind the bushes near Mr. Randall's house. Daniel's first thought was that the Grundy boys watched too many *Our Gang* reruns. After all, who actually waited in the bushes anymore?

Both boys had white-blond hair and angelic blue eyes, yet

they were no angels. Jim-Bob, the taller one, had been left back in the second and fourth grades and used his age and size advantage to inflict terror on his younger classmates. Elijah belonged in Daniel and Adrian's grade; a prodigy in the Grundy home, he was the first and only of six siblings never to get left back. What everyone knew, except for the Grundys, was that this feat was accomplished by years of complaints from parents about the Grundy clan's consistent cruelty toward the younger kids. The school decided to push the last of this brood out for the benefit of future generations.

Adrian was sweating like a race horse. His problem, as Daniel saw it, was he couldn't stand not to be liked. Adrian never risked an action that might make someone angry. The Grundys' animus disturbed him more than their beating. He was an unapologetic mama's boy, the target of those who fed off the desire to be accepted.

"You made us wait in the cold for five hours, fat stuff," said Jim-Bob. "Where the hell were you?"

"We didn't realize you'd made an appointment," Daniel said. "He'll do better tomorrow."

"Stay the fuck out of this, Hauer. 'Less you wanna get creamed, too," Elijah said.

"Does anyone need to get creamed?" Daniel asked.

Elijah shoved Daniel back and stood between him and Adrian.

"If you insist," Daniel said, and he stepped away from the scene. He surveyed the surroundings. Mr. Randall had been renovating, and there was a lot of construction trash on the side of the driveway.

"D-Danny, where're you g-going?" Adrian stammered.

Adrian and the Grundy boys disappeared into the darkness behind Daniel as he walked only twenty feet away.

"He knows enough to mind his own business," Jim-Bob's disembodied voice said.

Daniel heard Adrian take a punch to the stomach. He was sure it hurt less than Adrian's wailing implied. The boy had more natural padding than a walrus in winter. That didn't stop him from throwing up though. He heard Adrian crying, begging them to leave him alone.

Daniel had to get close to the trash before he spotted what he wanted. He picked up a discarded two-by-four post and headed back with it propped on his shoulder.

"You back, Hauer?" Jim-Bob said as Daniel emerged from the blackness. "What you think you're going to—"

Where Jim-Bob stood, Daniel imagined Josh Lundgren's mesomorphic form: his chiseled jaw, wavy hair, and fancy wool jacket with giant letter on the front—his lips tasting Katie's sweet breath, his fingers fondling her . . .

Daniel smashed his club into the side of Jim-Bob's head. Jim-Bob hit the ground at thirty-two feet per second squared and didn't move.

Elijah tripped backward over a tree root. Daniel walked over to him and thrust the end of the two-by-four into his face. Elijah was a bloody mess.

"Don't pick on my friends," Daniel said.

"Screw you, Hauer! When we get through with you, you'll—"

Daniel smashed his bludgeon into the boy's face again, this time resulting in a resounding crunch. The boy yowled, then passed out.

Daniel threw the weapon back on the trash pile.

Adrian trembled. "I can't believe you . . ."

"What can't you believe, Adrian? That they're bigger than us? Huh? They're bullies. They don't know how to deal with anyone who stands up to them."

"But . . ."

"All you had to do was hit Jim-Bob! You didn't even have to hurt him! You don't have to win a fight to make it not worth picking on you."

"Don't yell." Adrian kept crying.

"There are worse fucking things in the world than these losers! Things that are out of our control." Daniel realized he was crying, too. His face was flushed and tears streamed down his cheeks. "When are you going to stand up for yourself, Ade? When are you going to stop letting others pick on you?"

"Stop yelling at me!" Adrian screamed.

Daniel collapsed on the curb, shoulders hunched, breath coming in spurts, shivers, and gulps. "I don't want to go home," he said. A shudder started in his shoulders and ran down his legs.

Adrian put his hand on Daniel's shoulder. "Come to my house," he sniffled.

"I can't," Daniel said.

"Oh, come to my house, Danny, please. Don't go home."

"I have to. It'll be worse later if I don't."

Daniel stood up and started to walk. He didn't look to see if Adrian followed. He wasn't even sure if it was the right direction. He just walked. The air was cold. Layers of clothing couldn't stop his sweat from cooling to a chill. His muscles ached, as though he'd been moving for hours. Then he realized he was in front of his house.

5

Daniel took a deep breath as he opened the front door to his home. He walked into the dark vestibule, each step like a bare toe searching for glass shards. His blood hammered in his ears. The ground floor was dark, and for a moment, Daniel thought it might be empty, too. Maybe Clyde passed out on the floor of O'Leary's pub. He left his jacket on as he climbed the staircase. At the top, he heard a creak and froze.

Penny Knoffler, clutching a stuffed bear, stuck her head from around the corner and gave her older brother a big smile.

"Hi," Daniel whispered.

"Are we playing peek-a-boo?" she asked.

"No. Where's Pa?"

"Pa was mad. Mommy put me in my room."

"Where's Mommy?"

Penny waddled into their parents' room and pointed to the bed. Rita was asleep. An open bottle of Valium lay on its side on the nightstand. It was typical of Rita—evading conflict through chemistry.

Daniel picked up his sister and carried Penny to her bedroom.

"I'm not tired," she said as he put her on the bed.

"I know. But Mommy's sleeping and we don't know where Pa is."

"Pa's mad," she said again.

"I know. Did he go outside?"

Penny nodded. A trickle of snot ran down her nose and she used her bear to wipe it.

"Mr. Biggles is not a tissue." Daniel pulled out a Kleenex and wiped the toy. Then he put the paper up to Penny's nose. "Blow," he said. "Did you eat?"

Penny blew, then nodded.

"Stay in here tonight. Play with your dollies. Don't come out if you hear Pa come home."

Daniel went to the door and listened for any movement. When he thought it was safe he moved and shut the door behind him.

He crept down the dark hallway, entered his room, shut the door and locked it. Sweat trickled from his armpits, and he was breathing hard. He heard no one in the hall. A few seconds passed before he flipped the light switch.

On his bed, staring at him, was Clyde with a half-empty bottle of Jack Daniel's in his hand. His stained, white tank top showed off the semper fi tattoo on his deltoid. His stubble had dark lines where the drink ran down his chin.

A lump caught in Daniel's throat. From the look in Clyde's eye it was apparent that Conklin had called him. Clyde was in the zone, a domain of pure instinct beyond reason. He just sat on the bed glaring at the boy, daring him to try and make a run for it, but Daniel's legs felt like lead posts. Clyde stood up.

"You know who called me today, boy?" Clyde said in a deep growl. He took a step forward.

"I-I'll p-pay it out of my work money, promise," Daniel whimpered. "I swear, Clyde, it won't cost you anything," he pleaded. They both knew it for a lie, because most of what Daniel earned already went to Clyde. Daniel put his hands forward to ward off the impending strike. The hands fluttered about, not sure whether to protect his face, groin, or stomach. Clyde grabbed Daniel's right hand with his left, crushing his fingers.

"Clyde! Please. I swear it was an accident. It won't happen again." Daniel started to cry.

Clyde pulled the boy's fingers back until they crunched and popped. "Think you're so fuckin' talented, boy," Clyde grunted. "Think you're some fuckin' arteest! Try 'n' draw now, you good for nothin' piece of shit. You ungrateful piece of shit! I put a roof over your head!"

Clyde brought his knee up full force into Daniel's gut. The shock drove the air from the boy's lungs and made it impossible for him to draw another breath. While still exerting crushing force to Daniel's right hand, Clyde brought the bottle around into the side of his stepson's head. Tennessee whiskey splashed over the boy. He hit him again on the same spot. Daniel could feel his legs go from under him. As he went down Clyde would not relinquish his grip on Daniel's hand. There were more crunch and pop sounds as bones and ligaments stretched beyond their limits. The boy still could not catch his breath. Spots appeared before him, and he started to turn white.

Clyde let go of the hand and kicked him multiple times all over his body. It lasted an eternity.

"Draw now, you fuckin' piece of shit," Clyde muttered as he staggered out of the room.

Daniel could still hear Clyde muttering as he walked down the hall. Sobbing, he tenderly held his injured fingers in his good hand. He took stock of his condition, checking for broken ribs. There was a cut on his head. He had to hide it. No one at school could know. He didn't want people to look at him that way. Daniel sat on the floor of his room with his back against the wall. He thought of his life and asked the ceiling why this was happening to him. He remembered happier times when his mother was still coherent and married to a better man. He sat against the wall and sobbed.

CHAPTER 5

ONE OF THOSE DAYS

Cat MacDonnell waited for the e.p.t. results—two lines if pregnant, one if she wasn't. A miracle of modern science reduced the waiting time on these tests to less than five minutes, and yet, they were the longest five minutes of the day. She'd waited until Bree was sound asleep before taking the test. In spite of her daughter's predawn rendezvous with them, the girl didn't settle down until 10:00 P.M. She had to kick Maggie out of the room because Bree kept playing with her, and Cat finally coaxed her to bed with a bribe of allowing her school friend to sleep over the following weekend. The girl did run on nuclear energy, as Cal often pointed out. He once suggested an insidious plan to replace oil and coal with five-year-olds on treadmills attached to industrial batteries. The beauty of the plan, he said, was the kids would be so pooped by the end of the day, it would allow parents time to make more babies, thus ensuring an abundance of clean power for years to come. Cat smiled. Cal had his moments.

Cat had almost burst her bladder waiting to put Bree to bed. The snow from earlier that day had been replaced with a steady, freezing rain, and the drops tapping on the window didn't help as she tried to hold it in.

Waiting was stupid, like watching water boil. Cat put the test down on the side of the sink and turned on the TV in the living room with the volume low. MSNBC was rerunning a *Dateline* feature on indicted mob boss Dominic Tagliatore, "the Debonair Don" as he was called; who allegedly murdered and connived for the past decade to become head of the biggest drug and gambling network in the Northeast. There were people in the neighborhood who claimed they knew the Don from back in the day. "A standup guy, and a great cook," they would say. Cat picked up Brianna's toys and tossed them in a box as she listened.

The apartment was spic-and-span. The lights were low, and vanilla-scented candles burned on the stone island that separated the kitchen from the dining room. She was glad they had renovated their own apartment first. They had just finished tearing out the center wall, which opened up the space. The hallway, which once ran from the front door to the rear bedroom now started just past the kitchen. The hardwood floors added a cozy touch. Her only regret was not having more sound insulation between the living room and Bree's room, which were adjacent to each other.

After tonight's shift, Cal had three days off and Cat was determined to help him get a full night's sleep. She wore his favorite Victoria's Secret negligee. She had bought new satin sheets, and candles and oils were set by the bedside, as was a book on Swedish massage. Her hands were ready to knead Cal's back like pizza dough. She would even withhold the results of her test until the morning—one less thing for him to worry about. For breakfast there would be French toast with bacon, hominy grits, and a steaming cup of Swiss almond gourmet roast. Then, she'd surprise him with tickets for that evening's Jets game.

The building was quiet. Letting their tenants go so they could renovate the other two apartments was a risky maneuver. Their single paycheck was already stretched to its limits. Once renovated, though, they could charge more for the space. Cat had offered to go back to work early, but Cal insisted she wait until Bree hit the first grade. It was important to him that the baby have constant parental care at an early age. For a man who knew nothing of his origins, Cal had a devout sense of values. He was so old-fashioned, Cat believed he was born in the wrong era. He would have been happier in the Victorian age. She didn't know how to bring up the subject of graduate school.

She'd put aside her ambitions temporarily to make Cal happy, and in truth, she enjoyed raising Bree, more than she thought possible. But the bug to pursue her MBA was nagging her more than ever. If Cat spent another five years at home stuck with a daily vocabulary of polysyllabic simplicities like "Boo-boo" and "Da-da," she'd be fit to be tied. She was thirty, and this was the perfect age to practically apply an advanced degree for optimum effect. Cal would have to pick up some slack at home. How to sell it to him, though . . . ?

Thinking of her family and the man who was undoubtedly her best friend, Cat was amazed that she was even at this point in her life. In her youth, she would have been more likely to throw eggs and rotting fruit at her husband than kisses. When she attended Rutgers University, Cat marched in the "Take Back the Night" rallies; she once shaved her head at a sit-in to bring back the Equal Rights Amendment, chained herself to a tree in Oregon to save the old growth forests, and was a huge vocal advocate of homosexual and transgender rights, before it became the mainstream. How on earth did *she* end up with a cop?

They had met at a nightclub. Catherine wore jeans and a T-shirt. Her girlfriend pointed out Cal's interest in her, from across the club. In a room filled with dozens of prodded, preened, and scantily clad women, across a blaring dance floor, he was looking at her. He later admitted to her that his friends protested his becoming ensconced with the most hopelessly plain-looking woman in a club. She was glad Cal ignored his friends' objections (and his own inherent shyness toward women) and followed his instincts.

Almost immediately, Cat experienced the best vibe over any guy who had ever approached her. As they talked, she thought he was too good to be true. She was so used to guys putting on the act just to score, that she kept waiting for him to screw up; to look at her cleavage or touch her too soon. He never slipped once. He was perfect. The most decent man she'd ever met. She was embarrassed at her own betrayal to her feminist convictions when she realized (after three drinks) that she found him gorgeous, and went weak-kneed at the thought of his baby blue eyes.

Cal's conviction toward law and order and truth was almost priestly. To "protect and serve" was more than just a job to him. By the end of their fifth date (still unmolested) Cat knew she would never find a finer man. His antiquated convictions about marriage and motherhood were a small concern, but Cat knew if she let him go, she'd spend the rest of her life measuring new suitors by the standard Cal had set; and they would all fall short. She was on her guard at first, waiting for the neoconservative, the closet Promise Keeper in every cop to rear its ugly head, but it never showed. So it was a no-brainer. Over time and through lots of trust, her feminist shields (admittedly, a bit too militant in her youth) started to thin. She had tried the stay-at-home mom thing and was better for it, but now it was time for her to attend to her dreams. Grad school was possible. Cal would bend over backward to make it happen. She'd bet her soul on it.

A special live report interrupted the show. Cat wondered if all police wives had the same knot in their stomach whenever a *special report* came on. The odds were always against a cop's spouse. If the report was not about a policeman being killed, then chances were that police were rushing to whatever crisis was happening and placing themselves in harm's way while everyone else ran the other way. But, if Cal had been involved, they would have called her already, or more likely, sent a unit over to get her.

She was on the couch clutching Bree's Pooh bear when Hunt's Point was mentioned as the location of the incident. It was Cal's precinct. Cat began wringing the toy's arm. A graphic with a bloody rifle scope appeared next to the anchorman's head with the words *Cop Killed* in bright red and yellow. Her knot tightened. The report said the incident happened only an hour ago. Plenty of time to have sent over a squad car or called. She looked at the phone on the wall, still silent.

The reporter on the scene was a local celebrity, one of those Lois Lane types with the tenacity of a pit bull and the face of a soap star. *"An officer from the Forty-first precinct was killed in the line of duty tonight . . ."*

The seam on Pooh's arm began to fray, and then it burst.

Cat stared at the ruined toy. *They had had plenty of time to contact me,* she conveyed to the toy telepathically. It stared back at her with cold black eyes and a Disney-perfect smile that mocked the chaos in her head.

"*. . . decapitated by a sharp instrument in an abandoned tenement while chasing a suspect. There has been no sign of her partner, officer Callum MacD . . .*"

"No!" Cat threw the toy at the TV. She looked at the telephone, willing it to ring. When she picked it up, the line was dead.

"Mommy, is something wrong?" Brianna was standing by her bedroom door in the hallway past the kitchen.

"Go back to bed!" Cat snapped. Bree bit her lip to keep from crying and closed the door behind her.

It was Erin. Erin was dead. And Cal was missing.

Cat ran to her purse and got her cell phone, which she had set on vibrate so as not to interrupt getting Bree to bed, and had several voice-mail messages in the queue. She walked into the bedroom to change clothes. Mrs. Sullivan next door would come stay with Bree while she went to the station. She hated to wake the old woman at that hour, but her mother was too far away and it would waste precious time. The precinct's line was busy, no doubt reporters digging for a story and family members calling to see if their loved one was killed in action.

As she put on her clothes, she saw through the window that a police car was downstairs, parked at an angle facing the curb. Cat ran to the living room to get a better view. The rain on the window blurred the outside world, but she could see well enough to tell there was no activity around the car. The cruiser's headlights were on and the front doors were both open. From her vantage she couldn't see the driver's face, but his arm was slumped to his side, fingers dangling a few inches above the street. Then she noticed the other arm laying on the street, its owner obscured by the car.

"What the hell is going on?" Cat whispered to herself.

Maggie started barking and clawed at Bree's door.

"Not now, Maggie."

She heard a crash in Bree's bedroom and her child's scream. Cat didn't even remember opening the door; the scene before her was instantaneous: shattered fire-escape window, bits of glass like stars strewn about the carpet, rain and wind streaming in through the billowing drapes, and a strange swarthy man hoisting her daughter by the arm.

"Ah, the lady of the house." His smile was yellow. His long black hair billowed behind him.

Maggie rushed past Cat and lunged at the intruder, who dropped the girl to protect his throat. Cat scooped up her daughter and rushed into the hallway and turned right toward the front door. She skidded to a stop. Blocking the exit was the largest, ugliest man she'd ever seen. He lumbered toward her. Cat bolted the opposite way through the hall into the master bedroom at the end. She slammed the door behind her and locked it, well aware that it bought mere seconds. She heard a crack from Bree's room—Maggie whimpered and went silent.

Cat laid her daughter on the bed and began rummaging through her armoire at the far end of the room. She threw shoebox after shoebox over her shoulder, cursing every pair, until she picked up the one that weighed right. Inside was the Colt .32 caliber automatic pistol Cal had bought at a gun show. Under his supervision, she had fired it a dozen times at the Orchard Beach range but was now having trouble remembering the steps. She didn't even know if it was loaded. Cat jumped and almost fumbled the weapon when a large hand smashed through the door. She remembered the safety, snapped the catch and aimed at the door. Hinges and wood flew apart. Cat held her breath and fired.

CHAPTER 6

SAVING STRAY CATS

Seth summed up the day's events and concluded his life had been better before Lelani entered it.

This morning, he had been a photographer with a home, friends, and a job. Now, his home and job were gone, his roommate was dead, and none of his friends wanted anything to do with him. His life was in danger, he was fleeing a crime scene, leaving behind a decapitated cop and an abundance of his own blood, hair, and scraped skin all over the combat zone. Add to that, he was riding on a city bus with an unconscious police officer kidnapped from the crime scene and a woman who, among other things, refused to ever sit down.

Even now, she stood in the open corner reserved for wheelchairs, despite plenty of available seats. The driver and few passengers were oddly oblivious to Officer MacDonnell propped up on the bench, even after Lelani carried him aboard slung over her shoulder.

Seth nearly jumped out of his skin when the cop's radio blared, *"Officer MacDonnell, please respond!"* The few passengers in the bus looked around for the sound. Lelani searched the radio for the off button. The radio blared again and Seth jumped in to turn it off for her.

Seth stood up and began to pace.

"Stay close to me," Lelani said.

Seth wanted anything but to stay close to her. It was hard for him to believe that just a few hours earlier he had entertained notions of shooting her for a centerfold; that she would be his ticket to the big time like *Playboy* or *Maxim*. The longer he stayed with her, the more things unraveled. She was getting weirder by the hour. Earlier, she had insisted they wait until post-rush hour before taking the subway to the Bronx, citing lack of space in the cars. Then, she would only stand in the area between the port and starboard doors because the seats were "too thin." At 110th Street, a group of Hispanic teens came aboard and began making catcalls at all the young women. Seth had suggested moving into the next car. She refused. They continued harassing girls down the line until they came to Lelani. The tallest of them only reached her shoulders, but they had numbers. After one of them ran his finger down her arm, Lelani put her hand up, palm facing the hooligans, and in a foreign tongue, sang a verse from the most beautiful lullaby Seth had ever heard. The youths fell asleep where they stood, piled atop each other. The car erupted in applause. Lelani had spotted a baseball bat sticking out from under one of the teenagers' coats and handed it to Seth; a bad omen.

The bat! Seth remembered. He had left it at the crime scene; add another set of fingerprints for the forensics experts.

He studied the bus passengers: an old Hispanic woman in a maid's smock, a teenage couple making out, a tired construction worker, and a mother with her young daughter. None of them paid him any attention despite his overt gaze. It was as though he weren't there.

Lelani touched the rubber strip that signaled a stop request. The bus pulled over at the next stop, but nobody got up. Seth saw the driver searching the rearview mirror for someone getting off. After a moment, he resumed the route.

Seth watched her study the advertisements as the bus headed up Pelham Parkway. The babies were in at the Bronx Zoo, demonstrated by the bronzed webbed baby shoes of some exotic bird; Dr. Rajashkharappa guaranteed he could end your foot pain for only sixty dollars; and the language institute could teach immigrants English in only six months, provided they could read the ad to begin with.

Lelani hit the rubber strip again, and seemed amused by the sound of the bell. Seth studied her and realized a change in himself. Through her eyes everything took on a fresh perspective, as though the most obvious things were new and exotic. Sometimes she came off like a genius. But earlier, they had passed a street construction site and the pipes and wires beneath the street had enthralled her. "Everything flows here," she had said. Her outlook forced Seth to reconsider things he'd often taken for granted. Although a novel feeling, it wasn't worth going to prison for. Now, Seth needed a place to stay until he could sort out the mess that had become his life. Beyond that, he couldn't care less if he ever saw her again.

"Please signal a stop," Lelani asked.

Seth slapped the strip.

As before, Lelani effortlessly picked up Officer MacDonnell

and carried him off the bus. The driver shouted for whoever to "Cut that out!"

Lelani handed a fold-out transit map of New York to Seth.

"Find Mayflower Avenue," she said.

Seth pointed the way.

They passed Italian bakeries and delis, bodegas, dry cleaners, and Korean grocers, all gated shut at that late hour. A bar's canned music spilled onto the street along with a few stumbling patrons. The vibe was less claustrophobic than in Seth's neighborhood. Even in a cold drizzle at this time of night, Avenue A would be jumping with partygoers, diners, bar hoppers, dealers, addicts, musicians, artists, police, and transients. At the time Alphabet City had teemed with the denizens of eastern and southern Europe, huddled in rear tenements, the tranquil street they currently walked on had been farmland. This was where people who craved a slower pace came to settle. *All the better,* Seth thought. No one around to question their business.

"So these guys we fought," Seth said while they walked, "they blew up my apartment and killed Joe?"

"They thought Joe was you. It was a sloppy job."

"They're not . . . normal."

"'Normal' is a relative term."

"I mean, they're freaks."

"The swordsman is human. At least biologically."

So it would come down to space aliens. She gave off that "mother ship" vibe.

"A desert warrior, probably Verakhoon," she finished.

"So what planet did the other two come from?"

She threw him a furrowed glance to imply he was speaking

gibberish. "The big one is likely descended from frost giants. I'm sure even you noted his size."

"Frost giant? Like from an ice planet?"

"Star systems are too far apart to make travel between them practical. The odds of even a generational vessel completing a mission are approximately twenty-seven million, four hundred eighty-three thousand to one."

"That a fact?" Seth checked her ears for points.

"Is there something wrong?" Lelani asked.

"Never mind. What about the little gray guy?"

"He's part troll. Trolls are underground dwellers—excellent night vision, highly sensitive to light. Their skin is a strange hybrid of clay and organic flesh. It can bend and stretch to fantastic proportions, a trait developed to survive in their cramped universe. Their bones are soft, like cartilage, and a hormone they release at will makes their muscles, organs, and ligaments as malleable as putty. The ooze on their skin is a runoff of this process. I think it originates from their bone marrow. It's valued by magic users as a catalyst for spells. It's also extremely flammable, which is not a problem when you live in damp underground caves."

"Aren't you lil' Ms. Encyclopedia Freakanica?" Lelani ignored the snub. Seth realized that she believed everything she was saying. "Why would anyone have sex with a troll?" he continued.

"Most mixed breeds are not the result of consensual sex. There are stringent laws in almost every society about racial purity. To be half of one race is to risk ostracism from both. All living beings are naturally suspicious of things not quite like them. Years of war, however, have bent and broken the rules of . . ."

Lelani halted at a highway overpass. "Are we going the right way?" She took the map from Seth, studied it and groaned. She turned right and resumed walking. Seth hurried after her.

"You can be a little nicer. I don't need to be here."

"Where would you go?" she said.

"Anywhere. It's a free country. I have a life, you know."

"You had a life. Those 'freaks' are looking for you."

"Not for anything I did."

"You constitute a threat."

"I'm a porn photographer. The only thing I threaten is good taste and decency. Maybe I should take my chances on my own."

"Suit yourself. As long as you're with me, though, you can maintain the illusion that you are not friendless, homeless, and penniless."

Lelani was right. With her, there was shelter, more snippets about his past, and the possibility that in a weak moment she might sleep with him. This limbo of aiding her was better than what awaited without her. For the moment.

They approached Mayflower Avenue and turned the corner toward Cal's home.

"What are we going to tell this guy's wife?" Seth asked.

"I don't know. She complicates matters."

"You have to tell her something. You said yourself all this will cause problems for his family. You should warn her about the circus freaks."

"I didn't mean it complicated things for her. I was talking about his family in Aandor."

"He's got two wives?"

"Not quite. Captain MacDonnell comes from a very respected family of low noble stock. The higher nobility traditionally seek unions with MacDonnell's family for children not destined to inherit their fathers' titles. One such union was arranged with Lord Godwynn's child. I think her name is Chryslantha. This is a very important match for Cal. She is Godwynn's firstborn daughter; her dowry is huge and it includes property adjacent to the MacDonnells' ancestral lands. The union would elevate the MacDonnells in the aristocracy. But his marriage here constitutes a breach of contract between the families. This will cause problems for his father. At the very least, it sullies their excellent reputation. He will have to repudiate his American wife."

"What if he doesn't want to repudiate her? Hell, what if he doesn't want to go back to your 'Magic Kingdom'?"

Lelani turned sullen. She struck Seth as the type who liked to have every angle covered, and maybe she hadn't considered this possibility.

"Callum is captain of the Guard for Archduke Athelstan, High Regent of Aandor," she said. "He's here in service to his lord. Once he remembers who he truly is, he'll perform his duty and I will follow his orders."

Seth got the impression she was trying to convince herself.

"What if he's like me and can't remember?" he asked.

"There's a spell I can use to help him remember."

"Aha! You can't keep track of the big gaping holes in your own story. Why haven't you used this spell on me if I'm your guy?"

"There's an aura around you. You're inoculated from magic. It's an extremely elaborate enchantment. Captain MacDonnell does not have this barrier."

"An aura, huh? It's a little convenient for you that I can't remember all this crap because I put some whammy on myself."

"You did not 'whammy' yourself, Seth. The spell protecting you is beyond either of our abilities. I wouldn't know where to begin removing it. I'm not even sure I should. Right now, it serves you better than your memory would. Soon, I'll have the captain back, and the burden of leading this mission will be off my shoulders."

"You'd better hope his loyalty to this lord is as strong as you think it is."

"It has to be. The fate of my people is tied to House Athelstan. As it falls, so does my race. Others, too. Cal's family would have no place in a world ruled by Farrenheil. The enemy wishes to control every aspect of their subjects' lives. Dissidents and scholars disappear and are never heard from again. They use magic to torture and kill. Nations like this exist everywhere, even here. Aandor, for all its flaws, stands in opposition to this type of regime."

They heard a police call again and checked Cal's radio, which was still off. They followed the chatter to the police car up ahead in front of the three-story brick building the MacDonnells resided in. A uniformed cop in the driver's seat was unconscious, as was a detective on the ground by the rear tire.

The front door to the building was smashed in. Broken glass littered the walk, which they realized came from the window above the fire escape.

Lelani's terrified face said it all—she had miscalculated the enemy's intentions.

Gunshots thundered above.

Lelani bolted up the stairs with Cal mysteriously clinging to her back. Although unhindered, Seth could not keep pace with the redhead, even as he wondered whether following her was a smart choice.

When Seth reached the second floor, he cautiously peered

into the apartment. There was a living room on the left where Cal had been unceremoniously dumped on the couch. Some vanilla candles were lit in the kitchen on the far right. Vociferous noises, high winds, and a special effects light show emanated from a room down a short hallway in the back of the apartment. Seth sat on the couch back above the unconscious cop; after all, someone had to stay out front and guard him. He noticed the gun in Cal's holster and drew it.

The banging in the back room rattled the building. Seth imagined the rest of the building coming awake and a slew of noisy neighbors to contend with. A sound ripped through the air that could only be described as Chewbacca getting his leg amputated. Each footstep shook the floor; the china clanged, porcelain cracked, furniture hopped and crashed back to earth with loud thuds as the giant tread heavily from the bedroom toward Seth.

The gun shook in Seth's hand as he aimed at the running behemoth. He squeezed the trigger, but the safety was on. Seth shut his eyes expecting an impact, only to hear Hesz run past him as he bolted from the apartment. The hallway stairs splintered as Hesz blundered down them. Seth could hear his heart beat in his ears. He was shocked to be alive. It took him a few moments to spot the trail of blood leading from the bedroom and out the front door.

Seth stood, shaking. His first thought was to leave. It occurred to him that hulk could be on the sidewalk waiting to come back. He looked around the small apartment for a place to lay low. A rustling in the bedroom caught his attention. *Lelani,* he thought. Slowly he walked toward the back, past what looked like a child's room. A dog lay on the floor, its head at a sick angle. He played with the gun's latches until he was sure he had released the trigger. The master bedroom was at an angle to the hall, so he couldn't see inside unless he stepped through it.

"Lelani?"

He poked his head around the corner. The room looked like it had been put through a Cuisinart. A hasty exit was set in the wall where a window used to be. The cop's wife was helping a dazed Lelani stand. Then she spotted Seth, grabbed her gun off the floor, and aimed at him.

"I'm the good guy," Seth said, holding his hands up. He forgot he had the pistol.

"Drop it," the wife said.

"No, really. Your husband's on the couch."

"He's with me," Lelani said.

The woman kept her gun focused on Seth.

"If you're her friend, where were you when she was fighting those creeps?"

Lelani looked at Seth. She expected an answer, too. He was afraid. They both knew it and the truth lodged in his throat waiting for a lie to supplant it.

"He covered the front in case there were reinforcements," Lelani said. She let him off the hook. Seth gazed at the floor, unable to meet her eyes.

They heard crying.

"Bree!" The mother looked about frantic, the gun now abandoned.

The little girl pulled herself out from under the bed, the single-digit generation's refuge of choice.

"Are the bad men gone?" the girl asked. Mother wrapped daughter in her arms.

"Yes," she said.

"For now," Lelani added.

CHAPTER 7

DEAD ON HIS FEET

The scene was almost pastoral. A worn-down country road bordered by dirt, weeds, and gravel. Across the street an old wood-slatted New England–style church, steeple halfway to heaven, persevered like a white sentinel over the souls in the adjacent cemetery. Down the road the only gas station in town still washed your windshield and checked your oil. Across from it was the pastel blue-and-pink brick post office. Built in 1977, it was an enduring reminder of an era hell-bent on destroying traditional aesthetics. One lonely traffic light marked the center of town. It rehearsed unceasingly, waiting to reproach the next vehicle. The buildings were far enough apart, and the town high enough in elevation, that Colby could see the pines, birches, and rolling hills and fields of Dutchess County in the distance—a long way from the steel and glass canyons outside his office in New York City.

He watched the sunrise from the diner window as he ground the remainder of his cigarette into the ashtray. It was still long, mostly unused. He lit the damn things out of habit now, not because of the nicotine plea that had become his intimate companion for the past two decades.

He did everything out of habit at this point, like sitting in a country diner to avoid a chill, even though cold did not affect him anymore. Coffee packed no punch, food sat flavorless and undigested in his gut, and every nick and scrape he collected stayed with him unhealed. There was a tourniquet on his pinky where a paper cut had left him a quart low of A positive. His hair and nails continued to grow, but he didn't dare shave. Back in the city, Colby snorted cocaine for the first time in a decade in an attempt to jump-start his humanity. Nothing affected him.

Clammy described the overall sensation best. Like a humid, sealed attic on a hundred-degree day, except that the staleness was packed under his skin. Nothing moved internally, nothing vented. Gas occasionally emanated from a twist or a bend, the foulest smell imaginable. As the days wore on, the last vestiges of his humanity dwindled like the final swirl of water circling the drain. He looked at the old cemetery, and even the trepidation of realizing he belonged there was as absent as his heart.

Carla sat across from him. She was clearly more traumatized by what had happened to them and subsisted in a perpetual fazed state. Her hair was a mess and the buttons on her blouse misaligned. She had that "freshly fucked" look cosmopolitan women strived to imitate at great expense, except that Carla strove for nothing these days. She had lost her head the night of the attack and insisted they call the police. Colby convinced her otherwise. They would have been quarantined, subjected to study—two walking, talking, seemingly breathing beings without hearts. There was no guarantee the police could even handle Dorn and his crew. And then there was the matter of the million-dollar payoff, which would be jeopardized if they brought in the authorities.

Soon after, Carla had gone catatonic—unable to accept the reality of their plight. She had become incontinent until their bodies purged the last elements in their systems. Colby had dressed and bathed her at first, until he ran out of patience. She hadn't said a word in days. She followed Colby when he prompted her, like a puppy tracking snacks.

Colby's "friends" and acquaintances had disassociated themselves from him long ago. There was nothing like a government indictment for extortion to separate the faithful from the frivolous. There was an older sister living in a trailer park in the Carolinas, but they had not spoken in fifteen years, and this was not a situation that would aid any reconciliation. Even with Carla sharing the same nightmare, Colby felt forlorn. Even when he shamelessly fondled Carla in the bath in another vain attempt to reclaim his humanity and maybe help her snap out of her stupor, he was unable to attain an erection. Colby caught his reflection in the glass; his skin had become almost translucent. Purple veins and the bags under his eyes were darker, probably from the congealed blood. He stopped worrying about going to hell. He was already there.

The diner hadn't been redecorated since a great man sat in the White House; sparkling stars on glittery aqua-blue tabletops banded with corrugated tarnished steel. Holes dotted the hard plastic top where cigarettes lingered—small brown burns like sculpted phlegm. A graveyard of bug husks withered on the window ledge, held together by dust. The checkered linoleum was decades thick with grit and gristle, mopped around nightly in a futile effort to meet the health code. A fat, greasy-haired waitress in her forties who smelled like yesterday and cheap perfume walked up to the table with a pot of steaming coffee.

"Jeez mister, don't you get any sun down in the city? You look white as a ghost."

Colby just pointed at his cup. The waitress poured, glanced at Carla who just stared blankly, then shuffled off.

Colby drank the coffee straight. Milk would only cool it. Flavor and texture had become meaningless to him, but heat was a different story. It was his new addiction, the only sensation that registered. As the black liquid flowed down his gullet, he absorbed the energy from each excited molecule. It would be three to four minutes before the fluid in his stomach cooled to room temperature, and at least an hour before it ran through him, coming out coffee, exactly as it went in.

A yellow cab pulled up in front of the diner. Dorn and two new associates got out. No effort was made to compensate the driver. Colby wondered about the fare from New York City to Dutchess County. Dorn entered alone and sat next to Carla.

"Colby, my good man. Looking quite provincial," he said, with a rub at his jaw. "Any progress?"

Carla stirred for the first time. She backed as far into the booth as possible. Her arms floundered to get her even farther from Dorn, but the window prevented further regress. Dorn was oblivious. He exuded cold perfection. Chiseled jaw with azure, almost violet, eyes. A Scandinavian god from the scenes of an Abercrombie & Fitch polo game, who'd just as soon cut your heart out as say hello. His cell phone rang and he answered in one swift motion.

"Yes?" Dorn's mood darkened as the buzzing in his ear continued. He rubbed his temples with the thumb and middle finger of his other hand. "No," he said, cutting short the buzzing on the other end. The next thing he said was in a language

Colby had never heard. Dorn's tone betrayed all was not well. "I'll deal with them when I get back," Dorn said, slipping back to English.

Seeing his powerful employer upset gave Colby some vague sense of hope. Someone out there had disturbed his designs, which meant they were playing at his level—someone who could cross swords with a bona fide heart-stealing sorcerer.

Dorn cut the connection in the middle of the other person's sentence and then turned off the phone. "Mr. Colby, what have you discovered?" he asked again, in a mocked attempt at formality. He looked like he had a major migraine.

Carla's floundering increased. The gallery of insect husks shuddered off the ledge as she tried to push herself through the wall behind her.

"Can you let Carla out, please?" Colby asked.

Dorn looked to his side, seeing her for the first time. He made a face akin to discovering raw sewage on new shoes, and moved aside.

Carla stumbled out of the diner and ran across the street toward the church.

"That one didn't turn out as planned," Dorn said.

"No kidding."

Colby motioned to an emaciated nearly toothless Vietnam veteran in red flannel wearing a John Deere cap behind the counter. He came over like a man preparing to go onstage.

"This is Sweeny. He was working here thirteen years ago when a strange couple with a baby came in from the rain. Tell Mr. Dorn what you saw, Sweeny."

Sweeny gave the god the look tax cheats give an auditor. He sniffed, and with the reluctance of a man who had told the same story too many times said, "'Twas about October. I remember cause we was making cakes 'n' things for the Halloween party at the church. We was having mighty big weather that night. Couple came in to get out of the rain. The missus started changing diapers right here on this very table. I came out to tell her she can't do that on account of health codes. Woman had no good sense to be changing crap on a table what people eat on. The baby had the dangdest birthmark, like a tattoo of a Camero bird. What kind of damned freak'd ever tattoo a babe? I got me a tattoo in 'Nam. Hurt like hell. Dang if I didn't near pass out. And I had two bottles of sock-ee in me. Sock-ee couldn' cut it. Tequila is the best hootch, if you gonna get a tattoo—"

"Thank you, Sweeny," Colby said.

"Pitiful shame though what happened to them folks . . ."

"That will be all, Sweeny."

Sweeny's mouth gaped like a man who wasn't used to having the curtain drop on his act. "You gonna git anything to eat," he said to Dorn, "or just sit there like a fancy boy, taking up a customer's space?"

"We'll be going now," Colby said.

Outside, the detective met Dorn's new companions who were waiting by the cab. Both looked like Edward Gorey renditions of a Victorian butler. They wore black long-tail tuxedos with bowties, gray pinstriped trousers, and spats. Both held ornate walking sticks, the tall one with a brass ball handle, the other clutched a gnarled wooden cane. The shorter man was stocky, round of face, wore a bowler hat, and looked unkempt despite his classic ensemble. The fabric of his jacket was dusty and frayed. The cut tips of his white gloves revealed brown-stained fingernails. He was in need of a shave and teeth cleaning. The other was tall and thin, clean-shaven, impeccably manicured, and crowned by a silk-lined top hat. Colby half expected Queen Victoria's carriage to turn the corner any second. The smaller "twin's" eyes reminded Colby of a kid from grammar school who had been sent to juvenile hall for dousing a dog with gasoline and lighting it on fire. The cabbie, who still sat behind the wheel, was a Middle Eastern type with heavy bags under his eyes, who looked very unhappy.

"You didn't bring me all the way up here for one fool's walk down memory lane?" Dorn asked.

"Aren't you going to introduce me to your friends?"

"The last thing anyone wants, Colby, is an introduction to Oulfsan and Krebe. Why did you bring me up here?"

Colby motioned Dorn to walk. Now that he'd met Oulfsan and Krebe, he preferred to be far away.

"I did some checking in the county office. Since I had a definite time period I was hoping to find a property purchase, tax return, adoption record, speeding ticket, parking violation, you name it. What I found was an accident report." Colby pulled out forensic photos of a dead man and woman. "Sweeny identified them as the kid's parents. Said you couldn't mistake those two."

"How did they die?"

"Fatal car crash. Driving in a storm when they should have been indoors. They were blown off their lane and went head to head with a semi. The couple were a pair of Does. Their IDs were fake. No way to trace them, no history, no sense of having come from anywhere remotely familiar." Colby pulled out another photocopy. "They were in possession of a lot of cash and some strange coins, but not from any country the authorities could identify. The coins have since disappeared—they were made of eighteen-karat gold—but here's a photo of them." The profile of a nobleman adorned the head side, and an elaborate phoenix flew on the tail side. An unknown alphabet encircled the images.

Dorn's eyes lit up at the photo of the coins. "Are you telling me the child is dead?"

"No. The child is gone. It survived, but it's lost in the system. Illegally adopted, possibly kidnapped. For all we know Sweeny could have raised him and he's washing dishes in the diner for condom money. There's no trail."

"Not good enough. I have to see him—if he's not alive, I need a corpse."

"What the hell makes a thirteen-year-old kid so important, Dorn? Is there a shortage of acne where you come from?"

"Everything you need to know to do your job has been made available, detective."

"Not enough when it comes to politics and money. There are always people working for the other side, and that could get a man killed. Again. It is politics and money, right?"

Dorn looked away for a minute, considered Colby's remark, then said, "It's always politics. The boy, my second cousin, is an heir, the son of an archduke. What he stands to inherit is an empire."

"You mean that literally. We're not talking stock options?"

"Correct. Four hundred million inhabitants, twelve kingdoms, a treasury equal to the GDP of Europe. Head of state. Head of government. Head of religion . . . head of life itself. The power to shape our society in his image." There was contempt in the way Dorn ended that phrase.

"But you have other plans?"

"There are closer relations we'd prefer to see inherit the crown. We've waited just as long; they merely had a more successful breeding program."

"What're you going to do, get him to sign a waiver relinquishing his claim?" Colby said, sardonically. A devilish grin supplanted Dorn's calm indifference. Colby almost felt a chill. There wouldn't be any runes or spells used when Dorn went after this boy's heart.

"Didn't think so," Colby said.

They came to the graveyard and stopped. Two Doberman watchdogs approached from the other side of the picket fence. Dorn reached over and petted them. They accepted his graces.

"They recognize one of their own," Colby muttered.

"What's the price?" Dorn asked.

"Excuse me?"

"You brought me here to clarify the stakes and renegotiate our deal. I suppose you want your heart back before you go any farther."

"This kid can be anywhere in the country. Maybe farther."

"You know how I feel about loyalty, Colby."

"No one else can dig this kid up like I can. Half the tabloids in the country published off my leads."

"I don't negotiate with dead men."

"I'm not dead, goddamn you!"

"Enjoy any good meals lately?"

"How do I know you can fix me? How do I know you even want to? If you can't reverse what you did to me, you can go fuck yourself. No little lost cousin for you." Colby clammed up for dramatic effect, but it was wasted on Dorn.

"Just so we're clear," Colby continued, "there are a bunch of envelopes ready to get mailed to various law and news agencies in the event of my death."

"You *are* dead."

"There are still people in high places who will read my mail. I made some serious accusations that may or may not be true, but they would make any cop or reporter's career, and you can bet they'll investigate. You might work around the heat, but it'll slow you down, make life difficult. I'm betting time is of the essence."

Colby waited for a response. They were playing for high stakes. It warranted some reaction from the other player. Colby was now running on fumes. He needed to see that worried look again on Dorn's face to fuel his rebellion.

Dorn smiled at the dogs as he groomed them with his hands.

"Whenever one faction doesn't want to see a group gain power," the detective continued, "there's always another that does. My guess is you're in a race against people who'd be happy to see your cousin inherit his empire."

Dorn continued stroking the Doberman's head. "Look at you, Colby. One drawback to being heartless is the accompanying numbness, which always brings about a loss of fear. People forget to be afraid once you remove pain and emotion from their lives. Take Sweeny for example . . . at home, people have been flayed alive for talking to me that way. That toothless miscreant lacks fear. There isn't enough pain in his life. But . . ."

Dorn's attention wandered for a moment. When it returned, he surveyed the town around him. "I started this search for the prince cautiously, opting for a surgical approach in a world I barely understood," Dorn said. "A strange land of magical drought that I never knew existed. I've since found my footing, Colby—we're locating streams of magical energy here and there, buried deep. Enough to empower more ambitious sorceries. I'm reluctant because this place might yet have some uses for me and my ilk back in Aandor, but at some point, very soon, I will abandon my 'surgical' approach. And that will not bode well for the innocents of this world."

Dorn's words were too subtle for his tone. Colby thought of his son, Torrence, and the few others he still loved. It filled him with dread, just when he thought he'd exhausted his reservoir of that emotion. "You'll never find this kid without me, Dorn. I'm that good," Colby said, trying to reclaim his leverage.

Krebe approached silently with a large duffel bag from the taxi's trunk. He unzipped it, revealing dozens of thumping velvet sacks writhing about like a colony of rats. Dorn reached into the bag and pulled out a familiar velvet sack. Krebe and the bag went back to the cab. Dorn twirled the velvet sack around playfully on its drawstring before Colby.

"Is that mine?" Colby asked. He didn't expect Dorn to have his heart on him.

"I don't know. Is it?" Dorn pulled the heart out of the bag and scrutinized it as he turned it around. The dogs began to salivate at the scent of fresh meat. "Hmmm. Your left and right ventricles were quite clotted. Only a few years left from what Symian discerned. The color in this one looks healthy. But then, they all look the same from the outside. You know, Colby . . . we don't have to replace *your* heart to restore your life."

Colby suspected a con. "I don't follow."

"Any heart will do, as long as the blood type matches. There are a few spry but not so bright young men in my employ. Take

121

my friend, Salim, in the cab. Doesn't smoke, never drinks alcohol, and prays to God five times a day. Never underestimate the aerobic advantages of prayer, Colby. Think about it. What use would millions of dollars be if you could only enjoy it for the short while your heart has left."

"Millions?"

"Millions. My people live by the gold standard. Krakens, Gryphons . . . Phoenixes," he said shaking the photocopy of the coins. "It doesn't matter who adorns the coin, it's ninety-one percent pure gold. We don't care about green paper or dead presidents. My coffers here in the United States can be yours after I leave."

The word "millions" echoed through Colby's head like a scream escaping a canyon. With that kind of wealth, he could hire a dream team of lawyers; probably buy himself a pardon if he "donated" to the right political candidates. And, Tory would be set for life. Twenty-four-hour medical care with private nurses and the best doctors on earth. That much money bought life. Colby glimpsed at the driver in the taxi—the poster child for despondency.

"What about Salim?" he asked.

"He'll be grateful. His deity has promised him seventy-two virgins feeding him sweetmeats in a garden after he moves on. Everyone's happy."

Colby had known his days were numbered even before the forced coronary extraction. He could feel it in his wheezing breath after a four-story walk-up. Now, Dorn was offering seven figures with a few extra decades of debauchery added in—or redemption. It was the kind of offer that made for great German literature. Some slacker punk would get his decrepit ticker or buy the farm. This was the real thing—wealth and long life. He could find this kid, he knew that. But the offer didn't change the issue.

"It's a good deal. But it doesn't address why I brought you here. I'm not even sure you can reverse what you did to me and Carla. I want it now, before I find the kid. Otherwise, you can go to hell."

"You wouldn't be as motivated. Trust me, Colby, your heart is far more into completing the job sitting in my pocket."

"Goddamn it, Dorn . . . I've conned enough to know a con when I hear one! You don't give a rat's ass about anybody that works for you. Everyone's a mark to achieving your ends. You'll shaft me just for shits and giggles. Now is that my fucking heart or not?"

"Let's find out," Dorn said. He dropped the organ between the Dobermans.

"NO!" Colby cried.

The dogs tore at it. Colby clutched his chest in anticipation. Instead, he heard a tortured yowl. It came from the church.

"It would appear not," Dorn said.

Colby ran to the church and burst through the doors. Carla lay before the altar convulsing, screaming. A minister tried to help her as black blood shot from every orifice in her body. She was a perforated bag of soy sauce.

"I think she's having a seizure," the minister shrieked. "Please, call a doctor!"

No doctor could help her now. Colby sat on the end of a pew clutching his own chest as the aisle became a river. He wanted to cry, but was dry as a bone. Dead men didn't have tears. He ignored the minister shouting to call 911. Colby felt nauseated, but didn't even have enough life left in him to puke.

Carla's torso heaved and she gasped for breath. Her breathing slowed. Then, she just stopped.

The door creaked. Dorn stood at the entrance. He cut a dark silhouette against the winter sky. "A shame," he said.

"Is that what's in store for me, Dorn? For the cabdriver, for every other wretch unlucky enough to have entered your sphere?"

"I don't believe in fortune." Dorn held up four manila envelopes. Even from a distance Colby recognized them as his "insurance" letters. They burst into flames in Dorn's hands. He dropped them on the floor and watched them burn. The minister ran for the fire extinguisher, threatening to call the police.

"By the way . . . everyone these letters were addressed to will be dead within the hour. Don't ever try to blackmail me again. There are worse things than what she went through," he said, pointing to Carla. "I'm sure you'll take my word on that."

The cab pulled up in front of the church. Dorn turned to leave.

"Are you the devil?" Colby shouted.

Dorn considered the question. "I'm not as forgiving," he finally said. "Find the boy."

CHAPTER 8

ONION THEORY

Lelani and Seth placed the unconscious detective back in the police cruiser's passenger seat. They fastened the seat belt around him to hold him in place and shut the door. Seth turned off the car's headlights and put the driver's hand on the steering wheel. It was about 2:00 A.M. Lelani was grateful for the cold drizzle that kept everyone indoors at this hour.

"They'll both be okay," Lelani said. "I tended their wounds and gave them some sleep dust to keep them out a while longer."

The radio squawked. *"Four-One Adam, what is your status, over?"*

"Damn, they have to check in," Seth noted.

"You'll have to respond," Lelani answered.

"Great! Impersonating an officer on top of all the other charges."

"I cannot. There's no female in this unit," Lelani said.

"I don't know cop talk," Seth argued. "They have their own language."

"Four-One Adam, please respond."

"We need to buy a little time," Lelani said. "Keep it simple."

Seth picked up the radio and took a deep breath. "This is

125

Four-One Adam. We're at MacDonnell's home. Wife has been informed of situation. We're, uh . . . hanging tight."

Lelani pounded a fist on the car and gave Seth a grave look.

"What?!" Seth said. "Sounds like something a cop would say."

There was a long silence, or maybe it wasn't very long and just seemed that way.

"Affirmative Four-One Adam. Stay with the family until further notice. Over."

"See," Seth said.

"Just shut the car door," Lelani ordered, as she headed back into the building.

The family was in the living room sitting beside Callum, who rested on the couch. Lelani's hands were grimy and not suited for what had she had to do next. She found the kitchen sink at the end of a granite island that had been decorated with candles. The wife had been planning some sort of ritual for the evening.

Lelani watched from the kitchen as Catherine MacDonnell cooled her husband's forehead with a damp washcloth. The fever was a good sign that Cal was burning out the last of Symian's venom. The wife had insisted upon going to the hospital, but Lelani stressed that Cal would be dead by the time the doctors could develop an antitoxin. Lelani recognized a warrior's spirit in the woman, evident by her stand against Hesz. She was pleased to see this spirit tempered by wisdom after Catherine agreed to leave Cal's care in her hands.

The little girl sat near her parents, clutching her stuffed toy, eyes red from crying. *A true family,* Lelani noted. She regretted her earlier remark about Cal repudiating his American marriage. There would be much pain and hardship for this family in the days to come, decisions about continuing together, or not at all. Lelani had seen many families broken by politics and war. She began to resent her role. It bothered her that this was even an issue. After all, who were these people to her? What did she owe them? The success of this mission would determine her race's survival—the survival of many kingdoms—and possibly even the very world she found herself in at the moment. It was not her choice whether or not to help Cal recover his identity. And yet, if left alone, if she didn't recover the captain's memories, then no one need ever know, and his family here could persist. But could she complete the mission without MacDonnell's help?

This strange world ran at a hummingbird's pace. Life here moved on fossil fuels, the stewed and liquefied remnants of a billion, billion dead things. The most basic machines stirred faster than the swiftest beast. Even the peasants made life-altering decisions at the speed of thought. In addition, the world provided few places in which to recharge her arsenal of spells. It was a desert concerning magic. From the moment Lelani had arrived, she had felt overwhelmed.

She had read about this culture in Proust's records; tomes he'd penned during his decades of travel, yet they lacked many details and were incomplete. Lelani scribbled addenda in the margins of the text. It gave her an odd feeling to do this, not because she improved upon the work of a genius beyond her level, but because to do so implied that she believed this fool's quest had a chance of succeeding; that there would be a world left to go back to and its scholars would study her observations. There was no one but herself to depend on. Her race did not even exist on this planet anymore. Why did Proust choose her out of a multitude of students? She trusted his wisdom, and it was enough for her that he believed she could do this job. The opportunity, as unlikely as she was to succeed, was priceless. If she did succeed in safely bringing the boy home, however, Duke Athelstan would be indebted to her, and through her, to her people.

She had expected support from Seth—a former schoolmate, united by their shared loyalties and origins. She couldn't have been more wrong. Instead, he siphoned her energy, tested her spirit, challenged her resolve, and fragmented her focus. His maturity had arrested at thirteen. Lelani was mothering a delinquent adolescent. She was at a loss to explain the memory wipe. Perhaps an attack that affected the entire group?

A tug at her side broke Lelani from her thoughts. It was the girl.

"Can I have a glass of water?" Bree asked.

Lelani looked through the cupboards for a glass.

"Bree, I want you over here by me!" Cat said from the couch.

"But the nice horse-lady is getting me water," Bree said.

"Bree!"

"Go to your mother," Lelani said. "I will bring it to you."

Seth entered the apartment.

"What took you so long?" Lelani inquired. "All I said was shut the car door."

"Went to get cigs around the corner."

"We could have used some more peroxide and bandages for these cuts," Cat said.

"Sorry."

"Can you put the door downstairs back on its hinges?" Lelani asked.

"Not really. I just stuck it in the frame. I'm not a carpenter." He took out a Camel.

"No smoking," Cat said.

"Lady, I'm homeless and penniless because of all this shit, and my nerves are shot to hell. Have some consideration."

"Language, please. I have a five-year-old here. Smoke outside."

"There's fucking gratitude. We save her life and . . ."

"Seth!" Lelani shouted. "Either finish boarding up the bedroom window, or sit down and shut up."

Seth grabbed a Budweiser from the fridge, then took a seat in the corner and grumbled that if women were so equal, why were they always asking guys to do hard labor like fix doors or sleep on the wet spot. "Hey, maybe you can cast a spell that fixes doors," he said twiddling his fingers back and forth at Lelani.

Lelani brought water to the MacDonnells. She picked up the coffee table in front of the couch and moved it to the corner to make more room in the center. Then she placed herself between Cat and Seth.

"Do you have a last name?" Cat asked.

"Stormbringer," Lelani answered.

"What the hell kind of Norwegian death-metal name is that?" Seth asked. The unlit cigarette rolled along his lips.

"It's Centauran, and it's a prestigious name among my clan."

Seth snorted.

"Please have a seat," Cat said.

"Thank you. I prefer to stand."

"The horse-lady can't sit, Mommy," Bree said.

"Bree, that's not nice. I apologize. I don't know why she calls you that," Cat said.

Lelani smiled. "Brianna is every bit James MacDonnell's granddaughter. Where I'm from, the MacDonnells are legendary because of their inherent strong will and a gift for seeing through deception. It's why they are effective lawmen. Cal, too, could probably discern something odd about me if he were conscious."

"I don't need ESP to know that *you're* odd," Seth cut in.

"A child is far more accepting of the incredible than any adult," Lelani continued. "Their minds are not clouded by preconceived notions. And a MacDonnell child . . . ? Well, I have no doubt Bree can see flaws in my illusion."

"So, what are you really?" Seth asked. "'Cause I for one would really like to know."

"I told you . . . I'm a centaur."

"A what?" Cat asked.

"A centaur," Seth snorted. "Half man, half horse. Except," he added, gesturing toward her breasts with his beer, "you're a girl."

"Yes. That would be where baby centaurs come from. The one constant throughout the universe is that males could never handle the pain of childbirth."

Cat grinned.

Seth wasn't amused. "So you mean to tell me those long sexy legs aren't really there, and that at some point your beautiful body, the one I've been fantasizing about all day, turns into a horse's ass?"

"I wouldn't have put it quite as eloquently, but that is correct."

Seth turned to Cat. "You do know this girl's on medication?"

Cat turned to Lelani with a guarded look. "It does seem like a lot to swallow."

"Even after all you've witnessed?"

"It's not like there aren't eight-foot people in the world," Seth said. "Most of them just happen to play for the NBA."

"Is it true you're on medication?" Cat asked Lelani. Lelani noticed that Cat's breathing changed after asking the question. She was tense. Seth's game of devil's advocate was dangerous.

"To cope with pollutants in your atmosphere," Lelani said. "Aandor is a pristine world with little industry. I'm more susceptible to the airborne toxins than a human."

"Human?" Cat said.

Cat looked even more uncomfortable hearing language of that sort. Lelani held her husband's life in her hands and she realized talk of other worlds would undermine Cat's confidence.

"I told you she was nuts," Seth said.

"You are a feckless dullard, Seth Raincrest," Lelani scolded. "After what you've seen this night . . ."

"Everything has an explanation. I just don't know your bag of tricks." Turning to Cat, Seth went on. "She shows up at my door this morning claiming she knew me thirteen years ago. That would have made *her* about four or five years old. No one I know can remember spit about being four, much less me. Hell, I can't even remember being eleven."

"Are you exaggerating?" Cat asked, surprised.

"No. I have psychosomatic amnesia. I can't remember anything before thirteen years ago due to extreme trauma. My parents were burned to death in a house fire, not too far from here. The police found me dazed, wandering the streets with second-degree burns. They patched me up and threw me in a foster home. Life started at age thirteen far as I'm concerned. No relatives . . . just me. One thing I know for sure, I did not come from another planet like someone is implying."

"Cal can't remember before thirteen years ago either," Cat said.

Seth stopped rolling the cigarette along his lips. She had his attention.

"One day he woke up in a clinic upstate," Cat continued. "Some farmers found him unconscious in a field. They assumed he was in an accident. No one was looking for him, not a friend, not a relative. Months of inquiries and nothing. As far as Cal's concerned the day he opened his eyes in that clinic was the first day of his life."

"You're shitting me," Seth said.

"Watch the language," Cat snapped.

"What an amazing coincidence," Lelani said dryly. As the other two conversed, Lelani began to paint runes on Cal's forehead with black paste from her satchel.

"What are you doing?" Cat asked. She looked unsure at this point.

"It will help," Lelani said. She met Cat's gaze and with the most sympathetic expression she could produce, said, "Trust me."

"That still doesn't change the fact that Mrs. Ed here was only four years old when we supposedly first met," Seth continued.

Lelani finished painting the runes. She blew on them and the ink faded, the way water disappears into a sponge. "Time passes at different speeds throughout the multiverse," Lelani said. "Months on this end would have been minutes on our end, plenty of time for the first group to have settled in. We should have had immediate confirmation of your safe arrival. We didn't. Proust organized a rescue party, but we were betrayed by one of our own. An acolyte named Sazar. By the time the second party was ready to step through to this universe, Dorn and his hordes had broken into the sanctum and we were captured."

"Who the heck is Dorn?" Seth asked.

"The opposition . . . the nephew of the grand duke of Farrenheil. A proficient sorcerer . . . and a deadly swordsman. He's in command on this end."

"You mean there are more freaks than the three we met?"

"Dorn and his contingent used the link to arrive here. A fight broke out with our captors back in Aandor. While everyone was otherwise occupied, the rescue party rushed the link. I was the only one who made it through the hail of arrows and daggers alive. I entered the link only hours after your group left us, but I arrived here three weeks ago. Dorn's contingent was only minutes ahead of me, but he has been here almost two months. I had one major advantage. Dorn rushed through unprepared, unaware of the time differential. He thought he was right behind the first party, that he could track them, wipe them out, and be back in Aandor in time for dinner and gloating.

"Dorn had to scrounge for magical energies, which are rare here. He has wasted time coming up to speed. Proust had prepared me with language spells for your native tongues, maps, culture manuals, mana batteries, catalytic powder, and an assortment of other instruments. I was able to, as you say, 'hit the ground running.' Now it's a race."

"Where exactly is this 'other' world?" Cat asked.

"We're all part of a complex multiverse; countless universes that exist side by side on cosmic platforms called Branes. A good metaphor would be an onion. Each distinct universe is a thin layer of the onion, only slightly different from the next layer closest to it. At the core is the source of all, for lack of a better term, *magical* energy. The energy dissipates through the multiverse through veins and arteries extending outward. The outside of the onion is dry and hard because the farther one gets from the core, the fewer in number, and smaller, these channels become, until you reach the outer realms, where no magic exists at all. The universes at this extreme are stark and operate on pure scientific principle."

"You've been there?" Seth asked sarcastically.

Lelani noticed Cat became more distant the more she explained. Talk of other worlds did not boost her confidence.

"No one has ever gone to the edge of the multiverse," Lelani said. "Even our scholars are not sure about what constitutes life in those regions." She checked on Cal. Only a ghost image of the runes remained. If the spell did its job, Lelani could leave Cat's skepticism to Cal. The runes needed time to work, though. She continued her story.

"Between the core and the outside of the onion is a universe where magic and science are in perfect balance. We call it the Prime Meridian. Aandor exists halfway between the Prime Meridian and the center of the multiverse, thus magic exists in abundance. Earth exists halfway between the Prime Meridian and the outermost universe. Magic is sparse here. Where we use sorceries, enchantments, transmogrification, and so forth to manipulate our environment, you use physics, chemistry, and genetic engineering. In the end, each of us is manipulating our environment to suit our needs by whatever means available."

Cat and Seth were silent. Even Bree looked captivated by the tale.

"What an amazing story," Cat remarked.

"Well, it's a lot more original than thinking you're Napoleon Bonaparte," Seth added.

"Excuse me?"

"So show us. Pretend I'm from Missouri. Show me your horse's ass."

Cat watched intently. Despite the crudity of Seth's request, Cat wanted to see it, too. Lelani knew she was losing the woman's trust to Seth's cavalier attack.

"It's not that easy. There are limits to what . . ."

"Yeah, yeah. Blah, blah, blah. I'm just asking you to be yourself," Seth said. "Horse lady from an alternate universe. Or crazy woman missing from an asylum."

"Catherine, please believe you can trust me," Lelani said. "Take as an assurance the fact that I have saved you and your family tonight."

"I know. It's the only reason I've gone along this far, but . . . don't . . . I . . . I think . . . I should get Cal to a hospital." Cat looked to Seth for support after she said this.

It was all unraveling.

"I can get arrested for what went down tonight," Seth said. "I'm not going anywhere near where there are other cops. If he dies, they'll pin two cop murders on me on top of fleeing the scene. I have to look after my own ass."

For once, Lelani was grateful for Seth's selfish nature.

Seth stood up and headed for the door. "Maybe Red can take you to the hospital on her flying carpet."

As Seth passed them, a hand sprang from the couch and grabbed his wrist. In a grave whisper, Cal MacDonnell said, "Show them."

Cat cupped her husband's flushed, drenched face as he struggled to open his eyes. They were white with fever. "Cal," she pleaded.

Seth tried to break the grip. "Show them what?" he asked.

Cal looked at Lelani through cloudy eyes.

"My lord," Lelani said, "magical energy is in short supply here. My illusion has a high power cost. I . . ."

"Show them," he whispered one last time. He passed out again.

Cat stroked her husband's face, trying to revive him. Cal slept peacefully in her embrace.

Seth had difficulty breaking Cal's grip. "Jeez, this guy's stronger asleep than I am awake."

"It takes a considerable amount of magical energy to create an illusion such as the one I've been maintaining," Lelani explained. "I have a finite amount of energy with me, and I should be saving it for the mission ahead; however, I understand why a leap of faith on your part is too much to expect."

Lelani reached into her shirt and pulled out an amulet hanging from a silver chain about her neck. She took it off. Then she said, "*VATRAS ETRUS MEHA AEODIN.*

"Would you hold this for me," she asked Bree, handing her the amulet.

She felt nothing. She wasn't changing form; the energy field that altered photons around her now dissipated. Her legs vanished and in their place were the limbs of a thoroughbred. The area behind her, clear only moments ago, was now filled with the hindquarters of a horse that was bigger than a pony but smaller than a police horse. Cat froze. Seth's cigarette dropped, his mouth agape. Bree was smiling.

"I told you she was a horse-lady."

CHAPTER 9

WE'RE A HAPPY FAMILY

Cal MacDonnell saw white. No, that wasn't right. He experienced white—an ever-expanding, inestimable, infinite whiteness. Not the color of a complete spectral blend, but instead, an abyss; the absence of all matter and energy—the universe had been drained . . . a page sans ink. He turned; white behind him. He looked up; white above. He looked down; white below, and what's more, no *him*. He held his hand up . . . nothing. *Where am I?* He was sure he said it and yet the sounds, not sounds, reverberated in the void. It was not resonance as he remembered it. Cal yelled, uncertain he'd made a noise. A minute, an hour, nothing could be measured. He simply was, yet wasn't.

"This is your past," said a voice behind him.

He turned, and standing there like a cutout was a young girl, no more than ten, barefoot in a blue velvet dress with white lace trim. Her dark blond hair was pulled back into a ponytail. She looked almost like his daughter, Brianna.

Where am I? Cal asked again in the soundless voice. He wasn't sure if she heard him.

"I told you, this is your past. Don't you have ears?" The girl considered him for a second. "Oh, sorry. You understand me, though, don't you?"

Cal nodded, or thought he did. His sense of self was a strange sensation, like the phantom limbs of an amputee.

"Good."

You look familiar.

"I'm your sister, Meghan."

I don't have a sister.

"I just said you did. In fact, you have two. I'm the one you like best. Do you remember my nickname?"

No.

"Oh boy. Uphill all the way, I see. Please, look over here," she said, holding out her hand.

There was a dot in the distance. He drew closer to it, or it to him. It was an optometrist's eye chart, except the pyramid of stacked typescript was no alphabet Cal had ever seen. The letters reminded him of Sanskrit.

I can't read it.

"Did I ask you to read it?"

On the right of the bottom-most line of the chart, a tiny character turned red and began to squirm and wiggle. It leapt off the diagram and ran around them aimlessly in search of something.

"That rune is one of the details," Meghan said. "Very unorganized lot, the details. They're always getting lost." She put her fingers to her lips and issued a sharp whistle. The rune ran up to Meghan and studied her. Meghan thrust out her thumb like a hitchhiker and motioned to the right with quick jabs. It hopped into the empty air only to stick in the center of whiteness. It twisted and expanded like a bead of red ink dropped into a bath, then transformed into a black swirl. The swirl grew around them until they were enveloped in darkness. The air changed—humid and wet like summer in a swamp.

Where are we?

"Ground zero."

A violent slash of lightning cut the world open from sky to ground. Bright light emanated from this tear in the universe. Cold emanated from the light, an odd sensation for one lacking corporal form. Cal tried to remain still but a powerful force pushed him toward the light. He threw his phantom arms out to the sides, hoping to find a brace in the darkness. His head plunged through the phenomenon first and emerged from a thicket. He glimpsed a world of madness on the other end—freezing cold, bright, a world populated by giant heads. Two flesh-colored mountains framed him. He clung with all his strength but the force was too strong. Giant hands came toward him . . .

"That's enough of that," Meghan said.

Suddenly, Cal was standing in a room with stone walls, paintings, velvet draperies, furniture, a library, and a massive stone fireplace with two midwives assisting a woman on a bloody bearskin rug. The eye chart, minus one rune, hung over the fireplace.

Meghan walked to the fireplace.

"No one should have to go through that twice in one lifetime. Recognize the screaming woman on the rug?"

Is this another weird dream? I don't have time for this. I have to get back to . . . Erin. Oh my God, Erin is dead. I have to . . .

"You have to stick with the program if you hope to get your marbles back. So, this would be our mother. That's you putting her through hell."

Mother? Yes. I remember. Where's . . . ?

"Father's three rooms away with Uncle Ian, wearing a hole in a very expensive Verakhoon rug. Men can't handle childbirth. That's the one constant in the universe. Not so cute smothered in blood and jelly, are you?"

I was at my daughter's birth.

"I wouldn't brag about it in Aandor. Men and women have specific roles here. I've often begged Father to teach me fencing like he taught you and Laurence—but my job is to breed sons and the occasional daughter for some lovely, noble fat cat. I wouldn't even know which end of a sword to hold if it weren't for you. Remember our lessons . . ."

. . . In the stables, before supper. You had a great parry, but a lousy thrust.

Meghan beamed with pride. She addressed the eye chart. "Am I good or what?"

His mother and the midwives disappeared with a shimmer.

Cal studied the room. He'd been here before. Outside the tall arched windows lay the whiteness.

Where's the world?

"Listen to you . . . concerned with the world when you haven't even figured yourself out yet."

The scene changed. On a divan before the same great fireplace frolicked a young man and a woman, barely dressed. Cal recognized the lad as himself at fifteen. The girl was a few years older.

"Remember her?"

Loraine. She worked in the kitchen.

"Not the only place she worked."

She ushered in my manhood a week before. On this day, though . . .

". . . On this day, you made a very important decision. It defined you."

"Loraine, stop," whispered young Cal. The girl sat up. Her large smooth breasts bounced enticingly before him.

"What's the matter with you?" she asked. "There were no reservations when you took me the first time in the gardener's shed; or the servant's pantry the day after. Am I no longer appealing . . . ?" Loraine lowered a nipple to his lips. Young Cal suckled it, drawn in by the pink bud's exquisite sensuality. Then he lifted her off him. He sat up and covered himself with a blanket.

"It's not that. You're lovely. It's just—I've seen how lust draws men away from decent things—makes them spend their time and fortunes on decadent pleasures."

"My little lord's been spending nights in town, I see," she said. "Have I competition?"

"No, that's not it. I am very fond of you, Loraine, but I do not love you."

"Little lord, my legs part for you as winter parts for spring. I don't care who else you bed, and you don't have to spend anything to have me. Someday I'll be wed to the cook or the valet or the stable master, or if I'm lucky, a bejeweled, fat merchant, and I can look back on these days with a smile."

"Loraine, someday you'll be wed, and to have been used . . . to think of another over your own spouse . . . that does not sit well with me. Your husband should be your world, as my father is to my mother, as I will someday be to my wife."

"You mean Godwynn's child? You'd deny me for a girl you've only met twice? I doubt her blood has even flowed. She is a child."

"I'm resolute in this."

Loraine gathered her clothes and stormed to the exit. "Your father was a much better romp than you, anyway." She slammed the door.

"Somehow, I can't picture Father servicing the female help." It was a different voice that said this—a young lad of about twelve years, with sandy hair and green eyes. He wore a black tunic with gold trim and pantaloons. He didn't belong in the scene as Cal remembered it. "Personally, I think the slut was lying."

Laurence?

"At your service."

Where's Meghan?

"You mean the Pest? Her tour is done."

Pest. Yes, that's the nickname we gave her.

"Making progress, bro."

The runes on the bottom line of the eye chart were all gone, and the slightly larger ones on the next line were beginning to move and turn red. Outside the window, the whiteness had been replaced by rolling fields. A mountain distorted by distance loomed in the background.

"That's our piece of Aandor out there. Eight hundred acres of rolling fields (and one village), hitched to a minor, yet respected, noble title. The next eighty thousand acres, and the mountain, belong to Lord Godwynn. A bit of a tight ass, but he sires hot daughters. I'm hoping to get one myself."

It's coming back.

"It's the runes. We're rebooting your head. All this history is scrambled in there."

There are no computers in Aandor. We don't use words like "reboot."

"We're not in Aandor. We're in your brain, and everything in here is fair game to get you up to speed. Meghan and I are just coopted memories augmented by the spell to walk you through your life. But there's not enough self-awareness yet to manifest your self-image. The third will help you do that."

Is he the ghost of Christmas future?

"Hey, that was funny. When did you develop a sense of humor?"

The scene shifted. They were in a courtyard. Troops in black and gold uniforms stood in formation. Black banners with the symbol of a red flaming bird's wing on yellow circles were flying. Behind the dais, a large tapestry with the remnants of the eye chart was tacked behind a throne. Half the runes were gone. Cal watched his younger self lean on one knee, as though he were proposing. He was slightly older than the version with Loraine. In his left hand he held his battle helmet like a football. A tall, red-haired man touched his shoulders with a gleaming new sword. Then he turned the sword around and presented it to Cal hilt first. Cal accepted the sword and sheathed it. Trumpets blared and the crowd rejoiced. An older man with red cheeks, a white beard, and the biggest smile in the yard walked over and threw his arms around the boy.

Father? This is Aandor court . . . the day I joined the Dukesguarde.

"You made Father's year," Laurence said.

And the red-haired man . . .

". . . Archduke Athelstan. Well, gotta run."

Wait!

"Oh, let him go," said a female voice behind him.

Laurence's replacement was a beautiful young lady dressed in a white linen dress. She wore flowers in her sandy hair, done in a long French braid that fell to her hips.

"He has to go play with his toy soldiers."

Valeria.

"Handsome, noble brother." She walked up and took his hand. Cal realized he had a body now. He saw his reflection in a puddle and felt the pull of gravity on his bones. Valeria stood on her toes, took his face in her hands, and planted a gentle kiss on his mouth, tasting his lips with a flick of her tongue. "They broke the mold when they made you," she said.

Valeria?

"Oh, what do you know? I'm a manifestation of Valeria, tainted by your subconscious belief that no man is good enough for me. Remember this?" The scene shifted to a hidden glade in the woods. Valeria and a young knight are kissing. The knight had successfully maneuvered her out of her blouse. "Remember your childhood buddy? Gentle, handsome Salimon, born of the gentry and passionately in love with me? Ah, look, I let him get to second base. The ability of a supple nipple to draw a smile on the most stoic faces—*I* controlled that smile. Forget lances and swords, true power lies in the curves of a maiden. I had intended to let Salimon have his desire, but . . ."

Cal watched himself crash through the bushes. He pulled Salimon off with one arm and hurled him ten yards. Valeria screamed at Cal as he pounded Salimon. The paramour was outclassed and yielded often, but Cal would not relent. Other friends arrived and pulled him off his former friend.

"Double standard, wouldn't you say?" Valeria asked. "No one crashed the gardener's shed when Loraine rode you like a buck. Imagine how frustrated you would have been."

You were not Salimon's first. Nor were you even his thirtieth. He had a taste for whoring. Half the daughters of the gentry are diseased for being with him, including his half-sister. I was trying to help you . . .

"You were keeping the family's prize heifer pristine and pure. Daddy can't sell soiled goods to the highest bidder."

Why are you showing me this? How's this important to me?

"Because it's all about sex my dear, dear brother. Sex, sex, sex. Forget politics, forget war, forget religion—sex is the true power in Aandor." Valeria rested her head on Cal's chest. "Who beds whom determines the fate of millions. And the current mess? That came of the most calculated pairing in history." She gave his crotch a gentle squeeze.

"Vulgar girl," said an older woman on the dais. At first Cal thought she was part of the crowd that was ignoring them, but she looked right at Valeria. She walked down the steps and approached them. They were back in Aandor court. The woman's eyes were blue as an Alpine lake. She wore flowing green robes over a blue linen dress. The jewelry was sparse and tasteful. Her golden hair, tied in a bun, was wrapped in a gold and pearl net. Mina MacDonnell did not look like a mother of four.

Mother.

"Well, I'm out of here," Valeria said. She gave Cal one last kiss. Tasting him on her lips, she said, "Good luck, bro. You'll need it."

"Vile creature," Mina said.

Don't be hard on her.

"And why not? My opinion of her is tainted by your thoughts. You think her a slut."

She's not. I was . . . too hard on her. She's curious. Weren't we all curious once?

"Time has softened you. Or maybe it's the world you've lived in for more than a decade that is responsible. That's good. No one likes a zealot, Cal. Although, that's probably why you made captain so young. Even your most mature friends appeared undisciplined beside you."

I wasn't that uptight. Was I?

"Are you eating well? Where's your girth?"

I work out, Mother . . . I'm quite healthy.

"Nonsense. There's nothing like a roll around a man to help him through a lean winter. It's a sign of success."

What are you here to teach me, Mother?

"I was the daughter of landed gentry, Cal, and my father married me to James MacDonnell, a man twenty years my senior. At first I was devastated, for I loved another man. But I could not have asked for a finer husband in all the world. My children have titles, and you Cal, you are betrothed to one of the most powerful families in the kingdom."

I'm not betrothed to the family, Mother. I'm pledged to a woman.

"A good woman."

I know . . . but I'm already married to a good woman.

"Chryslantha's dowry triples our family's holdings, Cal. Your father might be considered for a political post. Some of the high nobility are looking to Valeria and Meghan for unions with their firstborn. Aandor's world order has served our family well. You must accomplish your mission."

I will, Mother—the minute I remember what it was.

"And you must remain true to who you are."

I'm a loyal husband and a father.

"I know. And it frightens me." Mina began to weep. She touched her son's cheek. "You are my greatest pleasure, Cal. You inspire goodness as easily as lust and greed tempt the weak. If

I were certain all my children would turn out as you, I'd have borne litters, five at a time, until the world were overrun with my offspring."

"And I'd sire them," said a voice to the side.

James MacDonnell took his place beside his wife. His thick white beard brought out the rose in his cheeks. He put his arm around Mina, drew her close to him and kissed her on the head. It was something he'd seen often, as natural as the course water takes to the sea. "She has seen only thirty and seven winters," he said, "but her wisdom is beyond her years."

Father.

"Aye."

Mina's color faded into a monochromatic red.

"Remember your duty," she said as she disappeared.

I've missed you, Father.

The scene changed. They were in a strategy room filled with parchments and maps of a large continent. There were topography maps, demographic maps, and political maps with boundaries that changed from era to era.

"Remember your world?" James asked. "The city of Aandor, seat to the Kingdom of Aandor, a great center of commerce, art, knowledge, politics, and former throne of the Twelve Kingdoms."

Vaguely.

"Once, it was a grand empire. Now, power is shared through a loose confederation. Peace between the fractured states rested on the lack of a true heir to the empire. No one man is descended from all the twelve kings who once ruled the continent prior to the empire; thus, no emperor. Many have striven to rectify this condition through alliances, purchase, war, kidnapping, rape—by any means necessary."

Did something upset the balance?

"Our duke married well. Or not. It depends on the point of view. Failed assassinations and bed tricks prompted a more direct approach. We were ambushed by multiple armies: Farrenheil, Verakhoon . . ."

Aandor is strong.

"Our friends failed to come to our aid. They have their own ambitions to consider."

So Valeria was right.

"In her own crude way."

Are we just another faction? Where is the virtue in our struggle?

James MacDonnell fingered his beard and considered this question carefully before answering. "Although he does not have the blood of twelve kings, Duke Athelstan is a direct descendent of the last emperor and the kings of Aandor," he said. "By rights, he could claim the throne, using Aandor's power to dominate much of the continent. But we've been down that road already. The whole continent was at each other's throat, my son. It almost destroyed our civilization. To keep the peace, Athelstan has honored the accord his grandsire agreed to seventy years earlier. The empire can only be unified by a man with the blood of twelve kings. If one of the other houses produces an emperor first, all titles of Aandor will be transferred to that child. Athelstan will lose his ancestral seat and his lands. To prevent counterclaims, he and his family would be jailed under dubious charges and executed. He does not deserve that fate."

They say war is hell. Politics is worse.

"War results from a failure of politics. See for yourself."

The scene shifted to a battle. Cal and his weary troops had their backs to a cliff. A larger force approached from the front.

Cal was cut, bleeding. Cuts and welts covered his face and body. His armor was shattered, his clothing shredded, his shin burned and blackened by ash.

This was the battle at Gagarnoth.

"Aye. Outnumbered three to one by fresh troops. Your captain had been slain. You were the ranking officer. It breaks my heart to see you so."

Warrior Cal clutched a fetish in his hands. It was a silk garter with pearls woven into the edges. A bow made of golden hair was tied to one end. Warrior Cal put the fetish to his nose and breathed deeply. His eyes lit from within. He rallied his men with a piercing cry and charged the approaching troops, who were caught off guard by their steel-curdling shrieks. In less than a minute, they were outnumbered only two to one, another minute one to one, then the remaining foes broke and ran leaving the Aandorans victorious over the disassembled corpses of their foes.

"Perhaps, if all the soldiers of Aandor possessed such a fetish, we would not be in this predicament today," James said, smiling.

"And would the noble James MacDonnell have his future daughter bed the entire army for such an advantage . . . ?" It was a woman's voice, sweet as honeyed nectar.

As he laid eyes on her, Cal MacDonnell remembered the sound, smell, feel, and look of his betrothed, etched in his mind like that of a beloved spouse recently deceased. Except, she was not dead. Wavy tresses of spun gold, eyes green as a forest in spring, and a smile that could warm a troll's heart, Chryslantha at seventeen was the most desired woman in all the realm; a girl by contemporary American standards, but in Aandor, primed to be the matriarch of a noble house. She wore a low-cut green velvet dress with gold and white fringe; the same dress she wore the last time Cal saw her.

". . . For surely you know, Father, that the scent of that fetish is the scent of my maidenhood. A gift to my beloved before the eve of his battle."

Chryslantha.

"How long since you last uttered that name, my lord? How long since you last thought of me?"

A lifetime.

Cal embraced her. She fit like the other side of a puzzle fragment.

"Excuse us, Lord MacDonnell," she said.

James bowed to her as he, too, turned the color of blood and faded away.

You are the last.

"A noble guess?"

Not a guess. The order of my guides has been relative to my closeness to them. There's no one left after you.

"Are you sure about that?"

Cal dropped his eyes. He couldn't look at her.

"I gave you my maidenhood. My value to my father as a bride is not as great as it once was."

There will be no shortage of suitors for your hand, Chryslantha—and not because of your dowry. You are the manifestation of beauty and wisdom. The ancients would have built you a temple. A fop would convert to your charms.

"Yet, I cannot convert you from your marriage bed . . ."

I . . . uh . . .

". . . Nor is it my place to, since I am only a manifestation of Chryslantha from your thoughts."

She placed her hand in his and guided him to a pool of water. In the reflection, Cal saw Cat, Brianna, and the two strangers from the tenement fight, sitting around in his living room. They were having a heated discussion.

"This is reality. The red-haired woman hails from the Blue Forest. She is losing her appeal for help from the others."

How do you know this?

"We are in the room. Your wife is prepared to take you to a hospice and bring the authorities into this matter."

That would be bad.

"Agreed. I will release you from this metaconscious trance to address this problem."

Wait! I need to know about the accident. How did the mission fall apart?

"The answer you seek is not mine to give. The runes are designed to reveal only your past in Aandor. The spell caster knows nothing of your years on this earth."

The world melted away to be replaced by the whiteness again. Cal felt as though he were hurdling upward at a fantastic rate, but there was no point on the horizon by which to measure this ascent, only whiteness and the sensation of defying gravity.

Suddenly, darkness surrounded him and a fantastic weight pressed his chest as gravity reasserted itself. He heard echoes.

"Maybe Red can take you to the hospital on her flying carpet," a male voice said. The body that belonged to the voice passed near him. It was the young man. Cal mustered all his remaining strength and reached out in the direction of the footsteps. He'd captured a wrist.

"Show them," Cal tried to shout, but heard only a whisper of himself.

"Show them what?" the young man said.

"My lord, magic is in short supply on this earth. My illusion has a high casting cost . . ."

"Show them," he whispered again.

The sensation of rising reversed itself. He fell through his own body, like Icarus from a blackened sky into an infinite achromatic sea. Such was the speed of his descent, the burn of the wind against his cheeks and forehead, that he lost all confidence in the knowledge this was a mental, not a physical, realm. The wind song deafened him. He thrust his arms before his face and shut his eyes tight in anticipation of the impact. And then silence.

He opened his eyes. His face was nestled in a silk pillow, his arms underneath it. He was in a perfumed feather bed with satin sheets. A soft hand touched his cheek. He looked to his side and there was Chryslantha, naked. He, too, was undressed. She rolled beside him, put her arms around his neck and straddled him with a smooth ivory leg.

"Let us finish the lesson, my lord," she said, and kissed him.

CHAPTER 10

SCHOOL AND HARD KNOCKS

1

Daniel awoke with a start. He was on the floor, back to the door, sitting in a puddle of his own urine. He opened the one eye that wasn't swollen and encrusted. His muscles ached, including some that hadn't been hit. He'd slept (if one could call it sleep) in an awkward position for most of the night. The tendons between his neck and left shoulder felt as if they'd been cut short and resoldered, and when he turned his head it was as though an embedded pick was jabbing at his sinews.

The dawn rays streamed through the blinds. The golden dust in the slanted beams danced and shimmered. His aching fingers were swollen and stiff. Slowly, the boy unbuttoned his shirt, wincing every so often from the pain. He had to sit on the bed to pull his pants off. When he was done, he took a moment to catch his breath. He opened the door to his room without apprehension. Clyde would be dead asleep at this hour.

Daniel slipped quietly into the bathroom, ran his trousers under the shower and wrung them before throwing them in the hamper. Then he stepped under the water and let the hot droplets pelt him. They stung as they hit the purple tie-dyed landscape of his skin. He cooled the water with a twist of the knob and remained a statue. His rib hurt when he turned, he maneuvered the soap across his body with mannequin-like perfection. He couldn't bend two fingers. Daniel put the wooded handle of the back washer between his teeth, grabbed one of the fingers and pulled until it popped into place. His brain swam in Tabasco for a moment until the finger settled into its slot. He did the same for the other finger—suddenly the floor of the tub rose toward him. He caught the edge of the tub with the last of his strength. Eyes closed, cheek on the porcelain, he was aware of the water dancing on his back. Daniel lay there, breathing the mildew on the grout until the spots in his head subsided. He only needed a few minutes.

Walking back to his room, Daniel froze outside his parents' slightly ajar bedroom door. He cocked his head just enough to peek in and confirm that Clyde was still passed out on the bed. The brute was on his back, head slightly off the bed and skewed downward, exposing his throat like he hadn't an enemy in the world. *This was the hour,* Daniel thought . . . if he ever wanted to do Clyde in, a razor across the throat in the early morning would be perfect. Like a vampire in its morning coffin, nothing would stir this monster before the act was accomplished. Clyde would sleep through his own bloodletting. But Daniel believed Clyde's end would come sooner than later—that aside from the possibility of getting hit on the road while drunk or being knifed in prison some day, Clyde's cause of death could likely be massive liver failure. So, Daniel moved on.

He dressed his wounds with some gauze wrap and an Ace bandage and went down to the kitchen. Penny sat at the table while Rita rinsed breakfast dishes in the sink. Rita kept a cigarette dry between her right index and middle fingers as she washed and maneuvered the sponge between her thumb and the last two digits of her hand.

"There's no eggs left," Rita said, without turning to see who it was.

Daniel poured himself a bowl of Cheerios and opened the fridge.

"We're out of milk," Rita added, with an edge.

Daniel realized he'd forgotten to buy groceries last night. He pulled the Brita from the top shelf and ate his Cheerios with water.

As Rita turned, she avoided eye contact. Daniel stared at her, daring her with his mind to notice the bruises. It was a game he played where he pretended to have telepathic powers and used them to help Rita notice the obvious.

"The principal called about some desks yesterday," Rita said.

"Yeah. Clyde already discussed it with me."

Rita turned and looked at him with that strange interest in trivial things one has when stirred by emotions for which one cannot find expression.

"Five hundred dollars is a lot of money," she said. "You know your father's out of work."

"Can't find a job, huh?" Daniel stressed.

Rita directed an agitated nod to the staircase and relaxed only when she confirmed it was vacant.

"Don't talk like that," she snapped. "I swear, Danny . . . you bring things on yourself. Don't write on the tables, don't sass your teachers . . . just don't do anything."

"I could sit in a closet all day."

"Clyde's trying."

"He's a short anchor and we're a leaky rowboat, Mom."

Rita glanced at the stairs again.

"When was the last time Clyde rolled out of bed before eleven o'clock?"

"You ought to be a little more grateful."

"How can I? I remember Dad. Clyde doesn't measure up."

"Right, it's all *my* fault," Rita shot back.

"No, I didn't mean . . ." Daniel regretted setting her in motion, something he knew better than to do.

"You think I planned to be a widow at thirty-three? Think it's easy starting over, alone, with a young child?"

He'd heard Rita's lament a dozen times, her shield against her own poor decisions. Daniel was only eight when Rita married Clyde. Too young to have a clue about his future stepfather's alcoholic and abusive nature. The truth that Rita never owned up to was that it was her fault; she had surrendered to loneliness.

"Mom . . ." She was shaking, and true to form, would soon be prying the cap off a bottle of mother's little helpers. Disturbed by the argument, Penny looked ready to bawl. Mr. Biggles lay on the floor by her high chair. Daniel picked it up and shook it before her with a smile. She grabbed the bear and squeezed it like a life preserver.

"We've got a roof over our heads," Rita continued. "There's food on the table . . ."

Yeah, thanks to me, Daniel thought.

"If you don't like it here, you can join the Marines. I'll sign the papers."

"Mom . . ."

Rita headed toward the stairs in a huff and stopped short of ascending. She stared at the top landing, then around the room, looking trapped where she stood. Her drugs were in the bedroom.

"I'm doing laundry," she said and headed for the basement. "You got anything needs washing?"

It was an innocent question, but it stung like a wasp. "In the hamper."

Penny, who wore as much food as she'd eaten, banged the table with a spoon. She moved her face around playfully as Daniel tried to wipe it with a napkin. "You need to change your clothes," he said.

"No," she giggled.

"No? That's a pretty powerful word for such a small girl."

"No."

"And you need to take a bath."

"No," she said again. She was in a good mood, just giving the word a test drive as she determined the limits of her power.

"Give me a kiss," Daniel said.

"No." She shook her head until it became a blur.

"Please."

"No."

"How about a hug?"

Penny gave Mr. Biggles a bear hug and thrashed side to side like she would love him to death.

"Not Biggles . . . me," he said.

"No," she said.

Daniel stopped coaxing. The toy glared at him, locked within Penny's arms. It disturbed him that he envied the bear.

2

Someone had replaced Daniel's desk in Algebra. On close inspection, though, Daniel realized it was his old desk after all. The top had been sanded down and restained with two coats of varnish. It was a half-assed, sloppy job. He could still see some remnants of the old grooves from his drawings. There weren't going to be any new desks. The realization gnawed at his gut. He could have refurbished all the desks himself for less than fifty dollars.

Katie Millar sat next to him. It was the only class they shared this year, an unexpected result of Daniel having gotten into many advanced courses. Fortunately, he sucked at math.

Katie wore a white turtleneck, but it couldn't completely hide the purple blotch that adorned her neck this morning. His heart sank at the thought of her with Josh; a spoiled, rich brat who probably had more than one girl and didn't care for any of them. Daniel daydreamed about the purple welts Katie could give him instead of the ones he drew from Clyde.

"I heard about your fight with the Grundys," Katie said. "Looks like they gave as good as they got."

"They never laid a hand on me."

"That's not what they said. Besides, you're wearing the evidence."

"This came from Clyde."

"Oh," she said. Katie turned away and searched for the day's lesson in her textbook.

Once, Katie was Daniel's Rock of Gibraltar. After one of Clyde's tirades, they'd lie against the trunk of a willow, his head on her lap, and she stroked his hair while he imagined himself in another life. It'd been months since they last did that. She was under pressure from her parents not to associate with him outside of school anymore. Clyde had worked for her father at the meat plant until he had been caught stealing prime cuts by the caseload for black market sales. It was as a favor to Daniel on behalf of his daughter that Mr. Millar did not press charges on Clyde. As an adopted child, Daniel had no traceable pedigree and everyone soon realized his legal guardians were trash badly masked by a single coat of whitewash. As the semester moved on, Katie withdrew her emotional attachment, as though Daniel might sully her with his bad fortune. A vacuum had emerged that made the day-to-day harder to bear than ever before. Adrian was a good friend but had no strength to lend him. If Daniel was to survive, he had to find untapped reserves of his own to draw upon. His universe was closing in on him.

Mr. Napolitano walked in and began handing out the morning's quiz, which Daniel had forgotten to study for.

"Mr. Hauer, your presence has been requested at the principal's office," the teacher said as he approached.

What now? Daniel thought. He collected his books and stood.

"No, take the quiz first," Napolitano said. "It should only take ten minutes if you know the material."

3

Conklin's secretary, Lacy McKnight, had taken a liking to Daniel. She told him he reminded her of her baby brother. Unlike the other delinquents who'd spent time in front of her desk,

Daniel found her a pleasant presence in a school full of antagonists. She was powerless to change school policy or suspend detention, but would often sneak him cookies and tell him about the latest escapades of her little brother who was in the Navy and stationed in Italy. That someone was standing in his corner made the trip to Conklin's easier to bear. Ms. McKnight treated him like family. Daniel would be sure to include her in his Oscar acceptance speech for Best Animated Short. Noticeably missing from the acknowledgments would be Clyde and Rita. Missing today was the jovial smile Lacy always greeted him with, an understanding that no matter what he did it was small potatoes in the world of great events and that everything would be okay no matter how much Conklin blustered. She shot Daniel a worried look as he approached. Daniel half felt he should turn around and run for his life. Raised voices emanated from the principal's office.

"Look at you," she said with a trace of mother hen.

"I'll be fine."

Lacy shook her head. "Go in."

Conklin was talking to Jim Grundy and Darlene Lebeaux, his nemeses' parents, and the local sheriff, Ed Maher, who wore his hat and sunglasses indoors and was, coincidently, the principal's third cousin. Mr. Grundy had yet to reach thirty-five, but looked like he was pushing fifty. He wore a few days' growth on his face and his emaciated thinness was emphasized by the stringy mullet he chose for his coif. Darlene was slightly older, but had a body as nubile as a woman half her age, which she tried to contain in the miniskirt she pulled on constantly because it was one size too small. Darlene was legendary among the boys in town. It was rumored that once a year she picked a graduate headed for military service and gave him a poke for good luck behind the strip club where she danced.

The parents sat on the couch, facing a chair reserved for Daniel. Conklin sat to his left, the sheriff to his right. Daniel realized he was on trial. Somehow, in the middle of this whole mess, Daniel had the wherewithal to realize that Darlene wasn't wearing any underwear.

"S'that the little fucker?" Jim Grundy asked. "Sure's hell took you long enough."

"I had a test. Why am I here?"

"Why . . . ? You whupped my boys!" Darlene said.

"There, there, Darlene," Conklin said. He reached forward and patted her on the thigh. "Don't get excited."

"They attacked us," Daniel said.

Conklin gave him a skeptical look. "Did you walk away from a conversation the Grundy boys were having with Adrian Lutz and then come back with a two-by-four post, which you then attacked them with?" he asked.

Reality had become skewed with that interpretation. A placid mood suddenly befell Daniel, like a shore when the tide withdraws before the onslaught of a tsunami. Daniel retreated to his mental battlement and took up arms. "Only if by *conversation* you mean Tony Soprano chatting with someone who's late on a payment."

Sheriff Maher chuckled.

"Smart-ass," Grundy said.

"Look, none of this happened during school time or on school property," Daniel added.

"The Grundys are planning a civil suit against you and your parents," Conklin said. "They came here to talk to Adrian, and to get your personal information. I called this meeting because I am disturbed by this incident, Daniel. This school has adopted a zero-tolerance policy. Certain behaviors have to be noted in this day and age, as the incident at Columbine clearly demonstrated. I have decided to suspend you until such time as we can determine whether expulsion is appropriate. It's for the safety of the other students."

Daniel only half heard what came after "civil suit" and "parents." He was numb. Clyde was already in a frenzy over the desks. "This is ridiculous," he said. He couldn't contain the quiver in his voice. "I am not a bully. Adrian will back me up."

The parents and Conklin looked at each other. Darlene shifted her legs and Daniel caught a peek of her shaved privates, which he was in no position to truly appreciate at that moment. The four adults said nothing.

"What?" Daniel asked.

"Adrian has stated that the Grundy boys are friends and that they were only horsing around," the sheriff said. "You know, joshing him . . . nothing serious."

The battlement took a hit. Someone brought a trebuchet to a sword fight. Daniel's innards sloughed down to the bottom of his gut; he was light-headed. A hundred thoughts flashed across his mind in anarchy, and he struggled to relate to what was happening right now. His friend Adrian was a coward who feared the Grundys coming after him when he wasn't around. Daniel pulled what wits he had left and said, "But, he was crying."

"He was laughing . . . ," Darlene retorted. "You overreacted. Now my poor baby needs new teeth."

"Adrian was screaming because your goons were—"

"That's enough," Conklin cut in. "Darlene, Mr. Grundy, we'll handle things from here."

On the way out, Jim Grundy shot Daniel a look that reminded him of Clyde. Darlene's glance made it clear Daniel would never get a poke, even if he won the medal of honor.

"Ed?" the principal said.

The sheriff didn't look happy. "Don't much like the direction of this, Roscoe. Boys will be boys. We all got into scraps when we was young. And them Grundy boys ain't exactly angels."

"When we was young, students didn't blow away their teachers and schoolmates with AK-47s. These are different times. Ed, bottom line, the boy assaulted two people with a deadly instrument. Are you gonna do your job or not?"

The sheriff put his large hand on Daniel's shoulder and patted him up. "Let's go, son. We'll go to the hospital first and check your injuries."

As they walked out, Lacy looked on the verge of tears. A cell was probably the safer place to be. It was when Clyde showed up to bail him out that concerned Daniel. Clyde would kill him over this.

The period bell rang; just in time for the whole school to come out and watch Daniel get escorted to jail.

CHAPTER 11

"HONEY, I'M GAY" WOULD HAVE BEEN FINE

1

"Jesus Christ, Cal, she's pumped us full of psychotropic drugs or something," Cat MacDonnell said. They sat opposite each other at the kitchen table, squared off like gunfighters at a high-stakes poker game. Cat's second mug of Irish coffee quivered in her hand. The woman Cal considered as solid as they come was one snowflake short of an avalanche. It pained him to see her like this.

On the other hand, another part of him felt better than it had in more than thirteen years. It was the first day of spring, and a window in his mind had been opened. Memories, like the scent of spring's first blossom, blew in on the breeze feeling both familiar and new. At the same time, any joy was countered by the seriousness of his failure to conduct his assigned mission.

It was 6:00 A.M., the sun was just breaking the horizon. Seth was dozing in the corner with an empty beer can in his hand, and Lelani was playing with Bree in the living room.

"You don't really believe you're some sort of knight from a feudal world?" Cat continued.

"Cat . . ."

"Erin is dead! Your career is in jeopardy. People are trying to kill us . . . there's no time for this fantasy shit!"

"Cat, your language . . ."

"Fuck my language! I always cuss when I'm high!"

"Cat, we're not on drugs."

Bree squealed as Lelani gave her a trot around the apartment.

"You get the hell off that *thing* this minute, Brianna Mac-Donnell!" Cat shouted.

"Please don't call her a 'thing,'" Cal said. "Centaurs are extremely proud. We owe her our lives."

"I don't know who you are," Cat said to her husband.

Lelani helped Bree down and stood in the corner with her arms folded.

"I'm Cal MacDonnell—husband, father, son, cop. None of those things has changed."

"Some trick," Seth said from the couch. "Breaking up a happy family usually involves drugs, greed, alcohol, or infidelity. She does it all by pulling a rabbit out of a hat; or rather, a horse's ass."

His wife's eyes, which Cal had gazed into a dozen times over, were surrounded by webs of crimson fatigue as they searched for a clue to his thoughts. The very structure of reality—time and space, God and science—had been thrown into flux. It wasn't just the attack or the craziness, Cal realized. The obvious was right there before him. His wife wasn't sure if there was a future for her in his new and former past. The confidence to handle anything life threw at her, which indelibly defined Cat, was shaken to its core. Cal had mistaken anxiety for anger.

He took Cat's hands into his own and rubbed them gently.

"This doesn't change how I feel about you," he said. "I'm not going anywhere without you." He hoped he sounded more sure than he felt. "Whatever the future brings, we'll do it together."

"Is that wise?" Lelani asked. "Consider your obligations."

"Queen of Tact strikes again," Seth said from his corner, still half asleep.

"Is what wise?" Cat asked.

"You. Shut up," Cal told Seth. "This whole mess is your fault."

"*My* fault?" Seth asked, coming full awake. "How the hell can this be my fault?"

"Call it a gut instinct."

"I don't remember any of this sci-fi shit!" Seth insisted.

"Well, I remember you. A pain in the ass."

"Hey man, I may be an ass sometimes, but I didn't cause your problems. Don't lay the blame at my feet. I'm a second away from walking out of here and forgetting this crap ever happened."

"You wouldn't last a day on your own," Lelani said.

"What did she mean, Cal? Is *what* wise?" Cat repeated.

Cal glared at Lelani, a reminder that she was his subordinate.

"I only meant that the road ahead is rife with danger," Lelani responded. "It might be wiser to put you and the girl somewhere safe."

"This is my family. I'm not getting 'put' anywhere," Cat said.

"You can stay with your mom for a few days," Cal suggested.

"I'm staying with you."

"Cat . . ."

"I'm staying with you. Case closed."

A high scream broke out from Bree's bedroom. The door was ajar when it should have been shut. Lelani vaulted the couch and reached the room before anyone else. Cal hobbled as quickly as he could. He still had a little vertigo but wasn't sure if it was because of the injuries or the spell. Bree was sitting on the floor crying with her arms around Maggie. The dog's neck twisted at a disturbing angle. Blood trickled from her mouth.

"Maggie needs a doctor," Bree wailed.

Cat lifted Bree and let the girl bury her face in her neck. "Maggie was very brave," she told her daughter. Cat rubbed Bree's back and made a shushing noise. She cast Lelani a resentful glance as she carried her daughter out of the room.

"Sorry about that," Cal said. "We really do appreciate your help."

A radio and car doors shutting sounded from the street.

Through Bree's window, Cal spied his lieutenant and the precinct chaplain tapping on the cruiser parked below to wake the cops that "dozed off" while on guard duty. They'd be put on report. How much did the cops remember? Maybe Cal could tell the chief they were gassed. How did that fit into the big picture?

"There are loose ends that need attending," Lelani said, beside him, as though reading his mind.

"How the hell am I going to explain all this to the brass?" Cal said.

Erin was dead. His home was in shambles. Cal realized he would be at the station house for hours as Internal Affairs debriefed him. If he left now, he could at least prevent them from coming up and having to explain why the apartment looked like a war zone. The mission ahead was full of travels, perhaps even a retreat into the remotest parts of the world. He needed to stay mobile and in the law's good graces. If only the boy was still alive . . .

EDWARD LAZELLARI

"What will you do while I'm at the precinct?" he asked
Lelani.

"Seth and I can address the damage to your home and other
matters," she said, looking down at the dead pet. "We—*I* will
guard your family. Although, I am fairly certain no other attempt will be made. Only a fool attacks a sorcerer without
backup, and I wounded theirs severely at the tenement."

"About your remark earlier . . . the one about obligations . . ."

"I meant only your obligations to Duke Athelstan. Whatever
your commitment to your betrothed, it is *your* concern. The boy's
survival is important to my race. That is *my* concern. Everything
I do, I do for my people."

"I am in a pickle, though, aren't I?"

"Pickle? A flip description. Your family's reputation is in
jeopardy. And I doubt Chryslantha's father will let the matter
go without reparations. His pride is at stake."

"You're assuming Cat will choose to come back with me."

"You are the victim of your own good judgment, Lord Mac-
Donnell. If your wife were of lesser character, the decision
would be easier. However, she is brave and will follow you to the
ends of the earth . . . and farther. You will eventually have to
make a decision. Whatever you choose does not change the fact
that you took a mate and sired a child. Your honor will not allow you to keep this news from Lady Chryslantha. Consider
this, though—if Athelstan's son is lost, even if we retake Aandor, the duke will be merciless in his judgment. He can use those
reparations to Lord Godwynn as his vehicle to strip your family
of titles and lands."

Cal pondered the ramifications. He had found his soul mate

on two different worlds. How could a man so lucky be so cursed at the same time?

"Of course the stakes are much higher than your complicated betrothal," Lelani continued. "Farrenheil will strip Aandor of everything decent. They will force its lords, including your father, to fealty, and those who do not submit will be publicly executed. Our citizens will be sold into slavery, our women carted off and raped. Scholars, clerics, and any other perceived threats will 'disappear' as agents of their secret guilds drag us out of our homes in the middle of night without a writ, and the last beacon of hope, prosperity, and fair rule in our world will be gone.

"And we have not even touched upon the dangers to this world should we not get on top of the situation," Lelani continued.

"This world?" Cal asked. "You mean the other guardians in our party?"

"They, too, are in mortal danger, but I actually meant the people of *this* world. Lord Dorn is as reckless as he is remorseless. You have no idea how many times he's been reprimanded by the Council of Wizards for engaging in the darkest arts— forbidden magicks that could lay waste to entire regions in a single stroke. There are no councils here to hold him in check. We're fortunate that magical energy is in short supply, but he will eventually find what he needs. Even if we find the prince and regroup the guardians, out of desperation, Dorn could resort to outlawed spells and kill tens of thousands here while trying to defeat us."

These revelations overwhelmed Cal. He thought about the line cops often used to avoid responsibility for FUBAR scenarios . . . *It's above my pay grade.* But that wasn't even the case here. In

Aandor, these types of responsibilities were exactly his pay grade. Three thousand men served under him, helping him keep order in the grandest city on his world.

The buzzer rang.

One problem at a time, Cal thought. "I'm going down to the station to get my interrogation over with."

"Wait," she said. Lelani delved into her satchel and pulled out a lapel pin that looked like a small silver flower. "Wear this somewhere in view of the people questioning you."

"What is it?"

"The pin is endowed with a credibility enchantment. As long as the person questioning you is in view of this pin, they will be more apt to believe your stories."

"I can tell them anything?"

"No. Try to make your explanation as realistic as possible. This is not strong magic. I confiscated this one from a novitiate who used it to bed tavern wenches in Aandor. If you told someone you were a cricket, they would get a terrible migraine trying to reject that lie. But if you told them you were five foot eight inches tall, they would accept that. The enchantment gives your own creativity an added edge."

Cal was grateful for the gift. He could paint Dorn's men as gangsters who kidnapped him from the scene and attacked the cruiser outside . . . that they didn't expect Cat to have a weapon much less be proficient with it, and with that distraction, he freed himself of his bonds and helped get the jump on them. He could put out an all-points bulletin on them as well. That would make it hard for them to travel in public, especially Hesz.

The buzzer rang again.

"Will they insist on coming up?" Lelani asked, worried about her appearance.

"No. I'll tell them Cat is having a fit. Her temper is legendary at the precinct. 'She's in a mood, hates the NYPD at the moment, and they risk having a coffeepot thrown at them.' They won't come up."

It was a stretch, but Cal had to keep the investigation in check. His original mission was the most important charge of his life. He had to resume it as soon as possible.

"I'll be back in a few hours. Try to formulate a plan of action. Take care of them. And keep an eye on Seth. I can't tell you how he did it yet, but my gut tells me he's the reason everything went to hell."

2

Seth entered the apartment with all the finesse of a drunken Marx brother. The wooden planks he carried caught on the door frame, and he slammed into them hard enough to drive the air from his lungs. He startled the young girl who sat on the living room window seat vigilantly watching for her dad. She looked exhausted.

"Sorry," Seth said to the girl.

Everyone had an assigned task to kill time until Cal returned. Seth's job was to raid the apartment being renovated upstairs for tools and materials to patch the bedroom windows that had been damaged during the fight. Cat was on the phone, telling her construction contractors to take the day off.

Lelani quietly came out of the girl's bedroom with the dog wrapped in bedsheets. A limp paw stuck out of one corner, an unfortunate oversight. The corners of the young girl's mouth drew down and began to tremble. She fell into another fit and buried her teary eyes on her forearm against the sill.

"She was engrossed with the view from the window only a moment ago," Lelani whispered. "I checked before coming out."

"My bad," Seth said.

Lelani hurried out of the apartment.

Seth looked toward Cat to tell her the girl was upset again.

"A family emergency, yes," Cat said into the phone. She was spinning around the kitchen, putting away candles and incense and doing other chores as she talked. "A death in the family," she continued. "And tomorrow, too. No, I'm not sure how long. You will definitely get paid for both days. No . . . I'll have to talk to my husband about that. I'll have to . . . Look, I don't know the answer to that right now."

The girl cried so hard she quivered. She soon developed the hiccups. Seth tried to break into Cat's phone conversation, but she was in her "zone" and the rest of the world didn't exist.

"I just don't know at the moment," Cat continued on the phone. "I'll call you as soon as I do. Yes, I know many people want to hire you, Mr. Pellegrini—you were highly recommended by the Kramers, but . . ."

Seth dropped the planks by the couch and gingerly approached the girl.

"Hi," he said. He was no better at starting a conversation with a five-year-old than a twenty-five-year-old. He realized how much of a crutch the porn gig had been.

The girl looked up. Her expression said *You're not my daddy.*

Seth already thought this was a bad idea right after "hi," but he couldn't abandon her now.

"I'm Seth. I'm a—*friend*—of your dad." Seth spotted a box of Kleenex on the end table and pulled a few tissues for her. "Here, for your eyes," he said with a smile.

She hiccupped, took the tissues, and honked a glob of snot into the pile. Then she held it out for Seth to take back.

"Uh—why don't you hold on to it," he said. "Just in case. So your name is . . . Britney?"

She gave him a quizzical look, the type with a pout. "Brianna." *Hiccup.* "Are you *sure* you're a friend of my daddy's? He tells all of his friends about me. *They* know my name."

"Maybe '*friend*' wasn't the right word. Anyway, I noticed you were sad. Thought maybe you'd like some company."

Bree shook her head.

"You're sad because of your pet," Seth continued.

Bree nodded.

"I have a pet, too. She never saved my life, though."

"Maggie loved me." *Hiccup.* "The bad man hurt her because she tried to help me."

"That's what dogs do. They protect the people they love."

"But, I miss her." Brianna started to tear up again. "I didn't want her to die."

Seth pulled out a fresh tissue for her.

"Maggie was a good dog," he said. "I know that she's in heaven right now looking down at you and she's very happy that you're okay. I think God gives dogs a special cookie when they save their masters. Sets them up in a doghouse as big as a barn; makes them the alpha dog in their pack in heaven."

"What's an alfafa dog?"

"The boss. The big dog who takes care of all the rest."

Bree nodded. She liked the sound of that.

"What kind of dog do you have?" she asked.

"I have a cat. Her name is Hoshi. It means 'star' in Japanese. She sits on my head in the mornings because I won't turn off the alarm clock. When bad men come after me, she runs under the bed and meows at them, but very angrily."

Bree smiled.

"It's true," Seth said with mock sincerity. "She says things—in cat language of course—like, 'Leave the food guy alone, you ugly wonk. He hasn't filled my dish yet.' Or, 'Get away from the food guy, you repulsive mooch, my litter needs cleaning.'"

"I'd like to meet Hoshi," Bree said.

"Sure. I'll have you up one day."

It took Seth a moment to realize there was nowhere to have her up to—he was homeless. He forced a smile. The talk of Hoshi chastising men who were after him also reminded Seth that Carmine wanted his kneecaps for wall trophies. Besides the freak show, there were normal everyday humans out for his head as well. He wasn't sure which set of goons were worse.

"Plumbers are the worst," Cat said, slamming the phone into its cradle.

"Excuse me?" Seth jumped.

"Plumbers. To get a good one, you have to book them months in advance and then you have a prima donna with butt crack to deal with."

"Right."

"Is the . . ." Cat made hand motions to signify the dog being out of the child's room.

"Yeah. Lelani took care of it."

"Poor thing."

"She was a brave dog."

"No, I mean Bree," she said pointing.

The girl was asleep on the window seat. Cat took the tissues from her hand and covered her baby with a quilt.

"Seth, *please* fix my bedroom window. Then I can put her down in there."

"Yeah." He picked up the planks and resumed his march toward the back.

3

Cat watched from her kitchen window as Lelani buried the dog under the small plot of grass behind the building. The patio umbrella was strategically positioned over her to block the centaur from the only other building with a bird's-eye view of the backyard. She was a beautiful woman in a turtleneck knit, with the ass end of a horse where her legs should have been. Her tail, which was also scarlet, was neatly banded by three gold ringlets one foot apart, forming spheres of hair with a tassel at the end. The fence and bushes around the backyard were high, but still, Cat wanted the horse-girl back inside as soon as possible. Things were already hard enough to explain without the neighbors spotting Lelani.

Seth made several phone attempts to get his photography career back. Someone named Carmine, with a cruel voice that the little plastic earpiece could not contain, made it clear that Seth would not only never work again, but that there were men combing the five boroughs ready to serve him his knees on a platter *plus* a court summons for breach of contract. To take his mind off his troubles, Seth tried boarding up the bedroom windows. He did everything badly.

Cat finished calling the contractors, then vacuumed for an hour, picking up glass and other debris from the fight. Bree was sleeping off the aftermath of her outbursts over Maggie's death. They all needed a time-out from life until everything was back to normal. *Would anything ever be normal again?* Cat wondered. How would this genie go back into the bottle? In all the years she pondered her husband's origin, nothing like this had crossed her mind. Was Cal really a knight, just like in the storybooks? A member of his country's nobility, heir to lands and a fortune? Did that make her Lady MacDonnell? She chuckled at the notion. No one ever mistook her for a lady. She soaped up a sponge and began washing the dishes.

When Cat was a little girl, she beat up boys, climbed trees, and spat farther than a camel. Her older sister Vanessa dressed in Barbie pink and pretended the decrepit jungle gym in the backyard was a castle tower from which a mysterious prince would rescue her. Vanessa ended up with Vinnie, an electrician from Fort Lee and her first child six months after the wedding. Cat allowed herself a second chuckle. Turned out *she* was getting the castle. Life was full of little ironies.

"Cut that out," she whispered to herself. "There's no castle. You need a reality check."

The monotony of the dishes caused her mind to wander, and she considered the lives of Cal's mother and sisters. Would it be like the movies—long gowns for the ladies and chivalry coming from every sword-wielding dork? A million rules of etiquette for every function: how to curtsy, present oneself to those of higher rank, where to sit at a table, how to hold in a fart and scratch one's ass properly. Cat did not know the first thing about being an aristocrat, nor did she want to. Cat avoided caviar, ballroom dancing, and hobnobbing with the pretentiously dull. She struggled to remember which side of the plate the utensils were set on when she had her own guests for dinner. She couldn't imagine putting Bree through all that.

"Ow!" she yelped, nicking herself on a chipped glass. "Serves me right for thinking nonsense."

She rinsed the cut in cold water and wrapped a paper towel around it. She went to the bathroom to find a Band-Aid and spotted the pregnancy test dissolving in a puddle in the tub. She'd forgotten it in the excitement. The result was ruined. Cat felt ready to vomit, but she didn't know if it was the cut, morning sickness, or the realization that Cal now had a family she'd have to meet—a family who had never gotten the chance to approve of her—that lived in a castle, had its own crest, traced its lineage for generations and had never heard of the Equal Rights Amendment. *My God,* she realized. *They're Republicans!*

"Excuse me, my lady . . ."

Lelani startled her. For a four-footed being, the horse-girl was surprisingly silent. Cat was also jumpier than usual. It would be some time before her nerves settled.

"Please, don't call me that," Cat said.

"How should I address you?"

"'Cat' is fine."

Lelani looked uncomfortable with the notion but pushed on regardless. "I was curious as to the duration of the captain's interrogation?"

"A few hours. It doesn't get more serious than a dead cop. He has to explain how and why he left the scene, without implicating you or Seth. He has to convince them that he was dazed and injured. That he got the jump on his assailants, but was too injured to pursue or radio for help. Otherwise there'll be disciplinary action."

"I see."

Cat found the centaur hard to read; she was so guarded with her emotions. She thought the girl might be judging Cal. "He'll bend the truth to its limits," Cat added, defensively. "It's not in his nature to lie outright."

"I know," the centaur responded.

Again, Cat couldn't make heads or tails of Lelani's enigmatic responses. She went to the kitchen and put a pot of water on the burner. This time Cat could hear soft clopping on the hardwood as Lelani followed her. For a large creature, the centaur was amazingly graceful navigating the cramped living space of bipedal humans. She wasn't as big as an actual horse, but big enough to have caused Cat some concern when Cal left her behind in their home. She had yet to knock over a lamp or break a piece of furniture. Cat wished she could say the same for the other one, as something, probably porcelain, just hit the ground and shattered in her bedroom. A weak, "Sorry!" emanated from the back of her apartment.

"Some tea?" Cat asked Lelani.

"Yes, thank you," the centaur responded. This time, Cat noted a smidgeon of pleasure in her response.

The horse-girl—horse-*woman*—was very polite. For some reason, Cat expected someone who was half horse to behave more like an animal. Was it even housebroken? Where would she do her business? Cat took out a few days' worth of old newspaper from the recycling bin and placed it on the kitchen table, just in case. There were a million questions Cat wanted to ask but didn't know how to begin. She prepared the tea and brought it into the living room on a tray with biscuits. She sat on the couch while Lelani lowered herself on the floor next to the coffee table. Folding her legs beneath her, the centaur still came up to eye level. If Cat concentrated on the woman's chest and up, she looked like any other gorgeous redhead in an olive-green turtle-neck knit.

"Isn't that dangerous?" Cat asked.

"Is what dangerous, my lady?"

"Squatting like that. I seldom see horses lie down, unless they're sick. Something to do with twisting their intestines or delicate leg bones. Do you sleep standing?"

"I am not a horse," Lelani responded, with a slight edge.

"Oh," Cat said. She scratched the *house-training* question from her list. "I've never met a centaur before."

"Clearly."

"I'm sorry if I offended you."

"My intelligence quotient measures in the top two percent of my class. I attend one of the finest schools in the Twelve Kingdoms. My family can trace its lineage for a thousand years."

Cal was right. These things were very proud—and very defensive.

Cat was off to a bad start. This being, strange as it was, had saved her family and restored her husband's past to him. Lelani was important to Cal. Whatever her trepidation about the future, Cat would try to remain on friendly terms with the centaur.

"Does your family also live in Aandor?" Cat asked. "If you don't mind my asking?"

"My tribe lives in the Blue Forest. We are hunter-gatherers. Archduke Athelstan has granted the forest safe haven from hunting and logging by humans. Centaurs patrol the single road that runs through it and keep it free of highwaymen. Traders breathe easily once their caravans reach the Blue. The road to Aandor City is the safest and most profitable in the Twelve Kingdoms."

"Is that where all centaurs live?"

"It is now. We numbered in the millions, once."

"What happened?"

"War. But nature, too. Our females need twelve months to carry a foal to term and almost two years before they can have another. Beyond a few hundred residents, our villages become burdened. Humans build sewers and aqueducts. They farm and produce enough goods to support large cities. My people cannot—or will not—adapt to a faster pace of life. Without treaties like the Blue Forest Accord and leaders like Athelstan, centaurs will fade from Aandor as they did from this world."

"Centaurs lived here?"

"Many races lived here who now no longer exist."

"Why?"

"No one is sure. Fear. Racism. I suspect peace was tenuous. Perhaps I'll research it and write a thesis one day."

"Is that what's happening on your world . . . why you came here? To escape?"

"Many are in jeopardy, not just centaurs, not just Aandor. Aandor is the anchor that steadies the ships of state in the Twelve Kingdoms. Our courts are fair, our economy strong, and the rights of minorities are protected. Through trade and diplomacy, we maintain peace with, and between, the kingdoms around us.

Coming here was a desperate attempt to keep Archduke Athelstan's claim to Aandor viable. Both the captain and I stand to lose everything if we fail."

The word "everything" unsettled Cat. She and Bree had once been Cal's everything. Her place in his life had diminished overnight.

"Ain't it funny?" Seth said from the hall. "Laws of physics might change from universe to universe, but the laws of human nature are exactly the same."

Cat didn't realize he had come into the room to eavesdrop. She poured more tea into both their cups and offered some to Seth.

"Thanks, I'll stick with beer," he said. "So what exactly happened on *your* world?"

"The concord between the kingdoms had loopholes," Lelani explained. "Many chose to exploit them."

"The fine print—another constant across multiple universes," Seth snorted. He sat down and put his feet on the coffee table. "Notice how charity and goodwill toward men are in short supply everywhere in creation? And people wonder why I'm a cynic."

"Let her finish," Cat said. "Get your feet off the table."

"In Aandor, titles are passed through sons," Lelani continued. "Women are valued for their pedigree and dowries. All the ruling families conspired to breed a boy with the blood of twelve kings, who, according to the continental treaty, would have the rightful claim to the title of emperor. A race began."

"A race?" Cat asked.

Seth shook his head and laughed. "A breeding contest. A royal fuckfest. 'Think of England' and all that."

"Because of his pedigree, and the bylaws of the continental

accord, the boy who was your husband's charge is the rightful prince regent of the Twelve Kingdoms. He will have more ruling powers than his father Duke Athelstan, the first regent, and he will most likely father the next true emperor of the Twelve Kingdoms. There isn't a family on the continent with the right lineage who would deny him a daughter for marriage. The boy is the penultimate step to House Athelstan reclaiming its empire."

"See, this is what happens when a society doesn't have soap operas," Seth said. "All this aristocratic sperm flying around, trying to find the right hole like a golf ball at the PGA Masters . . ."

"Please, shut up! I want to know what my husband is mixed up in."

"There's not much else," Lelani continued. "Certain factions had lost the breeding race. The most powerful of them, Farrenheil, became desperate, and rejected the treaty. Aandor was caught off guard. The castle was under siege. Magnus Proust, the court mage, devised a plan to spirit the child here, away from his enemies. A dozen guardians were sent along to care for the boy until he reached manhood. But he was lost. The archduke himself may already be dead. There are neutral kingdoms among the twelve that are staying out of the fight until they are sure Aandor's claim is still viable. There's no point in making war with Farrenheil over a dead prince. Everything in Aandor depends on finding this boy."

"Un-fucking-believable," Seth said. "This is why I'm homeless? Why Joe's dead? Our lives are turned inside out because of a handful of privileged brats with supercharged family trees playing pass-the-chromosomes. Who else bought the farm so these creeps can act like the Kennedys of Tolkien land? I ought to wring the little freak's neck if we ever find him."

Lelani vaulted the couch, a blur of rapidity, and hurled Seth against the wall. She braced him with her forearm pressed against his throat. Seth's feet dangled as he gasped for air.

Cat sprang up, unsure of what to do. How did one stop a four-hundred-pound angry horse-woman?

"You insignificant flea," Lelani hissed. "Proust picked you for the mission out of an unreasonable fondness, *not* because of your skills. My people have one haven left to them on our world and it exists by the grace of Duke Athelstan. Returning his child safe and unharmed means more to me than words can convey, so I'll give you this warning out of respect for our teacher—should you make any attempt to harm the boy, ever, I will burn you alive. That is not an exaggeration."

Cat put her hand on Lelani's arm. "Please, aren't we in enough of a mess without fighting among ourselves?" she said gently.

Lelani let go. Seth tumbled to the floor. His breath came in rasps.

"Is there a problem?" Cal asked, from the front door.

Cat rushed to give Cal a warm hug. "How'd it go?"

"Like spending four hours with the Spanish Inquisition. Thank God for my PBA representative . . . and for this," he said, holding up Lelani's silver pin. "Everyone's glad I'm okay, but the dazed-and-confused story has stretched my credibility to its limit. If I didn't have that pin, even my reputation couldn't have helped me square things with the brass. I arranged to have police stationed at your mother's house around the clock. I'm also scheduled to report for bereavement counseling in a few days. My PBA rep got me a few days to grieve for Erin before my next round of questioning." Cal stopped a second. "I haven't . . . I haven't had a second to think about Erin since . . . since she . . ."

Pride struggled to dam Cal's tears. Cat gave him another hug and found herself unable to let go.

"I need to call her life partner and offer condolences," he said. "God, so much to do."

He pulled away from her, took out a scrap of paper from his shirt pocket, and picked up the phone. "I'm hoping that since Seth and I kept our actual names, the rest of the guardians will also have kept theirs. Someone at the station looked up Tristan McLeod for me while I was being debriefed. He was my lieutenant in Aandor. We found one in Brooklyn that was the right age. If we can get Tristan back, it'll help with the search for the rest. Heck, maybe we'll catch a break and he's raising the prince himself."

The phone on the other end rang, and a woman picked up. Another wife that was about to have her world turned upside down, Cat thought. Cal introduced himself and asked to speak to Tristan. Then her husband's face went ashen. "How?" he said. "I'm sorry for your loss," he concluded, and hung up the phone.

Cal sat at the kitchen table in a daze, unaware that everyone was hanging on his next word.

"Cal?" Cat said, and placed her hand on his shoulder.

"Tristan was murdered two days ago," Cal said. "A mugging gone bad."

Cat looked to Lelani. The centaur was sad. She shook her head to say *It wasn't a mugging.*

"I was alone before today," Lelani said to Cal. "I had to make finding you and Seth my priorities."

Cal looked at Seth with disgust. Cat was sure he'd trade him for this Tristan in a heartbeat.

"My God," Cal said. "None of the others even know they're

being hunted by these psychopaths. They're helpless. We've got to find them. Where do we even start?"

Lelani approached with a handful of maps. "Perhaps at the beginning," she said. She opened a map of New York State. Notes, circles, equations, and runes were drawn throughout it. "The only way to travel between Branes is through lay lines, the rivers of magical energy that emanate from the core of the multi-verse. In Aandor, magical energy moves similar to radio waves here. It's in the air and everywhere where people attuned to it can access it. One cannot walk fifty yards without encountering a lay line, much like those Starbucks in Manhattan. Using magic on this earth is akin to a landline telephone. You have to find a line to tap into. They are spread miles apart. These energy lines vary in potency. Some are like rivers; some like streams, brooks, and so forth. The more energy that flows through a line, the easier and safer the transfer is between worlds." Lelani pointed to a zone north of the city. "This was the point of entry for your group."

"Dutchess County?" Cal said. "That's about two hours' drive from here. Is that where you came in?"

"No. Dorn may have posted guards at that transfer point. I used a smaller lay line running deep under Central Park. It was dangerous, but I was alone and thought I could navigate it. I would prefer not to use it again."

"You think going back to the original transfer point up north will give us a lead?"

"More than that, my lord."

Cat flinched as the horse-woman called Cal her *lord*. She looked for any sign of embarrassment in her husband's face. He barely noticed it. The ten-year veteran of the NYPD—this pretender to peasantry—was at home at the top of the food chain. He had an air about him now, like he expected others to serve him and his cause. Cat didn't like it.

"The last remaining magus on this earth resides somewhere near there," Lelani said. "An old friend of Master Proust's named Rosencrantz. He might know a way to give the others their memories back no matter where they are on this world. We should seek his aid."

"Okay. That's a start. What about you? You can't travel looking—well, like you are now."

"If I cast another illusion spell, I will deplete the last of my energy supplies. As I tried to explain earlier, bending photons is not simple. Illusion has a high-energy initiation cost."

"Can you recharge at the lay line?"

"Yes . . . but should we encounter sorceries on the way . . ."

"Do it. There isn't any choice."

He was a soldier again, Cat concluded—a commander. *Do it,* he says, and he expected it done. Would this change the partnership they had created?

"We're off to see the wizard, are we?" Cat said.

"Cat, I'll drop you and Bree off at your mother's . . ."

"I'm coming with you."

"No."

"I'm sorry. I meant, may I come with you . . . *your lordship.*" Cat attempted a curtsy.

"Catherine . . ."

"Should I bend lower? This is my first curtsy."

"It's dangerous."

"No fucking kidding, Cal. Did you think I didn't notice the

giant and the swordsman trying to cut our throats a few hours ago? Wizards and trolls? Where the hell is safe? You tell me."

Cal pursed his lips into a tight line. He looked taller. More rigid. Confident. He was still the man she loved and still just as much of a stranger. She had always held more ground in the marriage. He had spoiled her with power. She was not used to butting heads on serious decisions. Cat wondered how he saw her now. Was it through a new spectrum . . . his mother, his sisters, the kaleidoscope of women from his past? She owed him a victory, or three, for years of acquiescing. But this would not be one of them. He had left his family once before and it cost him thirteen years of his life. Cat could not stand to lose Cal for thirteen years or thirteen minutes. He had accepted a piece of her soul on the day they exchanged vows, and he could not just disappear with it. She would defend it.

"Bree goes to Mom," she said. "I go with you. Discussion closed."

"Fine."

"Hey, do I have to come?" Seth asked.

"Yes!" said the other three in unison.

CHAPTER 12

OFF TO SEE THE WIZARD . . .

1

A pothole jolted Cat back to the world. Her temple lay against the cold window, a string of dribble crept down her collar. The world whizzed by Cat's head at the speed of life. She peeled herself off the window and made note of her surroundings. They were driving north on Route 22 in the Ford Explorer. The rain had not made it this far north; the trees and pastures were bleached with frost, a shadowless cinereal landscape under the absent noon sun. Cal drove with a firm gaze and heavy thoughts on his brow. Cat pulled down the sun visor to wipe her chin in the mirror. Out of habit, she inspected the backseat through the reflection, forgetting that Bree was with her mother.

Seth, in the rear seat, had passed out. He had gone through a six-pack and was sleeping off the difference. *Better for everyone,* Cat thought. Lelani lay crouched in the rear of the Explorer. Her newly redisguised legs looked human enough, but she couldn't fool the car. Cat felt the extra weight at every acceleration. They were all quite tired from the previous night's activities. Cal and Lelani seemed to be handling it the best.

Lelani admitted to having a vague idea of where to find this

Earth-born sorcerer, Rosencrantz. He lived along the northern lay line, a virtual river of energy flowing from the center of all creation, in the vicinity of a major transdimensional gate. Dorn would likely have left guards behind, the centaur warned. Cal had taken his spare vest, both guns, and all the bullets.

Cat watched Lelani study the passing world. She had an appetite for knowledge, a mind like a glue trap, and a physique and dexterity that could make mincemeat out of Serena Williams on the tennis court. Cal said she was unique. In his experience, magi were the types whose cuffs soaked in their soup bowls while they absorbed text from a scroll. They were geniuses, but also awkward and clumsy in their youth—the types that seldom had girlfriends or boyfriends even in their own circles; in other words, nerds. Cal confessed to taunting a few with his friends when he was a child. Lelani, according to Cal, was a cut above the basic spell-tosser. Her bravery had returned his identity, made him complete for the first time in more than a decade. They were lucky she had been picked for this mission, Cal explained. A mixed blessing at best. Cat couldn't help wonder if a less able rescuer might not have been preferable, someone not as likely to have succeeded. After all, she'd earned her husband fair and square.

Cat had rescued Cal from an orphan's existence . . . a man with no beginnings. But he had rescued her as well, from an endless line of flawed, unintriguing men; a parade of players and insecure minds threatened by a strong will and a sharp psyche, or worse, ready to surrender their authority completely. Cal was the balance—the strongest man she'd ever met, not just in body, but also in his virtue. Chivalry became palatable through his sincerity. With Cal, it was possible to enjoy the comforts of feminine vulnerability and not surrender her self-respect. For that, she'd give him the world.

Bree's birth had marked a new beginning for Cal. Through nine months of pregnancy, and six hours of labor, Cat inaugurated her husband into the simple experience that many took for granted—a blood relative. And she'd do it again if they had the chance. They were on course for a happy life. A brother or sister for Bree, a promotion to ESU for Cal, her MBA and reentry in the workforce, and eventually a home in Westchester. Cal would retire at fifty with full benefits. When the kids were in college, they could travel while still relatively young. Lelani's failure would have left them content. Her husband would still be hers alone. No one would have known . . . not even Cal's tortured family in Aandor. Cat was embarrassed to have such selfish thoughts.

That damned guilt boomeranged and settled in the nape of her neck again. Previously, she'd have moved heaven and earth to discover his origins; it was the only thing missing from his life. Cat realized she wasn't thinking clearly. If Lelani had not come, Cal may not have survived Dorn's attack. She'd be a widow right now; another cop's wife filling out benefits forms. Sweeping Cal's history under the carpet as it threatened to unravel everything they'd built was not the solution. She wanted to protect him from the dangers his past brought with it. How far could she bend under the weight of his past before she broke, she wondered. Cat studied his profile like an art student replicating a sculpture. Cal kept his eyes on the road.

Cat hadn't said a word since leaving the Bronx. The man she'd shared a bed with for six years was holding something back.

He'd answered a dozen questions all with the response of a child who'd successfully pilfered the cookie jar and gladly confessed only to not having brushed his teeth yet. Cat was certain Cal would answer a million more questions so long as she avoided one important one.

"Penny for your thoughts," he asked. He kept his eyes on the road.

"I'm having ten-dollar thoughts."

"Hmm."

"And you? What's on your mind?"

"You have to bend a little lower," Cal said.

"Excuse me?"

"When you curtsy." Cal smiled. "Legs bent and torso and head bent forward as well. And it's not so slow. It's a quick motion. Your superiors don't want to be staring at the top of your head all day."

Cat smiled. "I'll try to remember that . . . in case I ever meet a superior."

Cal put his hand on her knee and stroked it. She laced her fingers on top of his and turned her attention to the road.

"Stop the carriage!" Lelani shouted.

"Shit, Mommy!" Seth screamed, rudely awakened. "What? What?"

They pulled onto the shoulder. Lelani bolted out the back and ran toward a dilapidated billboard.

"Christ! I thought we had an accident," Seth said.

Cal activated the hazards and backed the Explorer until they reached Lelani. She had a horrified expression on her face. They joined her.

The ad on the billboard was torn and faded, but there was

enough to see that it had been for an old carnie freak show in the area. It read, *Real Live Man-Horse! See the Eighth Wonder of The World at the Rogers' Farm, off Route 33.* The illustration was of a centaur rearing on his hind legs in all his glory.

"He looks familiar," Cal said.

"So what?" Seth said. "Carnies have been running crap like this for years. It's a guy in a harness. It's a con."

"The centaur in this drawing is Fronik," Lelani said. "He's from my clan and was one of the members of your party."

"Yeah," Cal confirmed. "I vaguely remember. Why aren't all my memories clear? They don't feel a part of me. More like old television shows I remember watching."

"The memory spell is still active. It transferred your memory anagrams to inactive neural tissue, and is rearranging them as it rewrites them back to the cerebrum in proper order."

"Huh?"

"She's defragmenting your hard drive," Seth said. "Haven't you ever used Norton's speed disk?"

"His memory will be complete by morning," Lelani answered.

"Should he be driving?" Cat asked.

"Probably not."

"Now she tells us," Seth snapped.

"You are inebriated, her ladyship is emotionally distraught, and I am incapable of operating this vehicle," Lelani stated. "There wasn't any other choice."

"We could have waited until tomorrow," Cat said.

"No. We have already wasted too much time," she replied.

"Why are we out here?" Cal asked. He was the least concerned with his mind's precarious state out of the group. "We should find the transfer site. Find Rosencrantz."

"Fronik's aid would be invaluable," Lelani said.

"This poster is ancient," Seth noted.

"He might know where to find Rosencrantz."

"It's a drawing. We don't even know for sure that it's him," Cal said.

"What happened to time not being a luxury?" Seth asked.

"This could shorten our investigation," Lelani said. It was almost a plea.

It occurred to Cat that until Cal's brain had caught up with his life, until he got a handle on everything that went wrong, he relied heavily on Lelani's judgment. She could hear his gears turning, trying to decide if this was a good idea or merely indulging her personal cause.

"Cal, she hasn't let us down so far," Cat said. "If my vote matters . . ."

"So much for the captain being leader of the pack," Seth said. "'I'll follow his orders,' yadda, yadda, yadda."

Lelani looked ready to drop-kick Seth. Cal stepped between them. "We'll go to this farm," he said. "It's only a few miles away. This Rogers could be Rosencrantz for all we know. Maybe Fronik got lucky."

"I'm driving," Cat said.

2

The dirt road ran for three miles before it came to the farmhouse—if one could even call it a house. Wooden slats barely held up a corrugated tin roof. The windows were caked with dust. The termite-infested porch was missing every other board. Ramshackle, broken, dilapidated, and deserted was what came to mind. Cal regretted the detour already. Cat pulled the vehicle around the gravel driveway and everyone spilled out.

Cal surveyed the scene, not sure what he was looking for. On a field between the house and the barn, pieces of an old canvas tent, flat and weathered with age, sporadically protruded from the snow. The poles leaned inward toward center, rusted at the bottom where they met the ground. Some had fallen over completely and turned the snow orange with oxidation. It hadn't been used in years.

"Don't stray," Cal said. "Lelani, you have twenty minutes to find something relevant."

She bolted toward the barn, which looked even worse than the house. Lelani looked like any coed running, but her tracks in the snow beyond the periphery of her spell betrayed her equestrian half.

Much to their surprise, the screen door creaked open soon after. A small Cabbage Patch–like woman with gray frizzled hair and a broom in one hand came onto the porch. Her puffy face had the texture of a walnut.

"You folks from the County?"

Cat looked less threatening, so Cal prodded her to speak.

"No, we're not," Cat said. "We are looking for an old friend. He looks like the actor who played the horse-man in the billboard on the road."

The woman eyed them suspiciously. "You friends of Fred?"

"Our friend grew up with him. She's by the barn right now." Cat said pointing to Lelani. "Would it be okay if we talked to Fred?"

The old woman studied Lelani with a squint that doubled the

creases in her face. She considered the request for a moment, then told them, "You can't talk to Fred."

"It's important. His family is really worried . . ."

"You can't talk to Fred on account'a he's dead. Been dead nine years." She pointed to a small dirty grave marker next to an old tree.

"I'm sorry," Cat said. She looked to her husband for suggestions. Cal checked his watch, looked at the waning sun, and watched Lelani pick things out of the snow. His impatience might be an effect of his impeded brain, so he suppressed an urge to scream. He turned back to the woman.

"Did you know him well, ma'am?" he asked.

"Well enough. He was my husband."

The three caught each other with odd expressions. The side trip was a bust as far as Cal was concerned. They ought to be heading to the lay line; they should be looking for the boy. Everyone else in the party was secondary.

"I think we may have made a mistake," he said. "We're sorry to bother you, ma'am."

"T'ain't no bother none." She scrutinized Lelani as best as she could from the distance, shutting one eye and squinting with the other. "You saying that filly is Fred's kin?"

"We thought so, but we were mistaken."

"Oh. That's too bad. Fred weren't no actor, you know. I was wondering if she could tell me which side of the family gave him that dang horse's ass."

They froze in their steps and exchanged looks again.

"Excuse me, but, you said Fred was your *husband*?" Cat asked.

"Got kids?" Seth cut in.

"You folks come in, and I'll make some tea."

Cal looked toward the barn, but Lelani was gone. The porch creaked under his weight. The house smelled of must and rot. Prominently displayed on the mantel was a blue ribbon from the county fair eleven years prior for best chili recipe. A wooden cross hung on the far wall. Coils stuck out of the couch and recliner. A steel and canvas wheelchair was folded in the corner behind a door. Yellowed lace doilies were draped over most of the furniture in a delusive attempt to cover the junkyard couture of the decor. The place reminded Cal of the living room on *Sanford and Son*. All that was missing was a toothless, old curmudgeon.

"That's my brother, Eustace, in the corner there," the woman said. The spot was badly lit. A man with no teeth, a week's worth of facial growth, and at least twenty years on his sister, grunted and raised his cane in a collective greeting and threat to knock someone's head.

"My name's Enid," she said. "Take a seat, now. I'll be right out."

Cal checked his watch. The twenty minutes were almost up and he wished they were on their way to the lay line. According to Lelani, this Rosencrantz might be able to cast a global memory enchantment. Not only could the events of the night they transferred to this world be revealed in one fell swoop, but every member of the original party would recall their true identities regardless of where they were. It could triple their numbers overnight. Lelani had tried it herself on her arrival, but it had proved too much. Global enchantments, she said, were considered highend mojo that even the best wizards had trouble with. All she had managed was to trigger Cal's nightmares.

Cal noticed a Polaroid picture of Enid and her groom on the end table. It was Fronik for sure. Fronik only came up to Enid's chest, as though he were a man proposing. Perhaps he was just being cautious about allowing his bottom half to be photographed. Cal looked out of a grime-covered window and wondered what Lelani was up to.

"Got any beer?" Seth shouted into the kitchen.

"Got any manners?" Cat scolded. "We apologize for Seth's behavior," she told Eustace.

The old geezer wore a stupid grin and bounced on the chair, excited. "Fursd prize. Heh. Fursd prize, heh," he repeated. A cloudy gray stream snaked from his nose and dropped from his grizzled chin.

"You won first prize at the fair," Cat said, politely. Cal marveled at his wife's patience with the old and the feebleminded. No one else received the benefit of such patience from her. Catherine MacDonnell did not suffer fools well. "I'm a sucker for a good chili recipe."

"See gret."

"Sea grete? Is that a spice?"

"See gret."

"Don't mind Eustace none," Enid said, bringing a plastic tray with a steaming pot and cups. "He ain't had a whole thought in years. Not since the stroke."

"I'm sorry," Cat said.

"Oh, he's more manageable this way. Fred and him never got on, you know. Eustace loved the hooch. I don't keep the snake water in my home no more," she told Seth.

Enid poured four cups and stretched two tea bags between

them. She took hers with cream. Cat opted for the lemon. Seth and Cal declined. Enid sat in a padded rocking chair, which made her look even more like a Cabbage Patch doll.

"How did you meet Fred?" Cal asked.

"Well . . . it was late October, we was having some mighty big weather if I remember rightly. Eustace was out in the barn when Fred just stumbled in. He weren't feeling right and just passed out."

"Did you attack him?"

"No, sir. He passed out all on his own. Eustace came into the house and got the shotgun on account of Fred looking so strange. I followed him back. Fred had a bad fever. We pulled him into a stall, got him a blanket, water, and set up a kerosene heater. I tended him 'til the fever broke. When he come to, he had no idea who he was. Couldn't even tell why he had a horse's ass 'stead of two legs like normal folks."

"And the carnie poster?" Seth asked.

"That was Eustace's idea. Had some problems with locusts that year. Crop was a bust. Thought it might bring in some extra money. But few people come. Too remote. Not like it is now, all hustle and bustle. We got a traffic light in town now. Most folks thought Fred was a trick. Even folks that did come din' believe it."

"And Fred was okay with this?" Cal asked.

"Would you like some more tea, hon?" Enid asked.

"Enid?"

"Fred cost us in fixins and medicine. Eustace put him to work. He had to earn his keep. Idle hands is the devil's tool. We ain't like you city folk with extra money hidden in the couch.

What you see is what we got. Fred didn't have nowhere to go anyways."

"Did you keep him here against his will?" Cal asked.

Enid fingered the doily on her armrest and studied the tea set on the table.

"Enid . . . ?" Cat prodded.

"We didn't encourage him to leave. Eustace had use for him, and I truly believed he would have been hurt if he ventured forth. Folks 'round here weren't as open-minded as us back then. Fred was a kindly man. A bit innocent. He was ill suited to handle a world of sinners. I kept him company so he wouldn't be lonesome, taught him to play checkers, read the Bible. Fred took to the Good Book in a big way. Surprising, when you consider his sin."

"His sin? Did he do something bad?"

"Not him. He was a kindly soul. Well, you know . . . ?"

"No, we really don't."

"How he got the way he was. It was clear to anyone with eyes. One of his kin had lain with a beast. The Lord Almighty frowns upon the laying with beasts. It's a dirty, vulgar sin. Wasn't Fred's fault what his mama or papa done, but he was begat of blasphemy."

Tension crept into Cal's spine. He could see it in Cat as well.

"Fursd prize, heh," Eustace repeated.

"But, Enid, you married him," Cat pointed out.

"I did." She smiled at the thought of Fred. "He was a gentle soul, twice as wise for only half the man. A good friend. I realized the sacrifice I'd have to make. I couldn't bring young'ins into the world. The devil's blood had to end with Fred."

"But that wasn't all . . . ?" Cal asked.

"He had to be purified. He was an offense to God."

"So, you baptized him?" Cal said. A nagging thought knocked on the policeman's brain. He ignored it. "You converted him to a born-again life."

"Yes, but more than that. Eustace said he'd be hung before he'd let a beast lay with his sister. He didn't trust me. Eustace said if I was going to be dang fool enough to tie my fortunes to Fred, he was going to exorcise the Devil from the man first."

"What are you saying?" Seth asked. "You got a priest to exorcise him?"

"None of them papal devils ever step foot in this home, no sir. We got Fred the chair," she said pointing to the folded wheelchair in the corner. "But he got terrible sick anyways after many weeks. Wasn't quite right again. Eustace said the devil ran too deep, that it even polluted the man. I cared for Fred best I could."

The knocking in Cal's brain became a physical tumult. The photo, the wheelchair . . . He rose so fast, he jolted the teacups on the table. "We have to be going," he said.

Cat looked confused. "Cal? Shouldn't we tell Lelani . . ."

"We have to go, now!"

Suddenly, a loud crash blew the front door off its hinges, shaking the home as it bounced off the wall on the far end. Lelani advanced, holding a brown horsetail fastened by four ornate gold rings, and in the other hand rusted iron shackles. She drifted toward Enid holding the horsetail before her.

"Where is Fronik?" she asked in an eerie, calm voice.

"He had to be cleansed," Enid cried. "I could not wed a filthy beast!"

"Where is Fronik?" Lelani demanded.

Eustace hopped excitedly in his chair, panting. "Fursd! Fursd! Fursd! Heh, Fursd!"

"Daughter of Lilith, I cast ye from my home!" Enid cried. "Leave this sanctuary of the Lord!"

"Lelani, let's go outside," Cal said.

"I want to know what happened to Fronik!"

"Now!" Cal ordered her.

"DEAD! HE'S DEAD! WE CUT THE DEVIL OUT, BUT HE WAS MORE BEAST THAN MAN!" Enid cried.

Cal stepped in front of Lelani and pushed her back. She nudged forward with blood in her eyes, moving him backward. Cat joined her husband, grabbing Lelani's shoulder from the side and pulling with all her strength. Seth sat frozen on the couch.

"HELL HE COME FROM, AND HELL HE GONE BACK TO WHEN THE DEVIL COME CALLED HIS OWN!" Enid continued shouting.

"Seth! Help us!" Cat cried.

Even with Seth's effort, Lelani crept forward.

Enid backed into the corner in fear. Eustace cackled, banging his cane against the end table. A wet spot grew in his crotch. "Fursd! Fursd!"

"Damn it, girl . . . I'm a cop," Cal yelled. "I can't let you hurt her! No matter what she did, you can't hurt her!"

"Monster!" Lelani screamed.

Cal sandwiched her face in his hands and locked his eyes on hers. She tried to look at Enid, but he touched his forehead to hers and filled her view. "Listen to me! We cannot leave a trail of corpses behind us. Think of the Blue Forest. Think of your tribe. How will we complete the mission if we're in jail? How could we search for the boy if we're dogged by the police?"

At first they thought she hadn't heard them, but soon, the bloodlust in Lelani's eyes abated. She pulled away toward the door, throwing off balance everyone who was already pulling in that direction. She went outside. Cat followed, as did Seth. Cal turned to Enid, but was unsure of what to say. These people were indeed monsters. The blue ribbon won eleven years ago taunted him from the mantel piece. Cal tried not to imagine how they disposed of Fronik's other half. There would be no stopping Lelani if she deduced Eustace's *secret* ingredient. They had to leave before Lelani collected her thoughts.

"Get out!" Enid cried. "I'll have no heathens in my house!"

"One last question. What direction did Fred come from the night he stumbled onto your farm?"

"Why should I help the devil's minions?"

"Because I'm going to stand right here until I get an answer." Cal stood there gazing at the old woman as the seconds ticked by. The old woman didn't realize her life was in danger. She was as ignorant now as she was the day she met Fronik. Centaur codes were clear and absolute in these matters. Every second they lingered there gave Lelani an opportunity to come back and exact justice.

"North," Enid said, begrudgingly. "Over the ridge. Now git!"

Her words rang true. She was too simple to lie well.

"We're sorry to have bothered you and your brother. Thanks for the tea."

Lelani and the others stood by the grave marker. Tears streamed down Lelani's cheeks. She sang a haunted tune in Centauran that reminded Cal of some old Gaelic dirges he'd heard at cops' funerals. He joined them, checking his watch sporadically. When she finished, she said, "I have to get off this world."

Cal opened a map on the hood of the truck.

"Fronik came from that direction. That's where we were headed before the detour. The gate is in the hills. If we took the road, we'd be spotted by sentries before we arrived."

"There can't be many sentries up here," Lelani said. "Not like a garrison. Dorn's assets are stretched thin and reinforcements are not likely for a few years our time. I went into the transfer soon after him and arrived six weeks later. There were no enemy forces behind me when I jumped."

"If the sentries are anything like Hesz or Symian, one is plenty. We're going to hike it from here, backtrack the path Fronik took over these hills—and hopefully gain some element of surprise."

"I can stay with the truck," Seth offered. "Make sure Ma and Pa Hackett don't mess with it."

"The truck will be fine behind the barn," Cal said.

"There's only a couple hours of daylight left," Seth argued. "I'm not the woodsy type."

"Let's move before the sun sets," Cal ordered.

CHAPTER 13

BY THE SHORT 'N' CURLIES

1

"Cough," Dr. Brown said, as he grabbed Daniel's scrotum. He was a kindly southern gent who reminded Daniel of the doctor on *Star Trek*.

Daniel stood shirtless and pantless in the examining room, braced against the medicinal atmosphere and the doctor's stethoscope, which sent a chill down his soul. When the doctor finished, he instructed the boy to sit on the examining table. The paper covering crinkled as he fidgeted; Daniel felt like a pork chop about to be wrapped.

Sheriff Maher stood in the corner, a toothpick sticking out from the bristles of his thick mustache and wearing mirrored sunglasses. The man seldom removed his hat even indoors. Daniel wondered if the sheriff took a crap wearing the hat and glasses, too. It was hard to tell exactly what the sheriff was looking at; perhaps at Nurse Shirley, who was one big smile as she assisted Dr. Brown. The nurse had retained her girlish beauty well into her forties, which, unfortunately, caused the half-dressed Daniel to be excited in a most embarrassing way.

The doctor examined the boy's welts with soft prodding, but Daniel winced when he brushed the injured rib.

"Might be cracked," the doctor said.

No shit, Daniel thought.

"You the kid whipped the Grundy boys?" the doctor asked.

"I plead the fifth," Daniel answered, shooting the sheriff a glare.

Maher smiled.

"I fixed them boys up last night. Gotta say, you sure don't look like the one who won the fight." The doctor examined the fingers. Daniel winced again when he applied pressure to one of the joints. "Gotta say, them boys had it coming."

"Wallace . . . ," the sheriff cut in.

"Now don't give me lip, Ed. Know how many kids I treated over the years, them boys put in here? It's a miracle no one's sued them out of house and home already. Delinquents! You did good, son."

"Wallace!"

"Just got to learn to duck once in a while."

The doctor pulled out a ruler and measured the wounds. His expression changed to one of uncomfortable puzzlement.

"Wallace, I need to get him to the station," the sheriff said. "Can we please take the photos?"

"That rib has to be wrapped, the fingers splinted . . . and . . ."

"And?"

"These marks . . . I'm not sure they were made by the Grundys."

"Let's talk outside," the sheriff said.

"Shirley, photos and bandages please," the doc said.

Nurse Shirley, it was easy to guess, was proud of her figure because she opted to wear an older style uniform, which accentuated it. Daniel used a pillow to hide his admiration for her curves. If she noticed, she revealed nothing as she took photos of his wounds.

"What's this?" she asked, fingering a mark over Daniel's left scapula. The warmth of her touch traveled down his spine to the spot he was trying to deflate. Daniel leaned further into the pillow.

"Birthmark."

"Almost looks like a tattoo."

"Yeah."

The nurse began to wrap his ribs.

"I knew your real father," she said, out of the blue. "We went to junior high together. John was a great guy. I was sorry to hear of his passing."

Daniel was only eight when John Hauer, Rita's first husband, died at the hands of a vicious testicular cancer. Most people believed John was Daniel's biological father, a belief Daniel seldom dissuaded. Even Rita didn't realize Daniel knew he was adopted. Clyde could never stand being compared to John, and revealed Daniel's adoption shortly after he married Rita. It had been a bomb. "You just a borrowed bastard," Clyde had said, with a smirk on his face.

But no matter how hard Clyde tried, he couldn't erase the memory of Daniel's childhood. John was a patient soul who had ushered joy into the boy's early years. His death was a harsh blow to their little family, which Daniel had coped with better than his mother. To fill the void in her life, Rita chose her new companion swiftly and badly. Clyde Knoffler was an opportunist and a predator. A woman of Rita's caliber would never have fallen for him under normal circumstances. Ignorant, penniless, he had a magnetism that gave him power over certain women.

Clyde exploited Rita's vulnerability and loneliness. Within months of their wedding he'd already spent the savings Rita and John took years to earn and pushed his new wife to the limits of her sanity. Avoiding reality was now Rita's primary occupation.

"I was having problems with algebra one year," Shirley continued, "and John tutored me to a B plus. He was also my first *real* kiss," she said with a smile. "Who knows . . . if things had gone differently, you might have been my kid."

As far as Daniel knew, he might very well be, anyway. He knew nothing of his heritage. Life was strange. Was it worth all the pain? Sometimes he worked too hard just to exist. He recognized that some people were very happy—couples who enjoyed each other, children whose primary worry was the gossip of who liked whom in school—but for the most part, people suffered. What was the point? It looked like good days only existed so that you would have somewhere to fall from.

Daniel stared out at the police station across the street from the hospital. He'd be going there next to take his mug shot and be fingerprinted. He was a juvenile delinquent, a danger to society. Just then, Clyde brushed past the window. Daniel's heart jumped.

"Whoa," the nurse said, navigating a roll of gauze around the boy's torso. "Did someone walk on your grave?"

"What?"

"Just an expression. You shuddered."

Daniel wanted to tell her that her grave remark wasn't too far from the truth. Clyde would fly into a rage over the lawsuit. Once Clyde was in the zone, anything was possible.

"Honey, you've got the sweats. Are you feeling okay?"

Daniel stared at the door, waiting to see his stepfather walk in. He considered telling Shirley the truth in the hope that she would defend him. After all, his dad and her kissed in the sixth grade. She was practically family. Maybe she was so fond of him that she'd risk life, limb, and fortune for the child of John Hauer (who was almost hers). A minute went by, then two. It wasn't that far from reception to his room. Maybe they were keeping Clyde out. The door opened, his heart caught in his throat. It was only the doctor and the sheriff.

"Just about done," Shirley said.

Daniel had some trepidation about leaving the room, but with the sheriff's hand on his shoulder he didn't have any choice. The hallway was busy with healers and patients. They reached the waiting area and turned left toward the exit. Just then, he saw Clyde at the end of the far hall, talking to a young staffer in an office doorway. His arm, braced against the door frame beside her, gave the appearance that the woman was trapped in his clutches. She giggled at something Clyde said just as Daniel walked out of view.

2

The sheriff let Daniel sit outside his office instead of in the tank with the real malfeasants. The boy suspected the lawman sympathized with him but had his hands tied in this matter. After all, if Daniel went postal one day and the authorities neglected an opportunity to prevent it, there would be hell to pay.

Daniel wondered if he'd be forced into aggression therapy. Maybe they'd place him on antidepressants? The thought of numbing out life was inviting to Daniel. He had occasionally contemplated the "stoner" lifestyle. They were numb to life's barbs. At least he'd belong to a clique. But that path was too similar to his stepfather's, and that meant there'd be another generation of asshole on the way. He wouldn't give Clyde the victory.

Rita walked into the squad room. Daniel let out a sigh of relief; a reprieve from the wrath of Clyde had been granted. He would, however, have to make arrangements to sleep elsewhere that evening. Before today, Adrian's house would have been the best refuge, but Daniel was now more inclined to help the Grundys pound on the fat boy. *No good deed goes unpunished,* he thought, recalling the satisfying crunch of the two-by-four into Elijah Grundy's face.

Rita ignored her son as she walked into the sheriff's office. The sheriff asked Daniel to come in. He sat to his mother's left. It was the first time all day he could see Sheriff Maher's eyes. He looked like a fair man.

"Will this take long?" Rita asked. "My neighbor is watching my four-year-old."

"Ma'am . . . ," the sheriff started—there was a sense of urgency in his tone, "Dr. Brown is of the mind that the size and impact of your boy's injuries were not made by another teenager."

"My son is free to go, then?"

The sheriff looked troubled that his point had been missed. "No, ma'am, it doesn't work like that. We know for a fact Daniel was involved in the altercation with those boys and whipped them good. But, I'm still concerned about his bruises. Those marks are the fist and foot imprints of a fully grown man. Perhaps another situation, maybe at home, is forcing him to act out against his schoolmates."

Rita sat in silence, her hands placed perfectly on her lap before her as if in prayer. Her eye contact with the sheriff never wavered. Daniel noticed the dimple, which occurred when his mother bit down on her inner cheek, sometimes to the point of bleeding.

"Ma'am?" the sheriff said.

"What are you implying?"

The sheriff rubbed his jaw and redoubled his efforts to communicate the facts to Rita.

"Mrs. Hauer . . ."

"Knoffler. Hauer was my former husband's name."

"God rest his soul," Daniel whispered. He tried to incite a response from Rita, but she just gripped her armrest tighter. The sheriff noted the exchange.

"Ma'am, a boy that's bullied is liable to act out in extreme ways. Possibly take things out against innocent people from sheer frustration. This is serious. Do you know anyone—adults—who have issues with your son?"

"No one has any issues with Danny. He's a good kid. I don't even understand why he's here. He's the one looks beat up."

"Them Grundys was sent to the emergency room, ma'am."

"Jim-Bob Grundy shaves almost daily," she said. "He's been left back so many times he's eligible for the draft. Have you checked the size of *his* fists?"

The sheriff braced himself and asked, "Mrs. Knoffler, is your husband physically abusive at home?"

Rita didn't flinch. "My husband is a good man going through hard times."

A glimmer of intelligence flickered in the sheriff's eyes; he was not convinced.

Rita seemed to waver for a moment, lost as to what to say next. Daniel stared into the well of his mother's thoughts. *Was she actually considering the truth?* He knew better than to hope. Rita was not strong, at least not since John's passing. She was terrified of loneliness and was adept at stretching the morsel of consideration Clyde bestowed her into a meal of affection.

"So, is that a yes?" the sheriff asked.

Daniel held his breath. The lawsuit, the cost of bail, these were enough to push Clyde into the zone. The world stopped on Rita's next breath. A single assertion could end this mess— protective custody; the sheriff would shield Daniel from Clyde's wrath.

"No," Rita said, in a steady, strong voice. "My husband does not abuse us."

The lie kicked Daniel as hard as Clyde's boot. His hope deflated. His mother said it so compellingly that Daniel almost believed she was right.

"Son, is that true?" the sheriff asked him.

Daniel wondered why the sheriff asked him this in front of his mother. It wasn't right. He looked at his mother, who still refused to acknowledge him. She was fixed on an imaginary point before her. Daniel realized Rita would waver under his pleading gaze if she turned. His mother teetered on a precipice. The sheriff realized this. Some part of her wanted to let loose.

Daniel had the power now to write a new chapter for them, but all the alternatives, all the things that might go wrong played in his head. Clyde might actually beat the rap. Daniel knew he couldn't depend on Rita to follow through on charges. She'd waver in the face of loneliness, fear, guilt, or a missed fix. If Clyde beat the rap, he'd probably kill them. What's more, Rita was in danger of being punished by the law, too. Besides his abuse, Clyde was involved in all sorts of welfare scams, food stamps, unemployment. She had lied about everything that was going on in that house, closed her eyes to the truth, and would be punished, maybe even jailed as an accessory after the fact.

Even if charges stuck and everything went right, a foster home loomed for Daniel and Penny; cold, industrial childrearing— guardians making a buck off the state while packs of children fight it out for attention and resources. He'd be trading one abusive jerk for a pack of smaller ones. There were no guarantees that Penny would be placed with him, so he couldn't even keep an eye on her. And then, when Clyde got out of prison in two or three years, as her biological father he'd get Penny back anyway since he never abused her. Daniel would be long gone from the house. She'd be left to grow up with an emotional invalid for a mother and an angry ex-con psychopath for a dad. There were more reasons to maintain the status quo than to plunge them all into a legal and social upheaval.

"I just told you my husband does not—"

"Yes, sir," Daniel cut in.

"Yes what?" the sheriff asked. "That your mother is telling the truth or that Mr. Knoffler is abusing you?"

Another chance to change—to get off the path that promised grief. Looking at his sneakers Daniel said, "My mother is telling the truth."

Disappointed, the sheriff leaned back in his chair with an air of surrender. The boy was grateful at least for the lawman's skeptical look. It was enough that someone important knew the truth despite the lies that were freely doled out.

Daniel realized his mother was watching him in wonder. He had every right to rat out his stepfather. Clyde would never acknowledge the boy's loyalty, only his troubles. All the precious money Daniel was costing him would send Clyde into a rage. Clyde might kill him, even if not on purpose. Once Clyde was in the zone . . . Daniel realized he'd just taken his life into his own hands.

CHAPTER 14

TIME WAITS FOR NO ONE

1

Of the four, only Lelani made the journey effortlessly, pausing every so often to let the others catch up. Wind that could freeze lava whipped the snow around them, but Lelani, impervious to the chill and warmed by a seething rage, trekked on. She had left Fronik's killers unharmed by Cal's decree. At first she suspected he might simply be protecting his own and suppressed a lifetime of prejudice against bipedals to follow his orders. But Cal's logic was sound, and everything she'd seen until now showed him to be a just man.

The forest soothed her. It reminded her of home, which she had been away from for three years. The parks and gardens of Aandor were poor substitutes for the Blue Forest. Too long since she was last surrounded by trees and other living greens in the wild, even hibernating ones. Her companions did not find the terrain friendly or relaxing. Cat had sprained her ankle on a loose rock coming down a hill. She piggybacked on Cal for a quarter mile until they reached a rock-strewn slope where the extra weight compromised his footing. The winter sun was waning, and they had less than an hour left before darkness covered them.

"Let me take her," Lelani offered.

"I'm okay," Cal said.

"You are not," Cat argued. "The last thing you need is a broken ankle."

"I've had training packs that weigh more than you," he responded.

"Oh jeez, will you let Seabiscuit take her?" Seth argued. "I'm freezing my fucking balls off out here. We're like the fucking Sopranos lost in the Pine Barrens."

"My lord, you should proceed unconstrained," Lelani said. "We don't know what we'll find ahead."

Cat hopped off her husband. Standing next to Lelani, she had the overwhelming urge to avoid approaching the empty area behind the redhead.

"Your instincts are telling you there's something your eyes are not seeing," Lelani explained. "It's part of the spell to make others want to avoid running into me."

"How do I . . ." Cat motioned to Lelani's back.

Lelani crouched. "Close your eyes," she said. "Put your left hand on my left shoulder. Now reach across and grab my other shoulder. Lift your leg up."

Lelani stood.

"Looks like a piggyback," Seth said.

"It feels like bareback riding," Cat said. She folded her arms across Lelani's breastbone.

"How far?" Cal asked the centaur.

"Down this ravine and up the next h—"

A crossbow shaft suddenly pierced the forearm Cat had braced around Lelani's shoulder. It continued through the centaur's shoulder and broke skin on Cat's chest. Lelani suppressed her scream with a grunt. Cat shrieked in the centaur's ear.

"CAT!" her husband yelled. A bolt grazed Cal's cheek, peeling a strip of skin like an orange. Seth ducked for cover.

Lelani jumped into a large ditch with Cat. The shaft had pierced beneath her clavicle and emerged out the back, where it continued to cut into Cat as they jostled. Cat slid back off the point, which ripped flesh. The tip was serrated.

"Break the end off!" Lelani yelled between sharp breaths.

Another bolt split a branch by Cal's head. He fired in the direction of the shot.

"My lady, break off the tip!"

Cat cut her fingers on the serrated tip, trying to snap it off, but the shaft wouldn't give. Lelani handed her a hunting knife.

"Cut through the wood."

"Seth, can you outflank him?" Cal asked, holding out his other pistol.

Seth had found a depression behind a fair-sized boulder to crouch in.

"I'm not moving my ass from this spot!"

Cat sliced through the shaft. Lelani grabbed the end in front of her and pulled in one quick motion. Cat screamed again from the wood scraping flesh out of her forearm. She fell off the centaur and landed on her back. Her shirt was stained dark red. She began hyperventilating. Lelani washed Cat's wound with water from her canteen. Even though Lelani was the more injured of the two, Cat was not trained to assimilate such shocks. After cleaning out the splinters, Lelani took out a vial of white powder and sprinkled it on Cat's wound. It fizzed in the blood like sodium bicarbonate in vinegar.

"Oh God! It burns," Cat wailed. "It feels like acid."

"You'll live," Lelani told her. She was starting to feel light-headed from her own loss of blood. "Wrap the gash with cloth and apply pressure."

"What about you?" Cat asked.

Lelani sprinkled the powder on the entrance of her own wound and handed the vial to Cat. "Pour this over the exit point." She put a branch in her mouth and bit down hard as the powder began to sew her shredded cells together. Cat poured the rest of the powder on the sorceress. The pain was intense, so much so, Lelani spasmed and bit through the branch. They both leaned back in the hole and caught their breath. No more bolts had flown for the past few minutes. "Is anyone coming?" she asked Cat.

"I don't know. Where's Cal?"

Cat took a peek. A series of bolts struck the tree above their makeshift foxhole. Cat ducked.

"I couldn't see anyone."

"Stay down!" they heard Cal yell, a few trees over.

Lelani reached into her backpack and pulled out a five-foot composite longbow and a quiver of arrows.

"How the hell did that fit in there?" Cat asked.

"I'm a good packer."

"Cat! Are you and Lelani okay?!" Cal had moved to a birch a few feet away and crouched low. Seth was still under his rock.

The centaur looked to Cal for instructions. He tossed his extra pistol to Cat and fell back behind the birch as a bolt slammed into the tree.

"Fire in that direction," Cal said. "Keep them down and keep them believing we're in this spot. Lelani and I will do the rest. Save one bullet."

"Why?"

"If Seth tries to run away . . . shoot him in the ass."

They took off. With Lelani's speed, she could outflank the assailant in time for the captain's frontal assault. She glided between the trees and brush, bounding over creeks and ravines with surefooted confidence of an equestrian champion. Bolts flew around her, hitting true at the places she'd been a heart-beat before. Cal fired from below, forcing the assailant's attention on him. Lelani's shoulder throbbed, but the pain only added to her focus. She slowed, waiting for some noise to betray the attacker's position. Her arrow was notched and ready to fly, but there was only foliage in her sight. She spotted the captain below, making his way up a ravine. The assailant had stopped firing. The frequency and limited origin of the bolts indicated only one attacker. Was his quiver empty? Had he left for reinforcements?

A twig snapped behind her. She caught a glimpse of reddish fur from the corner of her eye. She kicked back with her hind legs, surprising the assailant. He hit the tree behind him with such force an avalanche of snow fell from its branches, burying him. Before he could gather his wits, Lelani fired a shaft into his chest, pinning him to the tree. The creature's yowl echoed through the hills.

"Lelani, you okay?" Cal shouted.

"All is clear."

With its tongue hanging out, the creature panted rapidly, try-ing to take air through short bloody breaths. Froth and bloodspots stained its snout and fur. Its ears stuck up at Lelani's wary ap-proach. Its furry hands, which had only four stout fingers with thick black claws, shook violently. Cat and Seth soon joined them. She was leaning on Seth for support.

"Looks like a dog," Seth said.

"What is it?" Cat asked.

"A gnoll."

"That can't be right," Cal said. "Why would a gnoll work for Farrenheil—with Dorn?"

"Bad guys," Seth said. "They all stick together."

"Not that simple," Cal said.

"Dorn's uncle is intolerant of nonhuman species," Lelani explained. "He sponsored 'cleansing' campaigns into the forests and mountains of Farrenheil. Torturing, killing, and driving out everyone who didn't look right to him. As a child, I remember centaurs coming from Farrenheil as refugees. My parents fostered orphans. They'd lost everything. The gnolls didn't fare much better."

"Farrenheil and Verakhoon didn't have the numbers to hit every fortification, town, and port in Aandor," Cal said. "We couldn't find reinforcements anywhere in the kingdom. Our banner men were under siege in their own lands. If Farrenheil made war pacts with nonhuman races, though . . ."

"They could have tripled their forces," Lelani finished.

"Why would they join Dorn's uncle if he's out to 'purify' them?" Cat asked.

"A truce keeps his attention off the purge—off of them," Lelani said.

"And because there are always spoils to war," Cal added. "And Aandor is the biggest jewel in the box."

The gnoll whimpered. Its head fell forward, the spasms ceased, and it stopped breathing.

"I almost feel sorry for it," Seth said.

"Don't," Lelani replied. "We were fortunate to encounter the beast before nightfall. They're nocturnal. His bolts would have hit more true in the dark."

Seth took out his pack and pulled a Camel out with his lips. His hands shook as he tried to strike a match. Lelani grasped his wrist, preventing him from lighting up.

"Smoke will give away our position," she said.

"There are others?" Seth asked. He looked around the woods nervously. "Jeezus, I need a freakin' smoke."

Lelani looked ahead. The sky was in transition, the fading sunlight carved by the tree tips dwindled as the beams of shadow between them thickened. "The lay line is over that crest."

2

Cal told them to stay hidden until he and Lelani could recon. They were at the edge of the tree line and an open space materialized a few yards ahead of the last cluster of shrubs. Seth and Cat rested behind the skeleton of a snow-topped bush. The sky in twilight shifted from a light cerulean on the western horizon dabbed with traces of green and yellow, to a grayish blue above them, and finally a deep indigo in the east. The first stars that appeared in that indigo canvas would soon be covered as a cold front moved stubbornly down from the north.

Seth peered into the moist gray ceiling above them and was surprised to find himself thinking about his cat in the middle of this life and death struggle. They had dropped Hoshi off at the YMCA, where Lelani kept a room. He wondered if they had left enough food and water out, and if not, would anyone answer the mewling that was sure to follow. Girlfriends and models came and went, but Hoshi was one of the few constants in his life. The cat was always glad to see him, unlike his present company.

Seth resented every step dictated to him since Lelani entered his life. He had lost himself in the past forty-eight hours and couldn't remember the individual he was only yesterday. His friends had abandoned him, his home was a cinder, dog-men were shooting arrows at him, and his only companions were a mystical horse-girl, a moody fascist cop, and his humorless wife. His past had nothing to do with the present. One day he earned a living photographing and fornicating with beautiful desperate girls, and the next he was running for his life on the yellow brick road. A massive disconnect had occurred—an alignment of stars against him. And strange as it was, this felt more real than the past thirteen years of his life.

Cal signaled the all clear.

The tree line encircled a pristine meadow; in the center stood a grand old tree. Unlike its counterparts in the woods, this tree had all of its leaves, green as on a moist August day. Around the tree was a small zone of healthy green grass, untouched by the weather. A few yards away sat a small white RV trailer hitched to empty air. Smoke wafted from a pipe on the roof. No tracks led to or from. Either no one was in or no one had left home recently.

Seth walked a few steps and felt a snap underfoot that didn't feel like wood. The snow was spotted pink. He retrieved what had cracked. A bone. A slimy bone. *Some animal,* he thought. It was picked clean, notched with tooth marks and stray clinging liga-ment. He realized that there were bones all around him. He spotted a paw; a five-fingered paw—with opposable thumb.

"Uh, guys," he said.

Cal hushed him.

"Shush yourself, man. There are pieces of some dude all around me." That got their attention.

Lelani examined the bones.

"There are two people here," she said.

"Fuck," Seth said. "This place gives me the heebie-jeebies. Maybe the other sentries are worse than dog-boy."

Cal examined the scene also.

Lelani discovered shreds of scaled clothes, a spear, and some netting.

"These are the other guards," she said. "These items are from Aandor. One of them was a skilyte."

"A what?" Cat asked.

"Swamp dwellers," Cal said. "Not friends of Aandor."

"Perhaps we have an ally?" Lelani said. "Rosencrantz?"

"No." Cal picked up a thighbone and studied the nicks and scratches that covered it. "The gnoll got hungry." Cal handed the bone to Lelani for confirmation.

"It ate its partners?" Seth asked incredulously.

"Gnolls are terrible allies."

"Wouldn't their leader know this?" Cat asked.

"Dorn probably ordered the gnoll not to harm them," Lelani answered.

"And he didn't realize it wouldn't obey?"

"No. Treason and insubordination are rare in the Kingdom of Farrenheil. Dorn's uncle enjoys putting people on trial for the most minor infractions. Execution is the family hobby. Thinks it sends a good message to the masses. Sometimes they even coax children to divulge their parents' beliefs, then they arrest the parents and place the children in military orphanages. That's how they maintain such a large army." She threw the bone down with disgust. "What arrogance! They believe their whims can subvert nature. Their alliances with these base creatures will be everyone's undoing, including their own."

"Right now, that's a blessing," Cal said. "Two less sentries we need to deal with." He studied the trailer. "I assume that's where the mojo is?"

"Yes," Lelani said.

"And odds are, Rosencrantz is in that trailer."

"I'd take that bet," she answered.

"I'll go first," Cal offered.

"No," Cat responded. "We'll go together. How much safer can it be in a forest with man-eating gnolls?"

Seth chuckled. *Maybe not completely humorless,* he thought.

He helped Cat stand and volunteered to be her crutch as he'd done often since they'd dispatched the gnoll. The other two needed to be unencumbered in case something sprang up. It made sense to everyone, and it helped alleviate the sour mood that sprang between them after he had refused Cal's order to outflank the gnoll. It seemed like a *team-player* thing to do. Seth had a more practical motive for helping Cat. In the woods, you don't have to be able to outrun a bear to survive an attack. You just have to be faster than the person you're with.

They cut a path through the snow. The clearing reminded Seth of the Roman colosseum; the trees surrounding the clearing, bristling in the wind, were a thousand cheering spectators. This didn't bode well for the four of them, who were on stage. Seth felt vulnerable. Cloistered in the canyons of Manhattan, a person can't appreciate the reality of open ground. A tactical disadvantage when being hunted.

The trailer was about fifteen feet long and in need of a wash. Dents and dings decorated the pleated aluminum skin. Cinder blocks lifted the hitched end off the ground. Cal reached it first and was about to knock, when—

"Wait!" Seth said.

"What?"

"I don't know."

"You don't know what?"

"I . . ."

"Are we just going to stand out here?" Lelani asked.

"Oh, for Christ's sake," Cat said. She hobbled up and rapped on the door.

The vapors from their breath ceased in unison. Everything was silent. Then they heard clanging and banging within. The trailer rocked as the footsteps grew louder. The door creaked open and stopped at the limit of a chain, just enough space for a mouse to slip through. A single eye in the darkness took stock of them from the crack.

"No trespassing," it said in a low raspy voice.

"We're looking for Rosencrantz," Cal said.

The eye considered them, shifting from one to the other.

"Wizards are a temperamental lot. They're not like Jedi Masters—feed you soup and teach you tricks because you crash in on them. More likely to turn you into mice and feed you to their snakes. Go home . . . while you still can."

"I'm well aware of the temperament of wizards, sir," Lelani

said. "My own master, Magnus Proust, has turned a few assistants' heads prematurely white."

The eye pondered this. "Magnus Proust?"

The door shut. A chain rattled, then the door opened wide. He was a short, stocky man, bald on top with graying sides, red bulbous cheeks, and a little gray mustache. His skin was tanned, as though he recently returned from a cruise. He wore red-and-brown plaid pajama pants, slippers, and a black T-shirt that said, *What Is Good?* in stark white letters.

"Don't try nothing funny, or I'll cut ya," he said. There wasn't a knife in sight.

"We're not here to hurt anyone," Cat replied.

The man took a long look at Cat and smiled. "You know, you're the first people to show up around here that didn't give me the creeps. You ought to see the things popping up lately. There's a fucking gnoll in those woods. Kid you not. That damn thing howls at the moon and keeps us up all night. Sends shivers to my corns."

"Not anymore," Lelani said.

"You don't say? Well, hot damn. That's just great. The missus will be thrilled. Anything I can do to repay you folks?"

"Yeah," Seth said. "Blast the evildoers, find the kid, get me my job and apartment back, and send everyone else home."

"Uh . . . yeah," the man said. "I was thinking more like snacks, maybe some Tang or hot chocolate."

"Magi Rosencrantz, please forgive my companion's outburst," Lelani cut in. "Proust speaks very highly of your skills. We need help."

"Well, I'll do what I can, only . . . I'm not Rosencrantz. Name's Benito Reyes. Friends call me Ben."

"Can we see Rosencrantz?" Cal asked.

"You already have."

The four of them looked at each other hoping someone knew what he meant.

"We have?" Seth said.

"Please don't say he's a skilyte," Cat added.

"No. That's Rosencrantz," Ben said, pointing out the door.

The oak bristled in the wind.

"He lives in the tree?" Seth asked.

"No." Ben pointed again.

"Rosencrantz *is* the tree?" Cat said.

"Boggles the mind, dun it?" Ben responded.

"Of course," Lelani said. "I should have realized."

"How do you talk to a tree?" Seth asked.

"It can be done, but I lack magical energies."

"You can take your fill there," Ben said pointing to a rusty spigot sticking out of the trailer. "It's tapped into the lay line."

Lelani smiled and went to the spigot.

"Are you the . . . what? . . . butler, gardener?" Seth asked.

"Same difference when your boss is a tree. Say, you folks must be pretty cold. Come in for a spell and warm up."

"You go," Lelani said. "I want to recharge my cache first."

The trailer was filled top to bottom with periodicals, mostly yellowed with age: *Life* magazine, *National Geographic, Rolling Stone, Time, Saturday Evening Post, Scientific America, Better Home and Gardens, Vogue, New Republic, New York Times,* comic books, and countless trade publications from neurobiology to actuarial journals, going back to the turn of the twentieth century. They were stacked flat on the floor all the way to the ceiling, leaving just enough room for a single trail in the center. Seth spotted a copy of *Action Comics* number one, the first appearance of Superman. Each stack teetered and threatened the walkway.

Getting out of the wind was a good start, but Seth doubted any relaxing could be done in this mess. "Read a lot?" he asked.

"Actually I do," Ben responded. "But these belong to him."

"This is the tree's library?" Cat asked.

"Yeah. It's also a graveyard. All the pulp in here was made from Rosencrantz's friends; other sentient trees like himself. Creepy, huh?"

"How depressing. And you live here?" Seth asked.

"Not exactly."

Ben opened one of two doors in the back of the trailer. Sunlight and a warm breeze flowed through the doorway. They followed him in and found themselves in a spacious bright kitchen with terra-cotta floor tiles. The walls were cream-colored paper with pictures of bowls of fruit, sugar and flour bins, and other pleasant kitchen items, all rendered in lime green and lemon yellow. One photo stood apart, a black-and-white picture of a beautiful blonde in a one-piece bathing suit with a sash across her that read *Miss Flushing, Queens.* Open French doors revealed a patio with white wicker furniture overlooking a solitary beach and a beautiful sunset up on white crashing waves.

"Welcome to Puerto Rico," Ben said.

"Holy cow!" Seth said.

"For once, I agree with you," Cal added.

Seth stuck his arm back through the doorway and felt the cold sting of upstate New York. Once his mind accepted what had just occurred, he took off his jacket and claimed a padded lounge chair in the corner of the patio. "Finally, something good happens to me," he said.

"May I use the bathroom?" Cat asked.

"It's right in there, sweetie." He handed her a crutch that lay in the corner. "My daughter sprained her ankle last year. You look like you could use it."

"Thank you."

"Ben, is that you?" came a voice from another room.

"Be with you in a minute, honey. That's the missus," he said with a smile. Ben poured them lemonade and made each one a plate of freshly made *pasteles* from a tray on the stove. "Just finished a batch before you came knocking," he said. "Excuse me for a minute. Make yourselves at home." He went into the bedroom.

Cal kept checking his watch and looking back at the trailer door.

"Take a breather, man," Seth said. "Your brain's still being edited. Relax."

Cal considered him with a sour face.

It was in the forefront of Seth's thoughts that the cop blamed him for the current situation. If everything they claimed were true, Seth would only have been thirteen at the time. How could a teenager be relevant to a covert mission? Seth turned from the cop's scowl and studied the beach. A half-naked Puerto Rican girl, tanned and gorgeous, romped with her dog. Seth instinctively wanted to get his camera and pursue the opportunity. He watched—a neutered voyeur.

"We've got to go back," Cal said.

"Let's thaw out first," Seth whined.

"Now."

"Jeezus! I'm with the only guy in Puerto Rico who wants to work."

"Can it. Let's go."

"You go."

"You, too. You were there thirteen years ago. Might be important." Cal hovered over Seth. He wasn't going to take no for an answer.

Seth considered whacking the cop in the balls and running down the beach. He decided not to push his luck. "Well . . . so long as I'm important. What's the plan?"

"We talk to the tree."

"Of course. It's so obvious. Do you speak Tree?"

"Lelani will figure it out."

"Pretty convenient having your own living, breathing computerlike girl Friday. She's like your Mr. Spock."

"You're only as good as the people who help you. Aandor, NYPD . . . doesn't matter where." Cal's tone indicated Seth was the weak link on this team.

"What about Cat?" he sniped.

Cal's expression changed, like a stick prodding a wound; Seth had struck a nerve. Cat was a liability to the mission. In Cal's anal-retentive hierarchy, even Seth had more of a stake in this mission than Catherine.

"Quit stalling," Cal said.

Ben came back from the bedroom and with him was a slip of a woman with a slight hump, in mismatched sweat clothes and slippers.

"Hey guys, I want you to meet my wife, Helen Flannery Reyes. Helen was Miss Queens, New York, 1966, you know.

She gave those upstate girls a good run for their money in the Miss New York pageant, didn't you, hon?"

Helen shuffled over to the men slowly and took Cal's hands in hers. They were mottled and leathery, and she smelled of menthol. Seth was glad she chose to greet Cal.

"Don't you pay Ben any mind," she told them in a slightly slurred speech. Both men realized she was recovering from some sort of ailment, like a stroke. "He still sees me as that girl of seventeen, but you and I know there are a lot more miles on this ol' bucket than he cares to admit." She winked at them and smiled, mostly with the half of her mouth that was still mobile.

"It's a pleasure to meet you Mrs. Reyes," Cal said. "But if you could excuse us for a minute . . ."

"Are you leaving already?" Ben asked.

"Can you talk to Rosencrantz, Ben?"

"No."

"Please, it's very important."

"I didn't mean *no, I wouldn't*, I mean I can't. I inherited this gig from the former caretaker. Taught me everything I needed to do to maintain Rosencrantz's comfort and health. I don't even think the tree knows I exist."

"Is this portal back to New York permanent?"

"It's a fixed transfer," Ben said. "It'll still be there after you exit."

"Could I impose on you to let Catherine rest here a while? Her ankle . . ."

"I've got some Aleve and a cold pack we can throw on that baby," said Helen. "I think my daughter's old air cast is somewhere in here, too. Hey, when you come back, Ben will build a bonfire on the beach."

"Great idea," Ben said. "We can trade war stories. I was in the Big One back in 'forty-four."

"We're imposing too much as it is, Ben."

"What imposing?" Helen cut in. "We rarely get visitors anymore. The kids are so busy with their careers . . ."

"I've got eight bedrooms attached to this place," Ben said. "You guys look like you can use a rest."

"Yeah," Seth said. "At least do it for Cat."

Cal grabbed Seth by the cuff and pulled him toward the transfer. He smiled at the Reyeses and thanked them for their help while pushing Seth out the door. Seth barely managed to grab his coat before the cold breath of upstate New York kissed him again.

3

Outside the trailer, Lelani had painted two white concentric circles around the base of the tree. They were perfect circles, stark white on a green mass that reminded one of the boundaries of fair play at ball games. Viewed from the sky, Rosencrantz marked the green center of a bull's-eye. The four-foot-wide ring of grass between the two circles was painted with evenly spaced runes around the tree. Her brass compact was placed on Ben's propane grill, also within the circles, and she surrounded it with leaves, bark, soil, sap-coated twigs, and a plastic container of water. The lights of the device flickered brightly, casting a web of multicolored lasers on the smooth glassy surface of its inner lid. The compact hissed a steady stream of white noise. Lelani played with the controls, like tuning a radio station.

"Progress?" Cal asked.

"I'm about to contact Rosencrantz."

"So, the tree's going to talk?" Seth asked.

"In a manner. Sentient flora communicate through scent," Lelani explained. "Pheromones, sap, water, chlorophyll, nitrates—these are the components of their language. But they operate on a much slower plane than we do. To communicate in real time, I have to generate a time warp around Rosencrantz."

"If you speed time around him, won't the tree age rapidly?" Seth asked.

Lelani regarded Seth with pleasant surprise, as though such an observation was thought beyond his comprehension. Seth half expected her to award him a gold star.

"Yes," she said, in an encouraging tone. "Fortunately, trees have very long life spans. I've heard they rather enjoy the experience. It gives them a rush. Still, we should try and conclude our business as fast as possible. This device will utilize the elements I've placed around it to pose our questions and translate the tree's responses. Time within the inner ring will move rapidly. The buffer between the two circles is the event horizon. That's where we'll stand. Outside the outer ring is normal time. Don't move outside the buffer while the spell is in progress."

"Can I just wait in the trailer?" Seth whined.

Lelani touched a jewel on the compact. The sky beyond the tree danced like the aurora borealis. Strings of energy stirred around them, a proto-hurricane of photonic vibration. The tree shifted rapidly, like still shots taken on a windy day and flapped in succession.

"My God," Cal said, over the din of increasing white noise. "The power."

"Yes," Lelani agreed. "We could not attempt this away from the lay line."

"Hey, tree . . . are you there?" Seth asked.

The device squawked a raspy, rapturous, *"Yes."*

Seth was dumbfounded. Reality deteriorated every moment he spent with these people. He wanted his life back—the drugs, the raunch, the cheap sex, even the nagging roommate. Imperfect as it was, it was his; he could make sense of it, and it was safe.

"Tell these people I have nothing to do with them so I can go home," he said.

"Proust seed watered," came the reply. *"Remember you. Great feast of the waning joy, cycle of Zcqxbvxq."* A pit formed in Seth's belly.

"Do you remember me?" Cal asked.

"Great feast . . . waning joy. The wide trunk gives strength to its arms in the deluge."

"What does that mean?" Cal asked.

"'Joy' is also the word for 'sun' in flora speak," Lelani translated. "'Feast' is its word for 'rain.' Waning joy is autumn—large transdimensional crossings would have aggravated weather patterns. You probably arrived in a torrential rainstorm. 'Seed' is the flora word for both promise and potential. Perhaps it's referring to a debt to Proust. 'Wide trunk,' I believe, literally translates into 'something big on which smaller things depend on for prosperity.' My guess is it means leader. That would be you."

A shudder ran through Seth, the ghost of an old memory. He stepped back to the edge of the outer line. A sparrow chick caught in the event horizon with them hopped over the inner circle toward the tree. It aged like the subject of a time-lapse film.

"Remember."

"He knows why we're here," Lelani continued. "He's followed my progress since I arrived. Rosencrantz's consciousness can reach around the world through a green network, so long as there's a plant or a flower to tap into."

A surge of pressure poured into Seth's mind, as though all his sinus cavities were filled with fluid past their capacity. He grabbed his head and fell to the ground. The onslaught rushed in too quickly, too forcefully. His head was already on the brink of bursting when it was forced to take on more. He turned to Cal for help, but the cop was on the ground, too. Lelani was holding her own but looked like she'd succumb any second.

"Make it stop! Make it stop!" Seth shouted.

"What is it?" Cal screamed.

A ripple of air emanated outward from the tree accompanied by a deep bass vibration, which reverberated to the marrow.

The world changed. The wind-lashed forest was wrapped in a torrential downpour. Lightning stamped fleeting silhouettes of the surrounding tree line. A shimmer in the air preceded a vertical tear in open space, birthing a gaggle of weary travelers. There was a translucent quality to the beings. These were phantoms of another time. Men and women dressed in cloaks. A bearded man with the body of a horse. A crying infant cradled in one traveler's arm. And there, for the second time in a long age, Seth's parents Parham and Lita. He forced back his emotions, reminding himself it was all a lie. They were not his true parents. Yet the urge to throw his arms around them was overwhelming.

The phantoms took shelter under Rosencrantz. Seth recognized his own eyes in a boy on the cusp of manhood; frightened, confused. In his hand the boy held a rolled parchment. He broke the wax seal.

And then, it was Seth himself under that tree looking down on the scroll instead of his doppelganger. *As long as the spells remained uncast, they'd be vulnerable,* said a voice in his head. His voice. *Foreigners in a foreign land.* His orders were to delay for nothing. He unrolled the scroll, fighting the wind for its possession, and even as he did this, grown-up Seth struggled with inevitable history. Even without a conscious recollection of these events, he knew what was about to transpire, as though it were some late-night movie he'd once watched years ago. He couldn't stop. It was the past; it was done. He acted out the spellbound part in an enchanted script. The wind and rain took their toll on the parchment. The paper was saturated, the ink began to run. He would have to be quick or lose all the directives. He read the first line thirteen times, once for each member of the party. Then he recited their names, and then read the activation word, almost dissipated, at the bottom of the scroll.

A searing hot line of pain cleaved through his head. All the blood in his brain boiled like magma. Cal—both of them, old and young—screamed, too. Seth was again within the event horizon on his knees, holding his head. The cloaked travelers were once again third-party players in the drama. The phantoms staggered, dazed and confused, from their arborescent shelter in various directions, some standing, others crawling on their knees. They broke off into separate groups, some trailed off alone, with no regard for each other. The storm subsided. The phantoms faded from the world. Seth vomited.

"Oh God. What was that?" he said, gagging and spitting.

"Thirteen years ago," Lelani said. "Your repressed memories, or maybe Rosencrantz's own recollection of the events."

"Proust seed watered. The keeper, a cloud in the drought. The keeper's saplings will know fortune," said the tree. *"Water my seed."* And then it discontinued the time warp.

Seth passed out.

CHAPTER 15

DO THE RIGHT THING

1

Rita did not say a word until they were a block from the house.

Then, in a monotone she said, "This is a real mess, Danny."

Daniel could not tell if it was an accusation or a statement of fact. Rita's energy was such that she could spare none for inflection. Daniel tread carefully. It didn't take much to send his mother running for her little yellow pills.

"Them Grundys were messing with Ade," Daniel said.

"A lot of good helping him did."

"He's just scared."

Daniel was surprised to find himself defending a person who'd betrayed him. A part of him wanted to go back to the previous night and help the Grundys pummel the jerk. Deep down, though, Daniel understood his friend better than most. Mrs. Lutz, who kept an immaculate home, had a passion for baking that made Sara Lee look like a slacker. The house was always warm from the oven and smelled of cookies. Mr. Lutz was jovial, a tinkerer by nature and toy model builder with the patience of Job. Their house was in order and affection flowed copiously. Life behind those walls was as soft as Adrian's gut. Daniel took every opportunity to stay over. Unconditional affection, however, was not doled out in the real world, even when it was warranted. The world outside chez Lutz was a harsher place. Adrian squandered his energies trying to mold life into a facsimile of his home.

"You should pick your fights better," Rita said. They pulled into the driveway. The house was looking run-down, an eyesore on the block.

"Mom . . ."

Rita turned off the ignition and looked at the boy. Her eyes were alien. Nothing of Daniel's resided there.

"What?"

"Is Clyde looking for a job at the hospital?"

"Not that I know of. Why? Was he at the hospital today?"

"I thought he came for me."

"Where did you see him? Emergency room? Was he injured?"

"He was talking to a woman. A secretary. Or something."

Rita released a lungful in a huff and exited the car. She stormed into the house. Daniel dragged his feet going in.

The kitchen radio played "I Can See for Miles" by the Who. Rita threw dishes and cutlery onto the table, mumbling under her breath as the utensils clanged and clinked. Dinner was still at least two hours away. Rita had forgotten to retrieve her daughter from their neighbor.

"I'll get Penny," Daniel said.

He passed the phone, which blinked a fast red digital *4* on the display. Daniel pressed play. The hiss of an outdoor line, probably a pay phone, played for three seconds then clicked. *"Message received 3:58 P.M.,"* said the pseudo-feminine drone of the machine. Daniel thought he had heard a sniffle in that hiss. The second message played. This time he was sure there was crying on the other end before it clicked. *"Message received 4:07 P.M."* The third message Danny heard a sobbing girl mumble something that sounded like his name. *"Message received 4:15 P.M."* In the final message he recognized Katie Millar. *"Oh God Danny, Please be home. Pickuppickuppickup . . . Message received 4:21 P.M."*

Daniel star-sixty-nined the call but received an earful of that terrible static that informs one the call was from *"outside the class calling area."*

"Shit," Daniel said.

The phone rang. He picked it up before it occurred to him that Clyde might be on the other end. "Hello."

"Danny? Oh God. It's really you."

"Katie, what's going on?"

"Oh Dan . . . oh Dan, oh Dan . . ." More sobbing. Daniel wondered if anyone was having a good day.

"What happened?"

"C-ca-can you c-come g-get me?" Daniel could hear her shivering through the receiver.

"Where are you?"

"Outside O'Leary's."

Chills marched down Daniel's spine. His best friend, who was experiencing mortal terror, wanted him to come to the one place common sense dictated he should avoid. O'Leary's was Clyde's den, the place his stepfather ended up seven nights a week.

"Katie, what's going on?"

"He's looking for me. I can't stay here." Click. The line went dead. Daniel stared at the front door. His foot took a step toward it contrary to the little voice in his head telling him to stay put. From the kitchen, "Should I Stay or Should I Go" by the Clash wafted on the air. The whole day waxed ironic.

"Who was that?" Rita asked.

"Katie. Something's wrong."

"Something's wrong? Can you be a little more specific?"

"She sounded scared."

"And just like that, you're off to the rescue? In case you didn't get it already, you're grounded."

"Grounded? Clyde's going to find out about the arrest and the lawsuit. I don't want to be near this house when he comes home. I take enough crap here to get a lifetime pass on time-outs and groundings."

"Watch your mouth, Danny. We put food on the table. There's a roof over your . . ."

"And it gives that asshole the right to use me, to use *us* for punching bags?"

Rita slapped him hard. The sting lingered, his ear rang. He was alert. The whole day had been a bad dream; now he was awake. Clarity, emanating from the pain, fueled a burst of bravery.

"You let that man ruin us," Daniel said. "I remember having a childhood. Now we live on food stamps and public assistance. Dad bought this house, and we'll probably lose it because we can't keep up with the mortgage. Don't you know what people say about us? Clyde's an alcoholic. No one wants to hire him. You're doped on Valium half the time. I'm the one watching Penny when you're passed out. And get this . . . ," Daniel could no longer hold back the flood of repressed tears, "people think I'm a delinquent. Me! I'm the delinquent even though I stand behind my friends when they're bullied. I'm the delinquent even when I get into the hardest classes and get good grades. *I'm* the malcontent, when all I aspire to these days is for people to leave me the FUCK alone!"

Rita slapped him again.

"You can keep hitting me, but you don't have the guts to tell that piece of shit Clyde to get out. You're a fucking coward."

Rita tried to slap him again but Daniel stepped back out of the way. He headed for the front door.

"Don't you walk out!" Rita ordered, in tears.

Daniel was inclined to tell her that she was not his real mother. Instead, he bit his tongue. He took a deep breath.

"You didn't hear Katie's voice, Mom. She's terrified. Something really bad has happened."

"You're not a hero! You can't save everyone—you can't save the world!"

"I'm not brave enough to improve my own life. Might as well help my friends with theirs. Everyone turns to me when they need help."

"Danny! If you walk out that door . . . don't come back."

As he shut the door, the muffled cries of a desperate, lonely woman fell upon his ears.

2

It's a trap. That's what Daniel kept thinking over and over. Clyde beat the crap out of Katie to lure him to that side of town. Why else would she be in *that* neighborhood? Clyde wouldn't know their friendship was merely an ember of what it had once been; he had missed their last scheduled heart-to-heart chat.

Daniel stopped his bike about a block from the bar. It was a run-down block. With chipped wood siding and a sagging shingled roof, O'Leary's fit the scene. Coors, Budweiser, and Miller Lite glowed through the dust in the windows. The sidewalk was cracked and the lots to each side of the bar were overgrown with weeds and littered with broken beer bottles.

Daniel kept one eye out for Katie and the other for Clyde. There were very few cars parked on the street. A blue Ram pickup quivered on squeaky shocks—no doubt a trapped pet getting antsy while its owner downed a mug. Daniel rode the center line of the street, far from anything that might serve as an ambush point. His instincts said to go home.

Across the street from the bar stretched a poor excuse for a baseball field, boxed in by dilapidated dwellings and fences and bordered by a hedge. Next to the entrance by the right-field foul line was a solitary pay phone. Daniel rode onto the field, which was a big sand lot with the remnants of a mound in the middle. The roughness of the dirt caused his bike to shake, and it aggravated his bruised rib. Two depressed dugouts built from cinder blocks framed the sides of the invisible diamond. Empty beer bottles littered the whole bunker and graffiti covered the walls. Bundled in the corner of one dugout was a varsity jacket, number six. As Daniel approached, a cheerleading skirt and legs emerged from the bundle.

Katie was curled in a fetal position. She lifted her head with a start. Strangely, the look in this terrified girl's eye lifted Daniel's spirits. He had never met anyone so glad to see him. When he sat beside her, she unfurled and threw her arms around him. He put his own arms around her.

"What happened?" Daniel asked.

"We cut school after lunch. He said he had something he wanted to show me." The "he" she referred to was not Clyde. Daniel was relieved this wasn't a plot to get at him through a friend. Not everything that happened revolved around him.

Daniel realized there was booze on her breath.

"He has a hangout a few blocks from here," Katie continued. "Just an abandoned shed that Josh and his pals fixed up with old couches and some posters. We were alone. He turned the radio up, said it would give us privacy. He gave me a flask to sip and razzed me when I said no . . . said that was the reason he didn't like to date little girls."

Katie stopped and fell into a fit of tears. Daniel hugged her tighter and waited for the fit to subside.

"So you took a sip?" he asked.

"I took a gulp."

It was tough to compete with older kids. The senior girls wore their nascent bosoms as badges of honor, stuffing themselves into form-hugging tops any chance they got. The art of not staring was mastered better by some more than others, but every male noticed, every guy bragged when he brushed a gifted girl in a crowded hallway. Katie was still a work in progress.

"Burned your throat?"

"Heck, yes. He stopped razzing me about drinking and then we started . . . It was nice at first—it was . . . it was what I wanted. But he started putting his hands in places where I didn't . . . I said no, and he'd stop for a while; then try again. He got frustrated, said I was leading him on . . . kept calling me a little girl. My head was spinning. Somehow, he got his fingers underneath, in my . . . in my . . . and he was . . ." Katie succumbed to a second fit.

Through a fold in her skirt, Daniel realized Katie was miss-ing her underwear. He felt guilty that this excited him. In the past, Katie and him changed into swimming suits separated by no more than a shrub. Somehow this was different . . . or he was different. He was very aware of her sex just under that layer of rayon. The situation called on him to be stronger than his hor-mones. He focused on the moment. "What happened?"

"I didn't want to!" she sobbed. Anger edged into her voice. "I told him no! I told him *NO* more than once. I couldn't get off the couch. He was on top of me; he was too . . ."

"Jesus, Katie."

"And all of a sudden his pants were down . . ."

"Couldn't you knee him? Scratch his eyes?"

"He said just touch it . . . to help him out . . . since I . . . since I wouldn't . . . He said . . . I—I didn't think . . . I didn't think he . . ." Katie began to hyperventilate. Then she threw up, mostly the dry heaves. Daniel stroked her back. The retching soon sub-sided.

"HE WAS MY BOYFRIEND!" she cried in a torrent of grief.

Daniel stroked the back of her head. The gray fall sky was giving way to darkness on the horizon. There was a nip in the air and Daniel's skin where Katie's tears fell turned cold. His friend's ordeal had one unexpected result; it succeeded in taking his mind off his own problems.

Daniel heard the crunch of gravel behind him. He un-wrapped himself from Katie and stood, worried once more that Clyde had found them; only to be oddly relieved to be looking up at Josh Lundgren's well-chiseled face instead. One of Josh's cronies, Todd Harkness, stood uncomfortably behind him.

"There you are. I been looking all over for you," Josh said.

He tried to make eye contact with her. Katie used Daniel as a shield. Each time Josh moved to get a clear view of her, Daniel shifted to keep himself between them. "This ain't your business, Hauer. Keep out of things that don't concern you."

Daniel didn't respond. The warmth of Katie's breath on his neck, her arms on his shoulders, spurred his courage. He'd been dreaming of her arms around him for months, and odd as this situation was, it qualified. Todd looked more uncomfortable by the moment. Daniel knew him as a clean-cut, straight-B student. He played for the baseball team and hoped to get into college on an athletic scholarship. Helping Josh cover up an assault was not his style. He was only here because of Josh's persuasiveness. Handsome, strong, funny, rich—Josh's approval made your ho-hum existence a little more exciting.

"Hey, Todd," Daniel greeted. Todd looked upset that Daniel knew his name.

Josh stepped down into the dugout, clinking discards as he landed. He thumbed his nose, straightened his posture, took a deep breath, and put out his chest. Josh had a good six inches and twenty-five pounds on Daniel, and it was evident he thought this would be enough make Daniel move away from the girl. Daniel almost laughed out loud at the jerk's attempt to be intimidating.

"Hey, don't be stupid, kid," Todd said to Daniel. "Josh just wants to talk to her, that's all." Todd's plea was halfhearted. He didn't believe his own words and was worried the situation would escalate with *him* as an accessory.

"You know . . . Elijah Grundy told me to mind my own business too, before I inverted his face," Daniel said with a straight, albeit bruised, face.

There was something about cuts, welts, and splints on a young man that warned an antagonist, *You'll get hurt, too.* Josh hesitated. Todd appeared even more apprehensive. Although the events of the past twenty-four hours were not as dramatic as the buzz they generated, Daniel was aware that he now had a reputation. He'd been carted off to jail by the police in front of the whole school for single-handedly beating up two of the town troglodytes. There wasn't a person in town under twenty-one that didn't have a beef with one Grundy or another. This act was simply putting his juvenile delinquency to good use.

"And Elijah didn't rape anybody," Daniel added, for emphasis.

"Nobody got raped!" Josh shrieked.

"Fuck, man!" Todd cursed. The word rattled the jock.

"There was NO rape!" Josh repeated, more for himself than anyone else, but hearing the word again made Todd squirrelly.

"Screw this, man," Todd said. "This dude's nuts. Last thing I need is a busted arm or leg before the scouts see me play. I'm outta here, Josh. Sorry."

"Fuckin' hell, Todd! Get back here, you pussy." Todd kept walking.

"And then there was one," Daniel said.

"Shut up!" Josh didn't stand quite so tall anymore. He looked deflated. He looked alone in more ways than one.

Daniel was beginning to see a ray of sunshine in this situation. The last thing he needed was another fight. If Josh was shaken enough, they might walk out of the park unscathed.

"Think you can sweet-talk Katie into thinking she wasn't raped?" Daniel said in a mocking tone.

"Stop saying *that* word! I didn't force her into the shed."

"You can't even convince your best friend," Daniel said, motioning to the distant dot that was Todd.

"She wanted it. She got all funny *after* it happened."

"LIAR!" Katie bolted forward from her human shield, scratching and clawing at Josh. "GODDAMN LIAR!"

Shit, Daniel thought.

3

The five-fingered gash across Josh's face enraged him. He grabbed Katie's wrists and threw her to the ground into a pile of beer bottles. Daniel picked up a stray bottle by his foot and hit Josh square in the forehead with a solid throw. The jock staggered back, tripped on another empty and landed hard on his back. Daniel grabbed his friend's arm and pulled her out of the dugout. He dragged her toward his bike as she struggled to lunge at Josh. She had lost all sense about the reality of fighting a big, angry, dumb jock. Daniel shook her by the shoulders.

"Stop it, Katie! I know you're mad, but he's going to cream us when he gets up."

The sound of bottles rattling signaled the jock regaining his feet. Something about the look in Josh's eye snapped the girl from her fit; perhaps it was the same gleam of bad judgment with which he stole her virginity. Josh looked resolved to undertake new sins. It was time to go.

Daniel peddled for two toward the field exit. The dirt was terrible for traction, but he didn't dare look back. He turned right at the exit on a course for the better side of town, riding along the first-base line. Daniel barely registered that Josh had climbed over the chain-link fence ahead of him when all of a sudden he landed on them hard and knocked them down. Katie rolled into the street. Daniel was pinned, the bike frame cutting into his leg from his assailant's weight. His rib was on fire. A fist smashed his nose; pain swimming across a web of nerves. Another one hit him in the jaw. He saw spots before his eyes. Katie rammed Josh with her whole body and knocked him back. Daniel slid out from under the bike, trying not to pass out. His bandaged rib protested any further action. He staggered to his feet just as Josh grabbed Katie's wrist and twisted. There was a horrifying crack. She screamed. He clipped her in the cheek with a right jab and she crumpled to the ground like a rag doll.

Daniel was furious, angrier than he'd ever been in his life. Josh blocked his punch and returned a solid jab to the gut. The jock grabbed Daniel by the top of his shirt and almost lifted him off the ground as he shoved him back onto the hood of a parked Dodge Ram. Daniel struggled, but his assailant's arms were birch-tree thick.

"I am not going to jail for raping no one!" Josh shouted. "Especially for your little tramp girlfriend." Then, Josh stopped punching him and looked into the cab of the pickup.

Daniel looked, too, and saw a bare leg in a white lady's pump straddled over the steering wheel. The other leg lay over the headrest of the driver's seat. A well-manicured woman's hand gripped the passenger-side dashboard. And above the horizon of the dashboard were two pair of eyes looking straight at him. One of those pairs was Clyde's.

"Oh, crap."

4

She was the same woman Clyde had met in the hospital earlier. She struggled to put her tits back in her bra even as Clyde buckled his pants. Josh had stopped hitting Daniel, and hovered over him with a gaping mouth, confused by the distraction. Clyde looked incensed, which Daniel knew to be his default face.

"Shit," Josh said.

"Worse than that," Daniel responded. "That's my stepdad . . . ex-Marine."

Josh let Daniel go and backed up a few steps before turning and running off. *What a pussy,* Daniel thought. He rushed over to Katie, who was still out cold, and patted her face. She had a dark purple bruise where Josh hit her. *Even with welts, she is beautiful,* he thought.

"Katie, wake up," he whispered in her ear.

Clyde got out of the truck. "What the hell are you doing here, boy?"

The day's events had yet to catch up with Daniel's stepfather, but the boy realized catching Clyde in his extracurricular activity was enough to warrant a beating. Clyde wasn't stupid or drunk enough to do it in the middle of the street, in front of Daniel's friend whose father had some influence in the town . . . at least he hoped. He realized how silly he was earlier thinking that Clyde had attacked Katie. If she would only wake up.

"Katie," he repeated, tapping the back of her wrist lightly.

"Boy . . ."

"You know, Clyde," Daniel said, trying to keep the fear from his voice, "most dads would be proud to see their kid hold their own against someone bigger and older than they are."

"First off, runt, you wasn't holding your own. You were getting the shit kicked out of you. Second, you ain't *my* kid."

Katie groaned. She stirred, then opened her eyes. Clyde stood his ground. The woman staggered from the truck and joined them. They were both two sheets to the wind and would be adding a third before calling it a night. Daniel turned cold as he read the hospital name tag on her blouse: *Conklin.* That's why she looked familiar. He'd seen her in a photo in the principal's office. Clyde was banging Conklin's daughter.

The principal's animus toward him took on new dimensions. Clyde's actions, his lusts, greed, and poor character even polluted Daniel's sanctuary at school, the one place he had never had to worry about his stepfather. His collection of havens was shrinking. Clyde was his bane in an almost biblical sense. A new chapter had to be written for any possible future to exist. For the first time, Daniel feared Clyde less than the prospect of extricating him from his life. He should have ratted the bastard out to the sheriff earlier. It wasn't too late to go back and lodge that formal complaint. Rita would have to live with the consequences of her own lies. Penny would have to endure a house full of strangers. Daniel had had enough.

He helped Katie to her feet. She leaned on him for support, favoring her uninjured arm. "I'm going to take Katie home," he told his stepfather.

He picked up his bike and wheeled it by the handlebar while supporting Katie with the other arm. Daniel held his breath as they inched away. It felt like they were backing out of a lion's cage. Daniel hoped Clyde's lust for Conklin's brat was greater than the taste for his blood. After a few minutes they were around the corner and out of view. The boy sighed in relief.

"You ought to go," Katie mumbled.

"I'll see you home."

"No. My dad already thinks badly of you on account of being Clyde's boy. Here I am, welt on my face, no panties, bleeding between my legs, and smelling of liquor. I don't want to go home like this. I'll go to Samantha's house and clean up. Her mom works 'til seven."

"Your wrist is broken."

"I'll go to the emergency room after I clean up—say I took a spill on my bike. I need to clean up. I don't want to walk in looking like a . . ." She paused. She couldn't get the word out. "No one has to know."

Daniel restrained his surprise. He simply asked, "You're not pressing charges?"

Her eyes locked with his. "*No one* will ever know."

"Katie, what about the next girl Josh . . ."

"GODDAMN IT, DANNY!"

"Okay. Okay."

They walked in silence until they came to the fork that split their destinations.

"You know I don't have feelings for you the way you want me to," Katie said.

"Yeah."

"I do love you, though. More today than ever. You're a true friend. You're my hero."

Before Daniel could think of a response, Katie kissed him on the mouth. It was warm and lasting, or appeared to be. She tasted his lips before pulling away.

She moved on and never looked back. Daniel had the strangest sensation that he'd never see her again.

5

Daniel sprinted up to his room. He filled his backpack with underwear, some shirts, an extra pair of jeans, his toothbrush, and his copy of *We Can Build You* by Phillip K. Dick, which he had just started. In a tin that came with his X-Men trading cards, he pulled out seventy-eight dollars that he'd managed to hide from the step-monster. After his statement to the sheriff, they would likely place him in a temporary foster home. The thought scared him, but how much worse than Clyde could things actually get?

He crammed his duffel bag with some more clothes and as many course textbooks as he could. It was only three years until graduation. Then he could go anywhere, do anything, including the Navy or college on the West Coast, away from Rita, Clyde, Conklin, Adrian, Katie, and the state of Maryland. Three years until the rest of his life began. He would see it through, all aces.

From his pin collection, he chose the Green Lantern logo pin. He wanted to take everything, but space would be limited in foster care, and young couples were never in the market to adopt a thirteen-year-old. He looked around his room and wondered how much of his stuff he could reclaim one day. His library, his comic book collection, his clothes—it could be replaced. The only precious item was a Gil Kane original Green Lantern pencil sketch, which he had framed and hung on the wall. He wrapped it in a T-shirt and gingerly placed it in the duffel bag.

The hallway floorboards creaked outside his room, and he froze.

"Where are you going?" Rita asked.

"Away." Daniel resumed packing.

"Away where?"

"You told me not to came back if I walked out the door. So I'm out of here."

"To live where? What are you going to do?"

"Katie said I could stay at her house. I need time away from here."

"You're going to the sheriff, aren't you? You're going to lie. You're going to screw your family."

The family was screwed already. Denial was Rita's way of coping with her life. Daniel was just collateral damage—expendable. This made him angry.

"Lie? I lied earlier today to protect this freak show of a life," Daniel said. "You never lifted a finger to help me. Now I'm telling the truth."

"You ungrateful little bastard," Rita continued. "You don't know anything. How much we've sacrificed for you . . . *I've* sacrificed for you. Do you know how much easier it would have been for me to find a husband if I didn't have a brat clinging to my skirt? I kept you even after John died. That's right, you little shit. I'm *not* your real mother. John wanted a family, but he couldn't have kids. So we adopted you. Then he died and left me stuck with you."

Daniel was shocked. Not at the news, which he'd known for years thanks to Clyde's drunken rants, but the manner in which Rita chose to tell him. Like Clyde, she tried to poison his link to John Hauer, the only father he had ever known. Nothing of John endured in her anymore. Her transformation was complete—she was Clyde's handiwork, body and soul. So, Rita wanted to play the "truth" game. *The truth shall set you free,* he thought.

"I saw Clyde earlier," Daniel said. "He was having sex with

that woman from the hospital in the cab of her pickup. Turns out she's Principal Conklin's daughter. I think they've been *friends* for a while."

Rita's fists were balled. She filled the exit with her enraged presence. Daniel recognized a new crossroad in his life. One where Rita would start pounding on him, too, if he stuck around. More than just unwilling to let her hide reality from herself any longer, he challenged her place in the hierarchy, such as it was. Daniel was coming into his own, butting heads with the top, and she would either have to find some way to reclaim her station or yield to him. He felt sorry for her. She was a victim, a creation of Clyde Knoffler's, but he could no longer submit to her skewed view of the world.

"I'm tired, Mom. I can't do this anymore. I can't be a punching bag. I can't keep getting slammed for doing the right thing. This family is killing me, and I want out."

Rita walked up to Daniel and tried to slap him, but he grabbed her wrist and twisted until she was off balance, then he pushed her away. She lost her balance and hit her head on the bureau on the way down. She was dazed. A wave of guilt suddenly hit him. Daniel tried to help her up but she batted his hand away. He gave up, grabbed his bags, and walked out.

Descending the stairs, he stopped halfway just as Clyde wobbled in through the front door.

"Where the hell are *you* going?" Clyde said. His breath preceded him.

Clyde only ever returned home early to get money or beat his family. The fear that had paralyzed Daniel in the past, however, was kept in check this time. His decision to leave, to let loose the pretense of this family and all the chains that bound him to this existence, spurred him to new possibilities. The start of a new chapter in his story brought with it new reactions to old stimuli. Clyde no longer dictated the narrative. Cowering in fear in the face of his stepfather's wrath was an archaic response. If anything, catching Clyde in a crude act of adultery, in its prosaic glory, emphasized the man's base character. No one who spent the majority of his life staggering and stumbling as his primary mode of mobility could be the threat Daniel had envisioned him. Even Clyde was vulnerable.

Looking down on him from the middle of the stairs, Daniel said, "I'm out of here. That's what you wanted, right? You don't have to look at my ugly face anymore."

"Just like that? You think you can leave?"

"Yeah. Just like that."

"Think you can just leave and stick us with the bill for your lawsuit? That's right, I heard all about it. Uh-uh. No way."

"All the money we're paying out, the school desks, my expulsion, the lawsuit, it's all because you stuck your dick into Principal Conklin's daughter."

Clyde looked around nervously. "Shut your mouth, boy. You say one word about that to anyone and I'll kill you."

"Mom knows, but she's too beaten down to ever divorce your ass."

Clyde ascended the stairs with clenched fists. "You little shit . . ."

Daniel slammed him square in the face with his bag full of texts and sent the man reeling backward, grasping for the banister but too drunk to find it. Clyde landed on his back on the edge of the first stair and floor. Sprays of spit shot from his mouth as he yowled.

"I'm gonna rip you apart, you piece of shit," Clyde bellowed. "And not gentle, like before!"

Daniel jumped from the middle stair and landed on his stepfather's breadbasket. He heard a rib crack, and Clyde vomited the contents of his stomach over his own face. He choked on his own puke as Daniel leaped off him and made for the exit, but not before a hand grabbed his ankle, causing him to fall into the door headfirst. Daniel saw spots and struggled not to black out.

Clyde turned over, ready to get up. Daniel thrust his free foot into the man's face repeatedly, but Clyde was so drunk, his pain threshold was beyond Daniel's ability to breach. Clyde exposed his torso as he struggled to stand. Daniel let loose a solid shot to the cracked rib. Clyde yelped and let go. Daniel stood and swung his duffel bag into his foe to knock him down and nearly drove his own cracked rib into his lung in the process. He heard his picture frame crack within the bag.

Rita froze on the stairs. She stared silent and still at the scene unfolding below.

Clyde grabbed the duffel and threw it aside. Then he grabbed Daniel by the throat and dragged him into the dining room. He picked the boy up and slammed him into the dining room table, splintering it. Daniel grabbed one of the broken table legs, swung it, and missed. Clyde caught the piece on the backswing, pulled it from Daniel's hand, and threw it aside. Then he grabbed the boy by the throat again. The grip was a vise. Daniel clawed and scratched the arm to no avail. He thrashed his hands around trying to find something he could use as a weapon.

He remembered his pin. He unclasped it, bent the pin outward with his thumb and in one swift move jabbed it into Clyde's left eye. Clyde screamed and stumbled back. Daniel rushed him, blocking into his gut. He heard the rib crack again. They fell backward onto the shattered dining room table with Daniel on top. Clyde became still, almost frozen. His body tensed and then he coughed up blood. Daniel scrambled off and stood back. Clyde's one eye stared wide in shock. The man looked ludicrous with a Green Lantern monocle pinned to his eye. He coughed up more blood, and that's when Daniel noticed a section of Clyde's shirt, pitched up like a tent. A bloodstain soaked into the cotton at the point.

Daniel didn't need to be an anatomy expert to know that something important in Clyde had been pierced by a shattered table leg. Clyde extended one shaking hand upward toward the boy, but whether this was a plea for help or a last-ditch effort to throttle him was unknown. Clyde peed his trousers. His breathing became shallow.

"Oh God! Oh God!" Rita yelled, unfrozen and running down the rest of the stairs.

Penny waddled into the room. When she saw her daddy on the floor exhaling blood, she began to cry.

"Penny, go into the kitchen," Daniel ordered. But the girl just stared and wailed.

Clyde tried to roll onto his side but was staked to the spot. His breath was a gurgle, as though breathing submerged. He vomited more blood, but gravity forced it back into his throat. Clyde was drowning on many different levels; his face turned blue.

"Oh God," Rita repeated, hovering over her husband, frantic, but afraid to touch him.

Clyde convulsed, causing the shattered table leg to slide farther. He was having a seizure. Then as quickly as it started, Clyde just stopped.

He lay there with crimson streams running from him like a mountain in a spring rain.

"Oh my Lord," Rita whispered hoarsely. "Oh, God . . ."

Daniel went cold. He couldn't believe this was happening. It was a dream, a fantasy. Things like this happened on the nightly news to other people.

Daniel went to Penny and got down on one knee. "It was an accident," he pleaded. "I'm sorry . . ."

Howling, she pulled away from him.

"Penny . . ."

"You killed her father!" Rita cried. "You son of a bitch, you killed my husband."

The accusation shook him. Daniel couldn't remember the last time Rita referred to Clyde as her husband. For years he had cheated on her, squandered her fortune, basically shat on her, and all of a sudden he was her husband.

"He came at me . . ."

The boy collected his wits. There would be no finishing high school, no amending his friendship with Adrian, no second chance at Katie Millar, not even a kind word from his mother or his principal at his murder trial about what a good kid he was. His life, if he remained, was over.

Daniel grabbed his cap and jacket off the hook. He had to follow his instincts. After all, they were often correct. Over Rita's lamentations and Penny's sonic bawling, he walked out the door and never looked back.

CHAPTER 16

LOSER²

1

"The rumor is that he's Athelstan's bastard," Seth heard Lelani whisper.

Somewhere between sleep and consciousness, he was vaguely aware of lying on the couch in Ben's cabana. A pain in his temple throbbed like a tequila hangover, but he felt cheated out of the blissful state that always preceded one. He opened one eye the width of a hair. Cal, Lelani, and Cat sat around the dinette. A balmy breeze blowing in from the dark ocean carried their conversation to his curious ears.

"So, Cal's instincts were right," Cat said. "Seth did sabotage the mission. Maybe out of revenge for being abandoned by his father?"

It was true, Seth thought. He did ruin the mission. But not for any slight against him that he could remember. He still couldn't remember his life before the arrival. Even the memory of that night was like a lost scene out of a B film watched drunk at 4:00 A.M. back in high school. They were not a conscious part of him as though he lived the events, yet, he knew that what transpired was fact. The protection spell Lelani mentioned previously might be disrupting his memories of Aandor, but he was sure what he saw in Rosencrantz's memory enchantment was true. He just couldn't be sure whether he screwed up as usual or did it on purpose. He hoped it was an accident.

"No," said Lelani, adopting the unlikely role of his advocate. "Seth never knew who his father was even in Aandor. It would explain his scholarship, though. The nobility often sponsors apprenticeships for its bastards. It's considered bad form not to. Seth showed no interest for the craft, though. His presence in the school was a source of much speculation."

"You people have a strange way of running a society," Cat remarked.

"We saw him use that spell," Cal said irritably.

"That spell of false memory was prepared by Magnus Proust to superimpose fabricated identities and a working knowledge of English on your memory anagrams. Like a supplement to what you already knew, they were to be transparent memories, allowing you to remember your true origins, while functioning seamlessly in American society."

"So what went wrong?" Cal said. "What caused everyone to drift away and forget their duties . . . their very identities?"

I cast it wrong, Seth thought.

"He panicked," said Lelani. "Seth should have cast the spell for each of you individually. The parchment was imbued with a specific identity marker for each member. Instead, he tried to cast it en masse and read the initiation line multiple times, once for each member of the party, building up the potency of the spell. It was cast hundreds of times more powerfully than intended. It overrode your memories and submerged your true identities. A massive jumble; you were not even left with the unencumbered history of the fictional personalities that were created for you."

"They all got amnesia," Cat said.

"My God," Cal said. "We're lucky Galen and Linnea drifted off with the baby still in their arms. If they'd left the boy in the meadow . . ."

"That was the palace groundskeeper and his wife? Their spell was programmed to have them to act as the infant's parents, just as Lita and Parham Raincrest were to be Seth's guardians. The original mission was to find a safe community to blend into, purchase homes close to each other, and raise the boy to adulthood."

A catastrophic blunder, Seth thought.

"That idiot should never have been the group's mage," Cal said with the sureness of a military commander. "No matter who his father is."

Seth's headache grew worse, a pressure behind the eyes that felt strong enough to evict his orbs from their cavities.

"The duke would have sent his whole family across if it were possible," Lelani said. "There was a time limit and some concerns as to how many souls could be safely navigated through universes at one time."

"To save both sons, the duke jeopardized the life of the one that mattered," Cal said.

"We don't know for certain that Seth is . . ."

"And the team . . . all those people . . . ," Cal continued, lost in his anger.

"Rosencrantz cast that recollection spell across the planet," Lelani said. "It's too late for Fronik, but as of this moment, those who are still alive are waking up from a long dream. Now at least they know they might be in danger. If they are true to their oaths, they will attempt to find us."

The more Seth listened to their conversation, the more it drove the point that *he* had ruined all these people's lives. Fronik and Tristan were dead. So was his roommate, Joe. How many more were dead because of his mistakes? Was the infant, his possible half-brother, dead, too? Seth always hoped to reclaim the life his amnesia stole. He never imagined there'd be a day when he'd prefer to have his memories begin the day the fire killed his parents. At least in ignorance, the only life he knew to have ruined was his own. He didn't want to hear anymore about his screwup.

"I don't remember any life in another world," he said, in a raspy voice, revealing he was conscious.

"That's because of the shield protecting you," Lelani said. "Even Rosencrantz had trouble pulling you into his spell."

"Lucky me. What I need is a shield to protect me from traveling companions talking shit about me when I'm sleeping six feet away. Ben has eight bedrooms, you know." Seth glanced over to see their reactions.

Cat looked into her cup as she stirred her tea and Lelani processed him with a detached look. Cal looked fit for murder.

"The captain wanted you in plain sight," Lelani said.

Just then, Ben and Helen walked in from the beach holding freshly caught fish. The sun was past set, a faint line of yellow lay on the horizon, blending rapidly with the rich indigo sky. "Hiya, folks," Helen said. "Got us some dinner fresh from the backyard."

"We've already imposed enough," Cal said. "We should go."

"Go? Where?" Ben asked. "It's dark back in those woods up

north. I doubt you'd find your car before you froze to death, or worse, maybe run into a gnoll that you missed. Stay the night."

"Ben, you're an angel," Cat said. "We accept."

"But—" Cal started.

"But what?" Cat cut him off. "Rush back and freeze in the woods? We need sleep."

Seth could tell who wore the pants in the MacDonnell clan. They'd stay the night.

He retired to the patio, then onto the beach, and used Ben's campfire to light a cig. The fish were cooking on a spit above the fire, rubbed in spices and salt. They smelled good. The beautiful scenery and the fire's gentle heat conflicted with his feelings. He headed back into the kitchen. The group around the table ceased their conversation on his approach and remained silent, as though they had run out of words.

Seth exited through the kitchen portal and entered the trailer in New York State. The winter air was more simpatico with his mood. There, among the books and periodicals, Seth sat on the precipice of two worlds. It occurred to him a cigarette among so much yellowed paper might not be prudent. He went outside, where his breath painted a frosty path before him. The winter stars were bright in a way they could never be in Manhattan. Tomorrow would be a new day, but Seth could not escape the nagging revelation about his true nature. He was a loser in two universes.

He had always blamed his nature, admittedly selfish, on his abandonment—on his lack of a loving family. He just assumed no one cared enough to come find him. Life had dealt him a fucked-up hand, so what did he have to be happy about? His dead roommate was right—Seth never put his neck out for anything or anyone. After all, if he didn't try, he couldn't fail; and if he never tried, he could never be disappointed. But the last forty-eight hours changed all that. He was a screwup preamnesia, too. He came from a place where he was a part of something bigger than just himself, where he had history, and even this hadn't prevented him from committing a horrible mistake.

"Penny for your thoughts?" Ben said, coming out of the trailer. He hung a camping lantern on a hook by the door and approached Seth.

"They're not worth that much," Seth said.

"How can anyone look at a sky like this and wear such a sour puss?"

"Today I learned that I hurt a lot of people. A helpless baby was lost because of me. Three people are dead."

"That's pretty rough." Ben prodded a fallen branch with the tip of his boot. He considered Seth's confession.

Vocalizing his blunder made it more real. Seth couldn't remember the last time a mistake bothered him so deeply. He couldn't remember the last time he apologized for anything.

"Did ya mean to do it?" Ben asked.

"No!" That sounded more certain than Seth felt. How could he know for sure?

"Then, do better tomorrow."

"Easy to say. I'm not good at . . ." Seth lost his train of thought. He didn't know what he was trying to convey. He was not even certain about his own mind. He was emotionally detached from the events he witnessed, yet felt the remorse of failure. Remorse, like an unchallenged muscle, atrophies without use. It'd been a long time since he'd truly been sorry for actions of his that caused others pain. His role for the life that he knew was that of "the abandoned angry guy," who watched others get the breaks they took for granted. The world had always been in the position of owing him. Until today.

"I'm not good at anything," Seth finally said. "I'm not . . . good."

"Good?" Ben looked at him as an art teacher studies a student's work. "What the hell is 'good'?"

"You know . . . 'good.' As in, 'not bad.'"

Ben shifted like a welterweight, ready to go ten rounds. "No one knows what 'good' is. The concept of *good* is subjective."

Seth wasn't buying it. It trivialized his self-revelations and smacked of pop psychology. His silence must have broadcasted this to Ben. The old man retrenched and took on a more learned demeanor that belied his working-class façade.

"Look, son, there was this incident back in World War Two. My unit was ordered to take the town of Bernay from the Germans, see. We were a bunch of scared punks, bragging about women we didn't have and money we'd never earn. What did we know about anything? In the hoopla of a firefight, some young local farm kids got killed. It didn't take long to figure out our bullets killed them. Those Nazi cowards used them as shields. One young boy had his beautiful blue eyes blown out of his head. That boy's face still haunts me today, clear as the day it happened. His eyes looking up at me from the dirt, accusing me of killing him. We were ready to give it up right then. I thought of turning my pistol on my own head a couple of times. How could I go home, face my parents, my brothers and sisters after that? When we won, the townsfolk surrounded us with cheers and beers. No American soldier left Bernay a virgin. But I didn't feel like a hero. I didn't feel 'good.' None of us ever talked about it. Just kept it in, the shame, the guilt. Took me years to move beyond that day. I still look at my own kids sometimes and shudder. What if one of them got shot? There but for the grace of God . . ."

"Great story, Ben. Really cheered me up."

"Don't be a punk-ass," Ben said. "We didn't set out that day to do a bad thing. That mistake didn't represent my character, I know that now. But at the time I was too close to see it. Give it time, Seth. The past can drag you down like an anchor. It'll drown you. But the days ahead are unwritten. They're full of potential. So whatever you think good is, fix it in your head and work toward it."

"What if I thought good was ridding the world of American imperialism through suicide bombing?"

"You wouldn't be out here beating yourself up if you thought like that," Ben said. "Look, you remind me of my youngest son. The missus and I were working a lot, trying to put the older kids through college. As a teen, he got into gangs, drugs, petty theft, getting girls pregnant, you name it. Stayed that way until he was twenty-five. Today, he's a youth counselor earning his masters in social work.

"The way you carry yourself, thumb your nose at everything, you strike me as someone who didn't get enough attention as a kid," Ben continued. "Your antics are for getting everyone to notice that you don't care that no one cares about you, like some adolescent tantrum. Grow up. Be an adult. If you really want re-demption, you'll find it. Life always throws you opportunities when you least expect them."

Seth thought it unlikely. The weight of his history was more than his capacity to bear. Still, he considered Ben's words. "You still think about those kids?" Seth asked.

"Yes. They'd have been parents themselves today if they lived. But I won't let one bad moment define me. I'm Benito Hector Marin Reyes—father, husband, deacon of my church, town alderman, and retired draftsman. A good man who made a horrible mistake once." Ben swallowed with the strength of a general holding back tears.

Here was a man, living with a horrible act, who refused to give up and went on to accomplish great things, Seth realized. Out of all the people in the world, the last living sorcerer on earth picked him to be its guardian. Seth wasn't much older than Ben was when he stormed Bernay. Perhaps there was time to do better. Seth's eyelids grew heavy. He would kick Ben's words around in his head and decide how to apply them in the morning. Then he remembered something the tree said; something about Lelani's translations.

"Ben. Rosencrantz appreciates all you've done for it," Seth said with a strange confidence.

"Yeah?"

"Yeah. It said, 'the keeper's saplings will know fortune.'"

"What does that mean?"

"You're the keeper. Fortune will be with your descendants. Your family line is blessed because of your work here. It's the tree's way of paying you . . . of thanking you. Communicating this to you is its price for helping us. Don't ask me why I know this. But I'm pretty sure of it."

Ben smiled and finally gave way to the tears he'd been holding back. "Well how 'bout that," he said.

Seth grinned. Being the bearer of good news warmed him in the cold night air. It felt *good,* whatever that was.

Seth breathed deeply, grateful for the pristine northern

breeze. Suddenly, his hackles rose. There was something impure in that last whiff. He heard the distant crunching of snow from several directions in the darkness around them.

"Ben, walk back to the trailer slowly," Seth whispered. "Act like nothing's wrong." Seth walked in the opposite direction, away from the trailer and toward Rosencrantz.

"Seth?" Ben whispered.

"Just do it," Seth stressed, in hushed tones.

Seth pretended to pick up kindling wood around Rosencrantz's base. He hoped the tree wouldn't be offended. Ben made it to the door. The next moment, there were whistling sounds in the air. Seth ducked in time to avoid a bolt. It flew over him. Another hit Rosencrantz's trunk. From the trailer door, Ben let out an agonizing scream. A shaft had pierced his thigh. He fell into the trailer. Two more bolts penetrated the aluminum door just as Ben shut it behind him.

Seth heard more whistling and rolled to the other side of Rosencrantz. The tree took two more hits. Seth wondered if the tree suffered pain in real time. Seth found a fallen branch large enough to make a good club. The crunch of boots drew closer then stopped. Seth didn't dare move. Any sound would give away his position.

With the stars out in force, he could at least see a few feet around him. He made out two shapes approaching the trailer. The edge of the lantern light touched on their . . . *fur!* Gnolls!

Shit, he thought. Seth closed his eyes and listened for the ones that were still out in the darkness. The crunching was closer. They were creeping right toward him. *Shit, shit, shit!* Lelani had said gnolls were nocturnal. He was a sitting duck. But why weren't they on him already?

Seth sought out the ones closer to him. He saw their eyes floating in the darkness, reflecting the light from the lantern like possums on a country road. *The lantern!* Seth realized. It screwed up their night vision. They couldn't see him there. But it wouldn't last. Another second and the gnolls by the trailer would extinguish that light.

Seth searched for another branch within arm's reach, a smaller one than his club. He found one and lifted it quietly. Without getting up, he hurled it behind him as far as he could into the meadow. When it landed, he heard whistling and the thud of bolts hitting that spot. The crunches now headed toward that area. Seth crept to the other side of Rosencrantz with his makeshift club.

The two at the trailer smashed the lantern. The feeble light that eked out of the trailer window was useless. The earth became black under the starry heavens. Seth shivered, his clothes wet from lying on the ground.

With crossbows drawn, the gnolls at the trailer opened the door.

Ben! Seth panicked.

One gnoll's head exploded at the discharge of a pistol. The other gnoll shot a bolt into the trailer, just as a second blast painted the ground with its guts. Cal stepped out, a pistol in each hand. He put another round between the thing's eyes.

The group near Seth showered the trailer with bolts. The gnolls charged Cal even as the cop stormed into the night, firing two-fisted into their midst. The gnolls' path would take them past Rosencrantz and Seth. The one in the lead was huge, at least seven feet. The smallest in the group was about Seth's height. He stayed back to take what Seth thought was a drink, but was in fact putting his lips to a horn. Seth was frozen as the beastie blew out a long alarm into the night. The first two gnolls passed by him. The one with the horn moved to rejoin his brothers, but when he was close enough, Seth stuck his club out and tripped him.

The gnoll held on to its crossbow as it rolled. It fired at Seth, who held his club in front of him like a shield. The bolt punched through the branch and glanced off one of Seth's ribs.

"Fucking shit!" Seth yelled.

He raised the club and swung it down on the beast, who caught it before the branch could connect with its head. The gnoll twisted the club. Seth refused to let go and soon found himself off balance, then on his back. They rolled on the ground, struggling with the club between them. Seth managed to get on top. The thing had the most horrible breath, like a garbage truck in a heat wave. Behind them more gunshots, but Seth couldn't spare the concentration. Feral jaws snapped at him. Seth tried to bring the branch between him and the beast's canine teeth. He realized he was losing this tug-of-war just as a fourth and fifth gnoll entered his peripheral vision, charging from the night.

A whistling noise sounded. Seth braced for the arrow's impact but heard one of the rushing gnolls whimper and gurgle instead. Lelani vaulted over Seth, longbow in hand, as she charged the remaining gnoll.

"Hold tight," she shouted to Seth as she passed him, rushing the remaining gnoll.

Do I have a choice? Seth thought.

Seth lost his leverage and his opponent flipped him over. He landed on one of the dead gnolls. Its head had been blown apart. Seth caught a glance of Cal in hand-to-hand with the biggest brute of the pack as he tumbled over.

Seth's adversary was on its feet already. Seth's hand fell on the dead gnoll's crossbow. A drawn bolt was already in the chamber. His opponent lunged at him. He picked up the crossbow and fired in one motion, hitting the creature on its side below the rib cage. The creature landed on him, pushing him to the ground with the crossbow between their faces. Again, a small wooden obstacle came between him and a set of killer jaws. His luck couldn't last for long. The thing was enraged—thrashing wildly from the pain of the bolt. Its claws tore into Seth's arms and shoulders. Seth pulled his knees toward his chest and managed to get his feet under the gnoll's stomach. With all of his ebbing strength, he pushed the thing off him and scrambled away.

Cal and his gnoll were between Seth and the trailer; Lelani's battle was to his side. Seth found himself weaponless with Rosencrantz at his back. He leaned against the tree for support. The bark was warm as flesh. He became a conduit for the tree's energy. Heat traveled through Seth's body, tingling, giving him a boost.

The wounded gnoll lunged at him. Seth put his hands up and soon gripped fur. A gentle heat traveled through him, and where Seth touched the gnoll with his hand the thing's flesh melted into slag. The thing let out an inhuman howl of pain, nearly shattering Seth's eardrum. Not questioning how, Seth seized the gnoll at its throat and again the flesh melted at his touch. The energy from Rosencrantz flowed from his hand on the trunk and through his body. He held his grip, pushing farther back, like a hot poker driven into butter. The dripping sludge of muscle and bone could no longer hold the creature's head to its body. The gnoll's head rolled off its shoulders, frozen in its shocked expression as it hit the ground. Seth pushed the thing's hairy headless corpse away.

He looked around.

The giant gnoll had pinned Cal down. The cop jabbed it with his hunting knife, but the beast used his feral claws to rip apart Cal's body armor. A shot rang out in the night. The big gnoll howled in pain. He bled from the neck. Cat leaned against the trailer door, a smoking hunting rifle in hand. Helen came up right beside her holding a shotgun. The gnoll abandoned the cop and lunged at the women, but Cat stood her ground and fired again.

The beast fell on its face and skidded to their feet from sheer momentum. Helen fired once more into the back of its head for good measure. "That's for Ben, you son of a bitch," she said.

Seth relinquished his grip on the tree. The winter chill enveloped him, like exiting a Jacuzzi on a cool day. He ran toward Cal, picking up another thick branch en route. His hand was sticky with melted flesh and cooked blood. Cal rose and examined himself for wounds. Cat hobbled to him on her air cast and crutch, while Helen guarded the trailer door.

"Oh God!" Cat exclaimed. "Cal, are you . . ."

"Fine," said the cop. "My vest took the brunt of it."

The last remaining gnoll in the party, realizing he was outnumbered, backed into the darkness around them.

"Where'd that fucker go?" Seth asked.

"He's out there," Cal said. "We need to get after it."

"Not a good idea, dude," Seth said. "I think the little one got a call off to his buddies. He had a horn."

They heard a horn, emanating from the direction of the gnoll that had just left. The sound echoed through the night and sent a shiver of dread down Seth's back. "It sounded a lot like that," he added.

"Great! Good work, porn star."

Seth resisted the urge to tell Cal to go fuck himself. They heard a crunch to their left and raised their weapons.

"It's just me," said Lelani, coming out of the darkness.

Under the starry light, Seth glimpsed the silhouette of her equestrian half; her human legs were translucent. The image looked like movie projections superimposed. Her illusion was stronger in the day because it utilized light, and in its absence it waned. It was odd to Seth that he understood that . . . a law of magic that he recognized, the way a science student accepts planetary mass. It was starting to come back—cracks in the dam that concealed his earlier life.

"Lelani," Cal said, "we've got to brighten this area up before reinforcements arrive. We're dead in the dark."

Ben came out of the trailer with three more lanterns and two gallons of kerosene. His injured leg was bound with a tourniquet. Helen covered him as he hobbled about placing lights around the trailer.

"Ben, what are you doing out here, you old coot," his wife said.

"Stop nagging. I'm the same age as you are."

"Well I'm too old for this malarkey, too, but I wasn't shot in the leg with an arrow," she responded.

"That's not going to be enough," Cal said to them. "We need to really light this area up."

"What about Rosencrantz?" Seth asked. "He just helped me out." Seth held out his sludge-marked hands.

"Yes!" Lelani agreed. "Rosencrantz is an experienced mage, but he needs a conduit to cause effects in real time." She went to the tree and placed both hands on its trunk. Lelani closed her eyes and began to commune with the great wizard. Seth couldn't explain how, but he could see the tree's life energy flow through the centaur, and he was sure the others could not. Even from a few feet away, Seth felt heat radiate from her, the same sensation he experienced earlier. Lelani was wrapped in a warm glow; a rosiness filled her cheeks, similar to what you'd see on an expecting mother. Seth had a bunch of tree-hugging friends that had often talked about the health benefits of communing with nature. He always thought they were cool in their own odd, crunchy way, but he never thought in a million years they'd ever be proven right.

"They are close," Lelani said. "A large party approaches from the south, about three hundred yards. A mix of humans and gnolls. They have a sorcerer!"

Three whips of strong wind hit the lanterns and shattered them.

"Seth!" barked the cop.

What now? Seth thought.

"Grab an armful of magazines from the trailer and start building piles about fifteen feet apart to the south of us. Douse them with kerosene."

"Gee whiz, is that really necessary?" Ben whined.

"Ben!" Helen, scolded.

"What about the human dudes?" Seth asked. "Fire's just going to help them see us."

Helen was already in and out the trailer door with the first batch of magazines. "You always said these things would come in handy one day, Ben. Time to put them to good use, or we won't be around to read anything no more."

Ben picked up Helen's shotgun and helped Cat cover her as she piled magazines.

Seth stood his ground. "Look, we should go back to the cabana in Puerto Rico and shut the door behind us. Cut off the conduit. No death, no mayhem . . . easy breezy."

Cal grabbed the photographer by his collar and lifted him to within an inch of his face. "How do we get back then? Do we let them set up camp right beside Rosencrantz? What if they douse the tree with kerosene for helping us." He threw Seth to the ground in disgust. "You going to let that old woman do all the work?"

Seth fumed. It wasn't fair. He had risked his skin to help Ben get to safety. He had used a tree branch to fight these crossbow-wielding monsters while the cop was armed with pistols and wearing Kevlar.

"That's right!" Seth shouted back at the cop. "She's an old lady and he's an old man with a hole in his fucking leg! You're a dad with a kid in the Bronx and a wife with a busted ankle that's scared out of her wits! How am I the fucking bad guy for saying we get the hell out of here?"

Cal was about to respond, but Seth yelled first, "Go fuck yourself." He walked off muttering and took an armful of magazines from Helen for the fire.

Seth built up the pile that was farthest out from the trailer.

He knew the bad guys were gathering out there in the dark, but he wanted to get it at least three feet high. As he stacked and rolled the magazines, his hand fell across a copy of *Action Comics* number one, the first appearance of Superman. The artist in him was awestruck. It was one of the most iconic images ever created. In the picture, Superman lifted a car over his head and smashed it into a rock. There were a few others, too. *Whiz Comics, Detective Comics* . . . Seth wrapped them around his shins and snapped his tube socks over them, securing them to his legs. He realized what an optimistic gesture that was in light of what was coming toward them. Then again, if he survived, he'd never forgive himself for passing up the opportunity. *A few less magazines isn't going to make any difference in the end.*

Seth poured kerosene over the periodicals and lit his fire. He used a rolled-up issue of *Life* magazine from the 1940s to transfer the flame to the other piles Ben and Helen built. Four pyres in a line from west to east blocked the southern access to Rosencrantz and the trailer.

Cal surveyed the setup, then said, "Cat, how many rounds do you have?"

"Five."

"Climb up Lelani's back and take a position with the rifle in one of Rosencrantz's lower branches."

"Climb? Cal, I'm on one foot, and my arm still hurts from that arrow I took earlier."

"I know it's tough, honey, but gnolls are not good climbers. They're evolved canines, not felines. And you can cover Lelani from up there so she can stay with the tree longer." Cal looked to the caretakers. The temptation to send them back home was written all over his face. But he needed the old couple, and they wanted to help. "Helen, take a position in the doorway of the trailer. Ben, do you have a weapon?"

Ben reached into the trailer along the side of the doorway and produced a wood ax.

"Good," said Cal. "Crouch by the trailer hitch." Seth was impressed with Cal's strategy. He placed the couple close enough to the trailer for them to escape in case things went wrong. "Get back and sever the link if you have to," he told them. They both nodded *okay*.

The flames were already six feet high. Light flooded the area between the trailer and the tree. Seth was grateful for the heat that dried out his damp clothes.

"We don't have enough paper to keep this up too long," Seth noted. "They might just wait for these pyres to die out."

Cal considered this. "Lelani, where are they now?" he asked.

"They've stopped. About a hundred yards due south observing us; six gnolls and five humans. Rosencrantz and I have countered several spells from their mage already. They're confused. Based on the rudimentary nature of their sorcerer's spells, I don't think they are even aware of Rosencrantz's existence. It's likely when they came to this reality, Dorn walked right past him and did not realize he was sentient."

"That's our advantage," Cal said. "We need to go on the offensive. What I wouldn't give for a pair of night-vision goggles."

A light went on in Lelani's eyes. "I have an idea along those lines," she said. "But in the reverse . . . with Rosencrantz's help, of course." She closed her eyes and chanted, communing with the tree. The heat that emanated from her washed over them like a warm wind, and coursed into the woods beyond. Whatever this spell was, it was big. She released the tree and picked up her composite longbow and quiver.

"What are you doing?" Cat asked.

"Taking the battle to them." Lelani searched the meadow for a sign.

"That's suicide in the dark," Seth said.

"Darkness is relative," she said with a smile. "Sometimes you bring on the dark by turning up the light."

"Have you lost your marbles?" Seth asked her.

"This entire meadow and parts of the forest are within Rosencrantz's sphere of control."

"So we're going to ask Bambi to attack them for us?"

Lelani continued to search deeply into the night. "Seth, I will need you to stay in physical contact with Rosencrantz. He needs to be connected with one of us to effect change in real time."

"Cat's already in the tree," Seth pointed out.

"Cat is not attuned to the magical energies flowing through this meadow. It has to be a mage."

"I can't do magic," Seth argued. "I don't remember going to school or anything."

Lelani continued to search the darkness. "That doesn't matter," she said. "Once you are in a symbiotic connection with the tree, he will guide you. You are waiting for a particular spell I will cast once I've confronted their sorcerer. Rosencrantz will know what to do." Her eyebrow arched and she pointed into the field. "There!"

"Where?" Seth asked.

"There." A small speck of light, like a fallen star, meandered over a black section of the field.

"What is that?" Seth asked. Soon he noticed two more, and then several others—a convention of fireflies had been called. "Where'd the fireflies come from? It's freakin' winter."

"He woke them up early," Ben said. "He is a wizard, after all."

It occurred to Seth that there might be a shortage of fireflies in the area this summer. He didn't know why he had such stupid thoughts in light of what they were about to face—probably because he hoped to live long enough to see whether he was right. More flies poured in from the forest around them. Soon there were hundreds, then thousands, all convening around the enemy. Silhouettes in the shapes of men emerged in the glow.

"I can see them," Cat said. She took aim with her rifle.

"Please hold your fire until they charge you," Lelani said. With that, she bolted out into the night.

"What's going on?" Helen said from the trailer.

"We might actually have a chance," Cal said.

"Well, please explain it to us," a confused Ben inquired.

"Yeah, do some 'splaining," Seth agreed.

2

Lelani raced into the darkness and came to a stop at the snow line halfway between her friends and the strangers. She waited as the fireflies continued to grow in number. Her foes' voices conveyed alarm. They swatted to no avail. The fireflies broke off into separate groups around each enemy combatant. They swarmed over each gnoll's shoulder until a thick globe of swirling light hovered around each head. Now, the darkness served Lelani.

The centaur charged. She moved along the outskirts of the group, staying within the black of the meadow. She didn't need to see her targets clearly. The swirls of light around their heads marked them well. As she galloped, she strung an arrow and let it loose toward the center of the light. She heard the satisfying thud and squeal of a struck gnoll. The fireflies dropped with the gnoll to the ground before dispersing back into the night. She strung a second arrow and let it loose into another bright swirl of flies. This thud was followed by the gurgle and hacking of a punctured throat.

The enemy, in a panic, let fly a squadron of bolts from their crossbows. The first volley dropped fallow as Lelani raced away protected by the dark. They launched a second wild volley covering a wider area. One quarrel found its mark and sank into her hindquarter. She had no time to pull it out. She flew around them launching arrows at will. Three gnolls dead . . . four. The remaining troop abandoned their equipment and ran toward the light at the center of the meadow . . . toward her friends. One man with a staff remained behind. She fired an arrow at him, which he easily deflected with the staff. He stood his ground blocking Lelani's line of sight to his cohorts. But she was no longer interested in them. In the distance, Lelani heard the crack and echo of Cat's rifle. Her allies would deal with that rabble. She came here for *him*.

The man let loose a flame from the tip of his staff that burned the remaining fireflies about him. In the light, she saw that he wore a white polyester leisure suit over a wide-collard shirt. He was swarthy, with a blocky build, long coarse black hair, obsidian eyes, and a thick salt-and-pepper mustache that hung like a horseshoe on a nail. *One of Kraten's desert brethren, no doubt.* She aimed for his heart and let fly another arrow. With a wave, he burned it to a cinder before it touched him. He slammed his staff into the ground. A vibration emanated in a line toward the centaur, upturning snow and earth before finally knocking Lelani off her feet. She landed on the quarrel lodged in her rear; the serrated edges cut into the flesh around her wound. Lelani clenched her teeth through the pain.

She recovered, and vacated the spot a second before flame engulfed it. There was a crudeness to this sorcerer's technique. He had clearly been wielding magic longer than she, but there was no polish to his method. He was a brawler . . . a street fighter who learned his craft in the dusty back alleys of some desert city. His spells were limited in scope—fire and kinetic movement only. He lacked subtlety and had little imagination.

"They send an acolyte to battle me!" he barked at her, in a southern dialect of Verakhoon. "I am K'ttan Dhourobi of Aht Humaydah. I have killed a dozen wizards. You have no hope against me, child."

"And yet, four of your comrades are dead," she answered back.

"I care not for *dog*-men."

Lelani was sure they did not care for him either. She hoped there was a way her team could press that animosity toward their advantage . . . assuming they had a future after this night. Lelani pulled another arrow on her string and fired it. He deflected it easily. She had a good notion by now of his repertoire, his one-dimensional thinking. She needed to position him correctly to exploit these shortcomings. What worried Lelani was that she would have to cast two spells at once and drop her defensive posture. She was fairly sure that he would not counter with transmogrification and that she would not end up a cockroach, crushed under foot. It would be flame or flying knives . . . *a survivable risk.*

He cast a wall of vibration against her. The air between them shimmered, cracked, and boomed from circular vacuums shooting toward her like a tsunami. She got her hands up in time to counter the attack, but it pushed her back several feet, even with her digging into the cold hard ground.

"Defensive spells have their place, acolyte, but they are only half a battle," K'ttan Dhourobi said. "To win, you must attack! Consider this final lesson a gift."

Arrogant windbag. Lelani launched a half-dozen phosphorous spheres at him, which he dissipated with the fire from his staff. Flame and sparks erupted between them like a celebration. Immediately, Lelani cast her second spell and threw it wide. It bypassed K'ttan Dhourobi, and went toward the middle of the meadow. She prayed Seth remained with the tree. It would be her end if he didn't.

Even as she finished casting her spell, Dhourobi had already cast his response, a spell she knew well called *Sentient Wind.* Every dirk, dagger, throwing star, and arrow within his vicinity suddenly flew at her. *Knives it is,* Lelani mused as she tried to avoid them. A throwing star grazed her temple, leaving a long gash that bled into her eyes. A dagger sunk deep into the right side of her lower belly, arrows lodged into her right leg and deltoid, and a dirk shattered her right clavicle. Lelani's scream filled the woods.

She lay there struggling not to black out. K'ttan Dhourobi strolled confidently toward her as he readied his finishing blow. "A noble effort, but your aim was wide." He prepared a flame spell. "I see no reason to prolong your suffering, acolyte. This will only hurt for a minute."

Just as he was about to finish casting it, he spasmed and jerked as though struck from behind. The mage looked around and saw nothing but the clear winter night.

Still not quite sure what had happened to him, the mage returned his attention to Lelani and tried to recast his spell, only to find he could not. He was disoriented. He tried to speak.

"Glwaaaahgthooww blthezbed," he started. "Axxquernfing gbcxwi?"

K'ttan Dhourobi's eyes asked the questions his mouth was unable to construct.

"Brain hex," Lelani said, tapping her temple.

With Rosencrantz's help, Lelani's spell had boomeranged backed and hit the mage unawares. His thoughts muddled, the sorcerer from Verakhoon could not string together, in mind, motion, or tongue, the intricate and delicate motions needed to utilize magical energy; he couldn't cast anything more than a fart. Enraged, he charged Lelani prattling nonsense in a tone that communicated his intent to end her with his bare hands. Lelani pulled the dirk from her collarbone, making an effort not to pass out from the pain. She wasn't strong enough to throw it left-handed. She held it on her palm with the point aimed at her attacker and spoke the verse for *Sentient Wind*. It flew from her hand at K'ttan Dhourobi. Instinctively, he waved his arms in what he believed was the counterspell to ward off such an attack, but it was instead a blithering pantomime of no merit. The dirk pierced the underside of his forearm on the way through his throat and out the base of his skull, pinning his lower arm against him with the back of his wrist wedged against his chin. His hand dangled before his face in a foppish hello as he fell to his knees with a look of incredulous disbelief. The light left his eyes as the rest of him followed suit toward the ground. He landed on his face.

Lelani breathed relief. The blood in her eyes clouded her vision, and she could not tell how her friends fared at the trailer. She tried to get up, but the pain was intense. Lelani fell back under her own weight. Her head spun, darkness corralled her vision and spread toward the center of her remaining sight.

"Oh my," she said, as she finally passed out.

3

Seconds after Lelani bolted from their camp, the darkness swallowed her whole. Seth took his position by the tree and again felt the warmth flow through him. It was a calm, healing heat; even his corns felt great.

"What can you see?" Cal asked Cat, who was positioned above Seth on a thick branch.

"The fireflies are breaking into groups," she said. "Looks like a bunch of floating balls of light."

"They're blind," Cal noted. "The light shrinks their pupils . . . obliterates their night vision. Everyone get ready. They'll be at us soon."

"What?" Seth exclaimed.

"It's on our terms."

"Well, okay then," Seth responded sarcastically.

"Hey!" Cat shouted. "One of those light orbs just dropped and disappeared! And there goes another!"

The group could hear many bolts whistling through the air. They braced for impact, but nothing arrived.

"They're shooting the other way," said Cal. "Trying to take her down."

"Should I fire?" Cat asked.

"No," Cal said. "They'll be on us soon enough."

"Another one down," Cat reported. "Hey . . . !"

"What?" Seth asked.

"Two of those lights are heading this way, fast!"

Seth stepped on one of the dead gnolls by the tree to get a slightly better vantage on the field. Cat MacDonnell was right, the orbs were moving their way. Seth's heart began to race. Cat looked as scared as he felt. He smiled at her and put on a braver face. One ball of light broke off to their right heading west, away from their camp. Seth couldn't blame anyone, even the bad guys, from wanting to distance themselves from all this conflict. As the remaining group approached their well-lit area, Seth was able to make out the other people running alongside the gnoll.

"Cat! Take out that gnoll!" Cal ordered.

Cat aimed at the fireflies and fired. The border pyres were just starting to illuminate them. Seth could make out the fur on the gnoll's body. Cat fired again just below the head. The gnoll whimpered as it went down. The fireflies dispersed. The rest of the gang was on top of them.

Those that made it past the pyres appeared human enough. Two turned toward Cal. A tall Nordic-looking henchman managed to get a bolt off before the cop shot him. The quarrel lodged in a trough in the cop's vest where the gnoll had shredded it earlier. Seth could tell it had broken through when Cal winced. The cop kept firing at the other one, who continued to advance despite several direct hits.

The other two attackers headed toward Seth and Cat. One was tall and ugly, with a protruding lower jaw, similar to the fellow with the cold breath they fought in the tenement in the Bronx. Unlike his counterpart, he had long black hair which he kept tied back in a tail. He wore a white Judas Priest T-shirt and jeans, and nothing else despite the weather, not even shoes. He moved to the left of the tree while the other guy, a portly Mediterranean type in overalls who reminded Seth of Mario from the Donkey Kong games, moved to their right. Seth realized he was at a terrible disadvantage because he had to maintain contact with Rosencrantz.

Cat fired at the giant, but he was quicker than someone that size had a right to be. He rolled toward the pyre closest to the tree as she fired off shot after shot. She only grazed him. He got behind the pyre and kicked a pile of burning wood and paper at the tree with enough force to send streamers into the branches. A smattering of burning material singed Cat and Seth. "Mario" came around the other side.

Cat continued to shoot at the giant, keeping him at an honest distance. That left only the little guy for Seth. The man had heavy eyes with little life in them. His skin was sallow. He had a dagger in his right hand, but didn't have quite the same devotion as the other assailants. In fact, if Seth didn't know any better, this guy wanted to be there less than he did.

"What's the deal, bro," Seth said. "Wanna go home and we call it a night?"

"I wish I could, mister," the guy said with a slight Italian accent. "But they got'a my heart, and I gotta do what they say to get it back."

Seth didn't know what *they got'a my heart* implied, but this guy clearly didn't want to hurt anyone.

"Look man, it's never too late," Seth cajoled.

"I'm sorry," the man said. "But you gotta die."

The guy threw a half-hearted stab, which Seth easily caught at the wrist. Just as with the gnoll, the man's flesh melted under Seth's grasp. The hand with the knife fell away to the ground. The man didn't scream. He looked dumbfounded at his stump. No blood pumped forth . . . a congealed red gel oozed out.

"What the fuck are you?" Seth asked.

Frightened, the man said, "I was a person like you." The man sobbed, but produced no tears. "I no alive!" he shouted in anguish. He shook his head and tore open his shirt. He took out a small piece of paper with numbers on it and handed it to Seth. "You tella Matilda, Lorenzo love her so much," he said. The man took Seth's hand and pressed it to his chest. It melted through, past the empty chamber where his heart should have been, and came out the back. To both their surprise, Lorenzo was still standing, with a hole through his chest and Seth's arm deep into it.

"Oh shit!" Lorenzo shouted. He was in a bigger panic now. "What I gonna do? How I gonna die?"

"How the fuck should I know?" a distressed Seth responded. He had had his fill of bloody sludge for one night. Seth left the tree, pushing Lorenzo backward toward the nearest pyre. He braced his foot against the man's stomach, pulled out his arm from the guy's chest, and pushed him into the fire all in one motion. Lorenzo's cries of terror rang hollow. Seth doubted Lorenzo could actually feel the fire. After all, he took a hole in his chest with barely a whimper. The *idea* of burning alive was probably more than Lorenzo could handle. Seconds later, Lorenzo fell silent. Seth didn't know if he was truly ended or simply found peace with what was happening to him. If burning to ash did not kill that guy, Seth certainly didn't know what else would.

Cal and the other henchman rolled into Seth, knocking him on his butt. The goon had the same baggy eyes and sallow skin as Lorenzo. Cal outclassed his opponent and had him properly pinned, but could not render the man unconscious.

"Won't die?" Seth asked.

"Get back to the damn tree," Cal growled.

"Crap!" Seth said, getting up.

Ben hobbled out from his position near the trailer and hacked at Cal's assailant with his ax. "Get to the tree," Ben told Seth. "I'll help him."

Seth turned around to get back to position, only to find Mr. Seven-Foot Ugly in between him and his destination.

"Cat?" Seth called out. "I thought you were keeping this guy honest."

"Out of bullets," she yelled back.

The giant smiled. Seth realized he couldn't get around the guy to Rosencrantz. Buckshot rang through the air and the giant took a hit to the shoulder. He howled in rage at Helen Reyes on the trailer steps, who then took a second shot at him. Seth grabbed some burning paper and branches and threw it at the giant, singing his own hands in the process. "Shit!" he screamed, and blew on his hands.

The giant stumbled back against the tree, swatting the embers on his clothes. Cat, who was still on the branch above, took the rifle by its barrel turning it into a makeshift club and whacked him in the head with the butt. Seth saw his opportunity and squeaked by the big guy to lay hands on Rosencrantz again. He reached out and grabbed the giant by the arm, but nothing happened.

"I'm not a wight or a filthy gnoll," the giant said in a deep baritone voice that was peppered with nails. He took a swing at Seth, who ducked just in time to see a deep splintering indent punched into Rosencrantz's trunk, instead of his head.

Cat hit him again with the rifle. The giant grabbed the butt this time and yanked the weapon out of her hands. He smashed it against the tree and tried to grab Cat from her branch.

Ben came up from behind and lodged his ax a good three inches into the giant's right hamstring. The giant roared and backhanded Ben. The old man fell back several feet, his head almost falling into one of the pyres. Cal tackled the giant from the side shoving him away from the tree and past the border pyres. Seth wondered what happened to the henchman Cal had been fighting. Someone grabbed Seth's ankle. It was a severed hand. He shook his leg but it wouldn't let go. Ben had done a real good job on that guy with his ax, and now all the pieces were dragging themselves toward Seth. The hand on his ankle began to blister and melt, just like Lorenzo.

"I guess that's a wight," he said to Cat.

"Come here," she said. She placed her foot on his shoulder and then a large portion of her weight.

"What the heck?"

"Help me down," she said. She crouched until she was sitting on Seth's shoulder. Seth squatted until her good foot touched the earth. She grabbed the remnants of the rifle, hopped over to the dismembered man, and used it to sweep the pieces Ben had chopped into a pyre. The fires were getting smaller.

"Helen, we need more magazines," Cat said.

"Is Ben all right?" Helen asked.

Cat spotted Ben on the ground and rushed over to him. Ben had a cut across his head and a shiner on his cheek where the giant hit him. "Ben, are you okay?"

"I feel like Muhammad Ali in '71, when he was introduced to Frazier's left hook," Ben said. He smiled to advertise that he was fine.

Cat searched for Cal and the giant. They were beyond the compound, out there in the dark. Seth could hear the struggle. He didn't know what they would do if it was the giant that returned. Cat borrowed Helen's shotgun and walked into the dark toward the sounds. Seth wished Lelani would do her thing so he could go hide under the trailer.

"Come on tree . . . talk to me," Seth said. "Tell me what to do." Seth climbed up Rosencrantz, using the giant's indent in the trunk as a foothold, and took position on the big branch. In the meadow where Lelani fought, he saw a fireworks show like the type you see on the fourth of July. "Give 'em hell, Red," he muttered under his breath. Then he heard Lelani scream. The sound cut through the night like a razor and chilled him to the bone. Seth thought something went horribly wrong. *She failed.* Then everything slowed, moving as though underwater. Something was coming at him from the meadow, and he knew . . . Seth knew this was it. He somehow knew to open his arms wide as though to catch a medicine ball. The force entered his embrace still crackling with potency, looking for its target to rewrite laws of physics in a way this universe was not used to. The energy flowed through his right arm around to his left, which he aimed toward the spell's point of origin, and it exited back toward the south meadow. Time started again.

4

Cat walked out of their well-lit "safe" zone and into the dark after her husband. The giant wouldn't be able to see in the dark any better than Cal could, so he had no special advantage other than his size. At least, that's what she hoped. Cal could handle a larger assailant. He was the best hand-to-hand fighter in the NYPD. But everyone could use a little extra help. Cat kept her finger off the shotgun trigger; she didn't want to accidentally shoot her husband.

A few yards away from the pyres, the meadow was tranquil. It belied the actions going on around it. The earth was a solid black mass. She wouldn't see a mouse if it walked right up to her. The clouds from earlier in the day had moved on, the stars were out in force—spectators to the drama unfolding on the world stage below. Cat could see the top of the tree line along the edge of the meadow. She had forgotten how many shades of black were possible in the country.

In the distance, sparks and powerful flashes erupted, illuminating the tree line and revealing the two mages in heated battle. Cat was comforted that the centaur was still alive. The light also revealed two large silhouettes grappling about twenty-five feet ahead of her. The pyrotechnics died, but she was already halfway to her husband as the light faded.

Lelani let out a scream that made Cat freeze. She thought for a moment that the centaur might need her help more than Cal, but she made the difficult decision to look after her own first—and damn the guilt.

She walked south of the men to keep the camp's fires behind them; that way she could see them better. The giant had gotten the advantage over Cal, who was on his back with the big guy sitting on him. But Cal had a vise grip on his wrists, so he couldn't hit. The giant's arm was weak, torn up from the shotgun wound, and bled down. They were at a stalemate.

Cat came up to within a few feet, cocked the shotgun and aimed at the giant's head.

"Get the hell off my husband," she said.

The giant slowly did as ordered and backed away with his hands up.

Cal got off the ground and joined his wife. Another cry of pain from the sorcerer's battle echoed in the night. This cry was deeper . . . a man's voice. And then that part of the wood went still.

"Guess your man wasn't as good as you thought," Cal said.

It was hard to read the giant's expression in the dark. When Cal moved to relieve Cat of the shotgun, the giant rolled to the ground, disappearing into the darkness.

Cal fired where his adversary had been. After two shots, the gun clicked empty. Cat heard his footsteps crunching in the snow, heading toward the forest. The giant ran past where the mages had fought, then broke through a row of bushes in the tree line and was gone.

Cal and Cat followed. Cat tripped over something big on the ground. It was the centaur.

"Wait!" Cat told her husband.

"I have to go after him," Cal said.

Cat felt around her fallen companion's body and found the bolts that were lodged into her. She was warm and still breathing. Cat's hand came away wet and sticky. "Lelani's hurt."

Cal dropped beside her and looked the young mage over. He cradled the centaur's head in his hands. Her clavicle was broken in the same place the bolt hit her earlier in the day. There were several other knives and small bits of metal protruding from her. She breathed in rapid pants.

"If we pull these blades out here, she'll bleed to death before we reach the tree," Cal said. He looked out in the direction the giant had fled. "Cat, can you get Lelani back to Rosencrantz?"

"Where are you going?" she asked.

"After that guy."

Cat couldn't stand the thought of Cal in that pitch-black forest alone with that monster. More so, she didn't want to be left alone in the meadow.

"How am I going to get a four-hundred-pound centaur across this meadow without your help?" she said.

"We can't let him report to Dorn," her husband responded.

"It's pitch black in that forest, you're bleeding, and you can't even see five feet ahead of you," Cat insisted.

Cal stared into the night like a wolf that'd lost his pack.

"We won," she emphasized.

"Barely," Cal said. "Most of these guys clearly got here recently—no guns, no body armor—they were still using crossbows and daggers. Luck won't always be on our side."

Cat's attackers were scary enough without the modern weaponry in their arsenal. She did not think it could get any worse than it did this night.

"We're going to need Seth and Ben's help to get her back," Cal said, acceding to her wishes.

Cat looked inside Lelani's satchel. Something cold and cylindrical popped into her hand. She pulled it out. A flashlight.

"This thing won't shoot lasers, will it?" she asked.

"Only one way to find out," the cop said.

She clicked it on, and there was light. Cat surveyed the immediate area. The beam fell upon the other mage a few feet away who lay facedown in the snow.

"Cal, look."

Cal took the flashlight from his wife and examined the area around the fallen sorcerer. The footprints of a seven-foot man were around the body. "Our friend stopped here first before taking off into the woods. Cat, hand me one of Lelani's arrows from her quiver."

Cal gingerly searched the dead mage's pockets with the arrow. It clinked on something metallic in the inside jacket pocket. He pulled out a small, heavy metal canister with symbols on it.

Cat came up behind her husband and put a hand on his shoulder. "Cal, we have to get her to Rosencrantz," she urged.

He shone the light on the canister. It bore the infamous black and yellow symbol for radiation. Around the symbol it read, *Danger! Fissionable Material. Property of Indian Point Nuclear Facility.*

Cal and Cat gave each other worried looks.

"What the hell is Dorn up to?" he said.

5

Seth climbed down and went to check on Ben. The old man was next to one of the pyres brushing himself off.

"What's the score?" Ben asked him.

"I think we're okay, old-timer."

"In that case it's *pasteles* and rum by the fire in PR."

"Ben! Are you done getting your butt kicked?" Helen asked from the trailer door. "Get back home, now."

Seth and Ben smiled. Helen had earned the right to nag after this night.

Their smiles turned to abject fear when they realized a gnoll was on the roof of the trailer just above Helen. Before Ben could warn his wife, the creature reached down, grabbed Helen, and hauled her over the top of the trailer. It jumped off the roof on the other side and took off into the north meadow with Ben's wife.

"Helen!" Ben screamed. He hobbled after them as fast as he could.

"Ben, no!" Seth shouted. The old man did not heed him. Seth looked for Cat, but she was gone. Seth didn't know what to do. It was madness to go out there and face a nocturnal creature in the dark. But what choice did he have? The phrase *What is good?* popped into his head. Ben had delved into the realm of the amateur philosopher by questioning absolutes, but what Seth knew for sure was that abandoning your friends to the darkness was definitely *not* good. He had abandoned people who needed him all his life. It was second nature to him, and he needed to end it. Seth looked around for a weapon and spotted Ben's ax. He grabbed it, lit two rolled-up magazines and pocketed a few extra ones, picked up a can of kerosene, and followed Ben into the night.

Ben wasn't hard to locate. A few yards away from the trailer, where the grass met the snowline, he gripped a small hunting knife and yelled into the winter night, "Helen!"

"Ben, keep it down."

"Those things have night vision, punk. You think it doesn't know where we are?"

Seth was acutely aware of their tactical disadvantage. But he couldn't tell Ben to abandon his wife; even though that was the sane thing to do. All that would come of them chasing that gnoll in the dark was three dead people instead of one.

"It's a trap," said Seth.

"No reason we should feed it two mice," Ben responded. "You go back to that tree and see if the wizard can help us out."

"Nice try, but I'm not leaving you out here alone."

They heard Helen's weak cry in the distance. "Ben!" She was still in the meadow, at least—somewhere near the tree line.

"She's still alive," Ben whispered, relieved. *"Helen!"*

"Go back," Helen cried.

"Ben, we're fucked if we stay here."

Ben contemplated something big in a way that only a member of America's greatest generation could. He took the can of kerosene from Seth. "Listen up," he said, "it's a dog-man, right? I'm injured. It senses weakness, smells blood. I'm going to walk out along the edge of the snow line a couple of yards. It's going to come after me. I'm going to grab it and hold on for dear life. No matter what it does, I ain't letting it go. When you hear it, come to me and hack away. We won't even have a minute, so don't hesitate."

"Ben, I don't like the idea of you being bait."

"Well we're a few cans short of Alpo, kid. This is no time to split hairs."

"Ben, I can't even see out here."

Ben held up the can of kerosene. "You'll see me fine." He walked away into the dark.

Seth gripped his ax tight. His magazine was halfway gone so he rolled and lit another one. He closed his eyes and tried to listen. It was the more effective sense in this situation. He caught a whiff of something foul upwind, like a garbage scow. It was in the direction Ben had gone. *Damn!*

Seth started toward Ben before he heard the scuffling. Then he heard a shout. A circle of flame ignited before him, lighting up the meadow, and in the middle of the ring was Ben struggling on the ground with the creature. The gnoll was startled by the circle of flames around them. It clearly wanted to run. Ben wrapped his arms and legs around the gnoll and held it in place as it tore and snapped at the old man. Ben yelled, "NOW! NOW!"

Seth quickly hopped through the ring of fire and landed a solid hack with the ax into the gnoll's back. The creature howled and rolled on the ground bringing along Ben, whose legs were entangled with the gnoll's in a wrestling grip. They rolled through a corner of the ring, and the gnoll's fur caught. Ben went limp and the creature was able to push the old man off. It frantically patted the flames on its body. Seth picked up the can of kerosene and splashed the remains on the gnoll. Several embers on the fur lit up. The gnoll ran into the snow aflame. Seth chased it. The creature rolled around trying to extinguish the burning hair; Seth came upon it and swung a solid shot into the thing's gut with his ax. The creature cried out and swiped at Seth's legs. Seth continued to hack at it to his heart's content. The smell of burning hair filled Seth's nostrils. His fifth shot, a solid gash to the forehead, ended the creature.

Seth heard crunching in the snow. He lifted his ax to ward off another attack.

"Ben?" Helen queried.

"It's me," Seth said. "That thing is dead."

She was shaking with fear. Seth took her hand. "Where's Ben?" she asked.

Seth led her back to the spot where he left her husband. Ben hadn't moved from where Seth left him, and Helen rushed to her husband's side.

"Ben, talk to me."

The old man didn't respond. He had gashes all over and was bleeding out onto the ground. Ben's head tilted back when his wife tried to prop him up, and they saw the rip in his throat. Helen kept calling his name as she patted his face trying to revive him. His eyes fluttered, and he coughed blood. He reached out to his wife and touched her cheek.

"Helen," he slurred. His voice had turned into a raspy gurgle.

"You did it, Ben. I'm safe. We're both safe. You hold on now. We'll get you to the tree." She turned to Seth. "Help me get him back."

Seth was sure that moving Ben was a terrible idea, but he didn't have many options. He reached under the old man to lift him. His clothes were saturated with blood as was the ground beneath him. Seth only moved him a little when Ben started to convulse and spit up blood. His body spasmed; he gasped for air.

"What happened?" Seth asked.

"It's a heart attack!" Helen said. "Ben, hold on!"

Seth picked up the old man and struggled toward the tree with Helen right behind him. A few steps away from camp, Ben went completely limp. They got him to the tree and laid him beside the trunk. Nothing happened. Helen looked at Seth. Her face, streaming with tears conveyed the fears in her heart.

"Try touching the tree and holding Ben," she said to him.

Seth did so, and felt the warmth of the tree fill him again, but the flow stopped at his hand, not going into Ben. He tried touching Ben's forehead, his wounds, but nothing worked. Seth turned to Helen, who was looking to him for answers he couldn't provide. Seth was sobbing as well by now. "I don't know what to do," he said. "Lelani has this powder that heals, but it's out there with her."

Seth stood back and looked at the bloodied old man slumped against the tree. He had a peaceful expression. Ben had caught the moment he knew his wife was safe and made it his eternal mask.

"Nooo!" Helen wailed. She leaned down and embraced her husband. She had no care for all the blood. She kissed his cheeks and cried freely.

Seth kneeled beside her and put his arms around them both. They wept for an eternity.

CHAPTER 17

STRANGERS IN A STRANGE LAND

1

Dorn hated America. It lacked order. It coddled the weak. The rules of behavior were contrary to nature. Common women were arrogant, badly disciplined; peasants pressed for their rights; the wealthy kept the masses subservient through financial debt instead of fear; and leaders were subject to criticism and even ridicule, such as on the players' farce *Saturday Night Live*. Madness. Dorn rubbed his temples in an effort to relieve the growing pressure.

The Quinta do Noval '83 slid down his lordship's gullet and warmed the chill from his bones. He didn't like the Park Plaza's vented heating and longed for a real fire to stoke under a large stone mantel. Nothing was real in this world; the food was processed and bloodless and even the warmth was an illusion. The city smelled worse than brimstone, noxious waste belching from the asses of a million horseless carriages. Mass production by scientific trickery produced a lot of nothing. The masses hoarded material goods as if they were nobility—fooled into believing the purchase of soulless objects would overcome their ingrained defects. The right car or the toothpaste with a catchier tune will bring them closer to being noble. As wines went, though, port came closest to the spirits of home. It alleviated the throbbing in his temple, which had been growing worse since their arrival in this cursed world. It was also becoming harder to hide the pain from his underlings. He found himself drinking more of the wine the longer he remained here.

This world was not an easy place. Like hawks in a maelstrom, they struggled through it, denigrated in the effort of not drawing attention to themselves. Limited sorceries, restricted violence, and the inability to freely draw manpower from local denizens without leverage over them. More than that, there was no way to tell how high-grade magicks might react on this plane. Some unknown cosmic balance might be tipped. Such a thing could make the situation worse—the ensuing chaos might cause difficulty in their search. So they had to wade through the mire of orthodoxy, risking a spell only when needed, and slinking off like weasels after raiding the coop.

Dorn leaned against the mantel of his bedroom's faux fireplace and pulled an ornate silver locket from his pocket. It opened on a hinge and he studied the tiny portrait within—Lara, his mother's youngest sister. A few strands of her platinum-white hair encircled her image. He sniffed the strands, pining for any remnant of her scent. Lara had been more of a mother to Dorn than the woman who pushed him from her thighs could ever be. How long had it been since he had last seen her—her soft, scented skin, alabaster hair, and sympathetic amethyst eyes? The depiction, perfect as a photograph, followed him with its gaze. What was she doing at this moment? Was she free? Would Uncle keep his word? Dorn could not suspend his longing for her. It was there, below the surface, every moment of the day no matter what he did, as though he were under a spell. Even the port failed to dull its ache.

A renowned artist from Fhlee, whose race in adulthood grew to be no larger than a young child and were sought throughout the realm for their diminutive work, had painted the likeness with tiny hands. Dorn had set a few of their villages ablaze to bring them into line with his uncle's reign. Though the artist was a slave by conquest, so fine was the portrait of his aunt, that in a rare act of veneration, Dorn actually paid the painter with gold instead of a flogging. The portrait was his anchor to home.

A knock at the door reverberated through Dorn's headache.

"What?" he roared.

The gentleman entered—tall, lean, combed and manicured, in gray pinstripes, white gloves, and a black long-tail jacket.

"Oulfsan?" Dorn asked, pocketing the locket.

"No, master. Krebe."

Dorn noticed the slight hunch in the man, the nervous twiddling of fingers. Krebe's speech was heavy on the tongue.

"I'll never get used to you two switching about," Dorn said. "Well . . . ?"

"On their way up, they are, sire. Wounded it seems."

"I should hope so," Dorn said, as though this was the least they should be. "When does Oulfsan return?"

"It don't work like that, me lordship. 'Tis random."

Dorn considered the man, ill-suited for his body, and waited for something to change.

"Leave me," Dorn said.

2

The elevator, with some effort, carried the great weight of Hesz the giant and his two cohorts toward the upper levels of the hotel. Pools of blood from various wounds collected on the floor of the lift. Hesz supported Symian on his good arm. They had retrieved him from the sewer they'd stowed him in following the flare attack in the South Bronx tenement. The hope being that the dank, cool, darkness of the tunnels, similar to troll caves, would aid in his healing.

Hesz and Kraten ended up hiding down there with Symian for the better part of the day, much to Kraten's verbal dismay. A police officer had cornered Hesz for questioning as he attempted to buy bandages and alcohol at a drugstore in the early morning. MacDonnell had initiated an APB for Hesz and his companions, and unfortunately, the giant could not help but be indiscreet. Hesz dispatched the police officer with a quick snap to the neck, and they remained underground with the troll until well after the sun had set.

Symian was still in bad shape—blind, his normally gray skin was blackened and crunched into flakes beneath his raincoat wherever Hesz applied pressure to support him. Symian was only half conscious for the pain.

They had done no better without the troll in the North Bronx when they had attempted to kidnap MacDonnell's woman and child. Indeed, the woman herself had managed to wound Hesz before the sorceress appeared again with her magicks. Symian was one of a few besides Dorn in their group who knew how to wield magic—a fact that was lost on Kraten but was always in the forefront of Hesz's mind. Magic was power. It was the keystone of humankind's hold over their kingdoms and dominance over the nonhuman races.

The police swarmed the city looking for them. Because he was so unique looking in this world, they had to remain in the sewers and attempt to find their way back to the hotel underground. A city the size of New York had thousands of miles of tunnels beneath it. Hesz was angry, and in the true spirit of his forefathers, he wanted to smash things and break people. Dorn could have sent someone with an auto to pick them up, injured as they were, but his policy regarding failure was absolute. No mercy for failure. They were left to fend for themselves, not even a gurney for the injured lad. A stupid policy for such a fragile race as the purebloods. It would one day be their undoing. For now, Hesz drew on the three-fourths of his human blood to contain his temper.

"Stay your breath," Kraten ordered.

"What?" Hesz responded, pulled out of his thoughts.

"This lift is as cold as a grave," Kraten said, rubbing his arms for heat.

Hesz realized his anger caused him to breathe harder. Frost formed on the elevator walls. He held his breath to appease his cohort.

Hesz replayed the recent battles in his mind.

They had been outgunned and outclassed at MacDonnell's home. Who knew MacDonnell's wench had a firearm and the fortitude to use it? And then the sorceress appeared. But it never should have come to that anyway. It was Kraten who had forced the confrontation in the South Bronx tenement before they were ready. Symian was young and easily persuaded into action by the desert warrior. The swordsman was long on guts and glory but short on brains, a common trait among the desert folk of Verakhoon. Although a good warrior, Kraten was too brash and arrogant to be depended on, but he was Dorn's favorite: a childhood playmate, and more importantly, a pureblood. They should have waited. How lucky they were to remain alive depended on Lord Dorn's mood, which had become capricious with their extended stay in this world.

The group had been plagued by a series of blunders by Dorn's own hand. Jumping into the transfer on a whim left them unprepared to function in this world. They lost weeks locating enough magical energy to cast the proper language spells, produce currency, learn about social hierarchies, and get the general lay of the society. Then, Dorn divided the mission into two fronts: one to search for the objective and one to destroy the opposition's defenders—in hindsight a costly error. It had become apparent early on that none of the prince regent's guardians was a threat. They were ignorant of their origins. Bad fortune had fallen among that group. Dorn failed to press this advantage.

The first few detectives Dorn had procured to find the boy came up empty because the trail was long cold. These men simply withered away in despair, unable to come to terms with their "heartless" existence. They finally stumbled across some good luck when Hesz spotted the newspaper article about the disgraced detective Colby Dretch. Perhaps the other sleuths had been too honest with much to live for. Instead, they required a cunning, deceitful man, desperate to redeem himself when confronted by his own mortality. *Hesz* brought Dretch to Lord Dorn's attention, and finally they were on the boy's trail.

Now, it was a game of catch-up. Had Dorn marshaled all

their resources into finding the boy at the start of this escapade, and not put effort into eliminating the guardians, they might have cut the little bugger's throat before the centaur sorceress rallied even one ally. The ultimate irony, it occurred to Hesz, was that the best strategy might have been just to leave things alone; in stirring the wasps' nest, they'd set in motion the possible unearthing of the prince. This boy could have remained hidden forever: grown up, married, died an old man and, through union with commoners, bred his offspring out of any claim. He could even have been killed in a plane crash or drafted into a war. Anything was possible in this anarchic world. The odds had been in their favor. Now, it was a race.

The doors parted. Bellus, a skilyte, greeted Hesz, Kraten, and Symian with an oily smile. Two large humans stood guard at the entrance to the suite.

"The vanquished warriors return to the fold," Bellus sneered. "You've been gone for the better part of a day while there is much work to be done. What do you have to say?"

Bellus relished the failure of others because it was the easiest way to increase his own standing. He was short, hunched, and looked too small for his black suit. His skin glistened as though he'd just stepped out of a vat of olive oil. His eyes were bloodshot and puffy. He rarely made a decision or acted on information although he outranked Hesz and Symian by virtue of his pure blood only. Kraten could pummel the toady on their behalf, but at the moment the swordsman struggled to remain standing.

"Thanks for coming to retrieve us with the auto," Hesz said.

"Master's orders," Bellus said.

"We need healing."

"What you *need* depends on his lordship's mood. You've been gone a long time."

"We had to retrieve Symian." No one needed to know that they had gotten lost in the sewers. Hopefully, Kraten would have the good sense to keep his mouth shut.

Bellus looked suspicious of the explanation. His paranoia served him well. A whiff of the sewer's stink persuaded Bellus to back off from the trio. "Wait in the common room."

The suite took up half the floor and had four bedrooms attached to a common living area, including a kitchenette. By Manhattan standards, the fourteen-foot ceiling and Louis XIV décor with its gold-leaf molding were luxurious for a hotel room, but by Dorn's standards, this was roughing it. *There would be time for luxury after the boy is found,* Dorn drummed into them.

Kraten collapsed on the couch. Hesz laid the semiconscious Symian on the love seat.

The elegant gentleman approached.

"Krebe?" Hesz queried.

"Aye," the gentleman affirmed.

The *trick* unsettled Hesz. With these two, one rarely knew who one was dealing with. But Hesz was getting better at it. He had to—he couldn't rest easily when Krebe was about. Something about *that one* unsettled him.

"His lordship . . . ?" Hesz asked.

"In a mood. Been in his room since we returned from upstate. The headaches are growing worse."

An uncomfortable pause descended. They all knew better than to acknowledge Dorn's headaches when the man went to great lengths to hide it from them. The migraines were getting worse, but no one would broach the subject.

"Might want to come back later," Krebe suggested.

"Failed is failed," Bellus crowed. "Later won't change their incompetence."

"Symian will die without attention," the giant said. "Get him."

"His lordship is aware of your wounds," Bellus stated.

Hesz growled. He strode forward to rap on the bedroom door himself when it suddenly opened. Dorn walked forth, forcing Hesz to backtrack. His lordship studied the trio. He meandered toward Symian and pulled apart the troll's coverings. Symian's skin was the texture and color of strudel left in the oven too long. The gray man was now a being of caramelized soot. As the troll shifted, pieces of him flaked onto the cream-colored love seat. His bandaged eyes were stained blue with blood.

Dorn observed Kraten's wrapped, bloody arm and then Hesz's bandaged torso. Disgust filled the master's eyes.

"My liege—" Hesz started.

"Shut up."

Bellus sniggered.

Dorn walked around them slowly.

Symian tried to stand and teetered forward. Kraten and Hesz caught him before he spilled.

"Let him go," Dorn ordered. Hesz threw Kraten a quick glance. The desert warrior released his grip, as did Hesz a heart-beat later. The gray man fell with a soft crunch as skin broke into crumbs on the carpet. Symian whined in pain.

"That the captain might have prevailed against you," Dorn began, "despite his handicap of being unaware of his true iden-tity, was at least within the realm of possibility. After all, he is from the nobility. But a little girl and a common woman . . . ?"

"The centaur and the other took us unaware," Hesz said.

"Students. Not even adepts. And speaking of the other, you botched that one, too. Blew up a building, but failed to make sure he was in it."

"This world is complicated," Hesz said. "We thought . . ."

"Yes, it is complicated. That's why you are paid to act, not to think." Dorn stopped. He closed his eyes for a moment and pretended to brush his hair back, although it was obvious he rubbed his head to assuage another migraine. Dorn gave up the pretense and squeezed the point between his eyes. Everyone in the room felt the pain in Dorn's head by osmosis.

Dorn's eyes snapped open. The others looked away from his piercing gaze.

"I saved you half-breeds from the purge because of what you can contribute to Farrenheil's cause," Dorn continued. "Such a privilege is earned through success. You're fortunate my uncle is not here. We're operating on limited resources. This, and only this, affords you a chance to redeem yourselves, courtesy of this muddled and distant orb we find ourselves on."

The trio remained quiet.

"My liege," an agitated Bellus said, "surely at least one must be punished, as an example. They failed to carry out your orders. Your uncle frowns upon insubordination."

Hesz could have ripped off the little rodent's head. Mercy from Dorn was worth more than a pachyderm's weight in platinum. The little shit would report any failure of discipline to the archduke later, putting Dorn in an awkward position.

"I suppose you're right, Bellus," Dorn said.

Dorn pulled Kraten's sword from its sheath. He hefted its weight in his hand. Kraten was not alarmed. Everyone, including him, knew he wouldn't be the example. Hesz studied the desert warrior's face to see if he suspected whom Dorn would "exemplify," but Kraten betrayed nothing. Bellus rubbed his hands in anticipation. Hesz could tell the toady wanted him gone, there was no love lost between them.

Dorn faced Hesz and raised the sword straight up, balancing like a high diver before a plunge. Hesz had made his peace long before this day. It would go easier for his family if he didn't resist. He closed his eyes. Hesz felt the wind off the sword as it whipped by. It must have been a smooth clean cut because, except for a light knick at his throat, he didn't feel a thing. He opened his eyes and saw Dorn's back facing him.

In the corner, Krebe was snapping pictures with a disposable Kodak camera. Bellus's face had a look of total surprise. His head began to slide sideways off his shoulders. Hesz thought that Bellus, with his pleading eyes and questioning lips, should have brought his hands up to hold his head in place. He looked ludicrous with his arms just flailing at his sides while his skull went for a tumble, but of course, the connections had been severed. More shocking, Dorn had killed a full-blood instead of a half-breed. Hesz wiped a bead of blood from his nicked skin. A superficial wound. Kraten broke out in a loud laugh with his remaining strength. Krebe joined in the revelry. The troll had passed out long before the cut.

"Has everyone learned something?" Dorn asked.

"How to block his lordship's backhanded hook," Kraten guffawed.

Dorn smiled.

Hesz forced a grin, though he saw no humor in the events. He had become a master at appeasement—fitting in until the opportune time presented itself. Soon enough, he would act. Dorn and his ilk would count days past as their best of times.

Krebe dropped the camera and suddenly stiffened. His eyes blanked out, like he had been turned off.

"It's about bloody time," Dorn said.

A moment later, the elegant man shook his head. His posture straightened. He brushed off his clothes. An air of dignity prevailed that hadn't been there a moment earlier.

"Oulfsan?" Dorn asked.

"Yes, sir."

"The detective?"

"Delaware, sir. Driving south on Interstate Ninety-five. He's found the trail."

CHAPTER 18

DRIVING WITH ONE HEADLIGHT

1

The dates on the headstone matched. It read: John Doe, called to God early and spared the hardships of life. *Lelani had done most of the digging throughout the night. They broke through an hour before dawn. Cal thought the plain pine box could not hold the body of a prince. Not a rational thought, since no one on this world knew who he was.*

Cal MacDonnell, son of James, son of Mavis, son of Edmund, son of Chaucer, son of Edred, son of Henric, son of Sweyn, felt the pressure of his ancestors press against his sternum. They had been protectors of great houses since man left the safety of the caves. What was, or was not, in the casket determined the future of his line.

"Crowbar," Lelani said.

Cal was worlds away and didn't hear.

"Cal, crowbar," Chryslantha said, pointing to the tool by his feet.

He handed the centaur the bar. Seth, Ben, Cat, Chryslantha, Erin, and a shadowy group gathered around the grave. Cat was breast-feeding the baby. She eased him off her tit and handed the boy to Chryslantha.

"Cal needs me now. Would you mind?"

Chryslantha pulled out her breast and let the child resume feeding. "Not at all."

Lelani pried the lid open. An infant boy, dead for years, lay in the coffin.

"Doesn't mean it's him," Cat said.

"Turn him over," Cal said. "Take him out of the swaddling."

Lelani did this, careful not to peel the moldy rotting skin as well. The remnants of a birthmark were on the left shoulder. It was shaped like a phoenix.

"Is that him?" Cat asked. "Is this the boy you're looking for?"

Cal didn't know what to say. He had failed his ancestors and cursed his descendants. He looked to Chryslantha feeding his son.

"Bum deal, my love," she said. "I'm glad I didn't tie my fortunes to yours. I don't know what I'd have done if my children had been fathered by a loser like you. Better to spare anyone that fate." The hand she held the baby's head with twisted until there was a snap. "Ooh," she cried. "Got to take them off the tap first. These little buggers really clamp down."

"That's it for me," Cat said, throwing her hands up in defeat. "I'm done being an incubator for your useless family, Cal. I wasn't even your first choice. Just some runner-up after you lost your mind . . . and for what? A third-rate feudal nobility. I should have married the orthodontist like my mother wanted me to. Well, our kids are dead, the prince is dead, so I'm outta here. Chryslantha says she has a younger brother who's just my type."

Cal looked down at the dead prince as everyone moved off in his or her own direction. He was soon alone with the corpse, which was as dead as his own future.

2

Consciousness arrived like a former mistress—familiar and accepted reluctantly. Cal did not open his eyes but sampled the environment through his remaining senses like a blind man. The sheets and the mattress were not his own. The sun outside the window, higher than it usually was when he awoke, did not warm the skin, but a dull red glow radiated against his eyelids. The air smelled cool and damp and tinged with moss. Years of sleeping with a partner made him aware of the void beside him. A rarity, because he was the early riser in their home. He didn't hear anyone else in the room. Perhaps she had finally left; had enough of *his* mess. Her leaving would be a just dessert.

Eyes open. A vaulted ceiling with wooden beams; a circular chandelier made from deer antlers dropped from the ceiling's apex and hung on a single chain cutting down the center of the room. A spent blaze smoldered in the stone fireplace under a richly ornate oak mantel. It reminded him of Aandor. A stray thought suggested it was Scotland, a castle on the moors; one of the many bedrooms connected to Ben Reyes's nexus. *The late Ben Reyes.*

He had dreamt about Chryslantha before the nightmare about the grave. A hallucinatory vision of blissful peace and lust that culminated in a dry, sticky residue that coated his crotch. He hadn't done that since before his first woman, Loraine. Chryslantha had become a fixture in his dreams. He was grateful for the morning solitude. There was no satisfactory explanation he could offer his wife.

Cal considered living out his remaining life in this spot. He tried to lift his arm but it refused. Everything was still connected. The signal from his brain was sent. The arm simply didn't respond. The effort was akin to triggering the last mechanism of a Rube Goldberg device without setting the preceding steps in motion. A nameless force was at work. An empty space sat heavily on his chest and head and pressed down with a father's authority. Thoughts whizzed through three at a time. He couldn't focus. The jumble of images made lucidity difficult— his brain had been coopted by the chaos in his life; overwhelmed by his duty to his kingdom, his lost prince, his family in Aandor, his wife and daughter, the newly created widow Reyes, his responsibilities as a citizen of this world and, ultimately, to himself. All these forces vying for his faithfulness—he could not remain true to all of them by serving any one. Yet in the wings of his mind, like an invisible subprogram, a linear vein of reason watched the anarchy on the main stage. Was it a side effect? His mind had been twisted and prodded like taffy the past twenty-four hours. Consequences were only natural. Expected even.

Time stopped. The pressure in his head squeezed at the recesses of his memory. He shucked it aside, over and over, trying to shut it out, only to have the prodding claw return sharper, longer, with more fervor each round. A drunken barber had shaved his brain and culled his motivation like cream from a bucket. The problem pirouetted before him like an elephant in a tutu. The subprogram in his head yelled at him from under the din, scolding him with the natural authority of an elder.

Get up, get up, get up, get up! You useless sack of shit! Get your ass out of bed this instant! You're on a mission!

Semiconsciously, Cal knew the culprit yet resisted his own edification. Stress and anguish, much like with the roof jumper who was fired from his job and went home to find his wife in bed with his best friend, conspired to wring the last vestiges of chemical harmony from his worn-out mind.

Cal had attended many department seminars to sharpen his skills in negotiating with the mentally unhinged. Confronting suicides was a daily event for the NYPD. Apparently—and this was only a guess—his levels of neurofactor three (serotonin) were posting a low. His factors one, two, and seven weren't faring any better. Neurons fired with the efficiency of a gelding stud. He teetered on the precipice of despondency. If Cal could just get a modicum of cooperation from life, the universe, and everything else, things might be okay. *Is this what the "ledge jumpers" thought, too?*

Cal decided to roll on his side, an ambitious decision he was quite proud of. He lay on his back waiting for something to happen. The details on the ceiling beams were mesmerizing. The grains ran the length of the wood. Some beams were curved to follow the ceiling to its apex. Did they do that with water, the same way they bent drywall?

Drywall? Aandor has been invaded. Your family's been hunted, maybe tortured, the kid you took an oath to protect has been lost for thirteen years, Ben was mauled to death . . . and you're wondering about how they bend wood? Get up!

He pulled the sheet over his head.

Why was this so difficult? Just before the sleep wore off, for a nanosecond, he was the man he used to be. Then reality seeped in like poison. Couldn't he hold on to that moment—wrap it around him like a shield? Why couldn't he stay this mental hemlock? He'd led men through massacres; through battles whose likely outcome was a lacerated death. He was decisive, acute, confident. Why was turning over in bed arduous? *It's a spell.* Yes, that was it, a spell. Everything would be okay. Lelani would find a remedy. Probably an herbal tea made from yak's piss and eye of Newt Gingrich.

"Rise and shine, sleepyhead," came a familiar voice.

A grumbled whisper, "Chryslantha?"

The sizzling odor of sausage and maple syrup wafted through the covers. Cal shut his eyes. The bedsheet pulled back, like a magic trick, to reveal him. He peeked to find a Cheshire Cat hovering over him.

"No, it's not Christmas," his wife said. "Just thought you might like breakfast in bed." She pulled the drapes back the rest of the way and flooded the room with light. Cat notched the window open. A cold breeze blew through the room. "Sorry," she said. "Wanted some fresh air. Didn't think it'd be arctic. I can get the fire going."

"What time is it?" he rasped.

"Almost ten. You haven't slept this late since you did twelve to eights."

Cal pulled himself up and let Cat prop the pillow behind him. "Thanks," he said. "What's with the room service? Something else happen?"

"Can't a wife spoil her husband once in a while?" She was glad, he realized. Grateful to still have *her* spouse. "We've never been to Scotland, you know."

And technically, they still hadn't. The only access to the bedroom was through Ben's bungalow in Puerto Rico. Entry from the castle itself had been sealed with stone and mortar years earlier. To get to the moors they'd have to rappel three hundred feet down from the window and avoid the moat, which doubled as a sewage outlet.

Cat rested the bed tray over Cal's thighs and lifted the warming covers from the plates.

"Have some?" Cal offered.

"No."

"Did you eat already?"

"Skipped. Having trouble keeping things down. Probably nerves."

"Hmm," Cal said, swallowing java. One thought, a minor one until this moment, rose above the din in his brain. "Was that a pregnancy test box I saw in the bathroom trash at home?"

Cat was silent. She sat on the bed facing away from him with her hands on her lap.

"You coppers never miss a detail."

"Wouldn't be very good if we did. Is there something I should know?"

"The test results were ruined in the fight. I don't know for sure, but it sure feels like . . ." She didn't finish. Cal edged up to her and stroked her shoulders. "I didn't want to add to our problems," she said. "Not in the middle of all this."

He kissed her on the nape of her neck. "You've always been the solution to my problems," he said.

Chryslantha marched herself to the forefront of Cal's brain. For a moment, it was her scent he smelled, her voice he heard. Someone had hooked his navel from the inside and was pulling it back toward his spine. He smiled at his wife. Could Cat see the other woman in his eyes?

"What's the plan?" she asked him.

"We poke around the neighborhood up here, find a lead on the boy. Then, back to New York. The others from our group might head to the city looking for me." As an afterthought he added, "The ones who are still alive."

"And then?"

"Then we find the boy."

"And then?"

"One thing at a time."

"Let's say you're successful. Do we take the kid from his legal parents? Do we raise him ourselves? Do we move to his town? Buy the house next door to his? Do we bring him to the Bronx?"

"I don't know. Let's find him first."

"Do you have to take him back to Aandor? Or can Lelani do it?"

"Let's not talk about this right now."

"If not now, when? What's the plan? Are we actually making it up on the fly? We got lucky finding Ben and Helen up here."

Not so lucky for Ben and Helen.

"Who knows when we'll be able to catch our breath again," Cat continued.

"I'll know more later . . ."

"Have you made a decision about going back?"

"Can't we drop this, Cat?"

"Drop this?"

Cat stood up from the bed. She rubbed her arms, suddenly chilled, while she made her way to the doorway. Cal had a tinge of guilt. She was so distraught, she was out of character. The woman he married would never drop anything.

Suddenly, Cat stopped and turned to face him. "You're the guy who had every stage of his career with the NYPD mapped out before he graduated the academy!" she said. "You're the guy who had the colors of our apartment picked out before we even bought the building!"

Cat circled slowly back around toward Cal, still lying immobile in bed.

"You're the guy who plays chess five moves ahead of his turn. You have your endgame picked out after the first move and suddenly, in real life, you don't know what we're doing tomorrow or the next day. Are you delaying decisions you don't want to face, Cal, or have you made them already and don't want to tell me?" Cat demanded, hovering over him.

Cal would have preferred the battle at Gagarnoth to this moment. His back was again against a cliff, except he couldn't slash and hack his way out of this trap—he was an immovable object confronted by an unstoppable force . . . a slip of a woman who held the key to his heart. The problem was his heart now had a second lock, a backdoor key that led to his past, and more and more it looked like both keys needed to be turned in unison to keep him whole, like submarine commanders launching a ballistic missile.

"The first one," Cal finally said.

"The first what?"

"I'm delaying decisions I don't want to face. All options look like I'll have to go back if I'm successful. And I *have* to be successful."

"Or die trying?"

"Or die trying," he confirmed. "There are millions of people depending on me. Aandor is a city that became a nation that became an empire. A whole society. The entire balance of power is unraveling there. We need to preserve the succession and reclaim our seat of power over the empire to preserve peace on the continent. My family is depending on me."

The words "my family" struck Cat like a slap. She and Bree had been his whole family until yesterday.

Cat took a moment and then asked, "Is there room for your daughter—for me—in your new life? In whichever world you choose?"

"There has to be. I'll make it so. I have to sort things out first, then come back for you."

Cat stepped back from the bed, arms tense, fists clenched. A tear broke through her veneer.

"Cat . . . it's complicated."

"There's no guarantee that you'd even live through this war!" she said. "You could be hacked to pieces with those fucking meat cleavers you medieval jocks use."

"As opposed to getting blown apart cleanly in the Bronx by a drug dealer's bullet."

"Don't be smart with me, Cal! You don't have the right to be smart with me! If you did manage to live through that hell, if you go back, there's a good chance that the next time I see you Bree will have her own kids and I'll be an old crone. What the fuck am I supposed to do for the next thirty years? Pretend you're dead? Live my years never knowing for sure? What about Bree? What about our child inside me?"

"WHAT DO YOU WANT ME TO DO, CAT?"

Cal shoved the food tray off the bed. He leaned forward challenging Cat for answers.

"Tell me what to do!" he persisted. "Should I ignore that the prince exists? Go back to the Bronx and take my ESU training? Retire in twenty years with a beer gut, coach Little League, walk my daughter down the aisle, bounce fat grandkids on my lap, and fish until I keel over in my rowboat? Be content that I led a *good* life?"

"Fuck you," Cat said, in tears. For a moment, Cal thought she would slap him. Instead, she hugged him hard. "Yes. Damn it. Yes!" she whispered in his ear. And even as she repeated the word, Cal sensed Cat knew better. That she would never respect him or love him again with the same fervor if he could turn his back on his family and his responsibilities that way, even for her sake. Her tears rained on his shoulder.

"I love you, Catherine," he said.

"I know you do," she said, sniffling. "I'm just trying to figure out what our life is becoming. Has become. Will things ever be the same again?"

Cal took a moment to think things through. He was figuring out his strategy as much for himself as to give Cat her due. She deserved a straight answer. He got out of bed, pulling the comforter behind him for a cover. He threw kindling on the dying fire and a big log on top of that, then took a chair next to the hearth. Cat sat on the stone platform in front of the fireplace facing him.

"I know you came up here with me to defend our life—to help find a quick fix and make all these new people in our lives go away," Cal said. "For a brief moment in time, Cat, I believed we might do it, too. But it's not going to happen. There's no easy fix. I have to look for this boy, Cat. Not as a hobby or something I do in my spare time. I *have* to look for this boy," Cal emphasized. "If I can't find him during my sick leave, grieving over Erin's murder, then I'll cite psychological stress and use my vacation time, too."

"That's about four weeks in all. What if you still—?"

"Then I'll think of something else. With Lelani's help, I hope to find the prince in the next few days. I'll consider what to do with the boy as I search. It would depend on his current living situation."

"Fair enough," Cat said. "And if he's not alive?"

Cal stoked the fire. It popped a few cinders on Cat, which Cal quickly brushed off with his hands.

"If the prince is dead," Cal continued, "my mission is a failure—and House Athelstan loses its claim to the throne. If the prince is dead, it would be better for me not to go back. My family there would be better off for it."

"God forgive me, Cal . . ." Cat's eyes began to well. "Part of me wants the boy not to be alive. I feel like a selfish horrible monster. I want you back home."

"Catherine—"

"But if this little boy died because you weren't there to protect him, you'll never be the same man again. You'd never forgive yourself."

"Will I ever be the same again either way, Cat? Will anything?" Cal was scared, about his mission, his family, his very purpose for being, and Cat was the only person on earth he could ever admit such a thing to.

"I always wanted you to find your past," Cat said. "Be careful what you wish for, huh?"

"Let's take things one day at a time. One of the other guardians might have raised the boy. If we whip the bad guys, we might have years here before any big decision needs to be made."

"What if everything turns out okay? Are Bree and I even invited to join you in Aandor, Cal?"

Cal was surprised by the question. He had assumed Cat could join him if she wished. Yet did she want to be a nobleman's wife at court in a feudal society? Her family, friends, and history were here—Cal understood what it meant to not have those things in one's life. How could he place such a burden on someone who never bargained for problems of this magnitude? Or perhaps he didn't ask her to come because of Chryslantha. The thought of his wife and his betrothed actually meeting bothered him greatly. He felt he had betrayed them both. But what was he thinking . . . that he'd return to Aandor without Cat and Bree and take up with Chryslantha as though nothing had happened? Cat would haunt his memories in Aandor just as Chryslantha preoccupied them now.

"Cal, are you okay?"

"What?"

"You spaced out."

"I would never abandon you, but . . . do you really want to come to Aandor?"

The air hung heavy between them as Cat considered the question. A medieval life without modern conveniences; no electricity, television, motorcars, public education, women's equality, or even aspirin. How would Bree take to that change? What would she lose by going to a medieval world?

"I don't know," Cat answered honestly. "I'm trying to be a 'Stand By Your Man' type of woman. Fucking song! But this—"

"We don't have to figure it all out now," Cal said. He took her hands, leaned forward and kissed the tears on her cheeks. She moved to his lap and nuzzled her face in his neck. "Let's see how things play out," he added.

Cat laughed softly. "I always thought the worst scenario I'd have to contend with if we found your family was that they lived in trailer parks and were related even before they got married," she confessed. "Our problems never came this big."

"It's not the size, it's what you do with it that matters," Cal said, smiling.

Cat chuckled, even as she was tempted to punch him. She kissed him instead. "Dope," she teased.

With her arms around his neck, she asked, "What now, *my lord*?"

"We get out of this room and attend a good man's funeral. Come up with a plan to pick up the prince's trail. The sooner we accomplish this, the quicker we can get back to New York and see our daughter again."

CHAPTER 19

CANDLES IN THE WIND

The sky was a perfect blue and the wind strangely warm. Cal thought of Ben as the breeze caressed him, as though the air were made of Ben's essence and he wasn't truly gone. That idea brought solace to his troubled thoughts as they laid the old man to rest beneath Rosencrantz's shade.

Cat stood beside him. She hadn't let him out of her grasp since their talk in the Scottish bedroom. She was still angry at him for the secrets he held from her, but Helen's loss put things in perspective—a dark foreshadowing of what Cat might experience soon enough. Lelani leaned against the tree, drawing in its healing energies and recuperating from her injuries. Seth brooded in his own lonely corner.

Ben's children had argued with their mother that he needed to be autopsied and then put to rest with his ancestors at the family cemetery in Puerto Rico. But Helen would hear nothing of it. Ben had been caretaker of the world's only sentient tree . . . the world's last wizard. There were greater traditions to uphold.

It was a beautiful service. A local minister who knew of Ben's special circumstances led the service. He added elements into the service that reminded Cal of the Druid culture back home.

Ben's children each read from scripture. They sang hymns. His body had been anointed with lavender oil and wrapped in a clean white linen. He was placed directly into the earth without a coffin. In time, his flesh would become part of the meadow, and those who knew him in life would always feel his presence in this place. The Reyes children looked at Cal and his group as intruders who brought carnage to their parents' home. The bodies of men and monsters were still strewn about the meadow when the children had arrived. Cal and Seth had spent the rest of the morning throwing them into a pyre. They worried that the lingering smell of burnt flesh would pollute the ceremony, but a timely warm breeze cleared the air at the last moment. No doubt, the tree's doing. The kids hadn't said anything to Cal, but he knew they blamed him for their father's death. He agreed with them; another burden to carry.

Cal had gone to too many funerals in his day—too many fallen comrades on both worlds. It was part of being a soldier, a protector. As a young man, duty and honor motivated him. This conflict was not a job, though . . . it was about family. It was everything he held dear in the universe thrown like dice into a cosmic crapshoot of war and peace. So many pieces in flux. How could he possibly make it all right?

Seth was taking the death especially hard. He sat on a fold-out chair next to the trailer, smoking a cigarette, contemplating the grass. Seth hadn't spoken since Cal found him huddled with Helen and Ben. The cop couldn't understand it. The boy had no conscience, and yet he was broken up over a man he knew barely a day. He wished he could expel him from the mission, but Lelani insisted that Seth had a purpose. She had faith in her old teacher's decision.

The Reyes family headed back to Puerto Rico via the conduit, leaving the four of them alone. Lelani took out the lead canister Cal had found on the mage and turned it in her hand. Seth joined them, looking worriedly at the canister and its bright yellow and black markings.

"Well?" Cal prompted.

"It does not bode well," Lelani said.

"Our 'bodings' always suck," Seth said.

Cal gave Seth a stern look, and Seth dropped the attitude.

"There are certain forbidden magicks in Aandor," Lelani continued. "They are carefully monitored by wizard councils in every kingdom. I believe Dorn is taking advantage of the lack of oversight here to engage these taboo sorceries."

"And he needs plutonium?" Cat asked.

"These spells are unique. They cannot be powered by normal means. They need irradiated elements—radium, uranium—as catalysts. These are accelerators and increase the magic's potency exponentially."

"But . . . ," prodded Cal.

"But they are unpredictable; unstable. The energies can get away from sorcerer's control in the blink of an eye. Mages have killed thousands, entire villages, trying to harness this kind of power. No one has successfully tamed it. And this is with the elements we know of. We have no enrichment processes in Aandor. I have no idea how plutonium will react to magical energies. This world is in grave danger."

"That's just fantastic," said Seth. "A psychotic megalomaniac has found a way to supercharge his magic spells."

"Who is supposed to fight this guy?" Cat asked. "Didn't you say you're still just a student?"

Lelani looked at Seth.

Seth pointed at her accusingly. "No way!"

"It's us and Rosencrantz," Lelani explained. "You have to come up to speed and relearn how to wield magic. What we lack in power and experience, we must make up in numbers."

Seth looked morbid at the prospect.

Cal took a deep breath and tried to look commanding. "We still have a mission to find the prince," he said in his most confident voice. "He's out there and in serious trouble. Dorn is trying to find him before we do. There are a few towns nearby. I'll check their records to see what happened the night we all came through thirteen years ago. We also have the other members of our party waking up from their long sleep. Most will honor their obligations. We need to make ourselves accessible to them— help them. They will have families. Cat, I want you to come up with a strategy to help the guardians' families cope with this disruption to their lives. You're best suited for that. Once we find a trail, we'll divvy up the tasks according to our resources at the time. We'll figure out how to save the world along the way."

Seth remained bothered by his role in Cal's grand scheme. "I can't fight wizards and dog-men," he pleaded. "I just can't."

"You did fine last night," Cal said, coming dangerously close to a compliment.

"I'm a pornographer," Seth insisted. "I can't save the world."

Cal placed his hands on Seth's shoulders. He didn't know himself until he had done it whether he would thrash the young man or something else. Cat and Lelani became tense. Seth looked like he wanted to be punched . . . to be punished. Cal realized they'd had enough violence recently for a lifetime. He relaxed his grip and slid his hands down to Seth's upper arms. He looked the boy in the eye, and with a gentle shake said, "You've just been promoted."

Everyone breathed a sigh of relief.

"Let's go," Cal said with finality.

CHAPTER 20

HANGING ON IN QUIET DESPERATION

Dorn retired to his bedchamber. Symian would live, but healing his contingent's wounds had drained him. How much longer could he endure these delays—failures that kept them in this foul world.

The wind whistled along the panes like distant voices beckoning. He pressed his hands to his temple and squeezed to stay the growing pressure in his head.

Hard to think.

Dorn shot a panicked glance around the room. He was alone. At times voices spoke to him in fleeting whispers.

Dorn poured himself a glass of wine and downed it in one gulp. He gazed at the drained glass, studying it as the clear-violet film sloughed toward the bottom. Dorn ached for a refill, yet his trembling hands betrayed him. He cast the glass aside and took his wine straight from the bottle. The voices on the wind went silent; the pain and pressure subsided until only an ember of it remained—a promise of its return soon enough.

Something had happened to him in transit from Aandor to this place—barely noticeable at first, but growing more serious with time. If he had appropriate resources, he might have discerned the cause of his malady. One thing was certain, he was not getting better. The others seemed unaffected. That fact taunted Dorn—an affront in the face of his superiority over the half-breeds, dog-men, and swamp-dwellers he commanded. Even his heartless minions fared better than him. They could go on forever while his greatness faded away.

Time.

Yes, time was his enemy. If he accomplished his task soon, he could return to Farrenheil triumphant. There the knowledge to cure him of this malady awaited. Lara might even do it; she was a powerful witch, perhaps the most powerful on the continent. But if their task here took too long, he might not be in any condition to recreate the sorceries that brought them to this plane. Even in perfect health, he had concerns about his ability to execute such a transfer. Symian had talent, but Dorn did not trust him with that level of magical knowledge. It was bad enough the troll knew as much about sorcery as he did.

Rushing through that portal back in Aandor, unprepared and ignorant of the magicks being wielded, was a reckless act. The headaches reminded Dorn of this daily. He didn't realize he'd be separated from his lover, his world, for so long.

Dorn took out the locket and gazed upon Lara's image. Even despite the headache's pull, the longing for her would not abate. He was bound to her. It was as though he suffered a second bane alongside the malady. The pressures came at him from all directions.

Find the boy.

He looked around the room again. Still alone. Was it his conscience speaking to him? Had it achieved some ethereal state, offering its disembodied counsel?

It was good counsel. Find the boy, return home a hero, heal what ailed him, and embrace his love again. But he had to tread carefully in this alien place.

Do we?

"What?" Dorn whispered.

Have to tread carefully?

Money kept questions and prying eyes to a minimum, but there were too many laws to transgress. The denizens were coded and catalogued—Social Security numbers; licenses for cars, weapons, the right to work, even to hunt and fish; lists to restrict denizens from flying on airplanes—one minor infraction in this paranoid kingdom could reveal that none of Dorn's group had any measurable history. His greatness would not save him. Bernie Madoff, Martha Stewart, Michael Jackson; the populace here punished its nobility for mere bagatelles, for following human nature. This truly was a backward place.

"Too many rules," he responded to an empty room. "Too many eyes and too many rules."

You are great.

"Too many ways to run afoul of the powers that be. They'll want my secrets of sorcery!"

Sorcery can subjugate your enemies.

"Too many to fight them all. Can't find the boy if I'm in the dungeon!" Dorn spat.

The room spun. He didn't remember how he ended up on the floor. His arms wrapped around himself. He began to rock to and fro.

"My lord?" came Oulfsan's voice through the door.

"Let me be!" Dorn responded. Was he speaking to his lackey or his inner counselor?

Some secrets are worthier than others. Remember the satchel? The blood you spilled to claim its contents?

Dorn remembered the satchel.

Have you looked in it of late?

Dorn rushed into his bedroom closet and pulled out boxes from various clothiers in the city. He claimed the satchel that had been hidden behind the pile. He had trusted no one with its contents, so the bag had been with him the day he transferred to this world.

Dorn extracted two large scrolls from the satchel. Thick vellum parchments hung heavy over tarnished pewter rods with ornate ends prickly enough to tear careless skin.

He had "borrowed" the scrolls when they sacked the wizards' compound on the border of Aandor and Nurvenheim at the beginning of the war. He didn't know whether they had any practical use. No mage was idiot enough to fool around with exponential sorceries. He didn't even have the elements he needed to fuel such spells. Dorn had intended to study them at his leisure, for academic purposes of course, once returned home from the campaign.

Twelve wax seals fastened each scroll, one for each mage of the Twelve Kingdoms of Aandor. These were the forbidden magicks; the one area every powerful wizard agreed upon regardless of loyalties to various noble patrons. He had begged his uncle's court mage to let him study the scrolls that resided in Farrenheil. Dorn's uncle refused to intercede on his behalf. These sorceries scared everyone who knew of them.

Dorn's history of court mages was sketchy, but based on the seal of Farrenheil, he surmised these spells hadn't been opened in nearly two hundred years. He was curious about what material such a diverse group of geniuses—wizards whose beliefs, morals, and ethics ran along a wide spectrum—could actually agree on. He broke the seals and opened the first scroll.

There's much to work with here.

"Yes."

Power beyond imagining.

If Dorn could decipher the text coda, power to smite all adversaries and bring an end to his stay in this dreadful place. Dorn would no longer tread lightly on this earth; no longer fear to do what had to be done. These magicks were dangerous indeed, but what did he care for the equilibrium between natural forces here so long as Aandor would not be affected. The detective had found the trail. Soon the boy would be dead, if he wasn't already, and Dorn would be back in Aandor.

"My lord, news from up north," came Oulfsan's voice through the door again.

"Come in," ordered Dorn.

Oulfsan entered.

"Good news or bad?" Dorn asked.

"Both, my lord. Todgarten is en route to us from the portal."

"Why? He was ordered to patrol those woods—to keep out of sight and guard the portal."

"His party is dead," Oulfsan answered. "Lost in a battle with the centaur witch and Aandoran captain. Only Todgarten survived."

Dorn was agitated. The pressure in his head increased. "Do you know what this means?" he said. "Our forces are cut in half. No more are likely to come through in time to aid us." Dorn immediately regretted this show of emotion. Anything other than a cool demeanor broadcasted weakness. It was the damn headaches. "I should have that coward's ugly head on a pike for surviving. He should have fought to the death with his cohorts."

"Then we would not have the good news."

"What is it?"

"Todgarten was adamant that I inform you he has one of the canisters you had sent K'ttan Dhourobi to retrieve from the power station. He is heading back here with it."

Dorn waited a moment to ensure that he had heard correctly. He looked at the scrolls on his bed. They were no longer hypothetical devices. The fuel he desired was on its way.

"Maybe he can keep his head after all," Dorn said. "Make sure he has all the help he needs to get back here safely."

Oulfsan left.

Today started the endgame of this whole affair. The dawn of a new era.

Dorn raised a toast to his epiphany and drank heartily from the bottle. The voices in his head, pleased by his reborn commitment, laughed bravely in unison.

CHAPTER 21

EXODUS

Daniel wore his Orioles baseball cap low and eyed the station police just below the horizon of the bill. There was no way to know if they'd be looking for him yet. To most he'd appear like an average teen in jeans and with the ever-present stuffed backpack. No one could see the volcano of his turmoil beneath.

The bus station was almost empty. A few stragglers tried to get on the remaining buses heading out of town; the hour was filled with desperate people. Only one ticket attendant served the Greyhound passengers. Daniel stood in a roped line behind a punked-out girl in fishnet stockings, Doc Martens, leather skirt, and pink hair. Her black mascara was applied thickly, so much so, her blue eyes were luminescent by contrast. She'd popped the eyes out of her teddy-bear backpack and sewn black Xs in their place. A chain of metal rings and bolts festooned her eyebrows and nose. She had a nice butt.

Behind him skulked a college student with massive duffel bags. Around the station, old black men swept and mopped the terminal with perfunctory rhythm. How many runaways had *they* witnessed passing through this nexus in their years? A man, probably homeless, sat, or slept, on the wooden bench near the ticket counters.

Daniel was a killer. This new reality resonated through him like a vibration within a bell. He tried to think of ways to make it all better, but he couldn't undo it. A joke from a list of Confucius axioms looped in his brain: "Virginity like bubble, one prick, all gone." His bubble, the one that separated the ocean of chaos and violence from the good student, so fragile, had already dissipated like a raindrop into the sea. Daniel could barely remember a life prior to Clyde's dying eyes staring up at him.

Out of nowhere, a great pressure filled Daniel's head. He suddenly became nauseated and gripped the metal rope pole beside him to steady himself. Images forced their way into his head, a stormy night, a large tree, the sensation of being cradled in the arms of a woman wearing a hood. The pole wobbled under his weight, in danger of giving way. The pressure grew. Daniel knew he was about to go down, drawing the attention of everyone in the place. Strong hands grabbed and steadied him. The pressure began to subside. His stomach settled down. The images stopped coming.

"You okay, dude?" the college kid said, releasing Daniel.

"Yeah," was all Daniel could get out, finding his legs again and trying to catch his breath.

"What was that?"

What the hell was that? he repeated the question to himself. "I think I ate something bad," Daniel said.

"Next," the ticket lady said.

Daniel's state improved quickly. He let go of the pole and straightened himself. Those strange images haunted him.

"Next!" the woman repeated.

Daniel shuffled up to the counter and steadied himself against it. He had to get out of town. He would worry about the episode later. It was probably just anxiety, he lied to himself. "New York," he told the woman.

She had a slow methodical way about her. The end of creation couldn't rush this woman. "Next bus leaves at 11:00 P.M. That'll be sixty dollars."

"Sixty . . . ?" He would need some money for food wherever he ended up.

"Do you want the ticket?"

"Uh . . ."

"Step aside if you don't know where you are going, sir."

"What about Washington?"

"State or the District?"

"D.C."

"We have a Greyhound bus for twenty-five dollars leaving at 10:20 P.M. There's a local express service that starts at 6:30 A.M. that's only fifteen dollars—if you want cheap."

"No, I'll take the one tonight."

The ticket lady threw him a knowing glance. How much more obvious could it be that he wanted to be anywhere but here as soon as possible—a teen with no specific destination? A runaway. Daniel would have to find a ride out of Washington, D.C., fast. This woman would rat him out to the cops when they canvassed the station. Only a half hour until his bus left.

He took his ticket and looked for a place to sit. Most of the station was roped off for cleaning. There was a spot on the bench beside the homeless man.

The man's odor greeted Daniel ten feet from the bench. A scruffy, graying individual, he wore a trench coat that looked reasonably new (considering the stink) and a brimmed hat that looked like it belonged in a black-and-white movie, which the man wore low, covering his eyes. He looked to be sleeping sitting up, probably because the cops would eject him if he laid down.

Daniel sat at the farthest end of the bench from Stinky. A discarded newspaper helped him pass the time: a kidnapped baby in Cleveland was returned to its parents; India and Pakistan had backed down from nuclear annihilation; and Mafia capo Dominic Tagliatore was out on a million dollars' bail pending his trial for racketeering. He *should get out of town while he has the chance,* Daniel thought. The boy pondered his own options. South America was as good a place as any. He could learn Spanish. He could still go to art school. Life wasn't over. Not for him, anyway.

Clyde's dead body flashed in front of Daniel's eyes. The boy grappled with his new role as a murderer. Through reasonable justification of his actions—turning the events over and over again in his mind—he concocted a list, which included a column of positive ramifications regarding what he had done. Fact: His mother and little sister were better off without Clyde. Fact: With Clyde gone, Daniel would live to see his fourteenth birthday. Fact: The state of Maryland was short one worthless bum on its welfare rolls. Fact: Jessica Conklin wouldn't have to spread her legs for loser Clyde anymore. Fact . . . the list lost credibility after its first two particulars. Those reasons would have to carry Daniel's burden against his cumbersome list of sins.

"Running away?" said a voice beside Daniel.

Stinky's breath traveled like a cloud of sewer gases— everything about this man was rancid. This guy would sell him out for a sandwich and a bath if he got the chance.

"Visiting my aunt," Daniel replied.

"I had an aunt once," the man said.

Daniel pretended to read the newspaper.

"I ran away once, too," Stinky continued. "I was a little older than you, though . . . seventeen. Went to California. Life was good. I partied and screwed to my heart's content. You going to California, kid? 'Course, it isn't like the way it was when I was there. Flowers, free love, and few Republicans."

"Wasn't Reagan a Republican?"

He looked at Daniel with a spark of admiration. "You're pretty smart for a punk-ass kid. What the hell you running away for? Stick around here and finish school, you might get into Johns Hopkins or something."

Do they have an annex in Costa Rica? Daniel wondered.

A police officer approached their bench, his twenty-year love affair with the doughnut evident as it hung over his belt.

"Hey kid, you traveling alone?" he asked.

Daniel's heart dropped to his stomach and lodged in his throat at the same time.

"Kid's with me," Stinky said.

"Yeah, right," the cop said. "You running away, kid?" the cop asked Daniel.

"I said he's with me," the homeless man repeated.

"This true?" the cop asked Daniel.

"Yeah," Daniel said. Stinky was going to want something for this. Fair enough.

The cop did not look convinced.

"Officer," the homeless man said, "this is my sister's kid. I . . . I fell off the wagon. I'm not the best example of a righteous citizen. He came down here to get me."

"Where are you headed?" the cop asked.

"Washington," Daniel cut in. He regretted giving that much away, but he had the ticket as proof and he couldn't afford to get arrested.

"May I see your tickets?" the cop ordered.

Daniel waved his pass and tried to think of an explanation for Stinky. To his surprise, the homeless man pulled out his own Greyhound bus ticket. The cop scrutinized the tickets before handing both back to Daniel.

"You better hold on to these, kid," he said. "Your uncle's liable to cash them in for a pint."

Stinky laughed.

"Okay," Daniel said, confused. He looked at Stinky's ticket: Washington, D.C., at 10:20 P.M.

As soon as the cop left, he handed the man back his ticket. "Thanks."

"No problem. You look like a kid who could use some time to sort things out."

"Is it that obvious?"

The man shifted his weight on the bench and sat upright.

"Cop thought so," he said. "Look, it's none of my business why you're taking off. I had my reasons when I was younger and you have yours. But the world's a fucked-up place, kid. Sometimes traveling with a friend makes it a little better. I'm heading south. You're welcome to come with me for as long as you want. There's a hot meal, a shower, and a bed in North Carolina if you want it."

"What's in North Carolina?" Daniel asked.

"My sister's place. Except, I kind of ran out of money and

have to thumb it from Washington. Every little bit helps, right? Maybe we'll get lucky and pick up a ride."

Not with your stench, Daniel thought. The guy was smart. Daniel had enough money to buy food along the trip, and friends don't let friends go hungry. Stinky had earned his meal ticket. If not for him, Daniel would be on his way to a police station now.

"Okay," Daniel said. "For now."

The man put his hand out to the boy. "What's your name, kid?"

Daniel hesitated, wondering if the stench would rub off on him. Ignoring the hand would be an unceremonious way to begin a new partnership. He shook Stinky's hand, which was cold and clammy. "It's Daniel."

"Daniel. Dan. Dan the Man. Good to meet you, Dan." Stinky shook Daniel's hand heartily. "I've got a good feeling, Dan. Yessireebob, a good feeling. Helping you out will be like a karmic repair patch to my troubled and not so noble life. Just want to say thank you. You're helping me put my life back in order."

"Yeah, whatever," Daniel said, feeling like he'd missed something esoteric. "Uh, what should I call you, Mister . . . ?"

"Dretch. But my friends call me Colby. Yessiree, Dan the Man, everything from this day forward is going to be just fine."

EPILOGUE

The hum of the bus on the road had a soothing effect on Daniel. Or perhaps it was just the act of being in motion—moving away from the place that had caused him so much grief in his life.

The effects of the episode at the station had worn off. The speed with which it overcame him was troubling. The last thing he needed was health problems. There was more to it than just anxiety, though. Those images were as real as memories—as though recalling an experience. Daniel had a good recollection of his past until he was about three. He didn't remember any of that stuff during the incident. *What was happening to him?* He rested his head against the window using his rolled-up sweater for a pillow.

His new friend Colby slept in the seat next to him. There was something crafty about him—the way he talked—as though he knew more about the situation than he was letting on. At the same time, there was something comforting about having him on the aisle, like a sentinel positioned between Daniel and the world.

The man's smell was not as bad as when they had met; though reactions from the passengers passing Colby on their way to the toilet in back suggested Daniel had only acclimated to the stench. That was fine by him. Lots of fine-smelling people had let Daniel down in his thirteen years. One trustworthy companion, if that's what the man turned out to be, was worth a rank whiff.

The stars were bright against an inky sky over the Parkway between Baltimore and Washington. Mankind used to look into the heavens for portents of the future, but the light, traveling incredible distances, was actually a cosmic fossil of a billion years past. Whatever civilization circled a star by the time its light touched our eyes was probably long dead. Still, Daniel concluded, a talent for divination would have been useful—his future looked like a blank page, and he had no pen.

Everything that lived came from the spark of a great fire ignited long ago, a big bang. The universe existed in a cycle of expansion and contraction, recycling itself from its own dead matter over an incalculable number of years. One day, the sun would go nova, destroying the solar system, and the spent matter would collect into clouds that would at some point form a new star. If this was the way of the universe—a destructive end in order to begin anew—then why not the same for Daniel? Why couldn't *he* rise from the ashes of his own past?

"Stuck in a cycle?" Colby asked.

"You don't know the half of it," Daniel responded. "Thought you were asleep."

"Don't have much use for sleep," Colby said. "I might have more than I bargained for soon enough."

It was the first thing Colby had said that had the gravity of unadulterated truth.

"You sick or something?" Daniel asked.

"In a way. We all have our crosses to bear. Yours is fairly obvious."

"Really? What's my story?" Daniel asked. He was intrigued by the man's level of insight. There was more to this bum than what he projected.

"The cops want you for something."

Daniel regretted the game already. The man was, perhaps, too perceptive to be a safe traveling companion.

"You don't say," Daniel remarked, trying to play it cool.

"Relax, kid. I don't plan to sell you out. It was obvious back in the station."

"And this doesn't scare you? To get caught helping me?"

"How do you know I'm not running from the law, too?" Colby lobbed back.

"Good point. Still—"

"You have a good chance of dropping off the radar before any cop gets his hands on you."

"Had experience with the law, I take it?"

"On both sides. I used to be a cop once. Long ago."

"You don't even know what I did."

"Doesn't matter. Theft, rape . . . even murder, the logistics are in your favor," Colby explained. "Sure, they'll put an all-points bulletin out on you, but there's nothing remotely unique about you. Get a crew cut, change your jacket. You're about thirteen, right? In four months you'll be two inches taller."

"You seem awfully certain," Daniel said.

"The police force is outnumbered about a thousand to one in every city," Colby continued. "Only a third of the force is ever on duty at one time—unless there's a special event like the president coming to town, and then, they're all busy trying to keep his ass safe instead of looking for punks like you. You just have to be smart."

"Like?"

"Like don't get off at Central Station. Place is full of police. There's a stop before that. We get off there . . . avoid downtown."

Daniel hadn't thought of that. It made perfect sense, though, and that scared him. There was a world of things he didn't understand. There was also a lot more to Colby than met the eye.

"Thank you," Daniel said.

The man smiled.

"I like you, kid," Colby said this in a somber tone. Perhaps Daniel reminded him of a son. "You need time to sort out whatever mess you're in," Colby continued. "We could all use some time to ponder our messes."

"What if the mess is unsortable?"

"Yeah, that happens. You're a smart kid, Dan. There ain't two people on this bus with your wits. You have a . . . a bright future."

It was the first time Colby had outright lied to him. Daniel ascribed it to his companion's desire to perk his spirits. The boy took some cold comfort in the fact that he could read Colby so well. At least he'd have a chance if Colby planned to set him up.

"Good night, kid," Colby said, and turned aside, making a big deal about getting comfortable in his seat.

The lie put the notion of a future back in the boy's head. Daniel always believed he was destined to do something important. The belief that he could work his way out of the ditch that had become his life was what drove him to always try harder. He never imagined things at home would turn out the way that they did. He did not deserve to end up in a juvenile facility, or worse, death row, for what happened to Clyde. Clyde had choices too, and he often chose badly. He was the instrument of his own misfortune.

Daniel watched the lines on the road fly by. North Carolina was a ways off. The trailer park Colby's sister lived in was at least somewhere to go for the moment. Daniel would decide what to do from there. He knew he was wiser than many people twice his age. There was no reason he could not apply what he knew toward a fresh start—like the recycled remnants of an old universe giving birth to the new. For the first time in a long while, longer than he could remember, Daniel felt hopeful about the future.